CROSSFIRE

THE BULARI SAGA

JESSIE KWAK

ALSO BY JESSIE KWAK

The Bulari Saga

Double Edged

Crossfire

Pressure Point

Heat Death

Kill Shot

Bulari Saga Prequel Novellas

Starfall

Negative Return

Deviant Flux

Standalone Novels

From Earth and Bone: A Ramos Sisters Thriller

Nonfiction

*From Chaos to Creativity: Building a Productivity System
for Artists and Writers*

For my service industry family,
and anyone who's ever waited tables, poured beers,
pulled shots, flipped burgers, or bussed dishes.

This one's for you.

N
W
E
S
To the Maraka Valley
Geordi Jimenez
Space Terminal
Jet Park
Casinos
Downtown
To Julieta Yang's

Bulari
Dry Creek
Altamira
(Blackheart territory)
Tamarind District
University of Bulari
Carama Town

PROLOGUE

He'd been told this place was a temple.

Levi Acheta hasn't been in any temples or churches or whatevers before, but he watched plenty of religious promo vids in exchange for free meals back in rougher times. He knows what they look like: ornamental and opaque in a way meant to comfort believers and disorient outsiders.

This place? It looks like a fortress.

It's cavernous, an abandoned factory on the outskirts of Dry Creek, the northernmost of Bulari's Finger slums. If he takes this place, he'll push the farthest reaches that Blackheart's territory — Acheta's territory, he reminds himself — has ever stretched. Getting here before the Dry Creek crew did had been a gamble.

But Acheta's spent the past few days mopping up the remnants of the Dawn cult, taking the opening left after their leader, Bennion Zacharia, disappeared. And he isn't about to stop before he takes their prize.

This temple, or whatever it is, is definitely going to pay off in weaponry, and — if Acheta's very, very lucky — in some fancy relics and whatnot he can sell off. His crew's stuck with him this long, but the winds are going to shift if he puts off paying them any longer.

Only one problem.

There are plenty of signs of habitation here: sleeping cots in unorganized clusters, salvaged food rehydrators buried in reeking mounds of discarded containers, the shitters out back.

But no people. And no bodies, except for the ones he and his crew left in the street outside.

Maybe the cultists packed up and left after Zacharia's death, and to avoid the fighting between Acheta and the Dry Creek crew in the week that followed. Maybe the rumors are right and the Dawn actually was just a bunch of brainwashed rich kids who ran back to their mansions once things got tough.

Or maybe it's a trap.

The only nod to their weird-ass cult is a small shrine on the northern wall: a black-ink drawing of something that could be a desert mountaintop, a rickety bookshelf full of what looks like their prophet's holy ravings, and somebody's desiccated hand holding an unfilled shard tab. The tab's razor-sharp waffled edges glitter in the dark.

It's fucking disturbing.

"We hit the jackpot, man."

Acheta turns away from the shrine to find Aden Damyati behind him, his silver hair glinting blood red in the abandoned factory's emergency lighting. Acheta lifts his chin and Damyati continues.

"Some of the weapons lockers were emptied out, but they left behind some real good stuff," Damyati says. "Plasma carbines, shotguns. And check this out." He spins a grenade charge in the palm of his broad brown hand like an egg, flips it in his fingers to show the stamp on the back. Acheta winces inwardly at the oldtimer's lack of caution, then swears sharply under his breath at what Damyati's showing him.

The back of the grenade is stamped with the seal of the Indiran Alliance.

"Where'd the cult get Alliance shit?" Acheta says, and Damyati shrugs. "Pack it all up," he orders, and for a moment Damyati looks like he's got something else to say, but the oldtimer doesn't challenge him.

Not yet, at least.

Acheta'll need to get rid of him before too long, but Damyati hasn't done anything outwardly disloyal — and Acheta's not going to fool himself. He doesn't have a strong enough command to start killing people who've served this crew since Blackheart days. Not on a gut feeling.

Plus, the man's a magician with a gun. Acheta can't afford to be down by even one more good soldier while he's in a full-on fight with Dry Creek.

Damyati strolls back to the other side of the cavernous factory, shouting orders to fill duffel bags full of weaponry. Acheta should be feeling elated at the haul, but instead he feels uneasy. With this much firepower just sitting around, how did he and his crew manage to bring the Dawn to their knees?

Those aren't words he'll say aloud. But he also won't waltz into the next battle without some serious searching into what the hell.

"Almost clear here, boss," Sjel calls from the entrance to the factory's offices, just to the right of the altar. Acheta promoted Sjel to his lieutenant the moment he killed Naali Hinoja and took over the crew, and he hasn't regretted the decision. There's a man who knows the meaning of loyalty.

"You meet anyone?" Acheta asks.

"Just checking the back rooms for stragglers. All sugar, now," Sjel says; he's grinning, a good sign.

"And we found a stash of shard, gotta be a hundred thousand marks here."

A hundred thousand marks.

Acheta doesn't allow the relief to show on his face, but it flushes through his body just the same. They sell that shard and he can pay his crew. It's his lifeline until he gets the shard production facilities already captured from the Dawn up and running.

"Pack it up and ship it to the street dealers. Tonight."

"On it, boss."

"Keep sharp," snaps Acheta. "I don't like how easy this was."

Sjel ducks his head in agreement, then turns to bark orders down the chain, leaving Acheta staring at the abandoned shrine again as though it'll give him a clue.

Clue is, the Dawn lost.

The cultists got greedy, is what it was. They thought they could spin alliances with his crew and the Dry Creek crew, both. And Acheta ground them into sand.

Dry Creek is still fighting strong, but Acheta feels it in his bones that they're on the run. If he can just keep up the onslaught — and this new source of revenue will help — he'll wipe them off the map.

Then, all those who whisper that Levi Acheta isn't half the leader Blackheart was — that he isn't half the leader her lieutenant Naali Hinoja was — will either be dead or proven wrong.

Naali would never have seen the potential of joining with the Dawn to cement their hold on the drug trade. She wouldn't have had the strength or foresight to turn on them the minute Zacharia was killed and it looked like the deal would go bad. She didn't want anything to do with the shard — she'd said it again and again.

But without the shard they don't have the cash to operate.

Naali was the reason Blackheart's crew had been buckling under pressure from Dry Creek and the other crews on the edges of their territory. And Acheta is the reason Blackheart's crew — fuck that, *his* crew — is going to be feared in this city once more.

He's broken the Dawn, he'll break the Dry Creek crew, and he'll cement his control over the most lucrative business in the city. Everything in Dry Creek? That'll be his by the end of the week. All the shard manufacturing facilities, all the workers — so blitzed that none of them will even notice a change in masters so long as the masters keep feeding them what they're making.

It's all within his reach, provided he can keep his crew happy. Pay those that are grumbling for their hard-earned cash and shut down those —

like Damyati — who are putting him on shaky ground.

He's jostled from his thoughts by a disturbance at the door. Voices raised, menacing. The faint whine of pistols and carbines warming to their owners.

"Boss!" yells Bull.

Acheta jogs across the expanse of the old factory, shoulders loose and ready; he'd expected far more of a fight tonight, and he's floating high on unspent battle adrenaline.

Bull is arguing with someone outside the door. The two soldiers around him have weapons drawn, but Bull doesn't. He doesn't need to; his fists could pound rocks, his bulk fills the door.

"What is it?" Acheta calls.

Bull steps back to reveal a woman standing just outside the door to the factory. She's dressed outlandishly, like she's in some rom vid about a bounty hunter who falls for the scum she's supposed to kill: tight purple leggings and a practical yet formfitting biosilk baselayer top under a cropped black jacket that would provide a year's meals for some street kid if it was made out of real leather. Her black hair is pulled back in a short, shaggy ponytail; stray strands spear across copper cheeks.

"Says she's part of Blackheart's crew," Bull says. "But I ain't ever seen her before."

The woman examines Acheta, dark eyes glinting in the beams of tactical flashlights and red emergency lighting.

"You never ran with Blackheart," Acheta says. What kind of suicidal person thinks she can pull that line here? He rests his palm on his pistol. Everyone in the room tenses at the whine as it warms to his hand. "I been with Blackheart since before she ever left New Sarjun. Who the fuck are you?"

"I am Norah é Vega," the woman says, simply, like he should know the name. He doesn't, but at the Arquellian accent he knows one thing at least: that jacket probably *is* real leather. His first thought is that it will be a pity if it gets shot up.

His second thought is shame that the money stress of the past week has turned him back into the desperate kid he'd been before he started running with Blackheart, sizing up a woman's jacket for what it might be worth.

"And who's that?" Acheta asks. "I never heard of you."

"I was Blackheart's right hand on Indira."

And at that, the name does ring a bell, just vaguely. Maybe he read it in a memo. Maybe he heard Naali talking about her.

He doesn't let recognition show.

"And you're what," Acheta says. "Here to help?"

Here to challenge him is more likely. Adrenaline courses through him: Let her come. Let him have yet another chance to prove his strength to the unbelievers on his crew. Out of the corner of his eye he can see them — Damyati, Sui, Talla, all the others watching to see how he leads.

"I'm here to take revenge for Coeur's death," é Vega says.

Acheta lifts his chin at that, and é Vega seems to see the sea of weapons around her for the first time. "Revenge on the Dawn," she adds.

Beside him, Bull tilts his thick head. Pistols lower as people process what she said.

"Revenge?" Acheta asks.

"My way of showing respect," she says, like she doesn't get the question. "It's mine to avenge her death before taking her mantle back on Indira."

"Very nice," says Acheta. "Except seems you should've stayed on Indira, since that's where she got done."

She frowns at him. "I see you don't have that tradition here."

"We have our own ways of showing respect," says Acheta. "I'm showing mine by taking Dry Creek out at the knees and expanding her territory."

Or whatever. Let her think his actions had anything to do with avenging Blackheart, Acheta thinks. He'd been low and desperate in the crew back when the old bitch ran things. Cranky old Blackheart with her antiquated ways of doing things and her delusions that she could have it all. Then she'd hamstrung her own people for years by trying to run things from off-planet with Naali as her puppet. Refusing to go quietly into exile to Indira and let her people here run things on New Sarjun without her interference, that was what had driven this organization into the ground.

Good riddance. He's happy she's dead.

His crew will thrive now that there's a real leader at the helm.

Only.

Blackheart was killed on Indira in some random break-in, right? A weak way to go, he'd thought at the time. Fitting for a failed, exiled queen.

É Vega is watching him like he's missing a piece of the puzzle.

Fuck it, he'll bite.

"Let her in," he snaps at Bull, who pivots like a door to let the Arquellian woman pass. Acheta turns to Damyati and his team at the weapons lockers. "You done there or just gawking?" he yells. Damyati waves his team back to work.

The only place away from prying eyes and

pricked ears is by the disturbing shrine. A shadow in the doorway to the back rooms; Sjel has slunk out, watching his boss's back like a good lieutenant should. É Vega ignores Sjel, walking past Acheta to study the shrine. She tilts her chin as she takes in the desiccated hand with the unfilled shard tab in the palm.

"Blackheart died on Indira," Acheta says, voice low. "So why are you really on New Sarjun."

É Vega turns back to him; she doesn't seem scared. She has that same haughty look Naali Hinoja always had, like there wasn't a damned thing in the world worth losing her cool over. Blackheart had a type when it came to the tough bitches she picked for lieutenants, that's for sure.

"Thala didn't die on Indira," é Vega says. "She died ten blocks from here in a prison run by Dry Creek and financed by the Dawn. Do you want to know why?"

Until this moment, Acheta hadn't cared who offed Blackheart. He figured he owed them a nice bottle of gin, but he hadn't thought much more about it. "Why don't you tell me your theory?"

"It's no theory," é Vega says, the barest flick of her attention to Sjel. "The Dawn kidnapped Thala and paid Dry Creek to secure her in their territory. She was guarded and tortured by Dry Creek soldiers. They broke her hands. And they killed her."

"Well, it looks like I took care of your revenge for you, then," he says. "Sorry you made the trip."

"You don't need help?" É Vega raises her gaze to take in the whole abandoned factory, sweeping over the cots, the weapons lockers, the shrine.

"The Dawn are done," Acheta says. "This was their last stronghold."

"You're sure?"

No, no he's not. This shrine in front of them with its holy books and desiccated hand, that arsenal abandoned, nothing here feels like vanquishing an enemy should feel. Unease radiates out like an itch between his shoulder blades.

But he'll never show that. Acheta spreads his arms and turns a slow circle to show off the place, this last stronghold. He's not sure what's worse: turning his back on é Vega or on the strange shrine with its wilting books and eerie images.

"What do you think, yeah? They look dead to me."

He grins at her. She's not smiling. "And Dry Creek?"

"Why the fuck does the Dawn kidnap Blackheart?" he asks. Just so they could come straight to him with the shard connection? Blackheart would've been fine with it; it was leaving Naali Hinoja in charge that messed up their chances there.

É Vega's smiling like she knows something

that'll blow his mind. She turns back to the shrine, picking up the desiccated human hand with reverence.

"Have you heard of the Gift of the Fallen?" she asks.

Someone screams behind them and Acheta whirls from é Vega with his pistol drawn. A pair of his people — Masso and a new recruit named Liari — are dragging a struggling man between them.

"We found him hiding in one of these rooms," Masso says. "One of their priests, looks like. Do you want us to — "

But in that moment, the priest breaks a hand free, grabs something from his pocket, and slips it into his mouth.

The priest screams again, this time in rage, and throws Acheta's two crew back from him. Masso crashes against the wall, head cracking back and legs buckling as he slides to the floor. Liari isn't thrown quite as far. She stumbles, rolls, grabs her gun. With another screech, the priest flings him-self after Liari, wrestles the gun from her hand. But not before the new recruit gets off a pair of shots, both burying themselves in the priest's chest.

Acheta relaxes, but it's only a fraction of a second before the priest staggers back to his feet and lunges, grabbing Liari's head and snapping her neck with a sickening crunch.

The priest spins with animal frenzy in his eyes, blood washing down his torso from the bullet holes in his chest.

How is he still standing?

Acheta fires; the bullet tears through the man's shoulder but doesn't drop him. It only draws his attention.

"Aim for the head!" é Vega yells, and at her voice, the priest seems to find his focus once more, swiveling his head to notice Acheta and é Vega and the knot of crew running to surround them. He tenses as if to run, and Sjel wings him with a burst from his plasma carbine. The scents of ozone and scorched flesh fill the room.

The priest sprints towards Acheta and Sjel, howling. Acheta fires, the priest manages to dodge the bullets — how is he moving this fast? — and launches himself into the air towards Sjel.

Acheta lunges himself, tearing the priest off his lieutenant's back before he can do much damage. Acheta's tough, he knows, but this wiry priest? He's unimaginably strong. And none of his injuries seem to have slowed him down one bit. He writhes in Acheta's grasp, breaking free and wrapping his hands around Acheta's throat.

Acheta hears é Vega's shout and she slashes at

the priest's neck with a knife in her hand; the priest shifts and she misses, burying the blade in his shoulder.

It doesn't slow down him any more than the bullet wounds in his chest did, but it does divide his attention. Acheta kicks him off and rolls to a crouch with his gun in his hand just as the priest pivots and launches himself at é Vega. Acheta fires; the man's face disappears in a fine red mist.

Panting, Acheta rolls the man over to make sure he's really gone.

Alive, the priest had had the weight and strength of three men. Dead, he weighs as little as his scrawny frame looks like it should.

In the last weeks of fighting, the closest Acheta's come to dying is at the hands of this old man. The thought blooms bright and fiery and blinding, and he fights down adrenaline-fueled rage before he slips and turns it on his people. He didn't know what this man was — how could he expect it of any of them?

Except.

He turns to é Vega; she's radiating post-fight adrenaline. "You said to aim for the head. Why."

"I suspected once I saw what he was."

"And what was he?" Acheta asks coldly. "What did he take?"

"The Gift of the Fallen," she says, her Arquellian drawl sharpening with insistence. "I've never seen it in real life, I've only read about it in the Dawn's holy books."

Acheta suddenly realizes he's still crouched over the priest's body like a predator; he pushes himself to his feet. "Holy books." He glances at the shrine, though he doesn't turn his back on the priest. Not until he's sure the headshot is enough to keep him down.

"It's a drug. Zacharia and the Dawn were using it to make their people fast and strong. Invincible. It's what they killed Blackheart over."

Acheta frowns down at the priest's body, crumpled in a pool of blood on the factory floor. "He doesn't look very invincible to me."

"He wasn't a fighter. He was naturally weak." É Vega picks up the dried hand once more, touches a finger to the empty shard tab in its palm. "Still, you saw what he could do, how strong he was. Imagine giving that gift to a soldier."

Acheta is definitely imagining.

Imagining a world where finally defeating the Dry Creek crew is a given. Where he doesn't have to worry about someone coming after his position the way he came after Naali's. Because he may have gotten rid of her most vocal followers, but there are plenty in the crowd around him who are only waiting to see what kind of leader he'll be. To see if he'll be a strong, invincible commander, or if he'll simply be the next target.

No way is Levi Acheta a target.

"You said they killed Blackheart over this," he says. "Why."

"She was supposed to steal two cases of it from the Alliance on Indira and ship it to the Dawn here on New Sarjun," é Vega says. "But she double-crossed them, shipped it somewhere else instead. Somewhere only she could get it. One case was destroyed, but as far as I can tell the other is still intact."

"Where?" growls Acheta.

É Vega's watching him, he gets the sense that she sees his need, but he doesn't care. He's proven himself this far, and he'll continue to make good on his leadership. Especially once he has this gift.

"Where is it?" he asks, quieter.

"Do you know a man named Willem Jaantzen?"

1

———

BULARI

Fire is raining down over the city of Bulari.

Manu Juric spots another flash to the southwest, a long tail streaking through the night sky so bright, so brief, so enchanting, he can't help but become addicted to the search for the next spectacular death flash. It's one of the best of New Sarjun's annual meteor showers, Starla had told him. She'd been talking it up all day.

Manu's watching it from his balcony; she's probably back at Cobalt Tower watching it from the roof. Maybe she's even coaxed Jaantzen out to experience it.

He hopes so. They could all use a distraction after this last week.

Manu's apartment building is on the southern edge of the downtown core, and his apartment is on the far side of the building, so he's looking out over the dark desert plain and can actually see the night sky when he remembers to step out onto his balcony and look. The shield bubble surrounding the balcony is a blessing and a curse. Bulletproof for safety and reflective to give him privacy, and high-end enough that it doesn't buzz with its own energy from yards away like some of the cheap models. Doesn't even raise the hair on his arms.

But on dust-storm days it flickers like static as the dust sparks against it, obscuring the view.

Tonight it's blessedly clear.

Another meteor flashes in his periphery; he turns his head too slow to catch the whole thing. On another night he might have thought he imagined it, but tonight stars are falling all around him.

"You're still in your suit."

Manu glances over his shoulder. Oriol's standing in the doorway to the balcony, leaning forward on his crutches. He's showered and is wearing drawstring house slacks slung low on his hips, the empty left pant leg knotted at the thigh; the old scar scrawled up his hip glows white in the moonlight against the pale gold of his skin.

Manu's still in his funeral suit, wearing his

jacket even: black against the red of his shirt. Mourning colors. Oriol shed his funeral clothes almost even before they were through the door to the apartment.

"You okay?" Oriol asks.

"Nah, man," Manu says. "You?"

"Course not." Oriol shifts against the doorway, the end of one crutch scuffs against the tile. "C'mon in. I'm cooking."

"'Cooking?'"

"Yeah," Oriol says. "InstaMeals has a new flavor out, I picked up a couple this morning. 'Arquellian.' I already popped them in the rehydrator."

As if on cue, a cheery robotic tune plays distant from the kitchen. Dinner's ready.

Another flash in the sky, and Manu smiles for the first time all day. "Very gourmet of you." He leans against the balcony's railing, winces as pain lances through his bruised ribs. Concern flickers over Oriol's face. "How do you name a flavor after an entire country?" Manu says; he doesn't need Oriol remembering he should still be in bed. "What does 'Arquellian' even taste like?"

A smile tugs at Oriol's lips. "I'll show you later if you want."

Manu laughs — for real this time — and turns his back on the blazing finale of little dying rocks crashing through the atmosphere. He's seen enough death for one week.

Willem Jaantzen stands in a long, antiseptic white hallway with a bottle of whiskey in one hand and two glasses in the other. A pair of guards are standing at attention on either side of the medbay door while the medic, Elian, is trying gamely to face Jaantzen down.

"She shouldn't be drinking any of that," says Elian dubiously. He's eyeing the bottle, clearly wondering how much is swimming through Jaantzen's bloodstream tonight already.

None. At least, not yet.

"I don't care what's good for her health," Jaantzen says. "And I doubt she does much, either."

Elian's lips flatten. "I don't think it's a good idea."

Jaantzen doesn't bother answering. Earlier this week Elian wouldn't have talked back to a houseplant, but he's starting to test his new backbone. Now his attention has shifted from the whiskey bottle to the man whose fist it's in; Jaantzen can see the medic calculating if he has the guts to stop Willem Jaantzen from going into a room he damn well wants to enter.

Gia wouldn't let him in, but this kid is no Gia.

Elian loses the battle of glares and steps aside, Jaantzen walks past him.

"We need to talk when you're done," Elian says to his back.

Jaantzen doesn't answer.

Thala Coeur's eyes are closed, but she doesn't seem to be sleeping. He didn't think it was possible, but she seems to have lost even more weight in the past few days, her cheeks skeletal under bandages. Her cascade of braids — her signature for decades — had been singed beyond saving and have been shorn to her scalp, which is also blistered and bandaged.

She looks like Death.

Jaantzen sits stiffly on the stool beside her bed, his own burns and bruises screaming protest. He sets the glasses down on her bedside table with a clink, pours them each a shot. Coeur's eyes crack open.

"I thought you might need a drink," he says. "I certainly do."

She doesn't disagree, so he presses the button to raise her bed to a seated position. Her nostrils flare in pain. Another button lengthens the restraints on her wrists, and he hands her a glass. Coeur cradles it awkwardly in bandaged hands, staring at it with all the fury one world could possibly contain.

"We laid her down today," Jaantzen says.

A sharp nod. She still hasn't looked at him.

"It was . . . good," he says. How does one describe a funeral? "Quiet. Just me and mine. And Julieta."

"Where?"

"In the hills behind Julieta's. It can be — " He hates being at a loss for words. "Permanent," he says. "If you want it to be. Or we can move her. When things settle down."

"That's fine. Whatever works." Her expression is hellfire, but her voice is calm; Thala Coeur might be ordering a beer rather than discussing her sister's final resting place.

His cleanup crew has handled everything they could up at Julieta's greenhouse. The bodies have been dealt with, the glass and bullet casings swept up, the orchids repotted; the structure is on its way to being rebuilt. Even the road up to the hills has been repaired of the damage done when Coeur wrecked their spinner and Jaantzen shot the explosive case Bennion Zacharia had been running away with. The road had already been potholed beyond repair; now it just looks like a bunch of kids from the neighborhood went up and shot off fireworks.

He knows how to have a physical place scrubbed clean, so he did it. Nobody knows how to scrub clean a relationship, though, and that's what Julieta's left with after her youngest daughter betrayed them all to the Dawn.

He doesn't envy her.

He can't believe he's thinking this, but he'd rather be stuck with Blackheart than with whatever Julieta's having to deal with.

Coeur downs the whiskey, holds out her glass for another.

Jaantzen hesitates, then pours light. "We need to talk about your recovery," he says. "You need to eat if you're going to heal."

She glares at him. "Maybe I'll just let myself waste away."

"Then do it on somebody else's dime. I ain't got the time for that." He flinches internally at the phrasing, the more-than-hint of an accent. This day has gotten to him, and the street kid he thought he'd banished is starting to show back through. "I need to get this city back under control, and you dying isn't part of that plan."

"Find a different goddamned plan."

"You want to die so bad now? After your sister was killed trying to save your life?" Coeur flinches at that. "I know you're an ungrateful bitch," Jaantzen says. "But I thought you'd have more respect for Ximena."

"Fuck off." Coeur downs the second shot, holds out her glass.

Jaantzen takes it from her fumbling hands; she hisses in pain as she tries feebly to fight him for it, then turns her glare to the wall. He reduces the length of her restraints once more.

"Ximena's death wasn't your fault," he says. Kind. Firm. "But my wife? My children? They should still haunt you." He finishes his own glass, then stands and grabs the bottle. "Good night, Thala. We're going to keep trying to heal you. Co-operate because you want to live, or so you get well enough you can walk out of here and die a free woman on the street, I don't care which, but you're not dying in this building."

Coeur's gaze shifts to the bottle. "Leave that."

"No." Jaantzen shakes his head. "You can't pour, and Elian isn't going to do it for you."

"You worried I'll spill your good stuff, Willem?" He's waiting for an ironic smile that doesn't come. He feels the lack of it like a crack in the foundation of his world. "I'll drink straight from the bottle," she says; her eyes are pools of fathomless black.

He watches her a moment, uncertain. Is it pain she wants it for? He's never known how to help people in pain, whether the wound's emotional or physical. "I can have Elian give you something if — "

"Fuck off," she snarls.

"Gladly." Jaantzen's done with this game. "I'll see you tomorrow, Thala."

Elian is waiting in the antechamber when Jaantzen leaves, an array of charts and images open on the desk in front of him. Jaantzen recognizes the scan of Coeur's shattered hands with a sick lurch, but Elian's ignoring that file in favor of a scan Jaantzen can't place.

For a moment Jaantzen debates walking past him; whatever the medic wants to talk about can surely wait until the morning, and he's in too black a mood to calmly discuss Coeur's care at the moment. He checks the biolock again, though it's clear Coeur isn't going anywhere.

He has a demon in his medbay, one he desperately needs alive to keep this city from crumbling into open war. And the only person who could ever control Thala Coeur was her sister, Ximena, buried two meters down in the hills behind Julieta Yang's shattered greenhouse.

Jaantzen sighs, sets the whiskey bottle and glasses down on a shelf. "What did you want to talk about."

Elian taps on the unfamiliar scan, enlarging it to show a ribcage, black pooling beneath. Jaantzen doesn't understand what he's seeing, but he knows it's terribly wrong.

"You want her alive?" Elian asks. "Then we need to call Gia."

Music thrums through Starla Dusai's chest, beating like a fever through the packed dancers.

Simca's incandescent in hot pink, sequins shimmering off her minidress, stacks of rainbow neon cuffs glowing on her brown arms. Her black hair's in a thick queue, braided through with strands that spark in the light like starbugs, and the spikes of her stilettos flash a different color with every step.

Leti's in liquid turquoise from the band of her black fedora to the fine weave of her suit to the sharp-ass points of her gleaming dress shoes. Her tie drinks up the light, luminous black silk.

Starla's in silver that probably makes her pale skin gray and ghostly, but she loves the feel of the flounced skirt swishing against her thighs, loves the way it makes her look like she actually has curves.

And it must be working, because she's had no shortage of guys to dance with tonight. A Ganesh-class transport, the *Maria Elena III*, is still in orbit, and every nightclub in the city is flush with travelers and crew.

The beat transitions to double time, the bass

picking up to a low rumble that pulses once on one and twice on four and Starla loves this song, she claps and raises her hands with the rest of the crowd, lets her hips move how they want. The latest guy yells something to her but she's left her lens at home tonight and she closes her eyes to bask in the rhythm, ignoring him. Whatever he's trying to tell her doesn't matter. She's not going home with anyone.

The beat transitions again a few minutes later and the guy's gone. Leti is dancing in his place, her moves light-years beyond the grind he'd been attempting. Starla grins and takes Leti's proffered hand. Simca shimmies her hips through a gap in the dance floor to join them, and the whole world shrinks down to this moment: sweat and color and light and bodies against bodies, all shot through with the pulse of the music.

"Water," Simca signs after a moment, and Starla nods — she's been parched for ages, but having too much fun to leave the floor.

"You must be boiling alive," she signs to Leti. Starla's overheated in her skimpy dress, but where she and Simca are both gleaming with sweat, Leti is dapper as ever.

"Girl's gotta look good," Leti signs back. She pulls out a silk handkerchief and dabs at her dark brow, tucks it back in her pocket. "Sorry I ruined your chances tonight," she signs. "Every man on that dance floor thinks you're with me now."

"Good," Starla signs. "I'm not in the mood. But Simca . . ." She lifts her chin and Leti glances back to see Simca at the bar, trios of waters and shocking blue cocktails lined up in front of her. Guys on either side of her are trying to get her attention.

Leti laughs, elbows her way between Simca and one of the guys, gives her a *Hey, babe* look and a wink. She starts handing drinks back to Starla.

They find one of the few reasonably lit booths where they can see to talk. "Hopefully now I've ruined both your chances to go home with a boyfriend-of-the-week," Leti signs with a smile. "Tonight's supposed to be girls night."

It's a weekly chance for them to blow off steam, and the fact that it landed on the same day as Ximena's funeral means Starla has plenty of steam to blow. Simca, too; she's got an air of wild abandon about her tonight that's stronger than her usual, stronger than past times they've cheated at cards with Death and walked away grinning. Someone on their team didn't walk away this time. And following the initial numbness, that knowledge makes the crush of bodies more captivating, the cocktails sweeter, the beat more intoxicating.

Starla almost feels like she's in a trance, and

when she catches Simca's eye and sees her intensity, her fever, she knows Simca feels the same.

Leti works in media, some complicated consulting job helping vid stars and politicians and night club owners with messaging and news appearances. Starla understands just as much about her job as Leti understands about Starla's work designing security systems for Admant. Leti knows Starla's godfather is Willem Jaantzen, but she has no idea the nature of the jobs Starla sometimes hires Simca for.

Leti's only aware that something happened at work this week, and she accepted the usual brush-off when she asked about it. Tonight, she's slipped into the role of chaperone, letting her girlfriends work out whatever they need to on the dance floor and putting up enough guard for three.

And they need her tonight, god knows — this club is thick with horny single dudes from the *Maria Elena III*. Starla and her friends have barely claimed their booth when a man elbows up to the table, leans in with a conspiratorial smile to say something to Leti. Leti frowns at him. "I'm deaf," she yells. It looks like he's shouting louder — or maybe it's just loud in the club, because Simca yells back at him across the table.

The man abandons Leti and leans towards Simca. Starla can't read his lips, and Simca's angled away from her, but she recognizes the drug-pusher's gesture of one hand flashing open to reveal the glittering blue tab in his palm. Shard. He pops the tab under his tongue with a glassy grin, then pulls a bag from his pocket for Simca.

Simca's shaking her head, shooing him out of the booth. He gives her an apologetically wounded look — *Hey, just trying to offer a good deal* — and sidles off, ignoring Leti and Starla.

"Fucking pushers," Simca signs. She takes a drink and makes a face after the man's back.

Leti waves a hand to dismiss him. "Hey, did you end up signing with that new agent?" she asks Simca, and Simca rolls her eyes, the conversation swirling back to her latest search for a wrestling agent who's not scammy. It's not a night out without fending off at least one shard pusher, these days.

Starla follows along with the latest dramatic twist in Simca's agent saga, but only half-heartedly; talk isn't doing it for her tonight, and as soon as the last drops of cocktail are emptied from their glasses, she drags Leti and Simca impatiently back out to the dance floor.

Only now the energy is different. The beat is still steady, but a knot of people at the far edge of the crowd have stopped dancing, stillness rippling out from them as heads turn to see what's happening.

Starla elbows her way through — it's not her job, but sometimes there are fights, and if she can help she will. Plus, throwing a few punches might feel almost as good as dancing tonight.

She stops at the edge of the crowd, eyes wide.

Everyone's staring, and no one's helping. There's nothing to help.

The shard pusher from earlier is convulsing on the floor, mouth split open like he's screaming, tears of blood streaming from his eyes, black ichor leaking from his nostrils. His fingers claw protectively over his chest; bloody blisters form on the backs of his hands, his neck, his hairline as Starla watches in horror.

A scatter of his product has fallen out of his hand and is glittering on the dance floor. Starla hadn't been paying attention earlier, but now she sees his shard looks different from what she's used to seeing in clubs. Something about the color, the shape of the package is oddly familiar, and she realizes with a start where she's seen it before: in the drug-cooking operation that had been working out of the warehouse her godfather, Willem Jaantzen, is purchasing.

Others are pocketing the shard even as the pusher spasms in death. Starla signs for Leti to give her her handkerchief, then scoops up one of the strange shard tabs herself. She tucks it in her purse.

No one seems to notice, not with the screaming man acting out his dying moment on the dance floor.

Starla grabs Leti's and Simca's hands and drags them to the exit.

She's not going to stand around and watch yet another person die this week.

2

———

MANU

Manu's out of the bedroom in a gray suit and black silk tie and the turquoise shirt with the copper buttons that match his manicure. Beneath his jacket his holster is a familiar, comfortable weight against the right side of his ribs.

In the kitchen, Oriol's still in his workout clothes, his hair damp with sweat from the routine he put himself through while Manu was getting ready. When Manu walks in he swipes away whatever was on the kitchen-island counter — too fast — and reaches over his breakfast to pour Manu a cup of coffee.

"Morning," Oriol says, pushing the coffee across the counter. "You're looking good for your first day back."

"News that bad, you gotta hide it?" Manu asks, though he's got a sinking feeling it's not the news Oriol's been browsing this morning. Oriol never reads the news.

Oriol waves a hand. "News is always bad, you know how it is. Politics. Apparently one of the guys running for parliament supports joining the Alliance."

Manu would bet anything Oriol's hazarding a guess. It's an easy one — some far-outside candidate says that every run. "Saying shit like that is a sure way to shoot your chances in the foot," Manu says, holding Oriol's gaze, waiting. "Was it Oto? Or that other guy, the one from Ruby Basin?"

Oriol takes a bite of his toast, leans back in his chair. "Don't remember." He clears his throat. "Truth is, I read that yesterday. Right now I was just seeing what's out there."

Seeing what's out there on the job boards.

Manu's heart doesn't sink, it settles onto firm, aching ground.

Oriol's already scanning the job boards. It's not unexpected. For the last few days, Oriol's had that restlessness about his shoulders, that gaze drifting past Manu sometimes during conversation, like he's thinking of something — somewhere — that's not here.

Normally it's months before he starts to look for

the next gig. Once it was even a year. This time he's been home less than a week.

Manu leans a hip against the counter, too wired now to sit. He rests fingertips against the coffee mug but doesn't drink, just feels the heat, almost on the edge of burning.

"You just got back," he says, trying to keep his voice in neutral territory — not accusing, not upset, just stating. He fails.

"And you'll remember I got stiffed for my last job," Oriol says, defensive. He drums fingertips against his prosthetic thigh. "This ain't cheap."

Manu wants to remind him of the fat payday he made from Jaantzen for that business at Julieta's. Or the fact that Manu's got more than enough for them both to live on, on account of not ever going any-where fun himself.

"If you need a job, I'm trying to fill three," he says instead. "Two are desk jobs at RKE, but the third's driving. Long boring hours just like what you're used to on those security jobs you take in Durga's Belt, just you'll be home every night."

Oriol lifts a golden-blond eyebrow. "Driving?"

"If you'd rather get shot at, Starla's looking for a couple of soldiers she can trust for discreet jobs with high-level clients. She's asked me about you three times."

"She's got El and Simca."

"Simca's wrestling schedule is all over the place, and El hates making small talk." Manu's hand tightens on the coffee mug, nearly unbearable heat pressing into his palm. His comm buzzes in his pocket; he ignores it. "Pays way better than shipping security out in the Belt, plus I'd get to see you in a suit every now and again."

Oriol makes a face. "A suit?"

"You look good in suits. I'm just thinking selfishly." Manu says it lightly, like the suit's the only thing on his mind, but he's nowhere near successful. Oriol's watching him with a mixture of sadness and guilt that Manu can't handle.

His comm buzzes again, and he breaks free of Oriol's gaze to check it.

"Manu —"

"Hold on."

It's Gia.

AT THE TOWER ABOUT TO SEE THAT BITCH, WHERE ARE YOU.

Shit.

"I gotta go," he says. "Can we talk about this later?"

Oriol straightens in his chair. "Work stuff, or you need me along, or?"

"Nah, man, you're good." He slides his comm across the counter. "Gia found out about Coeur."

Oriol breathes out a curse. "You don't need me to come?" he asks. "I can put her in a sleeper hold."

Manu lets himself smile at that. "I can handle her."

Oriol tastes like the coffee Manu hasn't had a chance to drink, smells like aftershave and his recent workout, and already Manu misses him so much he could burn this whole place to the ground.

Manu catches Giaconda Áte in the lobby of Cobalt Tower; she's giving her name to the stone-eyed receptionist, Nadhi, spelling it calmly though her voice is tinged with a measure of slow-burning rage. Nadhi's taking it like a champ, but Manu guesses she's probably got one finger on the trigger of the stun carbine under her desk.

The lobby's filled with the usual midmorning traffic: office workers at one of Jaantzen's shell companies or one of the other organizations that rents space here, faces Manu recognizes but couldn't name. There are casual business meetings being held on the low orange couches in front of the double-height glass facade, the windows dimming already against the bright Bulari morning, heels clicking over the vast expanse of polished cream marble, the soft chime of the lifts, the indistinct rise and fall of office mates calling morning greetings.

And in the midst of all this downtown Bulari civility, two women are on the brink of a fistfight.

Nadhi is intimidating in a way that's hard to put your finger on. She's one of Jaantzen's direct hires from lord knows where, a stocky young woman with her rough street edges filed silky smooth. Today, her black hair's in a long, loose braid over one shoulder and her lips are the perfect shade of bronze for her warm brown skin and ruby red blouse. She looks like she could work any business tower front desk in downtown Bulari, until you start pushing her and feel steel not far beneath the surface.

Gia's plenty imposing herself. She's tall, lanky, with muscles kept toned and taut even though these days she's more likely to be putting the fear in a first-year med student than rushing into battle guns blazing. She wears her hair longer now, a crown of black twists that end just below her ears and hide her prison tattoos. She looks healthy, her dark skin glowing.

The straight and narrow has been treating her well.

Manu sidles up to the counter and flashes Nadhi a grin. "Giaconda!" he calls. "Morning, Nadhi, she's with me."

Nadhi doesn't take her watchful gaze off the

other woman. "Morning, Manu. You two heading up?"

"Yes," snaps Gia.

Manu turns his smile on her. "Gia, let's take a minute, yeah? Grab a cup of coffee?"

"He's waiting," Gia says, frosty calm, only her telltale hummingbird-fast foot tap shaking her right pant leg and betraying her nerves. Not at seeing Jaantzen, of course, though Manu can't think of many others who'd face down that wall of a man like it's no thing.

No, Blackheart has a way of getting inside your head, even when she's not around to do it in person.

"I'll call the lift, then," Nadhi says, a pretty smile at Manu that hardens to flint when she turns back to Gia.

"Thanks," Manu says with a wink. He ushers Gia past the reception desk — not towards the bank of blue-lit lifts that whisk office workers to their respective cubicles, but to the unobtrusive door directly behind Nadhi's desk. It's the only lift that goes all the way to the penthouse, the only lift that stops on certain floors.

"You look good," Manu says as the doors close behind them. He palms the biolock to get authorization for floor twelve. "Sorry it's been a while. I've been meaning to get out to see you and your man. Life just gets, you know." She's staring straight ahead, jaw clenched. "Oriol's back in town, though, we should come see you two before — " Before he disappears again. Manu stops himself from saying it. "Before we let too much more time go. How've you been? How's Tevi?"

Gia finally turns to him. "Coeur's alive," she says, voice low and dangerous.

"Turns out." Manu breathes deep. "Jaantzen call you?"

"Said she needs my help." She laughs, a harsh bark. "When you asked me to recommend a student last week, I figured it would be the usual pulling bullets out of meatheads. Not . . . this."

"Elian's done some good work with the bullet-pulling, too," Manu says. "This meathead is grateful."

He's almost forgotten this old Gia, the clear-eyed, angry woman he grew so fond of during the first, fateful job Willem Jaantzen asked him to take. They'd run side by side for almost a decade until just after the civil war that ousted Coeur in the first place, when Gia came home from a mission to Durga's Belt with a hottie doctor and a sense of peace that had secretly enraged Manu.

To Manu, it had seemed as though the religion Gia'd drunk during her childhood commune days and her Sulila Corp medical training was finally starting to sink in. Or maybe she was just matching

step with her new man. But either way, she was —
not a changed woman, he'd hardly say that. But the
restless, flickering energy in her soul now burned
bright in a single flame.

That's what had gotten between them, more
than her telling Jaantzen she was done with the
business, more than her new eye candy hating
everything Jaantzen — and, by extension, Manu —
stood for. More than the hour's drive out bumpy
desert roads to get to the nonprofit medical
training facility she and Tevi had founded (with
the endowment Jaantzen had given them,
unasked).

It was his jealousy over her new sense of peace.

Banish Coeur from New Sarjun, and suddenly
Gia was ready to move on with her life. It had taken
Manu years after the civil war to recover full func-
tion of his left arm, let alone anything he'd call
peace.

But now Coeur's back. And with a twinge of
shame, Manu realizes how perversely gratified he is
to see Gia's fragile peace crumble.

"Gia," he says quietly.

The lift doors open; Gia hesitates a fraction of a
breath.

"She doesn't need your help."

"She does if she's gonna live," Gia says.

"She doesn't deserve your help," Manu amends.

"No." That single syllable is sharp as a knife. "But Jaantzen does."

She steps out of the lift and onto the twelfth floor.

Jaantzen's already here, a pair of security guards just past him at the door to Medbay 1; one step past them and you'll enter the observation antechamber with its supplies and sleeping area. And you'll find Coeur in the medbay, behind one-way glass like a feral desert cat.

Caged. But always only for the moment.

Jaantzen sees them and straightens. "Giaconda," he murmurs. "Thank you for coming."

"When were you going to tell me?" she asks Jaantzen, tone going deeper than accusation; it hints at betrayal, though she's keeping it close in.

Barely.

"Gia," Manu says, the lightest touch of warning. "We should go somewhere else and talk."

Gia rounds on him, and finally her nerves at seeing Coeur are gone, washed away in white-hot anger. "You call me in like she's just one of your street soldiers needs a couple of stitches. Like I don't have need to know she's still alive. When were you going to tell me?"

"Never," Manu says coolly, and Gia's nostrils flare. He glances at Jaantzen, who nods; he hasn't misspoken. "We would never have told you. Not until we were sure she was going to stay alive and it would be important for you to know."

Gia rocks back on her heels at that, gives them both a skeptical mama bear look that must slay her students. "You were gonna kill her."

"We were keeping our options open," Jaantzen says, expression impassive. "But she's not dying today. Shall we?"

And Gia falls into step, walks with Jaantzen past guards who are politely ignoring the exchange. On her way to heal the woman who killed Jaantzen's family, who tortured Manu to death's door, who sucked away years of Gia's life into Redrock Prison. Manu bites back a curse and follows after.

Blackheart's awake.

Manu hasn't seen her since the night at Julieta's, but she looks like the devil dragged her to hell and she murdered him and dragged herself back. It turns his stomach, but he suspects he's looked worse, and he does his best to keep the horror off his face — not that she pays any attention to him. Her gaze slides to Jaantzen and then past, and for the rest of the meeting it's as though Manu's a shadow in the room. A ghost.

He's fine with that.

If she'd had her way at any time in the past, they'd all be ghosts.

"Giaconda," Coeur says with surprise.

Any nerves Gia'd shown earlier are gone, whisked away into doctor mode. She glances up from a monitor to regard Coeur with cool distance, then looks back down. "I liked it better when I thought you were dead," Gia says mildly.

"Yeah, I've been hearing that a lot." The words are light but Coeur's tone is weary, her lips pale and pressed. Like the joke's gone on long enough it's worn down her armor. Manu wants to feel happy seeing her so broken, but he can't find that emotion in him. He tries to conjure it up, imagines what she felt when their positions were swapped and she was standing over his shattered body.

His spine is electricity through water at the thought, and he leans back against the wall to watch Gia, slips his hands into his pockets.

"Look at you, sugar," Coeur says to Gia's back. "I heard you were doing humanitarian work now, is that true?"

"What the fuck else does it look like I'm doing?" Gia calls up Coeur's scans on the screen, angles them so her patient can't see. Manu can't see either, and he doesn't want to.

Coeur laughs, a rusty door forced open. "Touché. You gonna heal me up?"

At that, Gia finally turns to look her patient in the eye. "Depends on how quiet you can be," she says with enough venom that Blackheart herself falls silent.

Gia's frowning at whatever she sees on the charts, and after a moment she turns back to her patient, gently untucks the blanket from under stick-thin arms, and peels it down over Coeur's abdomen. Her fingers work over Coeur's hospital-gown-clad belly.

Gia's eyebrows knit together. "This hurt?"

"Nope," Coeur says, forced casual through clenched teeth.

"Liar." Gia prods further up, under the right side of the ribs. "How about now."

Coeur hisses with pain but doesn't answer.

"It's been getting worse every day, hasn't it?"

Coeur manages a shrug. "First time I noticed it."

"Bullshit."

Coeur's gaze narrows, deadly. "Leave me be, Giaconda," she growls. Gia's fingers pull back reflexively; Manu's left hand twitches towards the pistol slung over his ribs; but Coeur doesn't move, doesn't even shift her wrists against her restraints. Maybe she can't. Gia smooths the blanket back into place, swipes files from the monitor onto her tablet, and walks back out the door into the antechamber.

Jaantzen follows her, and Manu takes the rear, keeping his attention on Coeur. Doesn't matter how mortally wounded a predator is, her teeth are still strong and claws still sharp. And in Manu's experience, mortally wounded is when a predator's most willing to take the rest of the world with them.

But Coeur just lets her violently translucent eyelids close over red-rimmed eyes, each breath a rattle.

"We should have called you earlier," Jaantzen says to Gia as she calls up charts in the medbay's antechamber, with a hint of a wry smile Gia doesn't return. "It's much nicer when she shuts up."

The antechamber may not be pleasant, but it doesn't smell like death and feel like despair. The bright light chases a brief chill down Manu's spine; he hits the one-way window to full opacity, but he can still feel Blackheart on the other side of the wall.

"What's wrong with her?" Manu asks.

"Elian told me about her hands," Gia says. "But that's not the worst of it. What happened?"

The look Manu and Jaantzen share asks who wants to go first, but Gia sees it and lifts her chin, angry. "Or I don't get to know, is that right?"

"It's just a long, long story," Manu says.

Gia sighs harshly and calls up a screen for them all to see. She points; Manu can't make out a damned bit of the medical jargon there. "She's been bleeding internally, probably her spleen. Sometimes that gets better on its own, but in her case it's getting worse. She needs surgery."

Manu cuts his gaze to Jaantzen. "Elian told me late last night," Jaantzen tells him. "What are her chances?"

"Better now that you let Elian call me. You really want her alive?" When no one answers, she flips to a new screen. "Elian sent over everyone's files," she says. "Looks like you've all been having some fun. Anybody else in this room I should get up on an exam table?"

"We're fine," says Jaantzen.

"Right," says Gia. "Third-degree burns and a concussion are no laughing matter at your age, and Manu, I believe your diagnosis was . . ." She scrolls. "'Bruised ribs and a watch for internal bleeding.' But you're both fine. Of course."

"The concern right now is saving Coeur's life," Jaantzen says.

"For god's sake, she — "

And Manu doesn't know which of Coeur's past atrocities Gia was going to bring up, because she bites it off in a stream of profanity, jaw clenched.

"You gonna ask her about it?" Gia finally says instead. "If she wants me to cut her open? Because it looks to me like she knows she's dying and has been trying to hide it."

"She doesn't get a choice," Jaantzen answers. "We need her alive."

Three breaths, Gia's shoulders rising and falling as the strange weight of those words settles in the room. "I'm a good surgeon, but I'm not a magician," she says finally. "I can't keep someone alive if they want to die."

So let her die.

Manu doesn't say it, though. He and Jaantzen have had this conversation. It doesn't matter how much Manu hates it, Blackheart is their best chance at keeping the fighting in the Fingers from spiraling out of control.

Jaantzen meets his gaze and the older man's sober expression softens, something like sorrow or apology flickering there and gone before it's replaced by resolve.

"Can I borrow your gun?" he asks.

Manu lifts an eyebrow in surprise, but unbuttons his suit jacket and hands the pistol over. Jaantzen checks to see the chamber's loaded. Then, gun in hand, he pushes open the door to Coeur's medbay. Manu doesn't follow but stays in the antechamber, changing the window back to one-way just in time to see Coeur's startled expression at Jaantzen's arrival.

Her gaze trails down Jaantzen's arm to the pistol in his hand. A breath, and she smiles wearily.

"Prognosis that bad, doc?"

"You're dying, and you know it," Jaantzen says. "Gia's your best bet — the question is if you're going to make it worth our time to save you."

"So I can be your puppet," Coeur drawls.

"So you can do something goddamned good in your life."

Coeur bares her teeth with a sound that's almost a laugh. "You're going to fucking stand there in front of Gia, in front of Manu, here with the ghosts of Ximena and Tae and your kids, and say I'm worth saving? Tell me, Willem. Tell me you really believe that."

Jaantzen's expression hardens. He raises the gun, its barrel pausing inches from Coeur's forehead; it whines faintly, the safety off.

"I don't," he says quietly. "Do you want to live, Thala? Because if the answer is no, let's stop wasting both our time. I need to get on with another way to fix my Acheta problem."

The silence between stretches on, Coeur's labored breathing rasping rhythmically over the hum of medical equipment. When she answers, Manu nearly doesn't hear it.

"Yes," she whispers.

Another second, and Jaantzen lowers the pistol, clicks the safety back on. "Good," he says. "We'll get you into surgery immediately."

Manu takes a breath; he has no idea how long he's been holding it.

"Fuck you, Willem," Coeur says, but there's no venom in it.

Jaantzen breathes out a laugh, and for the first time in a week it sounds genuine. "Likewise," he says. As he returns to the antechamber, Manu watches Coeur through the one-way glass. She slumps back, her eyes clamped closed. A single tear squeezes free from her lashes, traces the lines of her red-earth cheek.

He activates the opacity settings once more as Jaantzen shuts the door.

"That settles that." Jaantzen hands the pistol back to Manu. There's a new levity to his voice, a looseness to his shoulders. Manu wishes he could feel so relaxed.

"Fine," Gia says. "You can tell me why later. But you." She holds up a slim black finger; it stops a handsbreadth from Willem Jaantzen's lapel. "Elian tells me you haven't let him examine your concussion for the past two days. Get back in bed until I clear you. It's your brain, man. It's what's got you here. Don't mess with it." The finger shifts to Manu. "And you — "

Manu holds up his hands. "I let your boy all over me with his scanner. He said I could work."

"Then you and I can talk later."

"What do you need?" Jaantzen asks.

"I need her set up in the surgery room."

"Done."

"And Elian wants me to make you promise you won't murder him in the desert for not being able to handle this himself."

A faint smile tugs at Jaantzen's lips. "I wasn't planning to."

Gia takes a deep breath. "And promise me that keeping her alive isn't a mistake."

"That I can't do."

In the silence surrounding them, the sharp hum of machinery and screens and computers seems to rise to a fever pitch, the whine of it all spiking sharply between Manu's eyes.

Finally, Gia takes a deep breath. "Well, I guess it's time for me to go cut on a bitch."

3

———————

JAANTZEN

W illem Jaantzen could use some rest. Would love some, but he's no longer just running off-hours illegal operations where he can pull a job and lie low while the heat fades. He's got real estate deals in the works. The hospitality supply business. His security business, Admant. One restaurant to run and another to begin planning. Hundreds of employees depending on him to put food on the table, whether they're aware they work for him or not.

Gia wants him on bed rest, but he's had two dozen messages show up in his inbox just in the time they spent dealing with Coeur, and now a voice call's coming from Cobalt Tower's reception-ist, Nadhi. And the only time he ever hears from her is when something urgently needs his attention.

Jaantzen sinks into a chair at the conference table. It's almost noon, and the floor-to-ceiling windows of the penthouse suite that doubles as his home and office have dimmed to keep out the glaring sunlight. Bulari's skyline is sketched jagged through the darkened glass. He catches a whiff of something sweet and floral and out of place and turns his head to the hydroponic garden that slices through the center of the room: lush, green, and courtesy of Julieta Yang. One of the vines is blooming, spiraled cream-colored leaves unfurling to reveal pale pink hearts.

Did it bloom just now? Today? Or is he only now noticing, in the chaos of the last week?

The chime of Nadhi's call sounds again; Jaantzen breathes deep, opens the channel.

"Sir?" she says. "You have someone here to see you. Phaera D?"

Jaantzen frowns at that. Phaera's come to see him here? He's known the Bulari businesswoman for almost five years, since she opened her luxury casino and began circulating in same rarified crowd Julieta Yang had introduced Jaantzen to. Phaera's always been friendly when they've met at social gatherings, but she's never sought him out.

But if Jaantzen knows anything about Phaera D, he knows she doesn't trek across town on a whim.

"I'll tell her it can wait if you're busy," Nadhi says, misinterpreting his hesitation.

"No, send her up," Jaantzen says. "Thank you, Nadhi."

The connection pops to silence and Jaantzen turns to survey the penthouse; it's been a while since anyone but his team has visited, but nothing's too out of place for entertaining.

Phaera's here to talk about Acheta. She must be. The last time he saw her was at Chief Justice Geum-ja Leone's dinner party, the one Acheta had strolled into to announce he'd killed Naali Hinoja and was there in her place. Phaera'd been one of many who'd seemed willing to do what was needed to get rid of the brash crew boss.

She's always been a mystery to Jaantzen. She floats perfectly in Julieta's world, Leone's world, as light and charming as any socialite. But in business she's ruthless. Despite the initial resistance she faced in pushing her way into the old money club of casino magnates, she's earned their grudging respect by being wildly successful with the Devil's Table. Enough that she was able to buy a second casino, the Lorelei, within only a few years. And earlier this year, she organized the casino district in a brutal campaign against an Arquellian casino chain that had tried to elbow in on the drag, drowning them in public relations fiascos and supply chain problems and so much general ill will that they never even opened their doors.

She's got claws behind the velvet facade she wears so easily at those fancy social gatherings. And the looks she gives him sometimes, when they're both enjoying hors d'oeuvres and listening to some patrician's old money complaints, it's like she sees straight through his own attempts to blend in and is sharing a joke with him.

It's unnerving. And intriguing.

The lift chimes and the lights flicker and Phaera steps into the penthouse with a smile. She's wrapped in some sort of complicated, expensive-looking tunic top in deep sapphire, paired with cream trousers. Her magenta bob brushes her shoulders, fringed with black at the tips.

She takes the room in with an appreciative expression. His office is really just the open living space of the penthouse suite; the bedrooms are all up the sweeping flight of stairs on the uppermost level. The furnishings are modern and colorful against the spare white palette, but the most striking feature is the dizzying view out over the city from sixty-eight stories up.

"This is gorgeous, Jaantzen." She steps past him to admire the view, then turns to take in Julieta's swath of plants. "An oasis. I'll admit I didn't expect it of you. I was anticipating a utilitarian war room with army surplus seating and mismatched carpets." She spots the flowering vine and leans in to breathe its perfume, eyelashes fluttering closed with pleasure. "I owe you an apology for underestimating your sense of style."

"Apology accepted," Jaantzen says with a faint smile. He's seen the surprise on other people's faces, but Phaera's the first to say it out loud.

She finally turns back to him, studying his face. He knows what she sees: the bruises have faded to mostly invisible under his rich brown skin, but he's still got a couple cuts on the mend and a scrape on his temple that people are going to be asking questions about for weeks.

Or maybe not. You don't acquire a reputation like the one Willem Jaantzen has in order to encourage small talk about mysterious cuts.

"So." Phaera gives him an appraising look. "The rumors are true."

"Which rumors."

Phaera lifts an eyebrow. "Oh, I didn't realize there were multiple," she says with a smile. "I'm sure there are some juicy ones I haven't even heard yet." She turns back to the vine, brushing a finger over the tip of a petal; the blossom contracts, petals spiraling closed. "What is this vine? I've never seen it before."

"There's one at the Jungle but I've never seen it

in bloom," Jaantzen says. "Julieta calls it Secret Heart. Please, make yourself comfortable." Jaantzen crosses to the kitchen, pulls out a pair of glasses and, after a moment's hesitation, a bottle of mezcal from a Ruby Basin distillery that he's positive he's heard Phaera mention. He pours them both a finger, then carries glasses and bottle back out to the pair of electric-blue couches Phaera's settled on.

"Thank you." Phaera clinks her glass against his and takes an appreciative sip.

"And what rumors have you been hearing about me," Jaantzen asks.

"That you got into a bit of trouble at Julieta Yang's place." The mischief on her face softens into something serious and searching, only for a moment. "Are you okay?"

"I'm fine. Everyone on my team is fine."

"I don't suppose I'll get any details." She gives him a secretive smile.

Jaantzen lets a smile touch his own lips. "There are none to give." As much as she drinks in gossip from others, he knows she doesn't pass it on. Neither does he. Some people revel in recounting stories, working over the little details in retelling after retelling until they're polished and pat. And maybe, he thinks, he just hasn't lived through many stories worth telling. Or maybe that's just not the sort of thing that gives him joy.

Either way, anyone who needs to know what happened at Julieta's greenhouse was there and already knows. Everyone else can get their voyeuristic rush from the latest thriller serial on the feeds.

"How can I help you?" he asks.

Phaera just leans back on the couch, holding the mezcal up to catch the light. It's the twenty-five year, a complex deep gold that he notices now is the exact same shade as her eyes.

"No business deals, no propositions," she tells him, then holds up a hand in apology. "Well, at least no business deals until later. I truly did just come by to see if you were all right."

He's not certain how to respond to that, so he just takes a sip, holds the taste of smoke on his tongue.

"Don't look so uncomfortable, Jaantzen," she says. "It's all right to have friends who don't work for you. But if it makes you feel better, I also wanted to pick your brain about something."

He doesn't bother to answer the first comment, but he does relax a fraction. Favors, problems, business propositions — that's firm ground. But he can't remember the last time someone who wasn't Starla or Manu made time in their day just to see how he was, let alone came halfway across the city for a social call.

No, he can.

His wife, Tae.

"What's on your mind?" he asks Phaera before he drifts anywhere near that lane.

"Acheta and Dry Creek," she says; he's guessed right. "Dry Creek shot up the corner store on Veritas and Third. Then the next morning, two of their thugs were found dead in the park on Fourth and Huaihai."

"Retaliation. I heard about that."

"Then you probably heard about the shoot-out on Fifteenth? By the Pearl Rabbit? A tourist got caught in the crossfire."

"I saw that."

"My books are in the red this week — the same goddamn month a Ganesh transport is docked," Phaera says. "The rest of the boys on the block are in the same boat. The dice are rolling on empty tables. Lounge singers are singing to nobody. The city is flooded with tourists wanting to spend their cash, and they're all too afraid to head outside the Tamarind and visit my casinos." She laughs harshly. "Though they're not even feeling safe in the Tamarind after what happened at the Brujería last night, did you see that?"

Jaantzen's vaguely aware of the club, but he hasn't heard any news about it this morning. He shakes his head.

"Someone was pushing bad shard, and a few

people died. Pretty horrifically, actually — do yourself a favor and stay off the news feeds today. Rumors are that it was part of a big batch Acheta just released, but no one can trace exactly where it went."

"I'd guess nobody's buying any shard today."

"Which is good for the state of humankind, but Acheta's starting to look for other revenue sources." Phaera sets her glass down, gold bangles jangling on her wrist. "Something needs to change. Tourists who've just spent weeks in space are turning around and taking Aiax Demosga's goddamn shuttle back up to orbit to play his tables instead of coming out to mine."

"What do you mean, Acheta's looking for other revenue?"

"He wants protection money," Phaera says, eyes narrowing. "From me and the other business owners in the casino district."

Now that was audacious. "He came to see you directly?"

Phaera shakes her head, the tips of her magenta bob brushing her cheek. "He sent some goons this morning, saying that all the trouble in the neighborhood is being caused by Dry Creek, and that if we pay him dues, he'll protect our businesses. Which is bullshit — half the trouble has been from his thugs," Phaera says with a roll of her eyes. "With Coeur there was never fighting on the streets. With Hinoja, even with Dry Creek. But now Acheta comes along and shoots up our businesses and thinks we'll pay him not to do it?"

"Will you pay?"

Phaera laughs. "Absolutely not."

"Phaera . . ."

"Acheta needs to go," she says. "This is getting out of hand. Even if I did pay, he's not strong enough to fight off Dry Creek. Not to mention his people will probably mutiny by the end of the week and turn the casino district into even more of a nightmare."

When Levi Acheta made his power play to take out Coeur's chosen successor, Naali Hinoja, he probably thought it made him powerful. But Hinoja was respected within Coeur's old crew in a way Acheta will never be. Especially if he's running low enough on cash to turn to extortion. That level of desperation is blood on the wind in a crew like that.

Jaantzen wonders if Phaera expects him to step in and take Acheta's territory — but that would simply mean more bloodshed, and he's not interested in a war for peace. The way he sees it, there are two ways this ends without intervention. Either Dry Creek forces Acheta back out of the neighborhood in a bloody pulp, or Acheta manages to win control of the territory but not his own crew.

There's no one Jaantzen knows of in Coeur's old team both strong enough to challenge Acheta and respected enough to win over the rest of the crew if they did. Nobody, except for Coeur herself.

Phaera is watching him curiously, like she expects him to have an answer. After all, he's billed himself as the man with the answers, hasn't he? The solver of other people's problems. It's the reason he's made any inroads at all into Julieta and Justice Leone's crowd.

"How's your security?" he asks.

"The best," she says. "For the casino business, though my people aren't prepared for the sort of violence Acheta and Dry Creek are bringing. But I don't want more guards, I want a neighborhood that's not riddled with bullet holes."

"I understand," Jaantzen says thoughtfully.

"I thought you might," Phaera says, and there's a hint of conspiracy in her voice that sets him to attention. She knows more than she's letting on. "Because I've heard some other rumors, too." She leans forward, elbows on knees. "I've been hearing that Thala Coeur is alive and on New Sarjun. You wouldn't happen to know anything about that."

Ah, good. Feeding that rumor mill has been delicate business — too much, and he'll have Leone knocking on his door demanding to know if it's true. Too little, and it won't reach the people in Acheta's organization whose ears might perk up in a good way. Too definite, and Acheta will have time to prepare. Too vague, and the rumors will be dismissed outright as wishful thinking.

Phaera's ear is clearly closer to the ground than Jaantzen anticipated, but if she's hearing that Coeur is alive — and wondering if it's true — then Manu's whisper network is working.

"And where have you been hearing these rumors?" Jaantzen asks.

"It's on the streets."

"You can't trust the streets, Phaera."

"Of course not. Especially when it's apparently Dry Creek doing the spreading. They know how fragile Acheta's loyalty is. But then I heard something else interesting." She taps an unvarnished nail against the side of her glass. "My chief of security at the Table, his little cousin runs with Dry Creek. He was hate-bragging at family dinner about taking shots at the great Willem Jaantzen last week. Sounds like he was running security for a very special prisoner when another crew came and busted her out."

She smiles; he's waiting for the catch, for the bribe in it, but there's only that quirk of conspiracy and camaraderie.

"And according to the rumors, it was a very

heroic and daring rescue," she says. "One for the action vids."

"Was it."

"Mmm. Some girls find daring rescues exciting." She tilts her head, watching him with topaz eyes. "The only thing I haven't been able to learn is why. If Dry Creek was hoping to take over Coeur's territory, they wouldn't kidnap her and bring her back to New Sarjun. And then what would be so important that her mortal enemy would bust her out?" She uncorks the mezcal bottle on the table, pours another finger into each of their glasses. "I prefer to gamble with other people's money. But if I were putting my own on the line I'd say the answer is the scandal of the century."

"Who else is talking about this?" Jaantzen asks.

"My security chief's little cousin was one of the Dry Creek bodies that showed up in the park yesterday. So he won't be telling anyone else. But he's hardly the only one who must've seen you there." Phaera sips. "What's your plan, Jaantzen?"

"I want this to be resolved as much as you do," he says. "But I can't make any promises."

"I'm not the kind of girl that demands promises," Phaera says with a slight smile. "I'm the kind who takes care of business."

Jaantzen leans back against the couch, waiting. She may truly have come just to see how he's doing, but the rest of this conversation has been a pre-amble of some sort.

And here's the pitch.

"I've been talking with other business owners on the north side, and there are plenty of like-minded people who are willing to do what it takes to make our neighborhood safe for commerce again," Phaera says. "And since you recently pur-chased a building in Jet Park — congratulations on that by the way — I thought you would make a good addition to our little association."

He takes a sip of his mezcal. "Inviting me won't make your other members uncomfortable?" Justice Leone may have made him a fixture at her little gatherings, but not all the upstanding members of Bulari's business community feel the same way about him.

She laughs. "Jaantzen, please. It's not a tea-par-ties-and-cigars kind of business association. This is a getting-shit-done sort of business association. That means mutual protection, sure. But more than that — we'll be patrolling the streets. Making sure the local trouble understands we don't pay protec-tion bribes and our neighborhood has rules. En-forcing those rules." She winks at him. "Please say yes. It'll be more fun with you around."

"Who else have you got?"

"Cavy and Tarri are on the fence, Ayisha's likely." She rattles off another half-dozen names of casino owners along Bulari's gambling drag. "And you know Lucky, of course?" she asks. Jaantzen nods; he does business with the shifty proprietor of Lucky's Palladium Coast through his restaurant supply business, RKE. "The dealer's union is on board, of course, and the mototaxi union. Still working on the cab drivers, Jaxon hasn't made time for me yet."

"You've talked to Seti?" The gentech magnate is the driving force behind developing Jet Park, and the one who convinced Jaantzen to start buying real estate there. But Seti's initial property holdings haven't developed into much of a stake in the neighborhood yet.

Phaera waves a hand. "Seti won't make up his mind until he knows who the winning team is. Maybe you can talk to him. The idea is the casinos provide the muscle, since we're all already bankrolling security teams. The others provide the eyes, the cash, and silence if needed."

"And you need someone for the dirty work," Jaantzen guesses. It's what Leone's crowd always needs from him — someone to do the work their hands are too clean to do.

Phaera's eyebrows shoot high; she looks honestly offended. "I'm not asking you for favors, Jaantzen. I don't need shit from you. I'm solving a problem in our neighborhood and figured since you're new to the area, you'd like to get involved."

She's gathering herself to stand, and Jaantzen holds up a hand. "My apologies," he says. "I assumed —"

"I know what you assumed. I know the sorts of favors Yang and Leone and Seti and all the rest of them ask you, but that's not why I'm here. I'm here to offer you a business opportunity. A chance for you to expand Admant Security into the casino market."

He takes his glass, sipping to cover his surprise. Julieta had introduced him to Leone and the rest of her world because they needed Coeur taken care of, and they needed to go outside their comfort zone to do it. And that dynamic had continued for the past decade: Jaantzen the problem solver, who will reach into the darkest corners of psyche and society where they don't dare look. He can count the times this crowd has wanted to do legitimate business with him on one hand.

"Nobody else is doing a good job in the casino security market at the moment," Phaera says. "Most of us are cobbling together what we need — and it's worked. But we run safes, not fortresses. Our money's sealed up tight, but we can't defend ourselves against someone like Acheta. And whether or not you have a way of dealing with Acheta" — she cocks an eyebrow at him — "I for one want to do better at security. Will you take a look at the Table and the Lorelei?"

Jaantzen clears his throat. "I can bring a team to see you tonight."

"I'll be at the Table tonight," she says. "Ayisha wanted to talk to you, too, and Ibn Rushd of the Aterciopelado. I'll let them know you're taking on casino clients."

"Thank you. Do you trust your security team?"

"Absolutely."

"Do you have a personal detail?"

"Like a bodyguard?" Phaera laughs. "Five years ago I was a waitress, Jaantzen. What the hell do I need with a bodyguard?"

"Phaera," Jaantzen says seriously. "The last time you organized the community against some-one, it was an Arquellian corporation. This time it's Levi Acheta. If you're going to stir the hornet's nest, you should have someone watching your back."

"I trust my team," she says. "I just need better weapons."

"We'll talk about what you need tonight."

"Excellent. To like-minded businesspeople," she says, toasting him with the last sip of her mezcal and setting the glass down on the table. "Now," she says, leaning forward. "When are you inviting me over for dinner?"

He frowns at the abrupt shift of conversation, feels a slow flush creeping up the back of his neck. That playful expression on her face, the tilt of her chin, the steady, even glimmer of her topaz eyes: she's flirting with him — with Willem Jaantzen. He doesn't have a conditioned response.

"I don't know if now is a good time," he says finally, and it's not the right thing to say — it's not what he wants to say — but it seems the safest course of action until he can figure out what she wants from him.

"Then I'll invite myself over, when you don't look like you've just been run over by a train," Phaera says with a wink. She taps a finger on her temple, right where his own is scraped raw. "And maybe then I'll get the story of how a quiet evening drinking tea at Julieta's resulted in all those cuts and bruises."

"I'll come by the Devil's Table tonight with my team," Jaantzen says, and Phaera rises, grasps his hand in a firm, business-like handshake; he's flooded with relief that she's keeping her distance, even as her grip burns against a bruise on his hand he hadn't noticed until now.

He presses the button and the lift doors open. "I look forward to it," she says over her shoulder as she wafts out of the suite.

4

———————

STARLA

Starla is going to have to buy Leti a new handkerchief.

By morning, when she finally pulled the strange little shard tab out of her purse, she could see that it was starting to eat specks through the silk, so she threw the whole mess into a glass jar, clamped the lid down tight, and that's what she now intends to deposit on Toshiyo's desk.

Manu's already there, kicked back in one of Toshiyo's office chairs, feet propped on the two inches of clear space on her desk, hands behind his head. Deep in conversation. Toshiyo is sitting cross-legged in another chair, elbow on her desk, fist to cheek.

Toshiyo only really opens up to Manu, as far as

Starla can tell. She and Starla can talk for hours about security system designs and wiring schematics and how to machine the exact right part they need for one of their projects — like that military satellite in the conference room — but they have never had a heart-to-heart.

Of course, Toshiyo and Manu have known each other for decades, since the fateful job when Jaantzen hired them both. The one where he and Coeur had their first break, that became a lifelong feud.

Seeing Toshiyo and Manu together like this is a familiar scene. Except for the fact that they're washed in pale pink by an angry-looking alien creature swimming in a too-small fishtank beside Toshiyo's desk. Its wings waft bioluminescent pink streaks through the fertilizer liquid. It's about the size of a newborn. Starla hopes it intends to stay that way.

"You have to tell him how you feel," Toshiyo is saying — Starla thinks she's saying. "It's only been a week, and — "

Starla deliberately knocks her heel against a scale model of a wind turbine so that it rocks against the table, and Toshiyo looks up, startled. Manu kicks down his feet and spins, then doubles over in pain. Starla ignores the stream of profanity scrolling across the bottom of her lens.

"Sorry for interrupting," Starla signs.

"It's fine, come on in," Manu signs, speaking aloud, too, as he often does when Toshiyo is around. Toshiyo's ability to understand USL isn't bad, but it's not perfect. Mostly, she just doesn't remember to pay attention visually to a multiperson conversation when there's so much around to tinker with.

Starla ducks underneath a swag of cables and edges around what looks like a full-sized wind turbine blade to get to Toshiyo's desk, then deposits her jar where Manu's feet had been. He leans forward, picking up the jar and gently turning it until the bright-blue shard tab works its way free from the silk handkerchief. He looks up at Starla, curious.

"The club last night? Some guy was pushing it," Starla signs. "He tried to sell some to me and the girls, and then he popped a tab himself. Next thing we saw he was on the dance floor, dead."

Not quite dead, of course. Starla can't get the image of his convulsing, blistering form out of her mind, and she's glad they didn't stay to see the end of it. Macabre human curiosity being what it is, others did — and even if Starla hadn't been looking for it this morning, she couldn't have missed the images of his death going viral throughout the networks.

Toshiyo's eyes widened. "You were at the Brujería?" she signs, as usual a flurry of mostly finger-spelling and scattered USL signs. Probably incomprehensible to most people, but Starla has known her long enough to understand it. "I saw pictures, but nobody seemed to know what caused it. His face was all black and scabby . . ."

Starla hadn't stayed for that part.

"What are you guys talking about?" Manu asks.

"I'll show you," Toshiyo says and signs. She carefully scoots a pile of LED rings to the edge of her desk, calls up a keyboard, and begins typing.

Starla raps on the desk, shaking her head. Toshiyo's fingers pause.

"I don't want to see it again," Starla signs. "Once is enough."

"Especially in real life I guess," Toshiyo signs; Starla nods.

Manu makes a face. "I'll take your word for it, and I've got enough horrible images in my head without adding one more." He clicks a gleaming copper fingernail against the glass jar. "You got this from him?" Manu asks.

"It was scattered all over the floor," Starla signs. "A couple others grabbed it, but hopefully they weren't stupid enough to take it after seeing what happened."

"God," breathes Manu.

"It looks like the same stuff we found in that old building Jaantzen bought," signs Toshiyo.

"That's why I grabbed it."

"I'll take a look. I've still got some of that old stuff in my lab." Toshiyo leans back in her chair, then glances over to the creature sitting beside her. "Pretty weird, huh, buddy?" she says out loud. The creature wafts back and forth; it could be a shrug.

"Have you named it yet?" Starla asks.

"Don't encourage her," Manu signs back with exasperation.

"Hey! I think it's cute!" Toshiyo says.

"I don't think cute is the right word for it," signs Manu. "Terrifying, maybe."

"Hellacious," spells Starla.

"Hellacious." Manu rolls the word around on his tongue. "I like it," he signs. "Perfect."

"Well, I think it's cute," signs Toshiyo.

Starla expects Manu to quip back, but he just checks his comm, preoccupied.

Starla turns her attention to the creature. The thing's only getting bigger; it's already starting to crowd against the confines of its aquarium globe. Pretty soon they're going to have to find a new home for their . . .

Adorable pet? Demon tormenter? Esteemed colleague?

It looks a bit like a murderous mermaid, and

Starla can't for the life of her figure out why it needs both bat wings and a fish's tail. Its eyes are ink black and glossy, and as it undulates gently in its aquarium, it's clearly plotting its escape and their murders.

The creature is unsettling enough on its own. But the worst part is how familiar it seems to Starla. She touches two fingers to the stone necklace resting against her breastbone, staring at the creature. The resemblance has to be in her imagination. It has to be.

Her mother had always worn the necklace, whenever she was home — a disk of stone carved in an intricate pattern that had seemed merely artistic when Starla was a child, but now reminds her of a small, fanged, winged creature.

Starla's mother had joked that it was her alien fertility goddess, found the night Starla was conceived — which was nothing Starla had wanted to know about. Then Starla arrived on New Sarjun in an Alliance prison jumpsuit, all of her previous belongings exploded into vapor, any memento she had of her parents destroyed in the Alliance attack that destroyed her family's home.

Everything except this necklace, which her cousin Mona had had in safekeeping and returned to her years later.

Where the hell had Starla's mother found this thing?

And why does it look so much like this creature?

There's a way to open the globe itself — Toshiyo got the other one open to extract the first black-eyed pea . . . or, embryo? . . . that they'd found just fine. It's now safely contained again — and hopefully dormant. But no one has suggested trying to open the globe containing the fully formed creature. Who wants to be responsible for unleashing an alien on New Sarjun?

Starla leans in to give the creature a closer look. It swirls in its liquid, tilts its terrifying head to get a better view of her, bares its fangs. Starla bares her own teeth, and it blinks a moment as though surprised by the return of aggression.

"Be careful, you're probably hitting on it," signs Manu.

Starla makes a face at him. "Its teeth? Double row," she signs. "Yikes. Make that a triple row."

There are scratches on the inside of the glass, some shallow, but others are deep, almost like cracks except that they run in parallel lines just about the same distance apart as the creature's claws. Starla traces one set with her fingertips, and the creature's clawed wings mimic her movement.

"We have to figure out what to do with this thing," Manu says and signs.

"I'm on it," Starla signs. "I've got a meeting with someone today."

"Who?"

"A biologist," she spells. "I sent you both the paper he wrote."

Toshiyo looks excited and palms her inbox open, scanning through messages. Manu blinks like he's searching through memory. "Right, I saw that," he signs. "And no, I didn't read it."

"'On the Possibility of Precursor Life in the Durga System,'" Toshiyo says, reading aloud. "Looks fun!" She opens the file above her desk and leans forward with chin on fists to read.

Above her, the creature is spinning in slow circles, enormous ears leaving streaks of hot-pink luminescence. It gnashes its horrific teeth in dainty little chops.

"I think it's hungry," signs Starla.

"Hungry?" Manu asks. "What the hell do we feed it?"

"Human flesh, obviously."

"Well, I'm not volunteering."

"I say we feed it Co — " Toshiyo bites off the name with a worried glance at Manu. He gives her a half smile, and she cracks her ring fingers in unison, takes a deep breath. "I've kept it alive this long by literally doing nothing but talking to it," she says. "But I don't think that's going to work for much longer."

"Be careful what you tell it," Starla signs. "It could be a spy."

"It's the cutest spy ever," Toshiyo says, giving the creature a smile.

"If you want a hell-beast we'll get you a cat, Tosh," Manu says and signs.

Starla straightens. Time to let them get back to talking about whatever's bothering Manu. If it pertains to her, she'll find out about it later.

"The weird shard, let me know what you find?" she asks.

Toshiyo nods. "I'll do some tests this afternoon," she signs. "Good luck!"

Manu gives her a thumbs-up.

The creature only glares, daring her to discover the truth.

Starla hasn't ever been to a university before. Back on Silk Station, her parents' home base in Durga's Belt, school was TUTOR, a Hypatia AI designed especially for kids in the off-planet colonies.

And which, Starla suspects, her parents probably stole.

She'd been expected to do the bare minimum, and beyond that, she'd been able to study whatever she felt like. In her youth, that had mostly been mechanics — if she couldn't take it apart with her hands, it didn't interest her. When she came to live with Jaantzen, it hadn't occurred to him to school her until after their first year together. By then, she was mostly just spending hours buried in books that reminded her of home. Mechanics, still, but astronomy and physics and fiction, too.

The University of Bulari is a Hypatia Educational Facilities Corporation feeder school providing indenture training for almost a hundred other companies. No technical track — that training all takes place out near the mines — but the university churns out made-to-order lawyers, mathematicians, writers, designers, and management personnel who graduate with a guaranteed job and an iron-clad contract to whichever company buys their schooling debt to Hypatia.

The whole campus is meticulously organized. Even the park she's walking through feels aggressively educational, with its carefully presented range of local flora: flowering tree aloes and thorny acacias and razor-leaf palms and silver-needle fern cacti. Everything is neatly labeled, feral desert plants tamed for show.

Starla dressed reasonably professional today,

but she's still gathering looks from the students who scurry in pairs and triples, each stuffing their brain full of the information and skills the indenture companies are paying for.

If that's the price of education, Starla will stick with her erratic patchwork, thank you very much.

The School of Life Sciences is at the top of a hill, a building of opalescent glass etched with an artistic mural that seems meant to depict the branches of life.

Biology is one of those gaping holes of topics that have never before interested her. Her body seems to work just fine, the things she eats are tasty, and she knows where to find a good doctor if she gets busted up on the job. What else is there to know? She's never going to gene-splice one of her cats with a fern or anything like that. A plant with claws and self-destructive tendencies just seems like a bad idea.

The thought makes her smile.

She palms in, and her visitor's credentials splash up on the screen: Starla Deyva. Citizen: Bulari, New Sarjun. As always, she feels a pang for not using her parents' name, but she also knows they would understand. In fact, more likely than not Dusai was a pseudonym itself — it's just a far too recognizable one in the right crowds.

A strand of blue lights embedded in the floor

pulses gently away from her, indicating that she should follow. Of course, she's already studied the building's floor plan, so she knows exactly where Dr. Sam Amrith's office is. And where all the exits are.

The blue lights in the floor are connected to pressure sensors, and when she stops in front of the professor's door, the doorframe pulses. She's installed these systems in office buildings before. If it's configured right, a chime will sound and the security AI will announce that Starla Deyva is here.

Or at least that the person who signed in with Starla Deyva's credentials and weighs the same as she does is here. This class of systems isn't terribly smart.

After a moment the door opens and the professor appears.

Starla blinks.

Dr. Amrith is not what she expected. Younger, for starters. Closer to her own age than how he looked in his fussy professorial profile photo. He's slender, with brown skin, short black hair, and russet eyes flecked with emerald.

"You must be Ms. Deyva," he says, holding the door open for her. His words glow on the bottom of her lens. "Come in. Can I offer you some tea?"

"No, thank you," she signs, and his eyes widen just a touch.

"Of course. How can I help you?"

He's smiling, but it's clear he's confused, and a touch worried.

She holds up a finger, then hands over her comm, presses Send on her gauntlet.

I JUST HAVE A FEW QUESTIONS.

He frowns at the words, then nods. For a second she's expecting that awkward thing where he stops talking, too, or — worse — starts using primitive hand gestures as though trying to communicate with a stranger through soundproof glass. "Of course. No, I'm sorry. Should I be typing?" He holds up the comm with thumbs poised, one expressive eyebrow arched in apology and inquisition. Even if her lens weren't able to capture his words, she'd understand him.

She taps a finger at the corner of her eye.

"Ah, a lens? And it's transcribing? Good. Please let me know, I can start talking fast when I get excited. Sit, sit."

He sits behind a state-of-the-art desk — it's a clutter of open screens and hand-scrawled annotations, two tablets and a paper book open to what might be drawings of grains. He sticks one tablet inside the book to mark his place, swipes all the open screens to vanish in a box in the corner. "If you like, we could key into my desk. It might be easier?"

Starla shakes her head with a *No, thank you* smile. Her comm and gauntlet operate in a shielded network that's almost impossible to hack, and she doesn't need Hypatia Corp seeing the sorts of questions she's about to ask. He seems to have asked in a spirit of genuine help, though, not because he's trying to maintain a record of their conversation. She relaxes.

"Are you a student here?" Dr. Amrith shakes his head at himself, laughs. "I'm sorry, of course you're not. My apologies."

She frowns. *What makes you say that?*

Her godfather has tried to instill his sense of sartorial language in her. To Jaantzen, clothing is armor, both a weapon and a defense to be carefully deployed. Starla prefers actual armor: her black combat fatigues, biosilk vest, bone-crusher boots. She's actually dolled herself up for this meeting, in a suit and the closest she's ever found to dress shoes she can still fight in. She knows she doesn't look like she belongs in a downtown Bulari office, not with her tattooed ears, her piercings, her bleached, spiked hair, her rangy restlessness. But surely she's mildly respectable?

"Oh, nothing, it's just — " Dr. Amrith tilts his head, examining her for a moment. She senses the moment when he decides to tell her the truth, instead of whatever it was he'd been going to say.

"You don't act like a person who's about to take on a lifetime indenture," he says finally. "May I ask what you do?"

I RUN A SECURITY BUSINESS.

"Fascinating!" he says, and though it can't possibly be, his expression doesn't seem forced. "And I'm guessing you grew up off-planet? Your height . . ."

Starla nods. She supposes the polite conversational thing is to offer up where, but she doesn't need anyone prying into her false identity. *I MOVED HERE FOR WORK,* she types, and he nods, satisfied. *I READ THAT YOU'RE FROM BULARI.*

"Born and raised," he says, with a pause and a little laugh like he'd made an inside joke. Maybe it was something in his inflection, or his accent? She's heard plenty of Indirans say the New Sarjunian accent is hard to understand. "Oh, sorry."

Starla shrugs, not certain what he's apologizing for. She's about to push Send on her next message — get down to business — but she finds herself distracted. His desk is pulsing faintly under his elbows, in a resting state of rotating starburst patterns that Starla finally begins to realize are microscopic images of cellular structures.

Dr. Amrith catches her looking and smiles. "Our world is incredible, especially when viewed from close up," he says.

The fibrous webs and brilliant colors could be nebulae, galaxies. She glances up, her memory sparked at something familiar she'd seen when she walked in. His walls are decorated with biological taxonomies, illustrations, and a scattering of stars: a poster of a familiar constellation. She smiles at it.

OR FAR AWAY, she types. THE PANGOLIN.

Dr. Amrith grins over his shoulder at the poster. "You know your constellations."

Damn right she does. MY HOBBY, she types.

"The stars look different from space," he says, and for a moment she's not sure if he's asking her a question; her lens doesn't assign question marks correctly if a speaker's inflection isn't standard. He smiles as if in memory. "The light's so steady. Almost colder. I always assumed I would feel closer to them, but they seemed so much more distant. The atmosphere makes them seem alive, doesn't it?"

He's waiting for her to answer, not just caught in his own private reverie. That serenity on his face, she doesn't want to crack it.

But, IT'S ONLY AN ILLUSION, she types.

His smile widens. "That's part of what makes the stars so fascinating, isn't it? Understanding them is as much about the emotions we bring to them as the astrophysics that creates and sustains them. I'm sorry, I'm not talking too fast, am I?"

The transcription is trailing behind him, but it

seems to be catching every word. At least, what it's displaying to her makes grammatical and contextual sense. He speaks with his hands and face more than most hearing people she's met, and he doesn't have that hesitation to stray from conversational safety with her that she senses in most hearing strangers, either. With those, it's all simple words, simple subjects, even when typing to her, when she can obviously read and write. It makes her want to tear her hair out.

She gives him a thumbs-up.

"But you didn't come to speak with a biology professor about astronomy, did you?" His gaze flickers to the time hologram floating in the far right corner of his desk; the numbers are formed of leafy sprouts that unfurl above the desk, waving gently as though in a breeze.

I'M HERE BECAUSE I READ A PAPER YOU WROTE. Starla has the link ready; she pushes it through so there's no confusion about what she's talking about.

She watches his face as he opens the link. Professional curiosity, confusion, then guarded worry.

"Oh," he says after a moment. "That paper. I don't do much with that topic anymore these days, I'm afraid."

It took Starla hours of searching before she found *On the Possibility of Precursor Life in the Durga System* buried in a dusty, dark corner of the network where few respectable scientists seemed to reside. It was partly an examination of unexplained artifacts and strange word-of-mouth stories — most of which Starla had already seen referenced in the works of crackpots around the net. But it also referenced another scientific paper, one Starla hadn't been able to find anywhere else: a genetic study on remains discovered in the Belt. Remains that the paper's author claimed couldn't possibly be human.

I JUST HAVE A FEW QUESTIONS, she types.

Dr. Amrith glances past her, then stands to close the door. He stares back down at the comm, his lips pursed to the side.

"A young man's wild imaginings," he says. He laughs ruefully. "I didn't think you could still find this. I suppose nothing truly disappears once it's been committed to a screen."

I HAVEN'T SHARED THIS WITH ANYONE. I JUST READ IT AND FOUND YOU.

"It's not — it's fine," he says. "I just don't . . ." He whirls a finger in the air, a gesture meant to indicate the office around him and, by extension, his employer. Hypatia Corp.

MY COMM IS ON A SELF-CONTAINED NETWORK.

She looks up at him, and he nods uncertainly.

IF YOU DON'T WANT TO SAY SOMETHING, JUST TYPE IT.

"Oh, it's not that at all," he says, but his demeanor's changed. The passion he showed when talking about the stars has been replaced by a careful politeness. "That was just something I wrote years ago. It's pure speculation, and I haven't thought about it in years. I'm sorry if you thought any of it was true."

His smile comes forced, and Starla feels a pang of sadness for him. She remembers his statement about how she didn't look like a student, didn't seem like someone about to take on a lifetime indenture.

She wonders just how many more years of his life Sam Amrith still owes to Hypatia for his own education.

She reaches behind her neck to undo the clasp, then slips the stone amulet out of her shirt. It feels cool in the palm of her hand, though it's been nestled against her skin since this morning.

Etched on one side is a stylized winged figure with a tail. The simple line drawing somehow carries motion, like the figure is spiraling towards the heavens.

Dr. Amrith is staring at it, eyes wide in recognition.

"Have you seen this before?" she signs.

For a long moment he doesn't say a word. Then he picks up her comm and types.

Can I meet you tomorrow? Somewhere else?

His message glows on her lens a moment and she lifts her gaze to meet his. His warm brown eyes hold wariness, but she doesn't sense it's of her.

"Of course," she signs, then holds up a finger and types. Lunch?

He nods. "I know this place — "

He turns his attention back down at the comm as her next message comes through. She's sent him the address to the Jungle, and his eyes widen.

My invitation, my treat, she types before he can object to the cost.

The food at the Jungle is amazing, and since Jaantzen owns it, it's one of the few places in town she feels comfortable meeting about something like this.

Plus, the man's a biologist. She can't wait to see his face when he sees the interior.

He smiles at her, but the wariness still remains under the surface. Then I look forward to it, he types.

He stands, and she does as well, takes the hand he gives her to shake. His hand is warm, the tendons in his forearm etch smooth lines beneath his skin before disappearing into his rolled-up sleeves.

Starla has to force herself to let go.

"It was nice to meet you, Ms. Deyva," he says. "I'm sorry I couldn't help you."

So he does think he's being recorded.

"Nice to meet you, too," she signs, and whether or not he understands, he smiles.

She lets herself back out, keeping tension and excitement from showing as she strolls back across the campus to where her moto is parked. If Hypatia is watching, she's not going to give them anything interesting to see.

The University of Bulari is set up above the city, where it sits on the wide, gentle slope that rises between Bulari's southernmost two Fingers. To the south, Carama Town spreads from its Finger of origin into the plain, obscured by the haze of the breezy, almost-stormy afternoon. The red brick roofs and corrugated metal shacks make the neighborhood look like a cheerful jumble of blocks, cut through with roadways that have no sense of plan.

Bulari's entire street grid has this tendency towards chaos. Throughout its history, rival settlers, rival city planners, and now rival crews have all sliced up the city without regard for convenience of navigation. In contrast, Starla has been out to a few small company towns in the countryside, where corporations threw down square grids of roads and proprietary little prefab houses over the landscape like a net to contain a wild planet. It makes her skin crawl.

Bulari feels organic, a chaotic early settlement left to its own devices until it was simply too late to do anything but put in a few ring roads and hope for the best.

The road up to the university is wide and smooth — it's one of the main ways out of town if you're headed east out of Bulari. Starla is letting herself enjoy the ride home, throttle open, leaning into turns. It's the middle of the day and traffic is thicker than usual thanks to the Ganesh in orbit, but the lanes are wide here and she has plenty of space. And no one else, whether city crawler, private spinner, or freight transport, has even tried to catch up or pass her.

So it catches her attention when a pearl-gray Bierat four-door appears in her rearview camera, gaining on her. She moves over to let it by, but it slows, moves to the lane behind her.

The spinner's passenger is holding a pistol.

Starla veers to the right and takes the moto into a slide, aiming to cross the gravelly median that separates the boulevard from the pedestrian and cycle path, which is nearly empty in the heat of the day. The pearl-gray spinner screeches to a halt just past her, half off the road, and both the passenger and the driver are firing at her now.

Starla's rear wheel spins in the gravel as she opens the throttle. The wheel catches — and she feels the moto shudder beneath her as something vital gives out.

She manages to crash into a roadside produce stand with a flourish that isn't quite controlled, and the moto skids to a stop in a tumble of casaba melon and yellow squash.

She hoists herself into a crouch — it's painful, but nothing seems broken — then pulls her own weapon out of its holster, using the side of the produce stand for cover. Traffic is piling up, and whether the men in the spinner think they got her or are worried about witnesses, the vehicle is fishtailing into a U-turn and heading back towards the university.

As they pass, a casaba explodes besides Starla, spraying pulp and seeds. She dives for the floor.

Her pulse is pounding, and she doesn't realize someone is in the booth with her until a hand grabs her arm. She spins, throwing them off.

It's just an elderly man, he seems to be screaming, and it's probably because of the pistol Starla has aimed at his forehead. Starla scans the area, tucks the weapon back into her holster. Her lens is trying to transcribe garbage words as the man shouts at her. She triple-blinks it off and crouches over her moto. There's a bullet hole through the nav panel, but when she tips it back up, the ignition system is blinking in standby. Nothing else seems seriously damaged, so while her moto's nav features may not work, so long as it starts, the mechanics of the beast should still get her home.

She takes a quick scan of the produce stand, a snapshot of the business sign with her helmet cam; she needs to get out of here, but she can still send something to help them pay for repairs. Anonymously.

The old man is still yelling, but he hasn't tried to touch her again, and she doubts he knows anything about whoever was trying to attack her. She palms her moto's ignition with a clench of apprehension and feels the low thrum of it between her thighs as it comes to life.

She breaths a sigh of relief, then kicks it into gear and peels away.

5

JAANTZEN

Manu hasn't stopped moving since he entered Jaantzen's penthouse. Even when he's settled into a conference table chair or perched on the arm of a couch, it's only a moment before he finds some excuse to stand once more — *You mind if I make coffee, boss? That new flower smells incredible. I need to take this call. The view's so clear today you can make out Mount Armayo, look.*

Jaantzen has survived this long because he trusts his ability to sense when a friend is thinking of double-crossing him, to identify an enemy's weakness, to estimate his trust of a potential ally — but when it comes to the tangled personal emotions of his crew, his solid footing's lost. He's learned to recognize their idiosyncratic moods, from Starla's sparks of frustration to Gia's slow-burning fury and Toshiyo's tendency to freeze like a rabbit at a single sharp word from him, even after two decades in his employ. And he's familiar with the signs that his lieutenant is agitated, those occasional black moods that bloom like bruises below Manu's polished poise of sharp dark suits and brightly colored hair.

Now Manu's leaning against the kitchen counter, stirring cream into coffee that's already well stirred, frowning at his mug. He has fresh copper highlights in his tousled black hair, and the appearance of new color is usually a good sign. But coming as it did following Coeur's return to their lives, Jaantzen suspects it may be more akin to armor.

Yes, Jaantzen notices his crew's moods. But he's not the one any of them come to if they want to talk about what's bothering them, and he wouldn't know what to do if they did.

Neither he nor Manu have the luxury of avoidance today.

Jaantzen clears his throat. "We need to talk about — "

Manu's comm chimes and he thumbs it on, then back off with a sigh. "No word from Gia," he says. "Sorry, boss. What was that?"

"Coeur." Jaantzen gives him a level look. Manu

reaches reflexively for the jar of cream, frowns at it when he sees the color his coffee already is, sets the cream back on the counter. "We need to talk about Coeur," Jaantzen says.

"I heard from my guy on Acheta's crew this morning." Manu's stirring his coffee once more. "He's starting to hear his own rumors about Coeur being alive whispered back to him."

"Good." But Jaantzen doesn't want to talk about strategy, not yet. "Manu, I need to know if you — "

Another chime, Manu thumbs the comm back on. And off.

"Sorry," he says, and fiddles with it before slipping it into his pocket. He runs a hand through his hair. "I turned off all notifications except for Gia," he says. "I should've done that earlier."

Jaantzen can't tell if Manu is deliberately trying to avoid this conversation or if he truly is so distracted that he doesn't realize what Jaantzen is trying to ask him. He decides to try an approach from the side. "Anything important?"

Manu shakes his head. "Mostly from Cedra Ardz." Jaantzen nods; he knows her name, though he doesn't have direct dealings with any of the people who work for Rosco Kudra Enterprises, his hotel and restaurant supply business. "Nothing important, just shit she can't figure out how to deal with on her own."

"You don't need to be personally managing RKE," Jaantzen says. "Hire yourself an assistant. Take some time off with Oriol." Jaantzen hesitates, then probes. "How is he?"

Manu stills a moment. "He's fine, had some damage to his hip interface, but that should be fixed soon."

"Have him send me the bill," Jaantzen says.

"I'll tell him that when I see him tonight."

A touch of bitterness there; Jaantzen has somehow struck close to a wound. He backpedals onto safer territory. Romantic troubles are definitely not his forte — he'd much rather talk about Coeur.

"What does your man know about Acheta's cash flow?" Jaantzen asks.

"Nobody's been paid in a week," Manu answers. "There doesn't seem to be money for supplies, so they're making do with looting. Which isn't endearing anyone in the neighborhood to Acheta."

"Phaera told me his most recent shipment of shard turned out to be lethal."

"Yeah, Tosh is taking a look at that now. Starla brought us a sample, it looks almost exactly like the stuff you guys found at the old spinner dealership."

Jaantzen frowns. "Starla brought you a sample?"

"She was at the Brujería last night." Manu glances up. "Did you hear about that?"

"I heard." Despite Phaera's warning, he had looked up the feeds from the club after all; he wishes he hadn't. "Acheta's stretched thin, his people aren't getting paid so they're looting the neighborhood, and nobody's going to buy his latest shipment of shard after watching a man blister to death in the middle of a dance club. Now he's desperate enough to turn on people like Phaera and the other casino owners who are actually powerful enough to do something about it." He's watching Manu carefully. "Sounds like things are prime for Coeur's return."

Manu flinches. "Did you want a coffee? Sorry."

Jaantzen sighs. "Yes, thank you." He rubs the back of his neck. "Tell me our options for getting rid of Acheta without much more violence. Working with Phaera is a bandage on a broken bone."

Mugs clinking in the cupboard while Manu buys time for his answer, the gurgle of pouring coffee. Jaantzen turns his attention out the window, where the horizon is blurred by a steady steam of launches and descents from the terminal as crews clean the last of the goods out of the Ganesh in orbit.

"Dry Creek aren't strong enough to try to expand their territory at the moment," Manu says finally. "Even if they could wipe out Acheta's crew. If we can get Acheta's crew to offer up something in peace, Dry Creek'll probably simmer down. Though, Acheta won't stop now that he smells blood, so going that route still requires getting rid of him." The hiss and sizzle of the coffee pot going back onto the warmer. "We might be able to spark some sort of revolt from within. My guy says plenty of people were more loyal to Naali and don't like the new direction."

"The shard."

"Right. Sounds like there's a faction ready for new leadership."

"Who's that leader?"

Silence. Manu doesn't have any better idea than he does.

"So Acheta's crew splinters, but no strong leader emerges," Jaantzen says. Manu sets the coffee in front of him, sinks into a chair at the conference table with his own cradled in his hands. "Which means even more fighting."

Jaantzen lets that sit in the air between them and takes a sip of the coffee Manu made. He coughs. It's thick and gritty.

Manu frowns at him. "Is it that bad?" He takes a sip of his own coffee and makes a face. "Oh, god. I'll make a fresh pot."

"Manu."

Manu pauses, half out of his chair.

"I need your head in the game right now,"

Jaantzen says quietly, holding Manu's gaze. His lieutenant's jaw sets tight. "I don't like the idea of putting Coeur in power. But it's our best option, and it's the plan until we come up with something better. We need to destabilize Acheta. Talk to your man on the inside about what he needs to do that. Weapons. Propaganda. Money. I'll talk to Phaera about putting pressure on him from the outside. If there's any part of this plan you're not going to be able to — "

"I'll set it up." Manu reaches for Jaantzen's coffee mug to take it back to the kitchen.

"Manu."

Manu stills, gaze steel.

"If there's any part of this plan you're not going to be able to handle, I need you to tell me now."

A muscle twitches in Manu's jaw. "I want that bitch out from under our roof," he says.

"Soon," Jaantzen answers.

"You can't trust her."

"I don't. But I will find a way to work with her."

"After everything." Manu's dark eyes are ice.

"After everything."

Manu lets out a furious curse and looks away, knuckles so tight Jaantzen's surprised the mug doesn't shatter. Jaantzen watches his lieutenant as he breathes deep, emotion warring on his face. In the silence, the mister drones whir quietly to life and begin their rounds in the garden.

"I hate everything about this," Manu finally says.

"I know. Can I count on you?"

"Yeah, boss." Manu slumps back in his chair and massages the bridge of his nose, his anger gone. "Of course."

"If you need anything . . ."

"I'm fine. I'll — "

"Manu."

The other man takes a slow breath, opens his eyes. "I'm fine, boss."

Jaantzen's jaw tightens. "I don't need you to be fine. None of us are fine right now. But I need you here. And if there's anything I can do to help, you need to tell me."

"Okay." Manu nods; he looks exhausted. "Okay. I'm gonna get ahold of my guy." He takes both mugs to dump in the kitchen sink, then pulls out his comm and leans back against the counter once more. It's not quite a casual lean, but the line of his shoulders is more relaxed, the stiff tension gone from his spine. It will do for now.

Coeur's not all that's bothering Manu this morning, but she's the bloodiest thorn in all their sides at the moment. If Jaantzen can just take care of that, he thinks, maybe the rest will sort itself out.

The lights flicker and a soft chime sounds as the lift arrives, right on time. Starla.

She sniffs the air as she steps out of the lift. "Coffee?" she signs. "I love you guys."

"Taste it first," Jaantzen signs back.

She lifts a quizzical eyebrow, then heads towards the coffee pot. She's not in her usual fatigues but in a nice pair of slacks and a black blouse, her makeup professional instead of moody. It's a look that goes surprisingly well with her half-shaved haircut and tattoos, though it does nothing to soften her. Even in this outfit his goddaughter has a dangerous sharpness to the way she holds herself, the way she moves.

A faint smile touches his lips; it fades as he sees how she's walking.

"Why are you limping?" he signs and says aloud. In the kitchen, Manu straightens and looks up from his comm.

"I'm all right," she signs back, waving away his concern. "Someone shot at me and I crashed my moto, but I'm okay." She pours herself a cup of coffee, then limps to the conference table and sinks into the chair Manu had just left.

Jaantzen's hands are frozen, every stitch of USL forgotten as he processes what she's just told him.

Manu swears under his breath. "What happened?" he signs. He grabs a glass from the cupboard, fills it with water and hands it to Starla.

She takes a long drink of the water before answering.

"I was heading back from the university when a spinner pulled up beside me, two guys with guns. I got away, but I slid out into a produce stand. Melons exploding everywhere." She's punctuating the exploding melons with little puffs of air. She shrugs like it's nothing, then smiles encouragingly at Jaantzen, whose chest is tightening with every breath.

"I'm fine," Starla signs. "The melons aren't." She takes a sip of coffee and grimaces. "This is terrible."

None of them are fine.

"Who?" Jaantzen growls. Adrenaline's rushing through him, blood risen to the surface of his skin. He just needs a name. "Who?" he asks again. The look in her eyes as she meets his is part wariness, part reproach. He forces himself to relax, to breathe.

Manu raps on the table, breaking their eye contact. "The shooters; did you recognize them?"

Starla shakes her head. "But I got a picture."

She swipes a photo from her gauntlet to the conference table, and Jaantzen leans in to see. It's a pearl-gray Bierat, a pair of figures inside. He doesn't recognize them, but he recognizes the amount of firepower they have, the intent to kill in their eyes. This image from Starla's helmet, it could have been one he found later, the last thing she saw and his only clue for revenge. His pulse pounds in his ears as he memorizes the faces of soon-to-be dead men.

A pale flash in his periphery, Starla's hand sliding across the table to his own, which is balled into a fist. He relaxes, lets her fingers open his and squeeze. Her hand is warm and dry.

"I'm fine," she signs with her other hand.

"I'm not," Jaantzen says, meeting her gaze. But he squeezes her hand back. She gives him a faint smile.

"I'll do a search," signs Manu. "We'll find these guys."

"Dry Creek or Acheta," Jaantzen says. He's not ready to release Starla's hand. "Someone's trying to draw us into the fight."

"Could be," Manu signs noncommittally, frowning like Jaantzen's not going to like his next suggestion. "Or it could be Phaera."

Jaantzen takes a long breath, but he can't pretend the thought hadn't crossed his mind. Starla makes a face at Manu: *Why the hell would you think that?*

"She came to Jaantzen earlier, she wants him to

join some sort of mutual protection group against Acheta."

Starla gives Jaantzen's hand a quick squeeze and lets go; his skin is suddenly cool where the warmth of her hand was. "Attacking me would light that fire," she signs. "And killing me would ensure you guys came in with guns blazing."

"You're sure they were trying to kill you?" Manu asks. "If it was Phaera, she may just want to scare us."

Starla shakes her head emphatically. "They shot to kill."

"I already told her we'd help," signs Jaantzen, and Manu lifts his hands to challenge him. Jaantzen cuts him off with a shake of his head. "Look into it. If Phaera is double-crossing me, I want to know."

"Sure thing, boss," Manu says.

"And find these men and bring them to me alive," Jaantzen signs. There's a flash of something on Starla's face that might be disapproval, but he doesn't care. He won't rest until whoever tried to take his goddaughter from him is dead.

"Consider it done," Manu says, voice practical and cool. He copies the image to his own comm. "By now they'll know they missed and have gone to ground," he signs. "But I know how to sniff out rats."

Starla just sighs. "Now that you two are done

planning how to avenge me, do you want to know what I learned?"

Jaantzen's anger is too close to the surface; at her joke it surges, but he catches Manu's quick glance and forces himself to be calm. Forces himself to remember being young. He does, of course. He remembers: not believing in his own mortality, not understanding the terror of loss — not until the day death came for him and took his wife and children instead.

He's not outliving any more family.

"Tell us," Manu signs to Starla.

"That professor, the one who wrote that paper I sent you?"

Jaantzen shares a look with Manu, trying to remember being sent a paper to read.

"What did she have to say? Or he?" Jaantzen waves a hand. "No, I didn't read it. But this professor knows something about our . . . ?" He can't even think of a USL sign to use for the creature, so he doesn't bother.

"He was too spooked about Hypatia to talk at the university."

Jaantzen frowns at that. "He's indentured?"

An emotion flickers across Starla's face, but it's gone before he can attempt to place it. "Almost everyone's indentured," Starla signs, dismissing his worry.

But you can't trust someone with an indenture, not really. It's nothing against the person, just the system. And it's one of the reasons Jaantzen's refused to use that model himself, even though it's ridiculously inefficient to buy out an employee's indenture before hiring them on at a decent wage. Even so, he'll take the security of knowing someone can leave if they don't like the gig over the uncertainty of never being able to know if an indenture is loyal.

As little as he's willing to trust someone whose indenture he holds himself, he's even less willing to trust someone whose indenture is owned by someone else. It doesn't matter how much this professor hates his employer. Hypatia holds his strings.

"Find someone else," Jaantzen says.

Starla cocks an eyebrow. "Do you know anyone else who's written a paper on alien biology?"

"We can talk to Gia."

"Anatomy and biology are different," Starla signs.

"I know that," Jaantzen snaps, then takes a deep breath. "I'm sorry," he signs.

"He knows something and he's willing to help," Starla signs. "His indenture; we can use that. He was afraid Hypatia would find out what we were talking about. If he talks, we pivot. Find a new plan. But him? He loses everything."

Jaantzen frowns. "When are you seeing him again?" he asks finally.

"We're having lunch tomorrow."

"Where?"

"The Jungle. And yes, I'll be safe," she adds belatedly, a strange expression of earnest kindness on her face; she's noticed how worked up he's gotten.

"Bring me empanadas?" Manu asks. Jaantzen frowns at him; he's joking, with what just happened? The look he gets in return is calm, deadly: *We will take care of this.*

If Starla notices the exchange, she doesn't react. "Order yourself; they deliver," she signs to Manu. "And that paper? At least check it out."

Jaantzen sighs and calls up his messages on the conference table, opens an unread one from Starla. "'On the Possibility of Precursor Life in the Durga System,'" he reads aloud. He notes the file size, raises an eyebrow at her.

"It's interesting," she signs, then makes a face like she misspoke. "Well, I mean it's mostly interesting. Phaera's plan: tell me more. What does she need from us?"

"Security and firepower."

"I'll see what Absolon has on-planet right now," Starla signs. "When are we looking at her security?"

"Are you free tonight?"

Starla nods and types something on her gauntlet.

"You think we can trust her?" Manu asks.

Jaantzen shakes his head. "I'm not planning on trusting her, not until we know who those men were."

"If she was behind the attack, it'll be good to be close to her," Starla signs. "I can build a back door into anything we install."

Jaantzen lets the comment go; if Phaera is still a suspect by the end of tonight, he'll be doing more than simply bugging her casino.

He hears the faint buzz of Starla's gauntlet, and she blinks at a message on her lens. "El's in for tonight," she signs.

"Tell him to be prepared for trouble."

Manu frowns. "If Phaera — "

"If Phaera sent people after Starla to draw us in, she's gotten her goal," Jaantzen signs. "Regardless, you should be prepared for trouble, too."

"Of course," Manu signs.

"Tell Oriol I'm sorry to keep you away for the evening," Jaantzen says aloud.

"He's used to it," Manu answers, but there's another flicker of something beneath the surface. Starla finishes sending a note to El, then glances at the clock on Jaantzen's wall. She grimaces at the time and pushes herself up from the table, obviously favoring her right leg.

"Do you need someone to look at your leg?" Manu signs. "Gia can if you wait."

Starla waves him away. "No, I only bruised my knee. It's just — " She frowns, finally realizing what he'd said. "Gia?"

"Coeur needed emergency surgery," Manu tells her. "Gia's operating on her right now."

Starla's eyes go wide, but she doesn't ask for further details. "I'll be fine. It's less stiff when I get moving, I just need some ice." She peers into the mirror beside the lift and makes a face at herself. "And to clean myself up before dinner. I smell like rotting melons."

"I hadn't noticed a difference." Manu grins, Starla punches him in the arm, and just like that, the woman Jaantzen considers his daughter and the man he loves like a son are bickering as only siblings can, teasing each other and throwing insults in rapid signs Jaantzen can't quite follow. They're both laughing, but there's no lightness in his heart.

If Starla hadn't been so quick. If the men hadn't waited to fire. If the moto crash had been worse, if she'd been on the edge of a cliff or a bridge instead of next to a produce stand —

A hundred or more ifs crush the breath from his lungs.

But when Starla turns to leave, she doesn't just wave him her usual careless goodbye. She leans in to kiss his cheek, then wraps her arms around him tight in places that are still bruised and burned and aching, but he doesn't notice.

He only notices what it feels like when she walks away.

6

———

MANU

Manu's got a to-do list long enough to strangle a man and three more "urgent" messages from Cedra since he left Jaantzen. Apparently a contractor is running behind schedule on an installation for their newest client, a hotel in the Tamarind District. The hotel's threatening to take business elsewhere.

Take business elsewhere.

Years ago, Jaantzen might have asked Manu to pay the hotel's owner a visit and remind him what it means to break a contract. These days, Jaantzen can afford lawyers, and they're both more effective and less likely to deter others in Bulari's high society from doing business with Jaantzen. It's an improvement, Manu guesses, but after the emotional rollercoaster this day has been, he could use someone to punch.

He blinks at the message in irritation. Of course, Cedra has no way of knowing what else is going on in Manu's life. She doesn't know there is no Rosco Kudra, that it's actually the notorious Willem Jaantzen who bankrolls her paycheck at the end of the day, and that Mr. Jaantzen and his lieutenant are currently in the middle of something way more serious than whether or not some hotel kitchen gets its refrigeration units installed on time.

He can't muster the energy to care about a contractor running behind schedule, or a pissed-off hotelier, or even losing the business. The woman who stole years of his life and murdered people he loved is in his home. Someone else tried to tear Starla out of his life. And Oriol isn't even going to stick around to the end.

He can't kill Coeur and he can't keep Oriol from leaving, but he can hunt the two men who attacked Starla. No matter how deep into the bowels of the city he needs to go to get them.

He clears Cedra's messages unanswered, swipes the image from Starla's helmet cam onto his desk, then pushes it through the network to Toshiyo. *Help me with an ID? Jail records, stuff like that.*

The reply comes back in seconds, because she

apparently never leaves her desk. *No prob*.

He sets his own desk to scan through records, then turns to the list of people he can start asking, too. People who owe him favors, who keep their ear to the ground in exchange for jobs here and there, for patronage, for keeping on the good side of Willem Jaantzen's man, for friendship.

His comm chimes with an incoming call, and he glares at it with a scowl that softens as soon as he sees the name.

Men like Hallelujah Oni, prosthetics repair man and one of the finest brokers of intel about Bulari's underground in the city.

Manu accepts the call. "Hallelujah."

"Manu, *mon ami*." Louis's rich voice always sounds like he's smiling. "What's going well with you?"

Louis's standard greeting catches Manu off guard as always. What *is* going well these days?

He's let the pause go too long. "I'm in one piece. You?"

Louis chuckles, deep and hearty. "Good, good. In the peak of health myself. Let your soldier know his hip plate is ready, he can come by for an install any time." Manu frowns at that. Is Louis calling him to pass on a message he could surely give himself? "I'd tell him myself, but I was calling you anyway," Louis continues, answering Manu's question before he can ask it. "Hey, I been hearing some rumors, about our Lady of the Black Heart, seems the Dry Creek crew's claiming she hasn't passed on."

Manu waits. Over a voice call he can't see Louis's expression and body language, can't tell if he's fishing for information or setting some loose. Knowing Louis, a bit of both.

A shifting creak on the other end of the call; Manu recognizes Louis's stool at his workbench. "I figured you deserved to know if she's out in the wild," Louis says gently.

"You hear it from somebody you know?"

"Dry Creek soldier. Been keeping his hand working longer than you've been alive."

Manu blinks at that. "I'm older than you think I am, then." Nobody's prosthetic is forty-five years old.

"Young pup," Louis says. "Summer-child boy. You don't seem surprised."

"I've been hearing that rumor, too. And I wouldn't bet on Acheta if it's true."

Silence as Louis processes that. "You want that?" he asks eventually.

"The man's got it under control."

"Hmm." A hum and a whir on the other end of the line, the clink of some tool against Louis's workbench. "Maybe it's an old man's folly, but I did prefer it back when business was business and shard was shard. Too much religion tangled in these days."

Manu frowns, trying to parse what Louis is telling him. "What do you mean?"

"You know the Gift of the Fallen? This new shard that hit the market last night?"

"The one that covers people in blisters then kills them."

"*Oui.* That's it." Louis sounds pleased he's heard of it.

"What do you know about it?" It's more direct than Manu normally is when it comes to Louis, but he doesn't have a lot of patience, considering everything that's not going well with this day.

"You ever read those Dawn holy books?"

"Negative."

"Might want to. They're the ones who made it."

Manu sighs deeply, racking his brain for someone to delegate that to. Maybe Toshiyo, since she never seems to sleep, and might actually find it interesting? "Thanks, man," he says.

"My pleasure," says Louis. "Hey, I've been curious. Seems nobody who knows is saying for sure, but the Dawn disappeared from town almost overnight, you know? Makes me wonder if they finally tangled with somebody they shouldn't've." Another creak of the chair and he gets more direct. "Makes me wonder what happened to Zacharia."

"He met his end," says Manu. It'll be common knowledge soon enough.

"May he rest in peace," murmurs Louis.

"I doubt it."

"His end have anything to do with what janked your soldier's hip plate so bad?" Manu doesn't answer, and Louis laughs. "Maybe someday I'll buy you a beer and you'll tell me the story in person."

"I'll take that beer, def," Manu says. "Next week?"

"Good, good." Manu can hear Louis grinning through the call. "You come see me when you're not so busy."

"Will do. Hey, Hallelujah?"

"Praise the Lord."

Manu smiles despite himself. "Can I get you to take a look at some faces for me?"

"They pretty?"

"Nah, man. And they're gonna be less so when I find them."

Louis laughs. "Send them over. Goodbye, *mon ami*."

"Bye, Louis."

The Dawn manufactured the tainted shard that Acheta's selling. But why? And — more importantly — why is he having to deal with fallout from this twisted cult on top of everything else? He laces his fingers behind his head and leans back in his chair, staring up at the ceiling. Bennion Zacharia, the Dawn's leader, hired Coeur to steal the cases he believed were filled with the serum he was using to turn his soldiers nearly unkillable. She — predictably — kept them for herself once she realized how valuable this "serum" was. Which is the reason her sister Ximena is dead, the reason Julieta's greenhouse is shattered, the reason Manu's ribs are killing him.

Unable to get their hands on the cases, had the Dawn started trying to re-create this serum for themselves?

And failed?

He pings Toshiyo. *Do you have a copy of dawn holy book? Need to find a phrase: gift of the fallen.* He pauses, realizing just how much shit has been put on her plate in even the last ten minutes. But he doesn't know who else to ask for work like this. *Can I hire you an asst?*

I'm good, comes the reply.

He doubts that, but before he can type back there's three taps at his door. It cracks open, and only one person ever does that. His secretary, Lo é Njeri. He tamps down his irritation — it's at the interruption more than at her — and beckons her in.

"Helloo!" she says. "Just saw you're in and wanted to run a few things by. Did you see the interview request? Cedra sent it this morning?"

Manu stares at her a second too long, having trouble making the mental switch to RKE publicity from his fantasy that the Dawn had simply killed Coeur.

"Should I come back?" Lo asks.

Manu breathes deep and calls up his inbox on his desk. "Now is fine," he says. He skims to the note, it's some profile on suppliers for a restaurant industry feature. "Fine. Ask MaeLin to talk to them, thanks."

He'd love for that to be all, but Lo leans one hip in the doorway and blinks up the next message, clearly settling in for a business chat. Light from her heads-up lens flickers in her hazel eyes. "And the charity request? From the homeless kitchen?"

Manu sighs. "Yeah, absolutely. Give them whatever we gave that street-kid theater troupe thing."

"Mm-hmm. D'Ondres came by this morning, about that new girl in accounting? He thinks she was a bad hire, she doesn't seem to even know basic math."

"Kill her and put her head on a pike in the lobby as a warning to our enemies."

Lo blinks in surprise, her gaze snapping from her lens to Manu. "What?"

"You don't need me to handle that, Lo," Manu says. "Besides, you stole the next hair color I was going to try."

She frowns at him.

"Your hair. It looks good on you, though."

In five years, he's never seen the natural color of her hair; today it's a deep burnt orange that brings out the dense spray of freckles peppering her light-brown cheeks and forehead.

"Oh!" Lo touches her pixie cut lightly. "I have plenty of dye left. We could be twinsies."

"Bring it in. Then maybe people will mistake you for me and stop bothering me with shit like this."

He doesn't mean for the frustration he feels to come through his voice, but Lo's eyebrows shoot up.

"I really can come back, if you'd rather?"

Manu shakes his head, weary, and waves her into the chair across from his desk. "Shut the door, Lo."

She does, then folds her lens away and sits on the edge of the chair, watching him with concern. "What's going on?" she asks.

Manu leans his elbows on his desk and digs his fingertips into his temples, staring down at the full, blinking inbox on his desk. "Lots. Everything is going on." He narrows his eyes up at her, trying to decide how much to tell her.

Lo is loyal, he knows it. She's not core crew, but he's considered more than once bringing her into the inner circle. After all, it's not like she's in any less danger being kept in the dark about the shadier things Manu gets up to for Jaantzen. And Manu has wished more than once that he could clone himself to keep up with everything that needs done.

She's a good person, though, from a respectable upper middle-class immigrant family who even had the cash to pay for her education outright so she didn't need to take on an indenture. She knows who Willem Jaantzen is, she knows that Manu's occasional split lips and bruised knuckles don't come from bar fights, and she knows her salary doesn't come entirely from refrigerator and alarm system sales.

But he's not ready to turn Lo into a criminal, too.

"I can't explain, but there are some things happening right now that need my full attention."

"Like a certain 'hostage exchange' situation that happened last week?" She'd been the one to take the call from Zacharia when he'd captured Jaantzen and Starla.

"That wasn't what it sounded like."

"Sure," Lo says, looking pointedly at Manu's right hand; the edge of a bandage is peeking from beneath his cuff. "What can I do to help?"

"You're capable of doing ninety percent of my job. I think it's time I promoted you."

Lo's eyebrows draw together. "Promote? I'm

not —"

"*Shh, shhh.* All of this" — Manu waves a hand at the glut of messages on his desk — "I'm leaving this all to you, my child. You don't need me to tell you if some trade magazine can get an interview with MaeLin, or if Jaantzen wants to donate to a charity. And whatever else you came in here to ask me, you already knew the answers, right?"

She nods slowly.

"Then you don't need my confirmation. Go forth and solve problems with my blessing. I trust you."

"Manu, what are you promoting me to?"

"Whatever you want. We'll come up with a title that works. And of course you'll get a raise."

Lo narrows her eyes and tilts her head, considering him. "And a new desk, mine is glitching out."

"You're also now in charge of approving new desk purchases." His own chimes with another message. "What the hell does Cedra want this time?"

Lo reaches forward and swipes his inbox away; a peaceful sunset scene glows in its place. "I'm now also in charge of Cedra," she says.

Manu sinks back into his chair, the tension draining from his shoulders. "You mean more to me than you'll ever know."

"You can thank me by approving the updated job description and salary I'll send by this afternoon," Lo says. "Unless I'm in charge of that now, too?"

She can't ask for anything he wouldn't approve, but still. "I should probably still sign that."

"Good." She stands. "I'll let everyone know."

"You're a goddess." He dares to smile. "This is fun already."

"Good. I prefer it when you're not a bundle of stress." Worry pinches between her brows. "Or limping. Is there anything —"

"You're an amazing help, thank you."

Lo gives him a small smile and heads towards the door. In her wake, she's left a dearth of small responsibilities and nagging chores — along with the sinking feeling that he's going to need to take her out to a nice dinner and formally answer some questions at some point in the near future.

And with how much she already probably suspects, he definitely needs to keep things solid with her.

Manu's staring down at the sunset screensaver on his desk when an alarm message pulses in the corner.

Do Not Disturb enabled by user Lo é Njeri. Override? Y/N

Manu hits the N with a sense of relief, then turns back to his searches.

He has some men to kill.

7

———————

JAANTZEN

B ulari's casino district is a slashing visual assault through an otherwise drab part of the city. Towering holograms vie for attention: the fifty-foot waterfall pooling into Phaera's Lorelei, the shimmering supernova exploding again and again at Orveto's Thousands, the dazzling lights and cut glass glittering on the facade of the venerable Desert Gem, the sinuous, writhing curves of the Aterciopelado.

Tourists come to the drag for the eye-catching displays and stunning illusions as much as to engage in gambling and other pursuits of vice they can't find back home in countries like Arquelle — or can't find at this scale out in Durga's Belt. Normally the casino drag is filled with gape-jawed tourists glad to pour money from their pockets, particularly when a craft the size of the *Maria Elena III* is in orbit. But tonight the wide pedestrian plaza connecting the casinos is nearly empty. It's a shock after the buzzing energy of downtown Bulari; even the hawkers have all taken their glowing baubles and good-luck charms and coca-caffeine tabs and noodle bowls and gone home tonight.

Starla pauses the spinner in the roundabout at the foot of the casino drag — no one else is behind them to care — so they can admire the view. Without the bustle of the crowds, the drag is eerily peaceful. An art installation in the emptiness of an industrial desert.

At the drag's farthest end, a gap in the glitz and glamour stands out like a burnt-out spot in the middle of a screen. Noticeable only for its lack of lights and holograms, the simple, blocky building with its throwback exterior of sand-scoured metal and reinforced glass doesn't attract many second glances. A pair of torches — real, not holograms — burn on either side of the door. Each blood-red flame is as tall as Jaantzen.

The nondescript building is not designed to draw the eye, but inside the Devil's Table, the most sophisticated high rollers in the Durga System are sparring with luck.

Starla's watching that dark building with a pensive expression on her face. She taps her fingers on the spinner's controls, then turns to give Jaantzen a look. "Do you really think she tried to have me killed?"

The more he's chewed at the thought today, the less he does. Phaera is direct and blunt, and even if he believed she meant him harm, this doesn't seem like her sort of game. It helps that Toshiyo spotted one of the shooters' faces in arrest records with the note that he was part of the Blackheart crew. But police information can be bad, and people can find new employers.

Starla is still watching him.

"No," he signs. "But I'm not willing to risk being wrong."

She nods and turns the spinner away from the display, exiting the roundabout into a glittering arched tunnel framed by spinning holograms of coins.

The majority of tourists will arrive at the casino district via underground train, emerging from the bank of golden lifts that shine in the center of the pedestrian plaza. But those who arrive in their own vehicles are funneled through this archway to a system of underground valets. Starla drives down a gleaming gold-painted road lined with scaled-down versions of the casinos' facades. Bored valets in themed uniforms wait in front of each. A few of the more industrious ones try to waylay Jaantzen's spinner with calls of too-good-to-be-true offers for their casino, but Starla heads past them all to the simple dock at the end.

A middle-aged woman in red-smoked glasses and a smart suit of pale gray shot through with blood-red pinstripe stands behind a counter. Her short black hair is slicked into finger waves; her lips are the same blood red as her pinstripes, only against dark brown instead of gray. Above her, a simple carved sign announces the Devil's Table in glowing red letters.

She steps out from behind the counter and smiles, a red-leather-gloved hand out to open Jaantzen's door. "Mr. Jaantzen, a pleasure," she says. Starla pulls herself from the spinner, leaving the engine running, and Manu and El Anahoy emerge from the back seat.

The woman turns her red-smoked glasses to take them all in. The augments are extremely subtle, but from this close, Jaantzen can see the light from their display playing in the woman's irises.

"I'm Vanessa," she says to Jaantzen. "Miss Phaera is expecting you upstairs." She holds open the door beside the valet counter. After the gaudiness of the other casinos' gold-plated, hologram-studded underground entries, the door to the Devil's Table is shockingly plain. Not a single adornment but the polished obsidian knob.

A man in the same gray and blood-red suit as the valet sits at a host stand just inside the door. He notices Starla and El as they surreptitiously check out the shielding on the door, but if it bothers him, it doesn't tarnish his smile.

"Welcome, Mr. Jaantzen," he says. "Please, follow me." There's a weapons locker behind the host stand, but he says nothing to them about that, only turns and leads them up a black lacquered staircase. It opens into the main floor of the casino — not into the back offices, as Jaantzen had expected.

Manu is a step behind him at his left hand. Starla and El are flanking him a few paces back, and Jaantzen motions for the two of them to fall back farther. They slip into companionable conversation near the top of the stairs, fingers flying. Jaantzen has already gotten a few glances from the nearest patrons on the casino floor and he's not intending on drawing more attention by walking in with a war entourage. He's already doing enough damage to Phaera's reputation by being here in the first place.

"Will we meet her in her office?" Jaantzen asks the host.

"She'll be here in a moment," the host says. "Excuse me." With a tip of his head he disappears back down the black lacquered stairs.

Despite its rustic exterior, the inside of the Devil's Table is opulent. And it's not the eye-catching pseudo-opulence of the other casinos on the drag — it's real. Real wood that must be imported from Indira. Real leather upholstering the chairs and card tables. Real workmanship in every single detail. And without the gaudy holograms to draw your eye in every direction, one could truly take the time to appreciate every single one of those details.

The room is maybe forty meters by thirty, low-ceilinged and moodily lit. The walls are painted a deep, textured maroon, and pairs of gold-fringed curtains in the same shade of velvet hide the entrances to what must be private gaming rooms and offices. A gorgeous carved wooden bar takes up the far edge of the room, dozens of colorful bottles on display on shelves behind it. The floor is dotted with antique armchairs and settees, and a handful of gaming tables are interspersed among the seating areas. Just as many of Phaera's clientele are sipping cocktails and conferring over potential new business gambles as are rolling the literal dice.

It feels more like an exclusive lounge than a casino, with eclectic lamps offering mood lighting and elegant waitstaff in sharp red uniforms stopping by to make sure guests have everything they need. A few more security in gray and blood-red striped suits are stationed discreetly around the room.

Across the room, Phaera sits on a low silk couch holding court with two women Jaantzen doesn't recognize. She's dressed in fine fabrics cut simply, her magenta bob held back in a complicated series of pins and her lips painted to match her hair. The row of opals studding the contour of her left ear and a simple gold cuff are her only jewelry. She has many ostentatious pieces, Jaantzen knows, having seen them at Justice Leone's dinner parties. But he supposes while in her den it's not good business to remind her prey she's likely to own them by the end of the evening.

She excuses herself as soon as she sees him, saying a word to her companions and casting a meaningful glance his way. The two women give Jaantzen an impressed look, then turn back to their own conversation.

Phaera offers a firm handshake first to him, then Manu. "I appreciate you coming, Jaantzen," she says. "Juric, it's nice to see you."

"I assumed you'd have us meet you somewhere a little less public," Jaantzen says.

"I thought you'd like to see the floor," Phaera answers. "And I don't mind my patrons knowing I'm hiring the best in the business." She winks at him. "The two women I was just talking with own the Blue Falcon hotel. They were impressed to hear Admant did the security for Leone's home. You'll be hearing from them."

The two women are still watching him from across the room; Jaantzen gives them what he hopes is a distinguished nod.

Phaera's attention turns to Starla and El. El's donned a suit and Starla's wearing something approximating evening wear that could best be described as assassin-chic, but neither look like they're here to mingle with this crowd. Not with her come-at-me smile and his electric-blue ponytail and even, deadly gaze.

Phaera holds a hand out to Starla with what looks like a genuine smile. "You must be Starla? It's a real pleasure, I've heard so much about you." Nothing in her manner says she tried to have Starla killed. She's either innocent, or she's incredibly talented. Or she's become a blind spot.

And blind spots are where the biggest dangers lurk.

At a glance from Starla, El steps in to interpret; the murmur and music from the casino floor must be reducing her lens's ability to transcribe.

"Starla will be handling the technical aspects of the installation," says Jaantzen. "El will be helping her."

Phaera holds out a hand to El expectantly

El clears his throat. "El Anahoy," he says, taking her hand. "I work for Starla."

Not "for Admant." Jaantzen has never heard the man phrase it that way; Starla's developed her own fastly loyal team.

At El's surname, Phaera lets out a gasp of recognition; El's expression becomes pained. "Any relation to Simca Anahoy, I hope?"

"My little sister," El says, wincing as though in anticipation of further questions.

"Simca sometimes works with us, too," Starla signs, and El falls back into interpretation with relief that someone else has taken up the mantle of small talk about his famous younger sister.

Phaera's eyes widen in delight. "I've always wanted to meet her," she says. "That win against Dreix last month? Incredible." She turns back to Jaantzen before El has to answer.

"I appreciate you coming," Phaera says. "Let's all go have a chat in my office, shall we? Everyone likes to know they're in the hands of the best security company in the business, but nothing makes you feel less safe than too much visible security." She smiles. "Especially in a certain crowd."

She leads them through a nearby set of curtains to a simple, utilitarian hallway that leads to the kitchen. The curtains had been muffling the sound of laughter and shouted orders, and the heady scent of orange peel and cinnamon. Jaantzen realizes with a start that he's caught that scent on Phaera before, always assuming it was some perfume, not that she had come to a social gathering straight from work.

"My office is through here, it's just — oh, Tam, I got it." She grabs a door for a woman in a chef's uniform struggling through with a massive pot of soup.

Phaera's office is just as spare and practical as the rest of the hallway, with none of the luxurious display of the casino's public spaces. It's simple, modern, and practical, with a state-of-the-art desk and a wall of AI-managed vid feeds that glow in a muted bar along the top of the ceiling. You can call them up if you need them; they don't become a distraction unless the AI decides there's something you need to see.

A big man in a dark suit is already there, examining the AI feed. He sweeps it away as they enter and turns expectantly.

"Hiro Matapang," Phaera says, holding out a hand to him. "My chief of security. Hiro, Willem Jaantzen."

Phaera's chief of security is even more physically imposing than Jaantzen, with another few inches of height and another few pounds of solid young muscle. His face is a few shades paler than

Jaantzen's. His handshake is courteous. "It's a pleasure," Matapang says, and his accent is faint: from New Sarjun, but from the hinterlands beyond Bulari.

"Likewise," says Jaantzen, hoping that will turn out to be true. The man is physically intimidating, but he still feels no sense of threat from him. "You'll be primarily dealing with my goddaughter, Starla Deyva. She runs Admant Security, and will be overseeing any projects with her team."

They shake hands, and Matapang signs, "Nice to meet you." It's clumsy, but Jaantzen relaxes a fraction. Starla's deafness isn't a surprise, then.

Phaera introduces El, then holds out her hand to Manu. "And, of course, Manu Juric," she says.

Matapang gives Manu a nod of respect and a careful handshake. That he apparently knows Manu's reputation makes Jaantzen wonder just where Phaera got her chief of security.

"Hiro, can you show Deyva and Anahoy around?" Phaera asks.

"Of course, ma'am." Matapang holds the door open. "Right this way."

Jaantzen nearly protests, but Starla gives him a look, softens it with a faint smile and a wink. She can handle herself. She's armed, and she's got El at her back. He returns her smile, but he doesn't bother keeping the worry from his expression.

When the door closes, Phaera waves at a pair of couches. Jaantzen chooses the one facing the door, Manu taking a seat at his left; Phaera crosses to the small bar on the far end of her office. "Can I offer you gentlemen a drink? Or are you on the clock."

"Please," says Jaantzen.

"Do you like jienja?"

Jaantzen's seen the name on his bar manager's inventory lists, but has no idea what it is. "Whatever you're having," he says.

"I like a man who's not picky about his liquors," she says. "Juric?"

"I love jienja."

"Good." Phaera pulls a selection of bottles down from the shelf, opens a small cupboard and extracts a trio of frozen glasses, and then busies herself measuring and stirring.

"I just got a call from Ayisha," Phaera says. She doesn't need to clarify which Ayisha she's talking about. Everyone who's seen a billboard or listened to a music feed in the past decade knows who the pop soprano is. For the past five years she's been belting out silken dance numbers from her club on the drag.

"She told me she had two people overdose on that awful new shard at her club earlier this evening. The police came, the whole thing. She had to cancel the rest of the show." The clink of ice.

"The guy selling it had hit a dozen people in the club, but only two got the bad stuff. It's just mixed in, impossible to tell if a tab's going to shred your brain over months or just kill you outright."

"Have you seen it around here or the Lorelei?" Manu asks.

"Not that I'm aware of." She turns back with three glasses on a tray, each with a dainty silver spoon balanced perfectly across the rim. A milky pearl sits in each spoon. "People are spooked off gambling, and they're spooked off shard," she says. "Acheta and Dry Creek are going to scare this whole town off sex with their fighting next. And then where will we be? Cheers."

Manu and Phaera both drop their spoons into their drinks, pearls dissolving in a stream of tiny ruby bubbles. Jaantzen lifts an eyebrow at the drink, then follows suit.

"It's the Table's signature," she says. "My bartender calls it Devil's Tears." She takes a long drink, then sets her glass on the low table between them.

"Very thematic," Jaantzen says.

Phaera smiles. "My clientele complain about the crassness of the other casinos, but they're as delighted at a good theme as anyone else. They just don't like it when commoners like us get to be in on the joke."

Jaantzen puts the drink to his lips but doesn't

sip; the scent is faintly sweet, undercut by something darker and more complex, and the more he thinks about it, the less he's able to put a finger on the scent.

"It's excellent," says Manu, though Jaantzen hasn't seen him drink, either. "Sage?"

"House secret," Phaera says with a sly smile before her expression fades to business. "But I have a question for you, and I need an honest answer: These rumors about Coeur, are they true? Because I'd love not to have to worry about our Acheta problem any longer." She holds up a hand. "And I know how that sounds, I don't need a history lesson."

"It's true," Jaantzen says.

Phaera nods slowly, the gloss of game play gone. Jaantzen decides he likes this side of her better. He's never been one for game play and intrigue, each holding back to see how much you can get the other to budge. And since they're laying it on the table . . .

"I have a question I need to ask you, Phaera."

"Anything," Phaera says, body language betraying curiosity, not nerves. Beside him, Manu shifts his glass to his right hand, leaving the left to go for his gun.

"Someone tried to kill my daughter today," Jaantzen says. The words come out distant and detached; he's rehearsed them enough in his head to dull them up. Phaera's lips part in shock. "I need to ask if it was you."

Phaera tilts her chin at him, curious for two beats; if she's bothered by Manu's still readiness she doesn't let on. "Ah," she says finally. "To blame Acheta or Dry Creek and give you a real stake in this turf war." She reaches carefully for her glass with an *It's just a drink* look at Manu — she's noticed him after all — then leans back against the couch.

"You're underestimating my faith in your word, Jaantzen. I asked you for help and you said yes — I'm not here to play games." She sips. "What happened? I did notice she's hiding a limp."

"A pair of men shot at her," Jaantzen says, trying not to let the words strike too close as he says them. "She crashed her moto. She just bruised her knee."

Phaera murmurs a curse, then sets her glass down with a sharp rap. Anger draws down the corners of her lips. "Did she get a look at them?"

"She did," Manu says. He takes a drink, then sets his glass down and pulls out his comm. A flush of relief eases its way through Jaantzen's chest. If Manu believes Phaera's telling the truth, Jaantzen is willing to trust his own instincts about her.

Manu thumbs on his comm, then slides it across

the coffee table. Phaera zooms in on the faces and tilts her head, considering. "I know this one," she says, unvarnished nail tapping on the face of the passenger. "He comes into the Lorelei every few days, he's got a thing for one of my dealers, though she doesn't much care for him. I don't know anything else about him, though. May I send this to the security team at the Lorelei?"

Manu nods and she swipes it onto her cuff, then types out a message. "We'll mistake him for someone with a debt to us next time he comes in," she says. "We can probably keep him in custody for an hour or so before clearing up the case of 'mistaken identity,' but if you can get here quickly enough?" Jaantzen nods. "Good."

"My apologies, Phaera," Jaantzen says. "I had to be sure."

She waves a hand. "I'm sure you're both relieved Juric didn't have to shoot me," she says, giving Manu a small smile. "Now. I've known Acheta for a decade from waiting tables and dealing cards in this neighborhood. He was an arrogant asshole and a shitty tipper before he got himself a crew, and now he's insufferable. Dry Creek and Acheta have made it clear they aren't willing to politely exterminate each other without getting the rest of us involved, and I'm over it."

"What would you like to happen?"

"What I'd like to see is Dry Creek and Black-heart's old crew swept off the streets entirely, but who's going to do that? The police?" Phaera laughs. "I'm a businesswoman, and I know how to hit Acheta in the finances: throw his street teams out of the casino district, maybe even hire somebody's seedy cousin to burn down a few of his stash houses. But that only works if others are working with me. Acheta's ability to retaliate is greater than my ability to defend myself."

"We can help with that."

"With increased security? Soldiers on patrol? Don't get me wrong, Jaantzen. I'm grateful. But he needs to be cut out of this city."

"There are others who want to see him gone," says Jaantzen. "Leone won't take a side and Julieta has her own things to deal with at the moment, but Teo Lordeur has offered funding, and Mizal Seti."

"Funding," Phaera says, dismissive. "And what, leave you to take the brunt of the fighting? It's what they expect you to do. But I'm not going to push you and yours into danger while the rest of us sit around wringing our hands."

She turns to Manu, curious. "You used to be freelance, right, Juric? How much would it have taken for you to contract on somebody as big as Acheta?"

Manu laughs, then glances at Jaantzen. "Depends on how desperate I was any given day," he says. "I took that contract on Jaantzen for a song because I was broke and a dumb kid. But I obviously didn't manage to kill him. You want to attract the best and get it done fast, I'd say look at the bounty boards and double the highest price. Between all the casino owners, Lordeur, Seti — you'd easily afford it."

"I'll have to get one of you to tell me that story some day," Phaera says.

"It's less interesting than you'd think," Jaantzen says, though in truth, everything with Coeur stems from that fateful meeting. "You're still throwing money at the problem and hiring someone else to do your dirty work."

The look Phaera gives him is inscrutable. "Yes, but I'm not throwing you and yours at the problem and expecting you to kiss my feet for the privilege." She smiles, suddenly lighter. "Though you're welcome to go after the bounty if you'd like."

"Killing Acheta without putting someone else in his place isn't going to solve any problems. And putting a bounty on his head will just make him more desperate."

"Or it will be a wake-up call. Last week he was walking into Leone's home with his suit on begging to play nice. Maybe this will be a good reminder that he can't rub elbows with us one night and demand protection payments from us the next."

"Acheta's not thick," Jaantzen says with a sigh. He's not entirely sure if she's serious. "He knows there are only a handful of people in this city with enough cash and enough hatred of him. The instant he learns someone's put a bounty on him, he'll guess it's you."

"Then let's get that security set up," Phaera says cheerfully. "Shall we go see what Hiro and — "

In the distance, something thunders, the deep, resonant rumble of an explosion.

The world around them plunges into darkness.

8

MANU

Manu's weapon is already in his hand and aimed at the door to Phaera's office by the time the generators at the Devil's Table kick on seconds later, yellow emergency lights near the ceiling casting the scene in flat dimensions. The bank of AI-managed vid feeds slowly flickers back on as they reboot.

Building backup power systems for the casino is going high on the list of security upgrades, Manu guesses.

Jaantzen is on his feet. "Starla," he says to Phaera. "Where are they."

"Hiro's office." She's pointing to her right. "Top of the stairs at the end of this hall."

Manu starts to rise, too, but Jaantzen stops him.

"Stay with Phaera. I'll make sure Starla is all right." He turns to Phaera. "Stay here. I'll give you the all clear."

As soon as he's out the door, Phaera smooths her palms on her thighs, then looks pointedly at the gun in Manu's hand. "You going to try to shoot me again, Juric?"

"Not planning on it."

"Good. Then let's go see what this is all about." She touches a finger to one of her opal earrings. "Hiro? Come in."

Phaera D stayed put in her office just about as long as Manu expected her to, despite Jaantzen's order. Manu does his best to scout doors and corners as Phaera hurries towards the casino floor. Despite the yellow emergency lights and the general feeling of panic, from what Manu can see — and hear, from Phaera's side of her conversation with her chief of security — there doesn't seem to be any breach of the casino. There are more people in the hallway than before, kitchen staff and waiters gathering in uncertain clumps as they wait to know what's going on.

He's waiting for an explosion, gunfire, anything to tell him the building is under attack. It doesn't come.

Maybe this was only a power outage.

Phaera's still talking to her security chief as they

head down the hall, flashing smiles and reassuring comments to employees as they pass; Manu's getting naked stares at the gun in his hands. "Send a sweep through to check the feeds in person," she says to Matapang. "I want to — hold on. Juric!" she snaps. "Not here."

He stops with one hand on the velvet curtains that lead to the casino floor. Phaera holds his gaze steady until he finally slips his pistol back into his shoulder holster.

"Send a sweep and report back," she says to Matapang over the feed. "We'll be on the floor."

She steps towards the curtain and Manu catches her arm. "Hitmen first," he says. He slips through the curtains, fingers brushing the butt of his gun.

Out on the floor of the casino, Phaera's staff seem to be handling the panic well. The emergency lights are running here, too, and most of the ambient lamps on the cocktail tables are still lit. The cocktail servers are circulating with reassuring small talk, the dealers are cashing out methodically, and the gray-and-red-suited security guards are flanking the doors.

"You're clear," he says to Phaera, and she steps past him, chin high and step brisk.

She leans down to pat the arm of an elderly woman and smile at her companion, a middle-aged man in a wheelchair. "We're finding out what happened, don't you worry," she says with a smile. "Probably just buildup from that last sandstorm. Can I bring you anything? Another glass of wine?"

Manu stays at her side as she works the room, garnering a few glances from people who noticed him come in earlier with Jaantzen, but otherwise being ignored. He gives out business-like smiles meant to be reassuringly professional to those who do meet his gaze.

"Don't worry, honey, my security guards say it was only a prank," Phaera is saying to a society matron who looks vaguely familiar; Manu is sure that if he heard her name he'd recognize her from some recent tabloid scandal. "Just some kids, we'll get it taken care of. Another drink?"

Her hostess smile fades as she turns away to intercept one of her bartenders, a small woman with a crown of black braids.

"Another jenever for the councillor and a glass of pinotage for the ambassador," Phaera says. "And when you're settling up, drinks tonight are on the house. I'll — "

Shots ring out outside the building. They could be muffled fireworks, if you didn't know what gunfire sounded like.

They're not.

A panicked chorus rises throughout the room;

all around them, posh Bulari socialites and off-world notables are clutching each other like they're in actual danger.

Phaera lets out a curse. "Comp everything, let everyone know," she says to the bartender, who nods and hurries back to the bar. "Whatever these assholes are playing at, they picked the wrong night. I am over their shit." Phaera touches one of her opal earrings. "Hiro? Tell me."

Manu's comm vibrates in his pocket: Jaantzen.

Not a direct attack. Stay with Phaera I will find you.

"Matapang says that last was a drive-by," Phaera says to Manu. "No damage he can tell, and no one else left in the vicinity. I heard from my security team at the Lorelei, sounds like the power's on at the south end of the drag." Her nostrils flare. "Not that it matters. A night like this, after everything else that's been going on? We're talking millions of marks lost up and down the drag. And millions more until this crowd decides it's safe enough to come back out. Oh, Judge Simcoe!"

Her expression becomes friendly once more as an older man approaches to ask about his spinner. "I'm speaking with my valet right now. My team is making sure everything's cleared up out there, and we'll get you on your way. It's been a long night for all of us." She blinks, fingers brushing her ear, then smiles and pats the man's arm. "And your dinner's on the house, of course. Now if you'll just excuse me, I'll go check in with the drivers' lounge."

She's making a beeline for the black lacquered staircase, Manu on her heels. "What is it?" It's obvious she heard something as she was talking with the judge.

"Vanessa says there's someone at the valet door," Phaera says under her breath, then smiles at another patron. "I'm just checking on the valet, love," she calls with a wave to another patron, then lowers her voice again. "Somebody whose neck I would very much like to break."

"Acheta?" Manu asks when they're out of earshot, and she nods, jaw tight. "I'll call Jaantzen."

"If he's with Hiro he's already seen. Anyway, Acheta is here for me."

Phaera's footsteps thud as she hurries down the staircase, jaw set and angry. The security guard at the host stand has a stun carbine slung over his shoulder now, but it won't do much against the type of weaponry Acheta is likely to have.

"Phaera," Manu calls, catching up beside her. "Let me go talk to him."

"He's not here to talk with you," she snaps, but it does slow her a pace, and at least now her security guard gets to the door before she does. The guard takes point and slowly opens the door, assesses the danger, then holds it open for Phaera to come through. Manu follows, hand on the butt of his pistol.

The long, black expanse of the valet tunnel is flickering with rebooting holograms. It's empty, except for a single black and green Kalai four-door with its engine on, sitting in front of the valet stand to the Devil's Table.

Acheta is leaning against the passenger door, flanked by a pair of his own. His lieutenant, Sjel, Manu recognizes. But the woman beside him is new. She's got light-brown skin and a shag of black hair pulled into a ponytail, and she's armed with a wicked-looking assault rifle. Though she doesn't look like she needs it — the way she holds herself, she's fit and deadly enough on her own. She studies him a moment, then turns her attention back to Phaera.

Phaera's valet — Vanessa — is acting every bit as polite as she had when greeting Jaantzen earlier, though now she's got her hand on the barrel of a shotgun hidden in the stand, and the smoke-red glasses are flickering data overtime. Manu hopes she's a good shot.

"Thank you for making a moment for me, Phaera," Acheta says. "Finally."

"I've been busy," Phaera says. "I have a business to run, and I honestly don't have time for whatever shit you think you're pulling tonight." She lifts her chin. "Get to your point."

A muscle tightens in Acheta's jaw, and Sjel's hand settles on the butt of his gun. Manu clears his throat in quiet warning.

At the noise, Acheta glances over Phaera's shoulder, seeing Manu for the first time as someone besides another one of Phaera's security team. His expression shifts to scorn.

"Jaantzen's secretary, huh?" he says to Phaera. "You slumming it with the help?" His grin slowly widens. "Or are you slumming it with the man himself?"

Phaera sighs. "Currently I'm being forced to slum it with you. I have a full house tonight, Acheta, powerful people who are ready to go home as soon as I sweep the trash out of my driveway."

Acheta bares his teeth. "Bitch, if you think — "

"What can we do for you folks?" Manu cuts in. "Since I assume you're not just here to trade insults."

Acheta takes a sharp breath at the interruption, but he relaxes, just a touch. "No," he snaps at Manu, then he smiles slyly at Phaera. "I'm here to remind you how much you need our help. I'm sorry about that power outage. Dry Creek messing with one of the substations. Pretty juvenile, but we took care of them. You shouldn't have another problem like that again."

Phaera laughs as though genuinely surprised. "I'm sorry, but you really expect me to believe — "

"I only regret that we couldn't of gotten there sooner and avoided this whole mess altogether," Acheta says smoothly. "Though I think you'll recall our earlier offer to keep this neighborhood safe."

"You mean, keep us safe from the power outages you cause and the guns your people are firing outside my place of business?"

Acheta lifts palms out, his gesture saying there's nothing to be done about it while his eyes say he's got one up on her.

"I don't understand your reluctance, Phaera. Other business owners in the area don't seem to have a problem with it. In fact, they're welcoming the peace that me and my people will bring. But you? Not only are you calling me a liar to my face, but you're telling the others not to do business with me. Spreading my name around in the dirt."

"Maybe I'm just the only one who sees through your bullshit," Phaera says.

Dammit.

Acheta growls. Sjel's pistol is halfway out of its holster; Vanessa's grip is tight on the shotgun; and Phaera's host raises his stun carbine. Only the mystery woman at Acheta's right hand looks relaxed, but Manu's watched trained fighters like Oriol often enough to recognize the zen before the storm of knives.

Manu can take out Acheta before somebody else draws — he knows he can — but he can't take out all three, and he has no idea how quickly Vanessa can draw that shotgun or if that stun carbine will do any damage. He steps forward, hands out in a peace offering.

"What's your offer, man?" Manu asks.

Acheta cuts him a sharp look. "What business is it for a secretary?"

"Just you keep saying you want to do business, but this environment isn't very conducive, what with all the guns. You know what I mean? Get your business done with the lady and let these people go home."

Acheta's nostrils flare, but he finally nods. "The deal hasn't changed," he says to Phaera. "You pay the fee, we make sure nothing happens to your place of business. Or your customers." The leer he gives Phaera makes Manu's skin crawl. "Or you."

"Fuck you," Phaera says.

"Not if you've been with Jaantzen first. You have three days to pay." And with a nod to his soldiers, he gets back into his spinner.

Manu tenses to stop her, but Phaera doesn't move except for the deep ragged breaths of pent-up fury. When Acheta's spinner disappears down the long tunnel, the host lowers his stun carbine and the valet finally lets go of the shotgun. Her hands are trembling.

Phaera's shaking, too. But it's not with fear.

"We could've handled that better," Manu says mildly.

"You could have put a bullet in him."

"Or we could have not antagonized the man with all the firepower while he has us surrounded."

"I don't need to be *managed*, Juric," Phaera snaps.

"The situation needed calming."

She rounds on him, pale cheeks flushed. "Would you have spoken over Seti like that? Leone?"

The rebuke is sharp and it stings. Manu feels an initial flush of frustration — if squeamish Mizal Seti was antagonizing Acheta, Manu would have definitely stepped in to calm things down. Phaera knows how desperate Acheta has become, and she still pushed his buttons. It could have turned deadly if he hadn't stepped in to defuse the situation.

But he isn't dealing with a pushover like Seti, nor is he standing beside Jaantzen, who expects him to step in when needed. The attack on Starla has brought out a custodial streak in him tonight.

Maybe he was out of line. Or maybe he kept them all from getting shot.

"I apologize, I was in the wrong," Manu says; he doesn't offer excuses. "Did you recognize the woman?"

Phaera shakes her head, but her valet answers. "She was Arquellian, I heard her talking," says Vanessa. The red-smoked glasses hide her eyes, but her lips are pressed bloodless beneath the paint. "Her face isn't bringing up any matches, though."

"Let me know what you find." Phaera swears under her breath. "I have three days to get rid of him."

"Would you like my opinion?" Manu asks.

A pause; Phaera's gaze is cool. "Yes."

"The bounty is a bad idea. I suggest you let him think you plan on paying him."

Phaera's nostrils flare. "I'm just supposed to turn the other cheek because this piece of trash thinks he can take away my livelihood?" Phaera flings a hand at the door to the Devil's Table. "Nobody gave me this. I didn't steal this. That door? I hung it myself. That staircase? My daddy built it. Every single one of those lamps inside, my mama found in somebody's trash heap and restored. This building? Ten years of saving tips from double shifts for the down payment, then three years dealing and playing cards down the road and working in my off-hours to restore it. And you think I should just let that asshole walk in here and demand a cut because he has a gun and I don't?"

"He's not saying any of that," comes a voice from the door. Jaantzen has appeared there somewhere during her diatribe.

"I want him gone," Phaera says.

"We'll take care of him," Jaantzen says quietly.

Phaera's jaw tightens. "See if you can beat me to it."

9

STARLA

Starla's been shot at before, and she's thought once or twice that her time was up. Most recently on the ground in Julieta's greenhouse with Bennion Zacharia's pistol aimed at her head. She knows just how close to death she'd been, then, and she knows it was sheer luck that she lived.

But, for her, danger has always been divided into clear categories. There are the times she goes looking for trouble, and there's everyday life where she goes about her business and people don't bother her. Never before has death slipped up to her with its evil-eyed grin in the middle of the day.

She's followed Jaantzen's nitpicky protocols. Been patient with Manu and Gia when they insisted on some paranoid backwards driving route, and with Oriol's refusal to eat at a restaurant that has too many windows. Intellectually, she's understood that those quirks come from a sixth sense of survival they earned fighting wars that hadn't touched her.

But now, what would normally be a routine walk from her apartment on Nidaly Square to the Jungle for her lunch meeting with Professor Amrith has become an exercise in ferreting out dangers, nerves strung taut and singing.

Starla tries to breathe deep and calm, lets the voice in her head that nags she's running late grow louder, lets it drown out the voice that screams for her to run from this crowd of office workers and downtown tourists.

Be calm.

Be calm.

Today's sun is harsh and dry, though Starla's sweating as much from adrenaline as the heat. She feels hungover, though she didn't have a drink last night, after they'd finally finished at the Devil's Table well past midnight. She slept past breakfast and needs some coffee. And some fried yucca in garlic sauce. And definitely some stuffed jalapeños in garlic sauce.

Or — maybe not in garlic sauce . . .

Or maybe she's getting ahead of herself.

The Jungle stands out from the rest of the angular modern architecture on this block. Cream-colored columns carved with vines and flowers form the restaurant's facade. They look to be made of marble, but the leaves rustle and flowers bloom as you watch — plastics, not holograms. Above the door, the words *The Jungle* scrawl in a giant's neon-green handwriting, are erased, scrawl again.

It's cheesy. She loves it.

She's also mystified by it. She recognizes nothing of her godfather in this place that he designed and owns. People who influenced him, maybe. But nothing of his quiet reserve in the stylish flourishes and overblown decor. He bought the original restaurant and relaunched it a few years after the civil war that ousted Coeur, and at the time, it had felt to Starla like a rebirth. A brand-new project with a lush new interior he could pour his energy into.

Something vibrant and alive and generative.

Maybe it was simply a way to impress Julieta Yang and Geum-ja Leone and Mizal Seti and the rest of that crowd. Maybe it was a fashionable way to launder money. Or maybe her godfather has a secret love of gaudy, lavish decor and the Jungle is his way of showing it.

Whatever the reason, it's the perfect place to impress a guest — and the food is incredible.

Sam Amrith is already here, perched on one of

the white faux leather couches in the entryway like he's afraid to touch anything, and for a moment she wonders if she's miscalculated, if this place is overkill. He's dressed up, wearing a suit that's a few seasons out of fashion, though it fits him well. But it's the sort of thing that would be more appropriate at an academic conference than at a nice restaurant.

Starla had thought about wearing a dress, but after the attack yesterday and the events of last night, she defaulted to the classiest outfit she has that still goes well with her bone-crusher boots and shoulder holster. Between the painkillers and the walk from her apartment, her stiff knee has relaxed, and she's lost her limp by the time Sam spots her.

Mostly.

Sam's eyes widen when she approaches. "Are you all right?" he asks, which is always the first thing you want to hear when meeting a good-looking professor for lunch.

Beyond the limp, she looks haggard from being up so late — not that her sleep was restful when she finally got it. There were gunmen around every corner in her dreams, only this time they didn't miss. She spent three times as long on her makeup this morning to see if there was anything she could do, but no amount of concealer would cover the dark circles under her eyes, and no shade of eyeliner or lipstick did much to distract from them.

She'd been hoping he wouldn't notice.

She makes an *It's nothing* face, then pulls out her comm. Late night at work, she writes.

"I didn't mean — you look great," he says, then backpedals, cheeks flushing. "I mean, this place looks great." He waves a hand vaguely at the yellow-streaked philodendron behind the couch.

Just wait until you try the food, she writes.

She's grateful when the host saunters up with a smile. "Good afternoon, ma'am," he says. "Right this way." Sam glances at her sideways; it's not missed on him that she didn't give her name.

She gestures for him to go on ahead. She doesn't want to miss a single moment of watching him appreciate the decor.

And she's not disappointed as the host leads them through the dining room floor. Hanging vines obscure the spaces between tables of couples in fancy dress, leaves giving off a muted fuchsia glow. Palm fronds glitter between the vines, a diamond-like light winking on the tip of each leaf like a star.

The glowing lights are tricks of the decorator, but Sam's not interested in those.

"I've never seen a *Monstera* like this," he says, brushing his fingers over the enormous leaves of a towering split-leaved vine. The host stands politely by, waiting for Sam to take it all in; it's a common enough occurrence among first-time guests to the Jungle.

Starla's never noticed this particular plant before. She assumes it's one of Julieta's creations, but to her it's just another leafy green thing. What she truly finds fascinating about this place is the fauna. She touches Sam's arm and points to the ceiling, where what looks at first glance like a golden-red vine uncoils to slither gracefully down a column, tasting the air with its forked tongue. At Sam's shoulder, a vivid pink orchid mantis unfurls its petal-like limbs; Sam starts back in surprise.

The host finally deposits them in a high-backed booth upholstered in synth leather so realistic that Sam does a double take and runs his palm over the cushioned back as he slides in. The host taps a panel as he leaves and a one-way privacy screen shimmers into place. They have a view out over the restaurant, but no one can see in — or hear their conversation. A pair of elegant silver switches at each end of the curved booth are labeled Do Not Disturb; switch them and the waitstaff know not to enter.

It makes the Jungle an excellent place for business meetings with skittish clients who are interested in Admant Security's less aboveboard offerings. Starla prefers not to think about the other reasons patrons might appreciate such an amenity.

Their waiter is an older man named Ivan, a trustworthy fixture here for as long as Starla can remember, and Starla's favorite because he speaks some USL. She orders coffee and fried yucca for them both, then chooses the daily special — lamb in a cilantro black beer sauce — to give Sam the freedom to order whatever he likes. He asks for the cheapest vegetarian dish on the menu, risotto-stuffed mushrooms, and she wonders if he doesn't eat meat, or he's simply worried about price.

Sam doesn't come from money, but Starla would have known that based on the fact that he took an indenture with Hypatia. He's self-conscious, but not about being out of place. Instead, his nerves seem directed at her.

Starla hands Sam her comm, but he sets it on the table, lifts his hands to sign. The motions are clumsy, but his intention is clear.

"How are you?"

Starla laughs. "I'm fine," she signs back. "How are you?"

"I'm fine." And then Sam shrugs, laughing. "That's all I've got," he says aloud.

IT'S MORE THAN MOST PEOPLE TRY, Starla types into her gauntlet.

"Oh, wait." He lifts his right hand and stares at it in concentration. Starla's heart melts with each letter. "S-T-A-R-L-A."

"Did I get that right?" he asks.

She's here for information, not a date, she reminds herself. And once she gets that information, she probably needs to get as far away from Sam as possible so he doesn't become a liability.

But he's not making this easy, is he?

She's dated far more hearing than deaf men in her life, but Sam's the first one who's bothered to learn even a single word in her language. Sure, she hasn't given most a second date — not because of them so much as because of her job. She's too busy and her hours too irregular for casual date nights. That, and there aren't many men in this town worth getting to know long enough to out herself as Willem Jaantzen's goddaughter.

She catches herself with a start. Jaantzen and Manu are currently hunting down the men who tried to kill her, Acheta is waging war against Phaera, and a probably actual alien lurks in Toshiyo's den.

Now's not the time to be thinking about dating.

Sam must have sensed a shift in her demeanor, because he's moved from the intimate vulnerability of trying to learn a new language into the safety of what he knows.

"The biodiversity of the flora here is incredible," Sam says. "I'd love to study some of them." He points out one with a scientific name her lens transcribes as garbage words. "I wonder where they've acquired all these specimens? The host, ah — " Sam clears his throat as he tries to put it into words. "Just, do you come here often?" he asks.

I BRING CLIENTS HERE FOR MEETINGS, Starla types, and he seems to relax — maybe more comfortable with the idea that she works with rich people than the fact she might have money herself? She can't quite tell. The small talk drifts into her line of work, and she finds herself accidentally explaining in detail one of the hacks she and Toshiyo are working on for a client. She starts to apologize — literally only she and Toshiyo have ever found this interesting — but he's nodding along, and his questions just lead her further into the explanation. She's sketching out the circuitry for him when the food arrives, and she realizes in horror how long she's been talking about security systems.

The fried yucca is golden and sizzling, the lamb fragrant, and even Sam's mushroom vegetarian thing looks incredible. Ivan's brought her a second side of garlic sauce because he's a god among men.

"Anything more?" Ivan signs, and Starla shakes her head.

When Ivan retreats from the table, Starla slides to the end of the booth and flips on the Do Not Disturb notice.

YOU'RE SAFE TO SAY ANYTHING HERE, she

types. *NO ONE CAN HEAR US. NO CAMERAS. NO RECORDINGS.* She nods at her comm lying on the table in front of him. *BUT YOU CAN USE THAT IF IT MAKES YOU MORE COMFORTABLE.*

Sam takes a deep breath. "What . . . what do you want?" he asks. "I mean, I'm sorry to have been so secretive back at school. I promise it wasn't just to get lunch with you." He hurries through that. "Though I do — this is nice," he finishes. He looks down and stabs awkwardly at a mushroom.

I HAVE QUESTIONS ABOUT THE PAPER YOU WROTE.

"I don't think I can help you. It's just that I wrote it years ago. Before I started working for Hypatia. It's — it's the sort of stupid thing kids in universities think about." His mouth sets firm after the words, and she's not sure if it's a statement of fact or an admonition to himself.

NOT HYPATIA PROFESSORS.

Sam shifts, uncomfortable. "I'm very focused on my discipline," he says finally.

Starla would love to probe more, but analyzing Hypatia Corp's stance on extracurricular studies isn't why she's here.

I NEED TO KNOW ABOUT YOUR PRIMARY SOURCES.

"May I ask why you're so interested in this paper?" He's guarded as he asks it, takes a bite of yucca and swallows too fast.

YOU HEAR THINGS GROWING UP IN DURGA'S BELT, Starla types. *WE*

She pauses before finishing, grateful she hadn't just signed words that couldn't be taken back. As nice as Sam seems, he's still indentured to an Alliance corporation, and she still has protocols from fifteen years of talking with those outside family: Don't volunteer information about herself, and if she has to give her name, birthplace, or anything else, she should stick with the bio details of her new identity, Starla Deyva.

She deletes the message and starts over.

WHEN I WAS GROWING UP, KIDS TOLD STORIES ABOUT DURGA'S BELT.

But she still doesn't push Send — that's not quite right, either.

He's said something she missed, the tail end flickers on her lens as she's considering what to say.

Finally she deletes her second message and reaches behind her neck to undo the clasp of her mother's stone amulet instead. It's cold in her hand despite having nestled against her breastbone all morning; she shivers involuntarily.

She pushes it across the table. "Tell me what this means to you," she signs.

Even if he could have understood her, his attention is only half on her hand movements; he gingerly picks up the amulet and traces a finger over the stylized sketch of the winged, tailed creature. She's having trouble reading his expression — it's somewhere between resignation and hope.

"Where did you get it?" he asks.

From my mother, Starla types. She's not sure how much to say without giving away some of her parentage, and anyway, she doesn't actually know where it came from initially. Given the far-reaching sticky fingers of her family, it could have come from anywhere in the system. She'd asked once, and her mother only said she'd tell her when she was older.

No chance of that now.

In your paper, you mentioned alien artifacts, but I couldn't find a version with images.

"You shouldn't have been able to find the paper at all." Sam turns the amulet over in his fingers. "But, yes. I've seen this symbol. There used to be this virtual museum of so-called alien artifacts that some old guy from Corusca curated." She nods; he mentioned it in his paper, but she hasn't been able to find it. "He had a few objects with this symbol. Mostly stone carvings like this."

He strokes a smooth finger over the surface of the necklace. "I was fascinated by the idea that maybe we weren't the first ones to visit these planets, even though at the time I figured they might just be artifacts the original colonists had brought from Old Earth. Or fakes."

He hands the necklace back to her and returns his attention to his food. "Anyway, that necklace, that's probably all it is," he says; his knuckles are white as he grips his fork. "And that paper I wrote was straight from the imagination of a bored grad student. I'm sorry if you wanted it to be something more."

What if it's true? What if this is from an alien?

He stares at the words on her comm a moment; she can see his heart beating in his throat.

"If it's true, it's an incredible conspiracy," he says finally. Sam leans in, but it's not with excitement. Not anymore. "And Hypatia has made it very clear that they're not interested in conspiracy theorists."

Losing your job as an indenture doesn't mean getting fired. It means having your indenture sold to another company. On New Sarjun, that other company is most likely a mining corporation, which means you can expect to be shipped out to the middle of nowhere and stay there for as long as you last.

Sam Amrith doesn't look like he'd last more than a few weeks in the mines.

"Who do you work for again?" he asks. He's folding his napkin with deliberate precision, lays it beside his plate even though he's barely halfway through his meal. "Because I'm loyal to Hypatia. Like I said, this is all from the imagination of a young kid."

WE'RE JUST SPECULATING, AND I DON'T WORK FOR HYPATIA.

He frowns at her comm, clearly wanting to trust her.

YOU WROTE THAT YOU DIDN'T BELIEVE THE ARTIFACTS WERE REAL, BUT THEN YOU FOUND EVIDENCE THAT CHANGED YOUR MIND. WHAT WAS IT?

His lips press together as he considers her.

"Who do you work for?" he asks.

I ALREADY TOLD YOU. SECURITY. COMPANY CALLED ADMANT. BUT THIS ISN'T FOR THEM, THIS IS FOR ME, MY MOTHER'S NECKLACE.

"I want to trust you," he says.

"You can," Starla signs. She types quickly, cursing the barrier to communication between them. I DON'T WANT TO CAUSE TROUBLE FOR YOU. POINT ME IN THE RIGHT DIRECTION AND I'LL BE GONE FOR GOOD.

His mouth opens at that, and she holds up a finger.

YOU CAN TRUST ME. THE ONLY WAY HYPATIA

FINDS OUT IS IF YOU SAY ANYTHING.

She can see in his face that he's reading that as a fact, not a threat, though it could be meant as both.

And he nods.

Reaches into his pocket and pulls out a flat case the size of Starla's thumb and slides it across the table. He keeps his fingers on it as she reaches for it, her pale fingers and his brown almost touching.

"The woman who did this research was murdered. The man who ran the museum was murdered. All traces of either of them were wiped from the nets, so I wiped all traces of that paper." He shakes his head. "Not well enough, apparently. I haven't been able to sleep since you told me it was still out there. I was an idiot for writing it."

Starla gives him a solemn nod of understanding, keeping her fingers on the case. It's warm from his pocket, and whatever's inside could change the world as she knows it.

Sam takes a deep breath, then releases the case.

Starla flicks it open to see the iridescent data chip inside, then tucks it into a secure pocket alongside the necklace.

Her fingers pause over her gauntlet, hesitating to send the next message though she knows it must be said. She got what she needed, and she's put him in enough danger by dragging this all back out into the open. Dr. Sam Amrith should go back to his standard biology classes, pumping out the scientists that agricorps and gentech labs and packaged food firms are paying Hypatia for. Starla has a creature to decode and a family to protect.

You won't see me again if you don't want to.

His lips part as he read the message, then close again. A crease pinches between his eyebrows as he considers it.

Sam looks up, gaze locked on hers. "What if I want to?" he asks.

Then you don't have a well-developed sense of self-preservation, Starla thinks. Instead, she lets a smile tug at the corner of her lips and pushes through a comm address, the untraceable number she keeps for the few flings she's ever thought safe enough to see again.

I would like that.

10

—————

ORIOL

Last time Oriol Sina was in a casino was in Aiax Demosga's *Dorothy Queen*, where he was thieving a ring for a mysterious religious organization and getting shot at by Bennion Zacharia and his undying supersoldier lady friend. Getting shot at isn't his favorite way to spend the day. But — and just playing devil's advocate here — logic says if he doesn't want it to happen again, he should probably learn cards and get a job as a dealer rather than the job he's in fact agreed to take.

As far as casinos go, the Lorelei is as gaudy as you would expect from a building where the exterior is shaped like an enormous holographic waterfall. There's a raised stage in the middle of the casino floor, surrounded by a fountain. At first Oriol figured that was a hologram, too, but no, it's real water. Guess nobody goes into the casino business to save money on showy stuff — or to save resources even if they are on a desert planet.

A sparse crowd has gathered around the stage, half listening to the trio of singers harmonizing in their diamond-studded gowns, half gawking at the water sprays. If you're from New Sarjun, you're not used to seeing anything like this, he supposes. If you're from Indira, you're probably just excited by the spectacle in general even though you're used to lakes and rivers and oceans.

And if you're from Indira but haven't been home for most of your life?

It's mesmerizing.

Because God, he misses swimming. Misses rivers. Misses those lazy summer days on leave, talking some recruit with family money into renting a boat and taking them all out on the lake. And, yeah, he'd have to buy a whole other prosthetic if he wanted to take a dip these days, but if he had the option on this planet, it'd be worth the cost.

Sometimes the thought strikes him: Manu doesn't even know how to swim. Oriol's got to fix that. Get Manu off this rock and take him on a tour of the old country, show him snow-capped mountains and clear blue rivers and thunderstorms and rice paddies as far as the eye can see.

First, though, he faces the epic challenge of convincing Manu to take time off from Jaantzen.

The singers' dresses scatter light like cut glass, their harmonies melting in perfect time with the water display. Oriol may have a high likelihood of getting shot at while stationed at the Lorelei, but at least he's not going to be bored while he's waiting for it to happen.

He asks around, finds a security guard, then finally finds his way to Phaera D herself. She's going over something with the bar manager, scrolling through line items and disagreeing about quantities. The security guard whispers in her ear and Phaera glances over, lifts her chin to Oriol to acknowledge his existence, then goes back to her conversation.

The security guard takes a step as though to head back to the front door, and Oriol starts to protest — the man still has his weapons. But then he gives Oriol another look and decides to stay in case Oriol's got bad intentions on his boss.

Good man? But if Oriol had been here to take Phaera out, she'd already be dead.

Oriol takes up a familiar stance, scanning the room, mind settling into the rhythm of checking for patterns in the crowd, looking for danger lurking among the revelers.

"How long you been in Bulari?"

Oriol blinks.

The security guard is attempting small talk.

"Twenty-some years?" Oriol smiles at him and continues scanning.

"Arquelle?" There's venom in the word.

"Yeah, man," Oriol says, another light smile and his attention back to the crowd. "How long *you* been in Bulari?"

That gets him a glare, he feels it burning on the edges of his attention. "Since my great-grandparents moved here from Corusca."

Corusca? Yeah, okay, fair enough with the anger. Especially when you're talking with someone who looks as much like ex-Alliance special ops as Oriol does.

"Nice, that's great," Oriol says easily, keeping his attention on the crowd. There's a man in a navy-and-teal suit who looks for a moment like he's about to pull a gun, then pukes on the lady he's next to. It's barely noon, man. Casinos are fun.

"What brought you to New Sarjun?" the security guard asks.

The first time? Oriol had come to assassinate a political refugee for the Alliance. A Coruscan freedom fighter, actually, he remembers with a smallish pang of guilt.

"Work," Oriol says. His new friend probably

doesn't want to hear about boring stuff like assassinating freedom fighters. "I loved it and stayed. Wouldn't go back home if you paid me." It's a solid line that normally gets grudging respect. And it's true — though it definitely depends on the amount you're paying him. Oriol will go a lot of places once there are enough commas in the fee.

The security guard seems satisfied with his attempt at a cursory interview after realizing he'd brought a trained fighter within yards of his boss. Now that Oriol's trashed Arquelle, though, the man wants to talk politics. "Can you believe the prime minister you all just elected?" the guard asks. "Because that woman …"

Oriol honestly has no clue what the man's going on about about, but he doesn't mind nodding and smiling — or frowning or whatever seems to be called for — until Phaera finally steps away from her bar manager. She gives Oriol the once-over. The security guard straightens like he has Oriol under control.

"And what are you here for?" Phaera asks.

"The man thought you could use a bodyguard," Oriol says, seeing realization dawning in her eyes. "Some worry about your bounty pissing the wrong people off." Manu's been swearing about it all morning.

Phaera tilts her head — whether at the accent or

the phrasing or both — and her second look takes in more than his hips and shoulders. "You're Oriol Sina."

Oriol inclines his head. "Yes, ma'am."

"It's a pleasure to meet you. When your boss suggested a bodyguard, I didn't figure he meant you."

"I'm in between jobs," he says. And her tourist clientele probably won't balk at his Arquellian accent, so it's a good deal all around.

"As I told him, I already have a security detail."

"But you don't have a bodyguard," Oriol says. "And I'm very good at standing around looking good in a suit until you need somebody shot."

Phaera laughs. "I thought your partner was, too. But in the end he preferred the diplomatic approach."

If Manu chose not to kill Acheta last night it was either because it was the smartest decision or because Jaantzen had ordered something different. Oriol, on the other hand, is being paid as a bodyguard for Phaera D — not as a soldier for Jaantzen.

"I'm under your order," Oriol says. "You need a man shot, I'll shoot him. Except you don't have to spend a dime; the man's footing my fee."

Her lips part in argument, then close.

"Thank you," she says. She dismisses the security guard who brought him here. "Thank you, Severs."

The man's about to leave, but Oriol clears his throat, holds out his hand for his weapons. The security guard grudgingly pulls out a pistol, which Oriol tucks into his holster, and a second magazine of bullets coated in neon green. Oriol tucks those in his pocket.

"What are those?" Phaera asks.

Oriol just winks. "They're special."

Truth is, he isn't entirely sure. Toshiyo gave them to him this morning and told him not to use them inside.

"Should I be worried?"

"Not about me," Oriol says.

"Good. Now if you'll — " She cuts herself off with a biting curse, then takes a deep breath. With the exhale her face smooths into a pleasant mask. "Hello!" she calls with a wave. A portly old man in an iridescent green suit is striding towards her from the front door, flanked by a pair of bodyguards. He lifts his chin in greeting, but does not smile.

"Herran Tarri," Phaera murmurs to Oriol. She doesn't bother to explain and she doesn't have to — Oriol actually recognizes this famous person's name. He owns Herran's down the street. "This isn't going to be good."

"Do you want me to shoot him?" Oriol says, and Phaera flashes him a look, allows herself a faint smile when she realizes he's joking.

"Just do bodyguarding, or whatever it is Jaantzen's paying you for. Tarri," she says, stepping forward to greet the older man with a handshake. "How can I help you today."

Oriol stays leaning against the bar, scanning the room and staying out of the way. Herran Tarri spares him only a glance, and after a quick evaluation, his bodyguards take up a stance behind their boss.

"Do you have a minute, Phaera?" Tarri's voice is a roughened baritone, no less commanding for the hoarseness of age. "We need to talk about this crusade you've started in the neighborhood."

Phaera laughs. "'Crusade,'" she repeats. "I'd love to. In my office?"

Oriol falls in line behind Tarri and his bodyguards as Phaera leads them diagonally through the maze of casino floor. He notes the looks they're getting. Phaera and Tarri are a recognizable pair, Phaera with her magenta bob and regal bearing, handing out waves as she spots regulars in the crowd, Tarri with his eye-catching suit, old money bearing, and chiseled brown face that's graced lifestyle and gossip feeds his entire life. The crowd is sparse, but it breaks around Phaera's entourage.

Oriol scans. If anyone has intentions beyond catching a photo with Phaera D and Herran Tarri in the background, they're hiding it well.

Her office is up a ramp marked Employees Only that Tarri takes huffing and puffing. The Lorelei's second-level balcony offers a view out over the casino floor; from above Oriol can see just how many tables are empty. Phaera opens her office door and waves Tarri through while his bodyguards take up positions on either side of the door. Oriol catches Phaera's eye and she gives him a slight shake of her head, so he leans up against an out-of-use Devilier table, watching Tarri's bodyguards watch the door.

"I never seen Mr. Tarri in person," Oriol says once the door's been shut a minute. He lets his accent shine through. "Even back home he was a legend, though. He good to work for?"

The shorter man, pale as Oriol himself, only glares at him. But the taller man — square-jawed, olive-skinned, serious black eyes — just shrugs.

"It's a good gig," the taller man says. "Pays well, not a lot of trouble. You looking for work?"

"Always looking." Oriol smiles. "I like not a lot of trouble. Trouble was fun when I was starting out, but now, I'd rather leave that to a younger set, you know?"

Shorty glares at him, but Talls just laughs. He's closer to Oriol's age anyhow. "I get that," he says.

"Tarri's the sort no one goes after. Doesn't like to stir the pot unnecessarily. Our work is lots of long, boring shifts with regular hours."

"Love that. Must be nice to work for someone who isn't hotheaded," Oriol says, leaving exactly who he's talking about open for interpretation.

Talls gives him a knowing laugh, taking the bait. "She a handful?"

"She doesn't take shit from anybody. And she doesn't sit down even a minute." From what Manu told him last night, the former is definitely true; from what Oriol's seen of her energy so far this morning, he's reasonably sure the latter is true, too.

"Tarri doesn't bow to anybody, if that's what you're suggesting," says Shorty gruffly, finally goaded into conversating. "There's not taking shit, and then there's going out of your way to pick fights like Phaera does."

Oriol raises his hands. "Ain't what I was saying. I'm just trying to get the lay of the land." He plays up his Arquellian drawl: He's just an outsider needs to be put in his place, told what it is. Shorty looks like he enjoys telling people what it is.

"Tarri didn't get to be where he is by making enemies out of powerful people," Shorty says. "You got to be smart about these sorts of things."

"You're saying Phaera's making enemies?" Oriol asks.

Talls steps in, trying to placate. "Not enemies, but she's making it harder to be friends with her. She maybe doesn't realize how much you need to play nice with the local color."

At that moment, Phaera's voice comes muddled through the door, her tone sharp, voice raised. Tarri's two bodyguards glance at each other.

Oriol gives them a wince. "I'm new to town. This all starts to go bad between Phaera and Acheta, who should I be looking for a job with? Your man hiring?"

"Always," says Talls. "And you might ask around Ayisha's Palace, or at the Aterciopelado, they know to stay out of trouble."

"The Horus," adds Shorty. "Angeliq's got a cool head, too."

"Good to know." Oriol files the names away. Very good to know. "Appreciate it, boys."

A thud sounds from within the office, and Oriol's left hand is on the door handle, his right on his pistol, before the other two bodyguards even react. But the handle turns as he touches it, Phaera flinging the door inward. Oriol steps back out of her way.

She holds the door for Tarri, her face a calm mask though her voice is icy with pent-up fury. "Thank you for stopping by, Tarri," she says.

Tarri steps past with an elegant tug on his cuffs.

"Come see me when you've got a handle on that temper, dear," he says, and his two bodyguards give Oriol a knowing look he doesn't return, but which Phaera doesn't miss. Anger flares in her golden eyes.

"And come see me when you've come to your senses," Phaera snaps. She shuts the door to her office without acknowledging Oriol.

Oriol waits until Tarri and his bodyguards are gone before knocking softly.

"What?"

It's not an invitation, but it's not a dismissal. Oriol slips inside. She's standing at her office window, jaw set in anger. A chair is on its side; Oriol rights it.

"Did you have a good laugh out there with Tarri's muscle?" she asks.

"No, ma'am," Oriol says. "But I did learn something you'll want to know."

"Did you learn I'm a hotheaded nobody who's trying to sleep and cheat my way into the good old boys' club?"

"That wasn't mentioned," Oriol says mildly. He makes a guess at her anger. "Tarri came to tell you he's siding with Acheta."

"Among other things. The spineless fucking coward." But now there's no venom in her voice when she says it, only annoyance. He can already see her mind whirling as she comes up with her next plan.

"Probably so is Angeliq at the Horus. And Ayisha, and the owner of the Aterciopelado."

Phaera gives him a sharp look.

"I asked Tarri's muscle who I might ask for employment if things go south with you and Acheta. I apologize if that was out of line, but I thought it might get some good intel."

Her mouth quirks to the side. "Clever."

"Which of those could you turn back?"

"Ayisha," Phaera says without hesitation. "Angeliq and Tarri are cowards, but Ayisha's smart enough to see reason. And others listen to her. Ibn Rushd and Cavy at the Aterciopelado will both do what she tells them to."

She takes a deep breath, and when she lets it out her eyes are bright and fierce. "Let's go see Ayisha," she says. "And Sina?"

"Yes, ma'am?"

"Thank you."

"Just doing my job, ma'am," Oriol says. "Acheta won't make it through the week."

She cocks an eyebrow at him. "Is that wishful thinking? Or are you telling me Jaantzen has a plan?"

"The man always has a plan."

Of course, this one about putting Coeur in Acheta's place is terrible. But nobody's asking Oriol.

Or, apparently, Phaera.

"Well," Phaera sighs. "He's not letting me in on it. Let's go make one of our own."

11

______

JAANTZEN

Jaantzen knocks once and gets Gia's distracted nod to enter the medbay.

Thala Coeur is watching some sort of game show projected over the bed, contestants currently suspended in vats of glowing amber liquid. When he enters, she rolls her head towards him with a rangy restlessness, then winces; half her face and scalp are still covered in bandages from the fire in the spinner. She taps a button on the controller with thickly bandaged fingers; the show blinks out.

"Willem, I am so fucking bored," Coeur says.

Without the sallow glow of the show playing over her face, she looks healthier than he's seen her since she returned from the dead. The ashy color is gone from her rust-red skin, the whites of her eyes are clear and bright. For good or bad, she almost looks like Blackheart again.

He turns to Gia; Coeur's steady gaze on his back no longer lifts the hairs on his neck.

"How is she?" he asks Gia.

"*She* is dying of boredom," Coeur answers. She coughs wetly, but it doesn't sound like the death rattle he's heard from her these last days.

"She'll live unless I kill her first." Gia angles her screen so he can see it, too. "We removed the spleen, and it looks like the internal bleeding is stopped. Her blood pressure is stable, now — so far no infection. Barring unforeseen complications, she's on the road to health."

"And her hands?"

"I did what I could, but almost every bone was shattered. The chance of full recovery is pretty slim."

"You underestimate me," Coeur says.

"Find a good physical therapy regime," Gia says bitterly over her shoulder. "It worked wonders for Manu."

Jaantzen expects a retort, but Coeur cuts her gaze away, a muscle clenching in her jaw. It doesn't look like anger to Jaantzen. Is that . . . shame?

Whatever she's feeling, he leaves her to it. "Thank you for your help," he says to Gia, who gives him a side-eye.

"I already regret it."

"I'm right here," Coeur says.

"How much longer do you want her on bed rest?" Jaantzen asks.

"At least a week."

"Vindictive bitch," Coeur says, but there's no venom in the words. She clicks the game show back on, amber light pooling in her eyes.

Jaantzen leans in towards Gia's monitor, tries to make sense of the jumble of words and images. The scans of Coeur's abdomen are blurred by staticky swaths of medical webbing; strokes of white metal and pins are bright highlights along the bones of her hands. "What can you do to get her ready for action sooner than a week?" he asks.

Gia's brows knit in suspicion. "What kind of action."

Coeur turns the game show back off and rolls her head towards them, gaze bright with sudden interest. A ghost of her old feral smile tugs at the corner of her lips.

"Can we have the room, please?" Jaantzen asks Gia.

Gia crosses her arms, watching him warily. "I disapprove of whatever you're planning with my patient."

"Noted," Jaantzen says, and if she considers arguing with him, she decides against it. But he can read anger in the set of her mouth and the cords of her neck, the stiffness of her movements as she swipes files from the monitors, adjusts settings on the various machines Coeur's plugged into, and lets herself out without a second look at either of them.

If he could change anything about this plan it would be to leave her and Manu and Toshiyo out of it. He's made his own decision when it comes to working with Coeur; in a fair world, he'd allow them each the same respect.

This is not that world.

Jaantzen settles onto a stool to the right of Coeur's bed, studying her.

"Please tell me you're going to let me go or kill me, or anything besides keep me chained to this bed watching shit vids," Coeur says.

"Nobody's choosing what you watch," Jaantzen says mildly. There's a spark of life behind her eyes that wasn't there a few days earlier. A glint of her old spirit. Good.

"You look like you're going to lecture me about something," she says. "Though I don't know what I could've done." She lifts her wrists an inch; the soft cuffs thud against the bed.

"No lecture," Jaantzen answers. "I'm here to make a deal. With Zacharia gone, Acheta is fighting with Dry Creek to take control of their territory. It's wreaking havoc in the city."

"So Acheta has ambition." Coeur shrugs, shoulders stabbing at the thin fabric of her hospital gown. "I didn't think you would be the first person to shit on that, Mister Street Kid in a Penthouse."

"He also tried to have my daughter killed."

Coeur's chapped lips part, then close; she looks away. She doesn't have a joke for that, and he can't read the complexity of the emotions playing over her face. As far as Jaantzen knows, Coeur doesn't have any children of her own. In fact, he's rarely known her to have a romantic partner, though rumors have always flown, generally about any man or woman whose name the gossiper was trying to drag through the mud.

He does know that Blackheart can be wounded by loss, now that her sister is dead. He just wishes he could have learned that fact without having to lose Ximena.

Jaantzen clears his throat. "Acheta needs — "

"Willem."

Coeur's been studying the wall to her left. Now she shifts with a wince to look directly at him, but though her jaw works, she doesn't speak. An IV admin whirs on, clicks back off, pumping some drug into her system.

"What is it." A knot is forming in Jaantzen's gut; he's not sure he wants her to answer.

Her bandaged hands ball to fists, slowly release.

"I'm sorry, Willem," she says finally.

"What Acheta did isn't your fault."

"Not about Starla," she says, and a door is flung open in his chest, a windswept void howling beyond. He stays utterly, deathly still; he's not sure he could move if he tried.

Coeur's gaze is level, her dark eyes now calm and clear. "I'm sorry about Tae," she says. "The kids. They were in the wrong place at the wrong time, and I regret that."

He forces his breathing into a steady rhythm, searches her face for the lie, the trick. "You regret your bomb didn't kill me instead."

One of Coeur's bony shoulders twitches in a shrug. "At the time, yeah. Of course. But I — " She takes a sharp breath, lets it out slowly. "But I was also sorry. I've left a lot of damage in my path, and I don't regret much. But they've always . . ." She cuts her gaze away again; he catches the sudden shine glossing her eyes, the moisture caught on her lashes as she blinks. "I regret that, Willem. I'm sorry."

"Thank you," he says when he trusts his voice. Coeur's eyes close, her shoulders relaxing against her pillows. For a moment, neither of them speak.

"What are you doing about Acheta?" she asks finally.

Relief washes through him; Acheta is safer ground.

"I'm getting rid of him," Jaantzen says. "But I'm not going to take over your territory, and I'm not going to let the neighborhood crumble. Word is there are plenty in your crew loyal to you and Hinoja, but no one with the strength to challenge Acheta."

Coeur stares up at the ceiling, thinking. "Rosa Nils?"

"Dead."

"D.W.?"

"Dead."

"Vira Llanos?"

"She's made the cut so far. Could mean she's loyal to Acheta."

"Bitch is loyal to me. And she could take out Acheta."

"Then why hasn't she? And even if she did, could she win over all those who are loyal to Acheta?" Coeur doesn't answer. "There's another problem. Acheta's broke, and that's going to plague whoever comes after him. It's one thing to hold together a fracturing crew. It's another entirely to do it without any cash to pay them."

She frowns into the air where her game show had been playing, gears turning as she processes what he's telling her.

"Tell me, Thala. If you take over Acheta's crew,

you're going to, what? Turn to dealing shard and petty theft? That's quite the fall from grace."

Her expression darkens.

"I need you," he says. "I need you to control your people. But if you're going to control your old crew, you need not only the strength to lead, but also a viable business plan. Something that makes you more than just another petty crew boss. Something that gets you cash immediately." He waits; she turns her gaze to meet his. "Something like what you came to me with originally."

She lifts her chin. "The terraforming technology? You destroyed it when you blew Zacharia up."

"Cut the bullshit, Thala. We both know you shipped two cases from Indira. And if you're planning on getting out of here and finding the other one for yourself, let me crush that dream right now."

"Fuck," she breathes; there's no heat behind it. "I was starting to wonder — not much slips past you." She laughs, her old ambition glinting bright and golden beneath the rasp of her voice.

"When Acheta goes, I'm not looking for a puppet to follow my orders," Jaantzen says. "But I'm also not looking for a knife in the back. I've debated ways to gain leverage over you, but every way backfires. I can't strong-arm you into helping, I can't bribe you, and I can't blackmail you. The only way I know you'll do what I want is if I have the upper hand, but I can't trust you long if I'm holding something over your head. So you can see my quandary."

"You're offering to go into business with me," she says. "Haven't you heard what a double-crossing bitch I am?"

"And I see where it's gotten you."

She lifts her bandaged hands. "A ghost of who I once was."

"That's hardly true." That little quirk of her lips could be a smile. "Thala. I need you, and you need me. Stabbing people in the back isn't the only way to get what you want."

"I'll have that tattooed on my arm."

"I think it was tattooed on your hands."

She sighs deeply. "Fine, Willem. Give me your pitch."

"You stole the cases with the serum fair and square, I consider those yours. But you didn't know you needed another part in order to sell a viable product to the Demosga family for development. Instructions. Plans for how to use the technology to terraform the desert."

She lifts an eyebrow. "And you have that?"

He does now, thanks to the ring Oriol stole from the Dawn — and Aiax Demosga. "I'm not interested in running yet another business," Jaantzen says. "But I am interested in investing. Part cash, part the goodwill offering of these plans."

"How do I know the plans are legit?"

"How do the Demosgas know your serum is legit? We have meetings to establish business partnerships. We do research to vet viability. We make educated decisions. It's much less of a thrill than stealing from the Alliance and selling to the highest bidder, but I promise it's a more sustainable way of doing business."

"But we don't sell the technology to the Demosgas."

Jaantzen shakes his head. "They have the infrastructure to develop and disseminate the product. But they'll need protection. Secure space to experiment. Maybe even someone who can be a figurehead — a historically vocal anti-Alliance mayor who risked her life to make sure they didn't use this technology to make New Sarjun dependent on them for our food."

Coeur laughs; it finishes in a cough which she muffles against her thin shoulder. "You're spinning quite the story," she says when she can breathe again. "If I remember, you got a nice payday from Leone and Seti and the others for running me out of town. How are you going to get them to swallow the 'Blackheart's actually a hero' bit?"

"They'll buy any story if it pads their bank accounts. You lost your crown because you were bad for business, Thala. Not because anybody had a moral problem with you. Anybody but me, anyway."

She holds his gaze a moment. "You and Seti," she says finally.

"Yes," Jaantzen agrees. "And Seti. You might consider apologizing for the hit on his father."

Coeur quirks her lips to the side, thinking. "But I don't regret that one."

"Then don't." Jaantzen pushes himself to his feet. "I'll let you think about my offer."

"I don't need to think," Coeur says. "I'm in. Lotta good people still on that crew who could be doing something better than pushing shard. I'd like to see what I can make of them."

"I'd like to see that, too."

She lifts her chin. "Get me out of this bed and somewhere I can fucking live again, and I'll show you."

"I'm not injecting you with mystery serum," Jaantzen says. "But I'll get in touch with the Demosgas and make preparations. You work on getting better. Watch something educational."

The rude sign she flips him is unimpressive, with her hands shackled; the little control slips off the edge of the armrest. Coeur swears and fumbles with the cord. Jaantzen hands it to her; her fingers are cool and dry.

"I'll watch whatever the hell I want," she says. "Hey, Willem. We trusting each other now?"

A long breath; around them, the machines keeping Coeur alive whir and chirp. Her hands are bandaged clubs. Her scalp seared with burns, her muscles atrophied, her organs held together with medical webbing and hope. How is any of this going to work?

"I suppose we are," Jaantzen answers.

Coeur lifts her cuffed wrists. "Please? I promise not to kill anyone."

Jaantzen types in the code that releases the cuffs, then helps Coeur ease each one off a bony wrist. Coeur cradles her arms to her chest with a hiss of pain.

"We're keeping the door locked," Jaantzen says.

"Course." She stretches her arms above her head, then drops them back to her chest with a fiery curse. "Thank you."

"I'll be in touch."

He hears a voice down the hall, coming from the second medbay. Toshiyo's chattering in half sentences followed by silence, which means she's either talking to herself, talking to the creature, or Starla is back from her lunch meeting.

From one imprisoned demon to another. Jaantzen sighs and steels himself to push open the door.

The creature is not happy to see him.

Maybe it doesn't like its new home in Medbay 2, where the lights are brighter than Toshiyo keeps them in her office. Or maybe it just doesn't like a crowd — with Toshiyo and Starla, along with the medical apparatus, there's not much space left in the medbay for Jaantzen.

Or maybe it's just evil.

Hard to tell.

In the early days, it only looked disgruntled. Now, its leathery, claw-tipped wings are crowded uncomfortably against the curved surface of the glass, and it pulses miserably in a space the size of a exosuit helmet. Wide, reptilian eyes track every human movement like a prisoner memorizing the faces of its captors.

"We're friends," Starla is signing to it. "We're just trying to figure what to do with you. We're here to help."

The creature bares its fangs.

Starla shares a look with Toshiyo, then catches a glimpse of Jaantzen over her shoulder and gives him a little smile. She signs something to him, but he doesn't catch it; his attention is fixated on the way she favors her right leg as she turns away from the creature.

Anger kindles below his sternum.

Acheta is walking dead.

"Hey boss," Toshiyo says. "We were just about to move him into the larger life support system. He's obviously getting a little cramped in there."

"The original tank, it's more like a carrying case," signs Starla. "Or an incubator."

"Right, but where are they supposed to go once they incubate?" Toshiyo asks. "Some alien sea? Hey buddy, hold on," she signs. "We're working on it."

"Do you think it understands USL?" Jaantzen asks.

Toshiyo just shrugs; Starla laughs.

It's incredible how quickly you can become accustomed to something. The creature is disconcerting, but only when he takes time to think about it. Over the course of a week, his mind has downgraded its categorization from Mind-Shatteringly Disturbing to Yet Another Problem. Starla is signing jokes to it, and Toshiyo seems to be treating it more like a roommate than an *ali* — He stops himself midword. A *creature of unknown origin*.

The new habitat sits on a table in the middle of the room, filled with clear liquid. It's a regen tank, long and wide enough for a person to lie comfortably inside while reknitting fluid is pumped around their body, and Jaantzen is certain they only have one of these. Which means the last time he saw it, Manu was inside, fighting for every breath.

He shuts the thought down.

Toshiyo has rigged a connecting tube with a series of locks between the original capsule and the new tank. The way Starla and Toshiyo are talking about it, they seem concerned primarily with how to get the creature from one sterile environment to another without exposing it to potential complications in the atmosphere.

There's another damn good reason to do things this way rather than just pop open the capsule and dump the creature in the tank, though: No one quite knows what it will do when it gets out.

Right now, it's mashing pitifully against the latch on its globe like it knows freedom is waiting on the other side of the glass. It sees him watching and bares its fangs.

"Almost there," Toshiyo says. She lifts an eyebrow at Starla, who nods.

When Toshiyo pops the hatch, the creature surges through the connecting tube and towards the tank, then thrashes as it realizes Toshiyo has trapped it for the time being in the connecting tube.

"Sorry, buddy," she murmurs, and she carefully maneuvers a needle in to take a sample from its neck, its haunch, its wing. The creature squirms ineffectually.

Toshiyo withdraws the last needle. "Okay, okayokay," she says, and Starla releases the gates to let the creature into the greater expanse of the tank. It surges into the open space and stretches its wings, clawed tips tracing paths through the liquid. Its wingspan is much bigger than Jaantzen had anticipated, stretching almost a meter. Starla's eyes widen.

"I wonder how much bigger it will get," Toshiyo says with an attempted laugh.

It wafts its wings, gives a flick of its tail, and spins in tight little circles, swirling the liquid into a miniature whirlpool.

After a few seconds, it stops propelling itself and rides the current, drifting in circles around the tank. It looks almost . . . happy?

"Its hind legs are already bigger, aren't they," Toshiyo says. "And its tail is definitely smaller."

"Have you ever seen a tadpole?" Starla asks.

"In vids," Toshiyo says. "Ruby Basin is about as far north as you can get into the Jupari Desert without needing environment domes. I didn't even know you could find water outside of plastic bottles until I came here."

The words slip out so nonchalantly, Jaantzen gives her a second look. She doesn't even crack her knuckles as she mentions her past indenture, so fixated is she on the creature. She traces a finger along the glass, following the clawed tip of a wing.

"The liquid, maybe it won't need to be in it forever," Starla signs. "Is that more or less terrifying?"

"More," says Jaantzen.

"I think it could be interesting," Toshiyo says.

"So long as it doesn't eat humans," signs Starla, then turns to it. "You don't eat humans, do you?" It's been watching their conversation with interest. Or maybe hunger, it's hard to tell. Starla makes the sign for humans, sweeps an arm to include them all, makes the sign again.

It bares its fangs.

"We're friendly, we want to help," Toshiyo signs. She turns away with a sigh. "We should feed it. It looks like it wants to start on us."

"Make your best guess and call down to the kitchen," Jaantzen says. He turns to Starla. "Did you learn anything more from your professor today?" he signs.

Starla's eyes widen and she signs something more like street kid slang for *This is going to blow your mind* than any USL he knows. "Are we good?" she signs to Toshiyo.

Toshiyo nods. "We got the genetic samples, the venom samples, and he's a lot more comfortable."

Jaantzen frowns. "The venom samples?"

"It's got little sacs in its neck," Starla signs, then strokes a finger behind her ear. "The diagrams say they're full of venom."

"Diagrams," Jaantzen says.

Starla waves him through the medbay door back into the anteroom, where there's a wash station, cabinets full of medical supplies, and a desk. She palms on the desk, which is already open to a series of anatomical drawings of something that looks exactly like the creature in the other room.

"The professor, he cited this research in his own paper," Starla signs. "I couldn't find it anywhere — he says the author is dead and the work was wiped out. But he had a copy."

"What do you mean, the work was 'wiped out'?" Jaantzen signs.

Starla shrugs. "His word. I'm looking into it. But it's a whole study on something the author calls a 'Fallen.' And it's definitely the same thing that we have in the other room."

"The fallen?" Jaantzen says, rolling the word in his mouth, trying to remember where he heard it before.

Toshiyo is closing the door to the other room; through the one-way security shield, Jaantzen can see the creature exploring every corner of its new home.

"The fallen?" Toshiyo says. "Manu asked me to

research it, and I completely forgot about it. The Gift of the Fallen, something that was supposed to be written in a Dawn holy book. God, I totally forgot."

Maybe it's the change from the bright lights of the medbay to the more dimly lit antechamber. Maybe it's that her attention is no longer consumed by the creature. Whatever the reason, Toshiyo looks suddenly exhausted.

"It's fine," Jaantzen signs. He turns to Starla. "I've heard the phrase before. From Zacharia. He said he was going to give you the Gift of the Fallen." She makes a face. "I forgot about that in everything else that happened."

"Whatever it is," Starla signs, "this author has anatomical drawings and genetic tests of something that's almost exactly like what we have in the other room."

"We're doing tests to make sure the genetics match," Toshiyo signs.

"Where was this other one found?" Jaantzen signs.

Something flickers over his goddaughter's face. "Durga's Belt," she signs. "No coordinates. Just Durga's Belt. The professor?" She shares a look with Toshiyo; they've obviously discussed how best to bring up the next point. "We need to bring him in."

Bring in someone who's bound by a corporate indenture?

"Not yet," signs Jaantzen.

"He won't talk. He'll lose his job if he talks about this."

Jaantzen frowns at that. Fear is a good motivator, and he's successfully worked with more than one outsider by virtue of how afraid they were. The key is that no matter how much this one fears crossing Hypatia Corp, he needs to fear crossing Willem Jaantzen a thousand times more.

Jaantzen can make someone fear him. But it's a balance — too much, and they become resentful of the power. Better is when someone is motivated by loyalty, but that takes time they don't have.

Jaantzen has already had Toshiyo scrub the network for this guy to see what kind of leverage he can get. No partner or kids to lean on, but he still has parents living, and a brother who works in the offices of some minor mining corp.

There's no dirt on him. He graduated top of his class at Hypatia's school in the nicer Santa Elena de Uairén neighborhood, one of the schools that train up and sell their students' mental acuity, not the strength of their backs. Sit in an office or crawl into a mine, though, an indenture is still an indenture. And the time commitment is usually more for the mental work than the physical. Sam Amrith has almost fifteen years left on his, after which he'll be free to take a contract with another company if he likes, or start his own business with whatever intellectual property Hypatia doesn't own.

The trade-off is guaranteed work, income, housing . . . Everything but the ability to decide what you want to do with your life.

Given the choice, Jaantzen had chosen the streets.

"See what you can learn on your own from this" — he sweeps an arm at the impossible drawings — "and come to me before talking to him again. If we have to bring him in, we will, but if we do I want to know we can control him."

"I'll find leverage," Starla signs.

There's something in her expression he can't put a finger on.

"It's late," he signs. He turns to Toshiyo. "Both of you, get some rest tonight. Starla, will you — "

"I need to feed my cats," Starla signs, cutting him off, and it takes everything in his willpower not to demand she stay here in Cobalt Tower. Or to insist on walking her the ten darkened blocks to her apartment on Nidaly Square.

"I'll call you a cab," he signs, and she doesn't argue, just kisses him on the cheek.

STARLA

You home?

Starla blinks at the message on her comm — she's taken her lens out for the night — and wonders who's in the mood. She's been in between flings for a while, so it must be an old flame. She's about to swipe the message away without answering when she notices the name.

Ah.

It's Manu.

Yep, she types.

Hungry?

Sure.

She's not, not really. But she can always eat, and she's just burned energy working out for the last hour. And while Manu never shows up empty-handed, dinner isn't the reason he's here at her Nidaly Square apartment.

Less than a minute later there's a knock on her door. Starla checks the security screen — it really is Manu. The AI doorman is trained to let him in, he probably pinged her from the lobby. He's still dressed for the office despite the hour, with a takeout bag in each hand.

"Hey, kid," he says as he slides past her; she holds the door open for him just a crack, then shuts it again as quickly as possible before one of the furballs decides to go for a midnight romp. Starla's apartment instantly smells like rich pork broth and ginger. She sets the locks again, reactivates the security field.

"You here to check on me?" she signs to Manu.

He shrugs, then sets his takeout bags on the one clear spot on the small kitchen table. "I was in the neighborhood," he signs.

"You're always in the neighborhood."

Cobalt Tower is ten blocks away, and though Manu lives farther outside the downtown core than she does, Starla's apartment is on his way home. It's not unusual for him to drop in unannounced, though it rarely happens when Oriol's in town. So he's got something on his mind.

Tonight she's guessing he was sent to make sure she got home safe. Jaantzen would prefer she stayed at the tower, she knows, but she can't leave her cats alone every night. Plus, she likes having her own space. She likes to feel the rumble of the commuter train a block over, likes the way her apartment smells like warm spice and yeast from the bakery on the street level, likes waking up to a tiny tongue licking her chin to demand breakfast.

And she's plenty secure here, even if she's not under her godfather's roof.

Jaantzen may not like it, but a girl needs her own space. Though the way Manu's surreptitiously scoping things out as he clears room for containers of soup dumplings and sauces, she's beginning to suspect he's not just here to make sure she's all right.

His gaze flickers down the hallway that leads to the bedroom, and it clicks.

"You're here to make sure I'm alone," she signs, raising an accusatory eyebrow.

Starla's wearing pajama pants and a tank top, no makeup. Hair still damp from her shower, muscles still warm from her workout. The small kitchen table is mostly covered with sketches for security at the Devil's Table and a product manual for the TR-X 17 partitioning shield system, though tonight Starla's made a nest on the couch, complete with a mug of steaming tea and a tablet still open to a scintillating page of the Dawn's holy scripture.

She's clearly here alone.

Manu winks at her and slips off his suit jacket, drapes it over the back of one of her mismatched dining chairs.

"He's cute," he signs. "I looked him up."

"Smart, too. Dr. Amrith has been a big help so far."

"Tosh told me."

She hadn't expected they'd be having this conversation so soon, but once she started getting interested in a man who could potentially guess they'd discovered a dangerous alien creature, Manu's tendency to snoop into her love life might well have gotten kicked into high gear. She shuffles technical drawings into a pile, annoyed, then stacks them on the rehydrator in the kitchen. She grabs chopsticks, spoons, napkins.

"Beer?" she asks him, and he gives her a thumbs-up. There's still a handful of lagers in the back of her fridge from the last time he swung by unannounced. She cracks one open for him, saves her tea on the coffee table from Pepper's curious nose, then scoops Mango off a dining chair so she can sit down. The calico gives her a disappointed scowl, then leaps into Manu's lap, stretching up to nuzzle against his chin. Manu ruffles Mango's ears before shuffling her back to the floor.

"Dr. Amrith. I think we should bring him in," Starla signs.

A tight, noncommittal smile. Manu passes her the ginger sauce and rolls up his shirt sleeves.

"Do you trust him around Tosh?" he asks.

Starla laughs at that. "They'll be nerd friends in seconds," she signs. "They're really going to get along."

But Manu's not smiling with her. "And your life, do you trust him with that?" He holds her gaze, expression serious. "With my life? With Jaantzen's?"

Does she? Starla can't lie to herself; she shakes her head. "Not without spending some more time with him. But my gut says he's trustworthy."

"Next time you meet him, I want to go."

"You'll scare him."

"Maybe he needs to be scared."

She lifts an eyebrow. "Maybe I know what I'm doing."

That earns her a long, evaluating look. Finally, Manu gives her a one-shouldered shrug. "Okay," he says.

He snares a dumpling and drops it into his spoon, snips a hole in the side with his chopsticks to let the soup drain out. They eat companionably a moment, Manu making methodical work of his plate, Starla only hungry enough to eat a few of the dumplings.

It's not Manu's implicit threat towards Sam that's bothering her; she knew that would be coming. In the past he's been even more explicit. "I need you to think hard before you let him get too close," he'd told her about the first man she'd ever gotten serious with. "I like him, but my job is to protect Jaantzen. You. Tosh. Everyone."

Starla had tried to lighten the mood, back then: "I know, I know. If he hurts me, you'll kill him."

But Manu hadn't been joking. "I love you, but if he becomes a liability, I will take care of it. Don't let him become a liability."

That guy hadn't been going to work out for a number of reasons, but Manu's solemn promise hadn't helped.

The old surgery scar snaking up the dark skin of his left forearm glints in the light as Manu reaches over the table to snatch one of Starla's dumplings with his chopsticks. She pushes her plate towards him; she's not going to finish.

Manu frowns at her. "I'm sorry," he signs.

She shakes her head. Manu's reminder that a serious relationship with an outsider isn't compatible with her family isn't what made her lose her appetite — she already knew that.

No, what's bothering her tonight is the fact that

the Dawn have apparently built their entire religion around Toshiyo's little lab buddy. Starla's been reading Dawn holy scripture nonstop since she got home, and what she's learned is unsettling as hell.

She surrenders the rest of her dumplings to Manu and crosses the two steps from the dining table to the couch to grab her tablet. Mango yawns plaintively at her — she was curled up on top of it. Starla cocks a hip against the couch and flips to the page she's looking for.

"This Dawn holy shit," she signs to Manu. "Have you read it?"

"I haven't had time."

"It's awful," she signs. "So repetitive, like just say it right the first time, I get it. But . . . here." She highlights a passage and sets the tablet on the table in front of him. *Through the Fallen, God has given us the means to create heaven on earth, to transform this broken planet and its unfaithful people as one.*

"What does it mean?" he signs.

"'The Fallen'? It was referenced in that new research Sam gave me. The scientist called the alien that."

She finds another passage for him: *It is the duty of the faithful to fulfill the prophecy by spreading the transformative power of the Fallen to cover the planet and its inhabitants.*

"Later it says the way they should spread it is by

exploiting vices. Starting with 'the lowly' and moving up in society."

"What does that mean?"

"The shard. Zacharia said it back at Julieta's, they're putting this 'Gift of the Fallen' in the shard to spread it to the masses. I think that's what happened to that shard pusher in the Brujería. This whole bad batch of shard, I think it has alien in it."

"Testing delivery that way?" Manu sighs. "So the Dawn had a serum that could transform people into superhumans — if it didn't kill them first — and they're just putting it in the shard to see how many druggies they can change?"

"It's not just shard."

She pulls up the news article she found earlier this evening, the one that's been bothering her the most. Some no-name company town up north, over a hundred people dying the same horrible death as the shard pusher she saw in the club.

Manu's face is expressionless as he reads it, the final few dumplings forgotten.

"Their water tank had been damaged, and an emergency shipment of water arrived. They think whatever killed them all was in the water."

"Shit," Manu breathes.

"The water, we need a sample. Do you know anybody who could get us one?"

"Yeah, maybe," Manu signs slowly.

"The bad shard Acheta is selling, that could have been made before Zacharia died," Starla signs. "But the water tank in this town was destroyed two days ago. Zacharia may be dead, but the Dawn is still trying to get their poison out into the world."

"Where are they getting it? We have the . . ." Manu makes a face, clearly not ready to sign the word *alien*. "Things."

"I don't know. We took samples this afternoon, and Toshiyo is going to match them against the DNA sequences in the research paper, and that shard tab I brought back from the Brujería."

Manu sighs and leans back in his chair, reaching down absently to run a finger along Pepper's back as the cat arches against his ankles. "So you're saying that whatever Tosh's creature is, it's not the only one out there."

"The ones the research paper talks about are dead."

"But there might be others. And not just on New Sarjun."

Starla flips back to the Dawn holy text. "This serum, called the Gift of the Fallen, they say it's a treasure that fell from the heavens and was buried in the sand. Whatever is going on with the Dawn, this shard, these creatures, it started out in the desert around Redrock."

"Which is where their prophet still is, yeah?"

Manu signs. "We took out Zacharia, but the prophet's influence obviously still reaches across the desert if they're poisoning water supplies down here."

Starla nods. "We need to know what's happening there."

Manu doesn't answer that, but his drawn expression says he's not happy about the idea.

Neither is Starla. The burning need to know what this creature is — and why her mother had a necklace with its likeness carved on it — has been eating her up these last few days. Tonight that need is tinged by the growing dread that it may require her to travel back to Redrock Prison in order to find out.

Manu pushes back from the table and says something to the floor. Pepper arches his back into Manu's shins, and Manu scoops him up with a wince; the cat drapes into a boneless gray puddle of fur in his arms, one white-socked paw batting contentedly at Manu's chin. Manu smiles down at the cat, but the smile doesn't stick.

Something's troubling him beyond the Dawn, beyond Sam, beyond Acheta; one more mysterious ping or electrical short or rusted-up pivot point to add to the work order of minor — and massive — failures needing attention these days.

She almost asks if he wants her to put on a vid

before she remembers that Oriol is still in town. Manu will be heading home.

She doesn't know if it's simple loneliness or malicious ghosts dancing around the corners of his memories that bring him here on those long, lonely stretches when Oriol's out of town. She's never been able to get him to talk about what's bothering him, but she's eternally grateful that he at least seeks her out.

He never asks for what he needs, simply shows up at her apartment every few weeks with food she's not hungry for or beers she's not going to help him drink, and although he says he's only stopping in to make sure she's all right, she knows when to offer to put on some cheesy old vid they've both watched a dozen times until he dozes off in suit pants and shirtsleeves with his feet kicked into her lap and Pepper curled under his chin. Sometimes he's still there when she wakes up, but more often than not he's gone, showing up at the tower the next day fresh and chipper with some quip about the vid from the night before.

They'd uncovered a shared love of bad entertainment years ago, back when no one was sure if he would ever walk again and she was trying to lighten the mood with the most ridiculous old comedies or bad dramas that took themselves so seriously as to be funny. She couldn't solve the problem, but she could lift his spirits. And that in itself eventually helped.

He kisses the top of Pepper's head, pours the cat back onto the floor. "I should go," he signs. "Did you get ahold of Chevalier?"

Most of Admant Security's clients need straightforward security systems, civilian-grade stunners for their guards. But for the small percentage — like Phaera — looking for something with more firepower, it's handy to know a weapons dealer like Absolon Chevalier. He's an old friend of her parents; she met him ten years ago when Jaantzen sent her and Gia out into Durga's Belt to negotiate a shipping deal with the local cartel at Maribi Station. As an Indiran, Absolon has access to some of the more interesting blackmarket firepower than what's available on New Sarjun.

"He'll have something ready for Phaera day after tomorrow," Starla signs. "Do you have someone we can send for it?"

"Definitely. I have a new driver I'm testing."

Shirtsleeves buttoned once more, suit jacket back in place, leftovers in the fridge, and takeout containers in the recycler. Manu pauses beside the door, smoothing dark fingers down Mango's back as the cat kneads contentedly at the top of the couch.

"Get some sleep tonight," he signs, ignoring Mango's indignant glare when the pets stop.

"You too," she signs back. "Say hi to Oriol."

A tight, brief smile. Not a good sign.

And after she sets the locks again behind him, Starla makes herself another cup of tea and sinks again into the couch.

She's not ready for sleep.

She pulls up the Dawn text again and finds where she left off.

And after the fire burns away the impure, the pure will become devout, she reads. *And when the pure become devout, we will see a new era unlike anything humanity has ever experienced . . .*

13

––––––––

ORIOL

Oriol is getting into the groove. His initial estimation of the gig was right — no matter how much standing around there is to do, when you're in a casino there's always something to keep your attention. Working as a bodyguard for a casino magnate comes with fantastic people-watching opportunities. Sure, he can get plenty of reading and studying done on a long-haul security job, but there's also a lot of hours of staring at gray sheet-metal counting rivets or laughing at the same tiny crew's same unfunny jokes. While Phaera's been complaining about just how dead business is right now, there's still a Ganesh in orbit, and there's still a decent hum along the drag. It's early afternoon. He can't imagine what this place must look like on a busy night in peacetime.

Only thing about this gig is, he's not sure how much longer he can get away with wearing the same suit. He hates to spend money on outfits for a temporary job, but Manu's suits are too narrow in the hips and shoulders for Oriol to raid his half of the closet. Might be time to torture himself with a shopping trip.

He's spent the morning trailing Phaera, who — he was right again — never sits still. She's got a few years on him, but her energy reserves are seemingly boundless. So far they've walked half the length of the drag visiting casino owners. Ayisha seems willing to play, and Phaera coaxed her into pledging her loyalty again. But Ibn Rushd at the Aterciopelado wouldn't budge, and Angeliq at the Horus wouldn't even see her.

"It's business," Ibn Rushd had told her simply. "Acheta makes working with you bad for business."

He hadn't offered any other explanation, but Oriol's learned a thing or two about reading people. Normally when he's acting as a guard in a meeting like that he's watching for the moment he has to pull out his weapon. But today he also saw the haggard look in Ibn Rushd's eyes, the gnawed lips. The frequent glances at the little holo-display of a pair of toddlers playing in a park.

"If you don't mind me offering, I'd bet Acheta's threatened his family," Oriol says as they leave the Aterciopelado. He scans the sparse crowds, scans the rooflines. "I'd rather we take a cab," he says.

"Sun too hot, Sina?"

"You're too exposed."

"Acheta doesn't get his money if he assassinates me."

You're making enemies, Oriol wants to tell her. But she's heard that from plenty of people in the last few days. She doesn't need it from him, too. He picks up his stroll to keep up with her brisk walk and keeps an eye on the crowd.

"Ibn Rushd did look like hell," Phaera says. "I wondered if something was wrong. You have kids, Sina?"

"No, ma'am. You?"

She laughs and waves a hand down the drag to where the Lorelei's cascading holographic waterfall is washed out and ethereal under the hot midday sun. "I have two. The Table and the Lorelei. Tell me what you think about Ibn Rushd."

Here's another difference in this bodyguard gig versus a long-haul security detail out in the Belt. Out there, nobody asks for his advice — and he likes it like that. He's got no interest in the responsibility and stress of a management job.

But Phaera keeps soliciting his opinion, and he

finds he actually enjoys the conversation. Finds it surprisingly satisfying to puzzle out strategy and motivation with her.

Who knew?

"You can count out Ibn Rushd's support for now," Oriol answers. "But if he's being threatened, at least he's not pulling his support out of malice. Keep him nearby for if the tide starts to turn."

Phaera waves a familiar greeting to a street magician, then sighs. "Acheta's threatening people's children," she says. "He must be desperate."

"Desperation is making him reach too far," Oriol says. "You can take advantage of that if you're quick when the right opportunity shows itself."

"And have the right plans in place." She winks at him.

Be careful, he wants to tell her. But she knows that, too.

The same security guard who brought Oriol to her yesterday, Severs, chief of the daytime crew, greets them just inside the door. He gives Oriol a nod — business-like camaraderie tinged still with suspicion.

"Ma'am, Jaxon is here to see you. He's in your office."

Phaera takes a sharp breath, chases it with a muttered curse. Oriol follows her across the casino floor to her office. He starts to settle a customary few paces behind, but she slows to talk with him.

"Dal Jaxon is the president of the cab drivers' union," Phaera says quietly. "It was a chore to get him and his crew to sign on in the first place, and I guarantee he's not here to see how I'm doing."

When they arrive at the office, Oriol takes up a position beside the door. Phaera beckons to him as she walks past.

"Oh, come in, Sina," she says.

Oriol inclines his head and follows her in, ears perked and gun hand ready.

Dal Jaxon stands as they enter. He's got another head on Oriol, but his height isn't intimidating; the union boss is lanky and angular as stick bug. Oriol tries to imagine him folded into the front seat of a cab all shift long and aches sympathetically for the man.

"Don't tell me you're pulling out, too, Jaxon," Phaera says in lieu of a greeting. She shakes his hand, then leans a hip on the corner of her desk to watch him expectantly. Jaxon glances at Oriol, but when Oriol doesn't get an introduction, Jaxon ignores him and settles back in one of Phaera's armchairs, all elbows and knees.

"I can't tell my people to put themselves at risk like this," he says. "We're vulnerable out on the streets. We pick up a fare, we don't know who they're loyal to." He juts his chin at Oriol. "Even you're walking around with muscle these days. My drivers can't hire bodyguards."

"I understand that," Phaera says. "But we're not fighting a war of muscle — you and I both know we'd never win that."

Jaxon throws up his wiry hands. "So we're fucked," he says. "What do you want me to do about it, Fay?"

"We can't win a muscle war, but we can win a business war," she says. She smiles at him, conspiratorial. "I remember last year. When that upstart cab union tried to edge in on your membership and steal your trade? By the time that was all done, how many rival cabs with 'faulty parking brakes' were at the bottom of Dry Creek Ravine, Jaxon?"

The man's lips twist into a lopsided smile and he allows himself a laugh. "They got what was coming to them," he says.

"And what does Acheta have coming to him?" Phaera asks. "How are fares lately? Because I haven't seen many people lining up to head back downtown at the end of the night. Are tourists even leaving the Tamarind these days?"

Jaxon's smile fades. "Fares are bad. You know that."

"Acheta's killing our business. Anybody else, you'd agree we should return the favor."

He's frowning at her. "Phaera . . ."

"You and I both know you can win a business war. Tell me. What would you do?"

"I would not fuck with Acheta."

"Play a game with me," Phaera says, a ghost of a smile. "What would you do if this were anybody *but* Acheta?"

Jaxon takes a deep breath, thinking. Leans elbows on knees, hands steepled over his lips.

"Well," he says slowly. "The shard trade's his money."

"Even after that bad batch?"

"Course. Addicts are still looking for a hit — he's ramping sales back up."

"How many of your drivers deal?" Phaera asks.

"Decent amount."

"Which means you can get an inside idea on where his stashes are."

Jaxon shakes his head firmly. "I won't put my people in harm's way to take out a stash. That's mad."

"I'm asking for intel. I know people who can start fires."

His gaze narrows, but he nods slightly. He's still willing to play her little thought experiment.

"That would hit him hard," Jaxon agrees, though he doesn't seem ready to agree to anything else yet. "Other thing I might do — if it was anybody but Acheta, mind — would be to look at where they get together. Say, maybe they meet at that cafe on the corner of Blackwood and Sol." He lifts an eyebrow at Phaera, who nods. "I might look at what they drink the most. Like maybe they're into a certain brand of vodxx."

"Such as?"

"Fang."

"Go on."

"If I happened to know the delivery driver, I might think about having him deliver a tainted batch. Nothing that would drive a crew out for blood, but something that puts muscle out of commission for a few days with the trots."

"I love it," says Phaera. "And might you also keep an eye out for Acheta's movements? Your people see a lot of the city."

Jaxon scrubs a hand over his dark stubble.

"This isn't going to happen overnight," Phaera says. "But you and I both aren't going to let anybody else edge in on our businesses. The way I chased out that Arquellian casino chain this spring? The way you shut down that rival union? Jaxon, we control this drag. And neither of us are going to pay protection money to somebody like Levi Acheta."

"He's not weak."

"He's killing your members' business, Jaxon. And how are you going to keep control of the union if you can't protect your drivers' income?" A slow smile grows on her lips. "You and me? We're not playing to lose."

A long beat, Jaxon's lips thin and tight as he considers. Finally: "I can get you some stash locations."

"Thank you."

"And I'll spread the word to the drivers I trust most. Have them keep an eye out for movement in Acheta's crew. I'll pass on anything interesting to you."

"I'd be much obliged." Phaera leans in. "And if you left here with a case of Fang, could you alter it and make sure it was being poured at a certain cafe tomorrow?"

"Dammit, Phaera."

A slow smile tugs at the corner of her mouth. "I'll make sure you also leave here with a very nice case of gin. Diamond Smoke is your brand, do I have it right?"

A pause, and Jaxon snorts out a laugh. "Dammit, Fay," he says again. "Fine."

Phaera stands and so does Jaxon, their handshake is firm, and this time Jaxon doesn't look chagrined.

"I owe you," Phaera says.

Jaxon shakes his head. "We'll see. This harebrained plan of yours works out, we'll all owe you."

"We'll see," Phaera repeats. "Stop by the Siren bar on your way out, I'll call the manager there and let her know you're coming."

Jaxon nods down at Oriol as he leaves, and Oriol shuts the door and turns back to Phaera. As soon as they're alone she claps her hands together, relief flooding her face. "My god, Sina," she breathes. "Finally a fucking win."

Don't celebrate in front of me, he wants to say, but that's a product of too many years working with Jaantzen. Instead, he returns her smile. "You've got quite the silver tongue."

"Jaxon doesn't want to roll over for Acheta," Phaera says with a wave of her hand. "He came here to get a bulletproof reason not to."

"And you were that reason."

She laughs, buoyed by the success. "I'll be the backbone he needs. I'll be a backbone for every damned one if I have to." She types something into her golden cuff and touches the line of opals in her ear. "Layli? Dal Jaxon will be coming by in a moment. Can you get him a case of Diamond Smoke? And do we have any Fang? Great, a case of that, too. Thank you."

A knock sounds at the door; the screen beside it shows her daytime security chief, Severs. At Phaera's nod, Oriol opens it. Severs's left eye is mercury silver as something plays on his ops lens.

"Excuse me, ma'am," he says around Oriol. He blinks, and his eye goes clear once more. "That man you wanted us to keep an eye out for? He's just shown up."

Oriol's never been much for revenge — it's not a useful emotion — but it takes everything he has to stay cool at the announcement that one of the men who tried to kill Starla is here in this casino.

Despite his best efforts to remain comfortably detached from other people after leaving Alliance special ops, he'd had the bad luck to fall hard for Manu. After that, it was impossible not to love who Manu loved: Toshiyo, Starla, Gia, Hallelujah Oni. Impossible not to develop a genuine if frustrated respect for Jaantzen.

And as much as he pretends he's still detached, he'll happily indulge in revenge on anyone who tried to lay a hand on Manu's family.

"Where?" Phaera asks Severs. Her voice is suddenly strained.

"The north fortune-luck table. Hassling Vy, as usual."

Phaera walks to the window overlooking the floor, scans the crowd. The brightly painted windmill of a fortune-luck table rises above the crowd. Oriol isn't sure who it is they're looking for, but he does spot a man leaning too close to speak with the dealer. Her face remains polite, but her body language says she wants him gone.

"Take him downstairs," Phaera says.

Severs relays the message, and a pair of security guards detach themselves from the edge of the crowd and make a beeline for the man from behind. "Do you want me to go with them?" Oriol asks.

Phaera lifts an eyebrow at him. "My team is more than capable of taking care of this. Kicking people out or hauling them downstairs without incident is pretty much our specialty."

Across the room, Oriol can see her team working. A man and a woman in the dark-blue suits of the security team approach discreetly, polite smiles and body language saying they're sorry for the interruption, but it would really be best if he came with them. If he knew what was good for him.

A few of the guests around have marked the incident, but no one pays it much mind. The man is babbling at the security team, confused but not yet scared, and whatever ruse they've told to get him to go quietly, it's working.

"Who knew the casino business could be so exciting," Oriol says.

But she doesn't acknowledge his attempt at a joke. The earlier elation has gone and her face is drawn tight and anxious as she watches the scene below.

"Is everything all right?" Oriol asks quietly.

"Fine," Phaera says, but the word comes quick and sharp. "Me, I get to be a hero twice over. My dealer doesn't have to worry about this asshole coming in to bother her on shift anymore, and your boss gets a punching bag."

She doesn't look fine, but Oriol doesn't press. His job isn't to get in the way of her game face. Phaera straightens, gives the dealer a little wave when she looks up at the office window. "I need to go make the call," she says.

14

STARLA

El Anahoy's eyebrow is cocked to say he just asked her a question, but Starla missed whatever it was he signed.

Her dreams last night were tinged with words of prophecy. She'd fallen asleep reading the Dawn scriptures to meet images of Bulari's streets snarled in cloying vines, her parents trapped and dying in malicious foliage, *now in the Jungle, now in Julieta's greenhouse, the floor slick with blood and littered with glass and bodies*, until a crushing pressure in her own chest distracted her from the horror of the scene. She looked down to see a single white calla lily bursting from her chest, slick and red with gore, then woke up with a scream that sent Pepper scrambling from his purring perch on her sternum.

El's frowning at her, and she snaps back into the present. They're at the Devil's Table, checking on the systems installation. The design Phaera approved is all defensive, some shielding and a drone swarm at the valet stand, better cameras all around, an upgraded AI designed to keep an eye out for body language that suggests malicious intent as well as cheating. Starla has planned for partitioning throughout the building as soon as they can get the TR-X 17 system delivered, which should be later today.

"I'm sorry, one more time?" she asks El.

El repeats Hiro Matapang's question about customizing the biosign recognition base data in the upgraded AI, and Starla rattles off the answer without really thinking about what she's saying.

The Devil's Table is getting dialed in. She's had a team working the Lorelei since yesterday, taking initial stock of the situation and drafting a proposal. And just this morning she had a new inquiry from the security lead at Ayisha's Palace, which on another day would have her messaging Simca and dying of excitement — Ayisha Amadule is a dance-hall *goddess* — but today it's just another sign of danger around every corner.

Well, protecting against that is her job.

She banishes distraction for the next few hours, walking Matapang and his crew through the rest of the AI training, finalizing the valet shielding, and taking the drone swarm for a test flight, which is always fun. She's showing Matapang a hack to boost his team's security-grade stun carbines — GHK's Wasp model is basically their Cobra with a limiter slapped on — when a message pops up on her lens.

CAN YOU MEET? I FOUND SOMETHING ELSE YOU NEED TO SEE. SAM.

Her pulse leaps, and she knows it's as much with anticipation of another clue to the alien creature as it is for a chance to see Sam again. The fact that he sought her out this time, despite the danger, is flattering — though her scintillating conversation is hardly the only reason, a practical voice says. He's just curious to learn the truth.

But whatever the reason, it's not even a decision not to go.

El notices her pause, pushes a strand of electric-blue hair out of his eyes. "All good?" he signs.

"Can you finish here? I need to deal with something."

"Do you need me?"

El's heard about the attempt on her life, of course, but she can't quite tell if the concern on his face is his usual desire to see if she needs any assistance or an offer of protection.

"I'll be fine. I'll see you back at the tower." She turns her attention to Matapang. "I need to take care of some other business. You're in good shape here, and El can answer any other questions you have."

She hurries down the black lacquered staircase to the valet stand, composing a message as she goes.

I'M FREE. WHERE?

I TAKE LUNCH IN 30 MINUTES. CEUTA PARK?

Not a park, it's too open, too exposed — and that one's too near Acheta's territory. She needs somewhere with a layout she knows. Safe exits and cover. It's not something she's spent a lot of time thinking about in the past, but it's first to mind now. She wonders if this is simply the way new Starla thinks, or if her knee-jerk caution will fade as time puts distance between herself and the attack.

PIONEER MUSEUM? she counters.

SEE YOU THERE.

Pioneer Museum is a tribute to the first people to decide life was too crowded and easy on water-rich Indira and figure they'd make their own way on New Sarjun instead. Sure, there were minerals to be mined and fortunes to be made by being the first to settle the more rugged planet. But Starla suspects the reason most of New Sarjun's early immigrants struck out from Indira was because they were too ornery for polite society.

Or they were escaping something else — conscription into never-ending wars, bad relationships, the long arm of the law. Misfits and hopeless cases who decided to do something about it rather than simply settling in to live the rest of their lives under someone else's rules.

So, her kind of people. The same sort that had washed up in her childhood home of Silk Station and been happily taken in by her parents. The same sort as her parents themselves, who'd fallen in love while fighting on opposite sides of Corusca's war for independence from the Alliance and had hightailed it out together when Corusca lost once again.

The plaza in front of the museum features one of the first shuttles to land on the surface of New Sarjun — along with a swarm of Indiran tourists and New Sarjunian school groups jostling for photos.

Starla walks past the shuttle — you'd've had to be desperate to trust your life to that hulking metal beast — and finds Sam pacing nervously near a display of early mining equipment. They've added a first-gen sandskimmer to that display since Starla was here last, and she'd love to check it out, but that's not what she's here for.

Sam looks tense, and she doesn't blame him.

But she also can't have him so nervous around her in public. She gives him a friendly wave and a smile and his lips quirk up — out of conditioned response or actual happiness to see her, or maybe both.

"How are you, Starla?" he signs, hands more confident than last time. "It's good to see you again."

"It's good to see you again, too," she signs back.

And the moment of friendliness on his face fades, his lips pressing together in worry. "I don't have much time before I have to get back," he says. "But you need to see this and I couldn't risk sending it." He takes a deep breath, glances over his shoulder. No one's around.

Starla pulls out her comm with a raised eyebrow, and he nods. It's unlikely anyone can hear them here, but she'd rather be safe.

"Remember the virtual museum I told you about?" he says.

Starla nods; of course she remembers. The one he'd mentioned in his paper, filled with supposedly alien artifacts. The one where he'd seen the same symbol that's on Starla's mother's necklace. The one that had been wiped from the nets when the curator was murdered.

Sam pulls a scrap of paper from his pocket and types a string of letters and numbers into Starla's comm — a network address. He hands the comm back and shreds the scrap of paper with his fingernails.

"It's back up," he says simply.

"How did you find it?" she signs, then starts to type the question into her gauntlet.

But either he understands her expression enough to get what she's asking, or it's the next thing he wants to tell her. "I couldn't stop thinking about it after I saw you," he says. "I know I should have left it alone, but I went searching on an anonymous terminal. I eventually found this."

God, she hopes he actually knew what he was doing hunting around like that. Anonymous, pay-by-the-minute terminal banks like the ones you can find at Geordi Jimenez Terminal and the seedy neighborhoods just outside of the downtown core still collect a lot of information if you don't know how to take the right precautions. If he's right, and both the scientist who did the DNA research and the curator who operated the virtual 'alien artifacts' museum were murdered, someone could be hunting for him, too.

Not to mention that companies like Hypatia sometimes have alerts set to track their employees' activity outside of corporation networks.

You visited it? Starla types.

He nods.

Is it the same as you remember?

Sam shakes his head. "The artif — " He clenches his jaw shut and types. *The artifacts are all the same I think. But the original curator's notes are gone. No information about where they were found, just poetry.*

How do you mean?

Sam frowns at the words. "Talking about the faithful, cleansing humanity, stuff like that," he says. "Weird religious stuff. And there's some sort of chanting in the background while you're visiting. Like a meditation."

A chill brushes up Starla's spine despite the heat of the day.

Do they mention the gift of the fallen?

Sam goes still, even the rise and fall of his shoulders frozen as though he's forgotten to breathe. His gaze jumps to meet hers. "Why do you know that?" he asks, suspicion drawing his brows together.

This cult, the dawn? They talk like that.

"I've never heard of them."

"Good," Starla signs, then goes back to her gauntlet. *They're bad news.* And they've apparently got longer fingers than anyone knew. Who knows how long they've been gathering information, putting plans in motion. Who knows how much power they actually have.

A disturbing thought occurs to her. *How long*

AGO WERE THE MUSEUM CURATOR AND DNA RE-
SEARCHER MURDERED?

Sam frowns. "Five years."

Meaning it's within the timeline where the Dawn have been operating, though that doesn't mean they had anything to do with it. Still, better safe than sorry.

LISTEN TO ME. LEAVE THIS STUFF ALONE, AND I'LL MAKE SURE ANY TRACES OF YOUR ORIGINAL PAPER ARE WIPED.

"What are you going to do?"

TAKE CARE OF IT.

It takes her a moment to realize the concern on his face isn't for himself. He lets his hand fall to brush against her forearm. The pressure is light as a bird, warm as the sun. "Starla," he says, leaning towards her with urgency. "Be careful."

"It's fine," she signs quickly. "I'll be all right." He frowns at her hands; god, this is frustrating. DON'T WORRY ABOUT ME, she types. I'M NOT IN DANGER, BUT I PUT YOU IN DANGER BY TALKING TO YOU.

"Let me know what I can do."

IF YOU FIND SOMETHING LET ME KNOW. BUT DON'T GO LOOKING ANYMORE.

She holds out her hand for the comm, her pale fingers brushing up against his warm brown ones and finding electricity there. He lets it go, then lifts his hands. "Can I see you again?" he signs stiffly.

Goddammit, he's not making this easy.

"I'll call you," she signs, big, easy gestures, and his smile slips straight between her ribs and into her chest to kindle there like fire. She turns on her heel before she can make a mistake; she can feel him watching her back as she walks away.

She opens a message to Manu as soon as she's out of the museum. *I NEED TO TALK TO YOU, YOU AROUND?*

The response is immediate. *CAN'T NOW, BUSY WITH THE BOSS. TONIGHT?*

Starla calls up Jaantzen's calendar as she's walking, but there's nothing there. Busy? With what?

FINE.

She has some more research to do.

15

____

JAANTZEN

The room is almost exactly what Jaantzen was expecting: bright, clean, the walls a gleaming white, floors spotless white tile. The holding area behind the forcefield is perfectly square, with a narrow cot, a table, and chair. The furniture is also white.

At first, it seems too cheerful — right down to the lounge music being piped into the white-grated speakers. But the longer Willem Jaantzen observes the room and its inhabitant, the more ingenious he finds it. This would be a hellish place to sleep off a bender, or to sit and think about what's about to happen now that you got caught cheating the house.

The man in the cell is cuffed to the table, and the way he's hunched over and pinching the bridge of the nose with the fingers of his bound hands, the pristine white must become blinding after a while. And Jaantzen can see how the music would be a torture all its own. It's already on his nerves.

"Can we turn the music off," Jaantzen says to Phaera. She nods and taps a code into her golden cuff.

And if Jaantzen had any reservations about this man's guilt, they disappear when he sees how the man stiffens at the sound of his voice. The fingers massaging the bridge of the nose go still. The unconscious toe-tapping along with the music stops. Even the gentle rise and fall of his shoulders ceases.

Slowly, like a man waking into a nightmare, the man opens his eyes to see Jaantzen standing beside Phaera on the other side of the shield. He screws his eyes shut again almost immediately, the blood draining from his face.

"He come in with that black eye?" Manu asks. He's leaning a shoulder against the wall to Jaantzen's right, arms and ankles crossed. Oriol's hanging back near the door, one eye on it though a couple of Phaera's security staff are waiting in the hallway outside.

"My staff are close to each other," Phaera says mildly. "I hadn't realized just how much of a bother he's been to my dealer. My security team enjoyed bringing him in a bit more than expected. I hope that won't be a problem."

"Not at all," Jaantzen says.

"Hey, man," the man calls, his voice reedy with fear. "I don't know what this bitch told you I did but — "

Phaera smooths a finger down a panel in the cell door and the volume of his protestations diminishes to nothing. It's a nice touch.

"I'd like some privacy, please," Jaantzen says to Phaera. He catches Oriol's eye, begins to sign that he doesn't want her to watch at all, then thinks better of it.

But Phaera's seen the gesture, and her nostrils flare. "Anything you have to say to Sina you can say to me."

She seems on edge today. It could be the late hours and the events of last night, or it could be a growing discomfort with Jaantzen's presence and what's about to happen. Either way, she's live wires under porcelain, the energy of her nerves humming so close to the surface she's practically vibrating. But the surface isn't going to crack in front of him. Not today. Maybe not ever.

"My apologies," he says. "I would like you to turn your cameras off."

"Of course. And you can have all the privacy

you need," Phaera says. "But I don't need you to protect my delicate sensibilities."

"Of course not," Jaantzen says, but how can he explain that's not what this is about? He's not trying to spare her a scene he doesn't think she can't handle. He's trying to earn himself one more day in which she doesn't think he's a monster.

The look she's giving him says they'll have a longer conversation about this later.

Behind the forcefield, the man is red-faced with anger, shouting, though he has to know they can't hear him. The bulk of his fury seems to be aimed at Phaera, as is the obscene gesture he manages even with his hands bound.

Phaera raises an eyebrow at him, then checks a message on her cuff. "Take your time," she says to Jaantzen. "I've got a business to run, and nobody'll miss this guy anytime soon."

"Nobody will miss him at all," Jaantzen says quietly, and he means it to be reassuring. That she won't have to worry about someone coming after her because of this man. That he'll take care of it.

But his words have the opposite effect.

Her gaze goes from feigned casual to steady and clear. The knowledge that this man is never coming back to her casino — to anyone's casino — has hit. A veil has dropped between them, and whatever story

Phaera's been telling herself about who Jaantzen is has burned away to ash.

It was going to happen sooner or later, and though Jaantzen thought he'd steeled himself for the loss, it still cuts like a knife.

Jaantzen clears his throat, preparing to give her an out; he can at least let her keep her own conscience clean. "If you prefer, we can — "

"Let me know if you need anything," Phaera says. She walks past him without another word, leaving a faint breath of something dusky and sweet in her wake. Oriol peels himself from the door to follow her, with a solemn nod to Jaantzen and a glance at Manu that Jaantzen can't read.

The door shuts behind them with a click. The scent of Phaera's perfume fades, and all Jaantzen can smell now is the sparkling antiseptic quality of the room.

And the sharp tang of the man's fear.

Jaantzen switches off the forcefield and finds silence, the man having yelled himself hoarse while the forcefield was up. Or having realized any chance he had of getting out of here in one piece left the room when Phaera did.

The man's gaze is locked on him as he walks past. Jaantzen can hear the man's breath ragged and fast. The faint tapping of his foot has started up again.

Jaantzen doesn't look at him.

He unbuttons his suit jacket, folds it precisely. Lays it gently on the bed. He rolls up one cuff, then the other, blue-gray crisp against the deep brown of his muscled forearms. He rolls his neck, letting his head hang heavy a moment to ease out the tension there until there's only clarity.

He cracks the knuckles of his right hand into his left.

"I only have one question for you," Jaantzen says to the blank white wall, and when he turns around, the man's face is gray with fear.

"Who sent you to kill my daughter?"

16

MANU

anu's almost lapped the Lorelei before he
finally finds Phaera. She's near the two-
hand tables talking to an old man in a suit that
would have been fashionable a few decades ago,
though it's still clean and sharp. She's at her most
charming, her hand light on his arm, her laugh
sparkling at whatever he's just told her.

She sees Manu coming and stiffens involuntarily before she catches herself and returns her
bright hostess smile to the old man. Oriol's standing
a few paces away; he gives Manu a slight nod, then
goes back to scanning the room.

"I'll tell Elva to come find you with a bottle of
our best champagne," she says to the old man.

"Congratulations, Tayib, I'm very happy for your family! Now if you'll excuse me." Phaera pats him on the arm and turns to Manu, gaze sliding past him for a moment. He can't quite tell if it's relief or disappointment on her face when she doesn't see Jaantzen there.

"This way," she says before he can speak. She unhooks a velvet rope and leads him into what is probably the quietest place in the whole casino: the high rollers room. The room is dimly lit and literally cave-like, watery blue-green light playing over the sculpted stalactites and stalagmites that are studded between translucent sapphire card tables. The room holds ten tables. A handful of Indiran tourists fill one of them.

Phaera waves Manu onto a cushioned stool at the farthest end of the empty bar, then slips onto the one beside him. Oriol leans with his back to the bar a few paces away, elbows behind him while he scans the room. Phaera ignores the bartender's look of inquiry, and the woman goes back to sidework.

"Did Jaantzen already leave?" Phaera asks, tone falsely light.

Manu nods. "He's sorry he left without thanking you in person. He needed to get back for some business." That's what Jaantzen told him, though Manu suspects Jaantzen's not ready to look into Phaera's eyes just yet. That might have been a good call. Phaera seems to relax at the news that Jaantzen is out of her casino.

"Thought I'd stick around to see when that new boy of yours gets off, though," Manu says with a wink Oriol doesn't return. "Unless me being here bothers you."

"Why would it bother me?" Phaera asks, too quickly.

Manu doesn't answer. She's smooth, but she has her tells same as anyone else. For some people, nerves make them more flighty. For Phaera D, nerves apparently shut down her constant multi-tasking and give her an intense focus. Phaera doesn't want to think about the fact that the man she handed over to Jaantzen left here wrecked and destined for the desert with Jaantzen's cleanup crew, but from the way she's acting, it's clear she can't put it out of her mind. And Manu being here isn't going to make forgetting it any easier.

"Do you want me to go?" Manu asks.

"Stay," Phaera says. She lifts her chin to the bartender, holds up three fingers. The woman pours three shots of something golden — Manu doesn't catch the label — and places one in front of each of them. Phaera clinks glasses with Manu; Oriol doesn't acknowledge the glass at his elbow, though she clinks it all the same. Manu rolls the liquid on his tongue: smoke and honey.

"Did you learn what you needed?" Phaera asks.

Manu shrugs. "Acheta gave the order, but that's about all this one knew. He was pretty low in rank."

"Why would Acheta send a nobody after such a high-profile target?" Phaera asks. "Especially since he botched it."

"Not sure Acheta cared much if the bullets took, or he would've sent someone he knew for sure would finish the job," Manu says. "Granted, he would've been delighted if they'd killed Starla, but I think this was more about sending a message." And using a disposable guy to do it. Manu doesn't add that part.

Phaera raps an unvarnished fingernail against the frosted glass bartop twice while she frowns into space, an unconscious tick.

"He's very grateful for your help," Manu says carefully. "And he hopes this doesn't mar your friendship."

Phaera gives him a sharp look. "Why would it do that?"

Manu just smiles and taps his glass. "What are we drinking?"

"Tobalà mezcal. Kyoshiri twenty-five year. Can I ask you a question?"

Manu sips, tastes distant brushfires, warm earth, caramel.

"How is he right now?" Phaera asks.

Manu frowns. In the trunk of a spinner, is the answer, on his way to digging his own grave in the desert. Surely she knows that.

"Jaantzen, I mean."

Manu lets out a breath Phaera doesn't seem to notice. She sweeps a hand at Manu. "You seem fine. Is he ... just as relaxed after murdering someone?"

"Nah, man," Manu says. Her gaze stills again, regarding him warily. "The asshole tried to put a bullet in his daughter, and I think the scumbag got what was coming to him. But the reason Jaantzen's not here having a drink with me is he still has one more person he blames."

"He can't think it's his own fault," Phaera says. "He can't keep Starla locked behind bulletproof glass." Phaera shifts to Oriol before Manu has a chance to answer that, the black tips of her magenta hair sweeping the dove-gray linen of her suit jacket. "And what do you think, Sina?"

Oriol laughs. "I think nobody is paying for me to speculate on your love life."

"My love life?"

Manu can't see her face, but she doesn't sound angry, just amused. After all, she doesn't strike

Manu as the sort of woman who shies away from stating what she wants.

Oriol returns his attention to the nearly empty room behind Phaera, but the amused quirk to his lips slowly fades. The sober expression transforms him by years, a reminder that the highlights in his hair aren't the sun, they're threads of silver in the brass. He keeps his eye on the door and clears his throat.

"They teach you a lot of things in Alliance special ops," Oriol says quietly. "One is to never kill angry, to not hold a grudge. You lose a lot of friends in terrible ways, but the Alliance drums out of you the urge to do anything about it. Except to fight harder the next time."

Phaera starts to say something and Oriol lifts his chin, just a touch; she falls silent. Manu stays as still as he can. Oriol never talks about his time in the Alliance; in twenty years Manu can count on one hand the number of times Oriol has let himself be raw like this.

"I ain't saying there's a right or wrong way, just that's what I was taught," Oriol continues. "And that's what I keep to. But I was also taught if you lost the gunner on your squad, you just plug another one in. Lose your sniper, your pilot, your interpreter, there's another one waiting back at base to replace them. Goes without saying there's somebody waiting to replace you, too, if you screw up. You get trained to think like that, why would you get all mad when somebody takes a potshot at someone on your team? I mean, obviously it's a pain in the ass to be down a person."

Oriol smiles, but there's no joke in it. "Jaantzen doesn't have a single goddamn replaceable person on his team. It's one of his biggest strengths, but it's gonna take him down."

"You think that justifies what — "

"Ain't no justifications here, ma'am. Just observations." Oriol turns to her, the profile of his pale cheek picking up the warm glow of the lights behind the bar. "And a warning, if you put yourself in that circle."

Manu wishes he could see Phaera's face; her shoulders straighten.

"A warning," she murmurs. Her left hand smooths flat against the bartop. "He's possessive."

Oriol shakes his head. "It's not like that. He protects, he doesn't hold. Anyone's free to go — if they want to." His gaze slips past her to Manu. It's only for a second, then he's back to watching the room.

Phaera shifts back in her seat so Manu can see her profile once more. Her jaw is tight as she takes another taste of her mezcal. "You two should go home. It's been a long day," she says. "I have some office work to finish up here, then I'm heading home as well."

"Apologies, ma'am," Oriol says. "But I'm here as long as you are."

Phaera sighs. "And you'll walk me home again, I assume?"

"I can be more discreet if you don't like feeling guarded."

"And hopefully it won't be necessary for much longer," Manu adds. Acheta signed his death warrant the moment he sent men after Starla. It's only a matter of time before Jaantzen makes it happen.

"It's fine, and I don't mind the company on my walk," she says. "But I don't want to keep you — just give me a few minutes to wrap up for the day. I —"

She goes silent, lips parted and gaze raised as she listens to whatever's coming through her earpiece.

Oriol's on his feet a second before Phaera, but not by much.

"What is it?" Manu asks, but then he doesn't need to have an ear on the Lorelei's security channel to bolt to his feet. He hears the shots himself.

"It's coming from the front entrance," Oriol tells him. "Two cars. Heavily armed."

"They trying to come in?"

"Not yet."

"Good. Stay with her. Let her team know I'm coming."

Manu breaks into a run.

The casino floor is packed, every gambler there standing and crowding the aisles either in panic or in hopes of catching a glimpse of the excitement. Manu shoves his way through the crowd. "Get down," he yells. "Take cover," and a few eyes widen; most remain oblivious. He vaults a low wall and finds the lobby mercifully clear — at least those closest to the door have realized the danger of gawking.

Manu stops on the verge of the cleared lobby, suit jacket unbuttoned and hands raised as one of Phaera's security team swings her weapon towards him.

"I'm Manu Juric," he calls to her, and she beckons him forward.

"It's Juric," she yells, and the memo goes down the line that he's a guy not to shoot.

The entrance to the Lorelei is a mess of splintered hologlass and bodies. The facade's holograms are flickering weirdly over cracks in the glass and dented panels, casting an eerie glow over the scene. Bullets are flying in, but Phaera's got a half-dozen security guards in reasonably defensible positions shooting out the door.

Manu finds a position next to the guard who first spotted him, a brown-skinned woman with a gold nose ring and a thick black ponytail.

"What's the situation?" he asks.

She lifts her chin at the door, then ducks as a round of fire shatters the skylight above them. "A spinner and a delivery truck," she yells as hologlass cascades around them. The larger pieces stutter-project flowing water for a few seconds before flickering out. The guard aims her woefully underpowered security-grade sidearm back at the front door and squeezes off a shot that would barely pierce skin at that distance.

Acheta's men, if that's who they are, are much better armed than Phaera's security team. The security team wasn't meant to defend themselves like this; what firepower they do have is for intimidating drunks and making sure cheaters can't run far. That's what Starla's weapons connect is designed to fix.

Tomorrow.

"Cover me," he says out of habit, not because he expects that security-grade pistol to do much damage. But the guard nods seriously, and he takes the next break in the gunfire to make his way closer to the entrance, ducks behind a blocky granite statue of a half-woman, half-fish nightmare with a bewitching smile and bared fangs. He shares a nod with another security guard behind the statue's twin sister, about five meters away, then leans out to the left and picks off the man in the spinner wielding the continuous pulse rifle.

Answering gunfire chews into the statue's base.

The gunfire ceases, and he leans out again to wing one man, catch another in the throat. He ducks back from the answering volley — it's lighter than last time — and in the aftermath he hears a woman shouting orders in an Arquellian accent.

Her again, the woman who was at Acheta's side last night.

He risks a peek to confirm: shaggy black ponytail, pale brown skin, cheekbones and jawline sharp enough to draw blood. She takes aim as he pulls himself back. Fire tears through his jaw, but when Manu presses a hand to the wound it's only a throbbing scrape. A ricocheting chip of granite, probably. He blinks, sparks of pain dancing in his eyes.

He recognizes most of Acheta's men — the leadership, at least. The newer ones he's seen in security videos and police reports. The older ones he knows from the long-ago days when Coeur still ran the crew.

Acheta is notoriously hostile to newcomers — the mole Manu has in his organization has been edging his way in for almost two years. Yet he's delegating a crew to a foreign woman no one seems to know a thing about.

Manu leans out to take a shot at her, but now she's an impossible twenty paces to his left, flanking him. She fires back, lightning fast, as he ducks, her bullet sending sparks flying from the hologram panel just behind him.

The display goes out. He'd been relying on the distortion from the holograms around him as much as the fish-woman statue for cover, now he finds himself flanked by the woman and visible. He launches himself back out of her line of sight to roll behind a cement planter.

He crouches in his new spot as a trio of bullets slam into the wall beside his head. The woman is shouting orders, closer. Any second now she's going to be around that statue and his cover will be gone. He's a fast shot, but he's never seen anyone move quite as fast as she just did. He readies his weapon. The least he can do is take her out, too.

And then something explodes on the other side of the statue.

Manu launches to his feet and pivots around the planter, pistols blazing. His first shot catches her in the back — she's wearing armor — and she spins and fires back at him, but her aim is off. She ducks his second shot then jumps into the spinner behind her. Manu's bullets thud into the reinforced doors;

the engine roars as it tears away. The truck is a roaring fire, those of Acheta's men who survived the blast scrambling free of the wreckage.

Silence.

Well, silence and the incongruous show tunes that are being piped out to accompany the hologram display. Now they're only narrating the shattered bodies of the dead in the lobby: "I have always loved you, come back darling, come back home . . ."

Manu shuts out the music, turns to figure out which of Phaera's team had access to something strong enough to make that explosion. Oriol's standing in the doorway behind, a pistol in his hand. He lifts his chin to the smoldering wreckage of a truck in the middle of the road. "I guess now we know what Tosh's new bullets do," he says. He shoves the gun back into his holster.

"You were supposed to stay with Phaera," Manu says.

"You're welcome, babe," Oriol says. And he hooks a thumb over his shoulder. Phaera is standing twenty paces away, conferring with her security guard.

"Well then, thank you." Manu breathes deep, massages the lump on his jaw with two fingers. Pain blazes through the joint when he tests the range of motion. His hand comes away bloody.

Oriol's fingers are warm on his chin, concern

flaring in his golden eyes as he turns Manu's face to see the wound. "You shot?"

"Nah, got punched by a chunk of granite or whatever this is." Manu waves a hand at the fish-woman statue. "How's it look?"

Oriol steals a kiss before releasing Manu's chin, then hands him a handkerchief. "Not deep. You'll probably live."

The kiss and the concern over an obviously non-life-threatening wound when he should be shadowing Phaera: beneath his glass-smooth exterior, Oriol'd been afraid for him. It's gratifying after the week Manu's spent wondering when Oriol's going to pack up and leave.

"Did you see that Arquellian woman?" Manu asks. He presses the handkerchief to his jaw; his eyes water with the searing pain.

"Seen her," Oriol drawls, and the look on his face says he didn't like whatever he saw.

"You think she's one of those supersoldiers Zacharia had?"

Oriol shakes his head slowly. "Ain't that," he says. "I'd guess it's something worse. That armor, that speed? She's Alliance. They train you to blend in, but it's tough to pretend to be shit at fighting when your life's on the line."

"Alliance working with Acheta?"

"Alliance working," Oriol says noncommittally.

"That a good thing?" Manu asks. One can hope.

Oriol doesn't smile. "Gonna guess bad."

Manu takes a deep breath, trying to process what it would mean for Acheta to have an Alliance special operative embedded on his team. But his jaw's aching and he's suddenly got a splitting headache, and he's not sure whether the latter has to do with the former or if it's informationally induced.

"Juric."

Manu turns to Phaera. And maybe it's not nerves this time making her still and focused, maybe it's resolve. She's turning slowly to take in the whole scene, every body of security guard and civilian, every shard of glass, every drop of blood. He wouldn't call what he sees on her face fear. He'd call it vengeance.

"This was Acheta," Phaera says.

"Yes."

"He told me I had until tomorrow night."

"You should get back inside," Oriol says.

She's not looking at him, she's staring at the old man in the outdated suit she'd been talking to before Manu arrived. He's lying in a pool of his own blood. In the distance, police sirens are starting to get closer.

"Juric. I need you to answer me," she says quietly.

"Of course."

"Did he attack me because of the man your boss murdered."

No beating around that bush anymore, it seems.

"I doubt it," Manu says. "Could be since Acheta saw you and me together the other night, he knew attacking you would be an indirect attack against the man."

She takes a sharp breath; he holds up his hands.

"But most likely it's a direct attack on you," Manu says. "You did put a bounty on his head, and you weren't very complimentary last time you saw him."

"And I will be less so next time." Each word holds venom. "Now answer me this. If I had paid him, would he have done this?"

She's still staring at the body of the old man.

Manu's not going to lie to her. "Probably not." A muscle tenses in her jaw, but it's what she was expecting to hear. "Though it wouldn't have stopped him — it would have taught him that you were an easy target. It would have led to this eventually."

"And if I pay him now?"

"He's not going away, Phaera."

"That bastard's going to have to try harder to shut me down." She turns to Oriol. "I might be here later tonight than I thought."

"I never say no to overtime."

"I'm not going anywhere, either," Manu says. "Not until you're home safe. Let me know how I can help."

The fury in her eyes is electric.

"Get me your boss on a call."

17

JAANTZEN

"I'm sorry, Jaantzen," says Aiax Demosga. "I was with you until now. But Blackheart is dead."

Even meeting virtually, the casino magnate's deep voice booms through the speakers. Jaantzen equals Aiax when it comes to size, but when it comes to filling a room, Jaantzen spent years speaking softly to fight a reputation gained from growing up on the streets, while Aiax can shake a building's foundation with his laugh and somehow still not make the society matrons clutch their purses. And maybe with good reason; Jaantzen's fist still aches from questioning Starla's attacker last night.

Like Aiax Demosga's never broken a skull or ten himself.

Aiax's older sister, Lhasa, will never fill a room with her slight frame and soft voice. But she's whip smart when it comes to running the agricultural arm of the Demosga family's empire and — it turns out — one of the few people who isn't automatically blown over by her brother's bombast.

Lhasa's hand flashes out beyond the edge of her hologram as she reaches for her cup of tea. Jaantzen hasn't dimmed his office windows against the morning sun, and both Demosgas' holograms glitter in the bright light.

"Aiax, think who we're talking to," Lhasa scolds. "You really think Willem Jaantzen's called to play some prank? If he says Thala's alive, she's alive. Or have the rumors not reached you in orbit?" She turns back to Jaantzen. "Where is she?"

"Recovering from a bad turn," Jaantzen says, hiding satisfaction — letting rumors fly free is tricky business, but they've reached Lhasa with just the right timing to lend credibility to Jaantzen's claim in the moment he was ready to approach her. And if rumors have reached Lhasa Demosga, with her head full of triticale harvest and soybean futures trading, they've certainly reached everyone else who matters.

It's a perfect plan, unless things go terribly wrong tonight. In which case Jaantzen doesn't need this deal with the Demosgas to help keep Coeur under control. He can simply expand into a new business on his own without the additional complication.

Well, without the Coeur complication. There are still plenty of complications when it comes to figuring out what to do with the terraforming plans Oriol stole and the creature Coeur dropped in his lap. But every new business venture has its learning curves.

"We'll need to meet with her as well before we agree to anything," Aiax says.

"You will, I'm simply sounding things out," Jaantzen says. He leans forward. "And it sounds like you're interested."

Aiax and Lhasa share a look.

"We'll have to talk." Lhasa takes another sip of her tea to hide her mouth.

She's interested.

"Take what time you need," Jaantzen says. "But we want to make a decision next week."

"Who else are you talking to?" Aiax demands.

Lhasa rolls her eyes at her brother. "You'll hear from us tomorrow. Aiax, come planetside for dinner tonight and let's run some numbers. We need to work on our strategy for the trade agreement talks anyway." She turns back to Jaantzen. "I only have one last question for you, Willem." She lifts an eyebrow. "You. And *her*?"

"We've come to an agreement," Jaantzen says.

Each of them is using a top-of-the-line meeting rig, but even so it's difficult to catch all the nuance of body language and biological sign with a hologram. Still, Jaantzen can feel Lhasa Demosga searching his face, see her running calculations on his relationship with Coeur: How solid a partnership does twenty years of betrayal plus one dead family plus a decade in exile equal?

"I didn't come to this lightly," Jaantzen says. He lets show the flicker of emotion Lhasa's probably expecting to see; her lips thin. "But we've started a new era. Mutually."

"A blank slate," Lhasa says.

Jaantzen smiles tightly. "There's no such thing. But you've known me for years, Lhasa. Aiax. I don't enter into a business deal I don't believe is solid."

He lets that settle. Lhasa gives him a tiny nod. Aiax breaks into a grin.

"Good talking, Jaantzen," he says, voice booming. "Lhas, I'll see you tonight."

The connection cuts, and Jaantzen leans back in his chair. Takes a deep breath. He already knows that the Demosgas are interested in new agricultural technology on account of the fact they were willing to buy the plans from the Dawn in the first place. He isn't worried about them having a problem working with Coeur — she helped them pass several lucrative agricultural bills when she was mayor, and the Demosgas must be one of the few families she hasn't yet stabbed in the back.

The *yet* in that thought is reflexive — and hopefully not prescient.

Though it's good to be prepared for the worst.

Two messages blink into place as soon as the call is finished, having come in while he was speaking with the Demosgas. The first is from Teo Lordeur, private investor and number one financier of Bulari's underground. In person, Teo can take three hours to tell a ten-minute story; in text he's mercifully concise: *HE'S AGREED. DINNER.*

A knot loosens in Jaantzen's chest, but he doesn't have time to celebrate another brick of his plan slotting into place. Because the second message is from Cobalt Tower's stone-eyed receptionist, Nadhi.

THE LAWYER IS HERE.

Jaantzen checks the time — he's only left her waiting three minutes — then tells Nadhi to send her up. A moment later the lift chimes, the lights dimming momentarily, and out steps Calanthe Yang, Julieta Yang's oldest child. She's dressed in sensible cream pumps, matching drop pearl earrings, and a rose-colored sheath dress of raw silk pleated at the side seams to accommodate a growing belly.

Jaantzen rises to greet her with a pair of kisses and catches a whiff of her perfume, faintly floral with a warmth that reminds him of honey.

"It's good to see you," Jaantzen says, pulling out a chair for her at the conference table. "Can I get you anything besides tea?"

"Water would be lovely." Calanthe leans back with a sigh, smoothing a hand over her belly. "It seems like this one is always thirsty."

"Congratulations."

"Thank you," she says, accepting the glass he hands her. "It's a girl, finally. Three boys would've been two too many boys."

Her tone is bittersweet. A birth should be celebrated, but he can't imagine Calanthe and her family feel very celebratory at the moment. Not since her younger sister Aster betrayed her mother and Jaantzen to the Dawn and nearly got them all killed. Jaantzen still hasn't been able to reconcile the vicious Aster he saw at Bennion Zacharia's side with the shy girl he'd known since she was a baby. He can't imagine how Calanthe and her mother and brother must feel.

He clears his throat. "And . . . your family?"

"We'll be fine," Calanthe says, waving a hand, though there's darkness below the surface of her voice. "Mother wishes you would call."

"Oh?" At Ximena's funeral a few evenings past,

Julieta had seemed withdrawn; he'd assumed she was there for the formality of it, that she would want some space from him after the near destruction of her greenhouse, the bloodshed on her property. Perhaps he was mistaken.

He'll call her.

Once this mess with Acheta is all over.

He's already had tea sent up in anticipation of Calanthe's arrival, and he pours for her: sweet and aromatic. The kitchen included the tea cakes she's commented on in the past, and Calanthe's eyes light up when he removes the lid to the tray.

"Do you need anything else?" Jaantzen asks.

"I would kill for a rare steak," Calanthe says with a sigh. "But no, I'm fine. Though I warn you I will eat every last one of these pastries if you're not quick."

Jaantzen smiles at that. Unlike her timid — and apparently quite impressionable — younger sister, Aster, Calanthe is a firebrand both in and outside of the courtroom. The pale pinks and rose golds she favors only serve to make others underestimate her, leaving them wide open to her cutting legal attacks.

Jaantzen's had her on retainer for years, and not just because of his long friendship with her mother. He's not alone. Calanthe has an exclusive clientele of businesspeople whose business specialties tend to land them in murky legal waters. Fortunately,

Jaantzen has only ever needed her in an advisory role. And to act as a go-between.

If everything goes as planned tonight, it won't do for Jaantzen to have been seen meeting with a series of local businesspeople who have grudges against Levi Acheta and would benefit from his death. But Calanthe can make the calls without suspicion. And, of course, she can make his case far more eloquently than he could.

She's tapping excess powdered sugar from a tea cake, watching him.

"I'll get to the point," Jaantzen says. "Acheta. I need to take care of a problem that affects us all."

"Don't you think that's a bit drastic? Acheta could still be reasoned with." Calanthe takes a delicate bite of a cake.

"You heard about the Lorelei last night?"

Calanthe swears under her breath, pats a speck of powdered sugar from the corner of her mouth. "I didn't realize that was him."

"He's been trying to shake Phaera and the other casino owners down for protection money, and she pushed back."

"The idiot. So we have Leone talk to him."

Jaantzen reaches to refresh her tea. "He also tried to have Starla killed," he says, and Calanthe's eyes widen in shock, then narrow in anger, hardness setting into the lines of her face as he relates the story as Starla told him.

"Do you have evidence he ordered the hit?" she says when he's finished.

"I have a confession from one of the men."

Calanthe winces at his even tone. "Any way this man's still alive to witness against Acheta?" she asks, then waves a hand. "Nevermind, don't tell me. You recorded the confession, at least? Well. None of the others will dispute your side of things. Acheta doesn't have any allies, really, but only a handful would put themselves in his enemies camp." She arches an eyebrow; he's asking a lot of professionally neutral people to throw their support behind him, an act that could be disastrous for them if Acheta survives — or if someone else in Acheta's organization decides they want revenge.

"You know Leone better than I," Jaantzen says. Chief Justice Geum-ja Leone is the only one whose opinion really matters here. Jaantzen can weather getting on the wrong side of any other influential person in this town. "What will she think?"

"She'll think you're reaching above your pay grade." Calanthe holds his gaze a moment in warning. "And Geum-ja doesn't like to see violence, you know that."

"Acheta is committing plenty of violence in the streets as we speak." Jaantzen ignores her first comment. It's not like Leone is stepping up to take care of Acheta; he'll deal with her displeasure with his initiative when it comes.

Calanthe sighs. "Violence among the family heads, I mean. I know, I know. I'm on your side. But some — Leone, the Lordeurs, Seti, the Demosgas — they only pay attention to what happens above a certain income bracket."

Jaantzen knows it's an act; for all he genuinely likes her, Calanthe isn't losing sleep over the street kids who are dying in this war between Dry Creek and Acheta's crew. But she's willing to give him the nod for it, which is more than some in her family's circle do.

Of course, Leone and others have already made their displeasure with Acheta known, in their own way. Though Acheta could only guess it was Phaera who put his number on the bounty boards, he had to understand for certain that Leone and the others approved of it by the fact it didn't get rescinded immediately.

Spreading a name on the streets is a warning as much as an attempt to solve a problem. Maybe Phaera hadn't meant it as such — she'd meant it for real — but Acheta should have seen it for the second chance it was and gone to see Leone about what could be done to get rid of it. Instead, he shot up the Lorelei.

"Acheta is done with their way of doing business," Jaantzen says. "He killed Naali Hinoja without coming to Leone first. He's been shaking casino owners down for protection money, and he turned the Lorelei into a war zone. And he tried to kill my daughter." He lets himself feel it this time, lets the grief show in his voice. For a moment he fears he won't actually be able to draw it back.

Calanthe is watching him, banked anger simmering just below the calmness of her expression.

"I can already tell you my family will support you, Willem," she says quietly. "And I'll make your case to Geum-ja and the others. But there's one question they're all going to want to ask me." She leans forward, and Jaantzen knows what she's going to say. "What's your plan for his territory?"

Selling taking care of Acheta to the others will be a simple thing. But selling the rest of the plan is going to take all of Calanthe's skill.

"You've heard the rumors by now?" he asks. "About a certain old player back in town?"

Calanthe goes still. She sets her teacup and saucer back on the table with too sharp a clatter, her eyebrows high in two perfect arches. "No goddamned way," she says. "Please don't be about to tell me that Blackheart is alive and you intend to put her back on her throne."

Jaantzen holds her gaze; it's the answer she

needs, and Calanthe just shakes her head. "That puts a kink in things. They already paid you to push her out. What do I tell them, that she's a changed woman? That you can control her? Seti won't agree to it — Blackheart had his father killed. And Leone? She's terrified of Blackheart gunning for her after how Leone helped push her out. Anjali Balçe? She threw a *party* when Coeur went into exile. It lasted a *goddamned week.*"

"But your mother won't mind," Jaantzen reasons. "Neither will the Lordeurs, and neither will the Demosgas. I just got off a call with Aiax and Lhasa." The Yangs, Lordeurs, and Demosgas had all managed to walk both sides of the Coeur problem back during the civil war. It's been a sticking point between him and Julieta for years, but he's grateful for her diplomacy now.

Calanthe claps her palms together, leaning elbows on the table and pressing the knuckles of her thumbs into her lips in thought. "Oh, Willem," she says finally. "How do you expect me to sell this?"

"Tell them I'm taking care of it," he says. The corners of Calanthe's lips pull downward, skeptical. "Do you think I would go into this lightly? She and I have made an agreement."

Calanthe suddenly straightens in realization. "Wait, is Blackheart here? In this building? No —

nevermind, don't tell me." She takes a deep breath. "Do you two have a contract written up?"

"Would it matter?"

"Ugh. No. Not with her, would it?" Calanthe sighs, then picks up her teacup again. "I'll talk to them. I know Seti's having an impossible time moving forward on construction in Jet Park with all the fighting, and Geum-ja had been doing business with Naali for the past ten years, so maybe she'll be willing to mend her bad blood with Blackheart. Surely they can come to some sort of understanding." She lifts an eyebrow at him. "You do not make easy requests of me."

"I look forward to your invoice."

"Oh, you'll see it." She pats her belly. "You're buying this little one a very nice education."

"It won't be the last gift she sees from me."

"I'm sure it won't." Calanthe goes to stand, and Jaantzen beats her to his feet, holds out a hand to help her up. She gives a little groan. "Come over for dinner soon, the boys have been asking about you."

Jaantzen frowns at that. "They have?" He still doesn't understand the attachment Calanthe's young boys seem to have to him.

"'When will Uncle Lillem come?'" Calanthe says with a smile, mimicking their high voices. "Oh," — she winks — "and bring Phaera."

Jaantzen opens his mouth, closes it again without reply.

"I'll call you as soon as I hear," Calanthe says with a pair of parting air kisses and another waft of her honey-sweet perfume.

"Thank you," Jaantzen says. "It will be done by tomorrow, whether they agree or not."

A sharp breath, but she understands the need to strike while the iron is hot.

"Good to know," she says. "Be careful, I'll be in touch."

18

STARLA

The first thing she sees when her vision clears is a mummified human hand.

Starla flinches back from the grisly relic with a curse, adrenaline seizing her chest like a bass drop. She steps back, forcing her heart rate back to calm — *It's only virtual.*

Nothing can hurt her in virtual.

Especially not a dried-up old human hand.

She leans back in for a closer look.

It's dead. It can't reach out and grab her, this isn't some horror vid. That knowledge doesn't keep the hairs on the back of Starla's neck from rising, though. Every object in this virtual museum exists in the real world, which means some actual human is missing their hand, and the Dawn took the time to preserve it for their horrifying museum.

That's legitimately terrifying.

In the hand's palm is a shard tab, the same sort of new tab that killed the dealer at the Brujería. The inscription on the museum label reads, *And the Gift of the Fallen will purify them.*

Charming.

The simulation is forbidding snapshots, so Starla jots down the inscription and reference in her notebook and straightens to take in the rest of the artifacts. She's standing in a dimly lit room of unknown size; she can't see the walls in any direction, though there doesn't seem to be anything to explore beyond the beams of ethereal blue light stabbing down from the ceiling every five paces or so in a perfect circle around her. Like deadly spears pinning the objects they illuminate to the floor.

She shivers. She knows she's actually sitting in the sun-warm conference room on Cobalt Tower's fourth floor, but the virtual museum's graphics are real enough that she can almost feel a subterranean breeze on her skin. At least she's being spared the background chanting Sam mentioned.

A shadow shifts at the edge of her field of vision; Starla spins to face it, adrenaline thrumming once more.

Nothing.

She takes a deep breath and moves on.

The next pedestal holds a pile of worn leather notebooks — real paper — covered with spidery writing. *Our Prophet's original words,* reads the label.

Starla pauses despite herself. She can make out more interesting-looking artifacts in the murky light ahead, but something about this captures her attention. Some of the earlier notebooks are pieced together from scraps of paper and packaging, their bindings hand-stitched. But eventually the prophet must have convinced one of his guards at Redrock to get him some real writing materials.

She picks up one of the hand-stitched books and pages through it, recognizing snippets from the finished text she's been reading. Out of habit, she takes a snapshot and gets an error message yet again: *Recording not allowed.*

The words blink red and angry.

Fine.

She moves to the next pedestal to find a capsule like the one their creature arrived in, and her heart picks up a beat, this time with excitement. *The Vessel of the Fallen,* reads the label.

The next pedestal holds another sphere, and she almost moves on, impatient to find something new, when she realizes it's made of metal, not glass.

And some sort of markings are scratched into the surface.

It's like no language she's ever seen, but the precise lines of hatchmarks and spirals march in even rows like writing. Chiseled in with an implement — or maybe a claw? She lifts the metal sphere in her hands, turning it slowly. Another snapshot — she stops herself with a curse and begins to copy a sample of the writing into her notebook, fingers awkward at the strange lines.

She has to come back here with Toshiyo.

She's still examining the sphere when something about the light changes. She straightens. Things have shifted in a way she can't put her finger on — were those streaks in the dark beyond the circle of light beams always there, or are they a trick of her eyes?

And — are they getting closer?

Nothing here can physically hurt her, but her pulse spikes again, her palms sweaty as she pivots. A quick security check and she breathes a sigh of relief that her encryptions are all still in place. Whatever program is running here, no one should be able to trace her.

She hurries to the next pedestal then pauses to scan the room around her. The shadows are definitely getting closer. In the center of the pedestal is a carved chunk of glossy black rock — obsidian, maybe — cut in the shape of a diamond. It's polished and gleaming in the ghostly bluish light. As it slowly spins, light catches in the lines engraved on its flat surface.

Starla's heart is in her throat as she reaches for it, cradling it in her palm to see the lines of the carving.

A stylized image of a winged, tailed creature spiraling up towards the heavens.

Exactly like the carving on her mother's pendant.

WHO ARE YOU.

Starla looks up, heart pounding. An old man is standing in front of her, where seconds ago there had been no one. He's pale, white beard neatly trimmed, hands folded into his robe. She risks a glance away from him to find that the shadows she noticed earlier are closer, still just outside the pool of light she's standing in.

They're people: hooded, robed. And armed.

They can't hurt you, she tells herself.

WHO ARE YOU, the old man asks again, the user-to-user message pinging in the center of Starla's field of vision.

She backs away from the old man. Around her, the figures step forward, blue light glinting on the edges of wicked knives. She's still holding the obsidian diamond in one hand, having forgotten to put it back, and when she looks back at the old man, he snatches it from her hand and throws it to the ground. It shatters, obsidian shards glittering around them.

HOW DID YOU FIND THIS PLACE.

It's just virtual.

She can feel them closing in.

They can't hurt her.

The old man reaches for her, and she's not wearing a fancy haptics suit, she shouldn't be able to feel it, but his grip is tight around her wrist. A knife appears in his other hand, slashing upward at her face, and she's on her moto again with shots fired and melons exploding around her, she's tied up and helpless with Zacharia's pistol against her forehead, and the sharp spike of terror nearly freezes her.

She forces herself to move, severing the connection, tearing the goggles from her face.

Toshiyo barely ducks as Starla lashes out at whoever's still holding her, and Starla comes back into reality with a rush of panic.

She's panting, she can smell the adrenaline stink of her sweat, her heart pounding against her sternum. Toshiyo massages Starla's hand gently in hers a moment longer, then releases it.

"I'm sorry I startled you," she signs.

"It's fine." Starla scrubs a hand over her face. "Things were getting tense."

Toshiyo frowns. "In virtual? Were you playing a game?"

Starla shakes her head. How to explain it. "You know that virtual museum Sam Amrith mentioned in his paper? He found it. Only now I think it's run by the Dawn."

"And you just went there? By yourself?" Toshiyo gives her a disapproving look. "You should have asked me to help."

Starla should have; she can't exactly explain why she didn't. Except that one part of her still thinks she's lost it for believing her mother's pendant has anything to do with the creature. She had to see it for herself before she showed anyone else. And all the conspiracy stuff about the Dawn — there's a part of her that was hoping it would all turn out to be a figment of her imagination.

But.

Starla drops the virtual kit on the conference table and pulls up a search for the Dawn's prophet, heart pounding. There aren't many photos after his intake shot at Redrock Prison, almost twenty years ago, but in it she recognizes the man whose avatar she just saw.

Felipe Zacharia.

Starla slides the image over to Toshiyo and

quickly explains what Sam told her about the museum. "This man was there. I don't think he got through my encryptions, but he kept asking who I was. And he grabbed me the same time you did."

Toshiyo winces. "Sorry again. Did you get any snaps of the museum?"

"It was blocked." Starla takes a deep breath. "But I took some notes. And I saw a stone carved with this image."

She's been wearing her mother's necklace ever since she first dug it out of storage to show to Sam. She never feels it, the stone is lighter than it looks, and after the initial cool touch against her skin it drinks her heat like blood until it's warm as her own skin. She pulls it out now.

What's that, Toshiyo's face says, and she holds out a hand for the pendant.

And her eyes widen.

"Oh my god," Toshiyo says, and then in her hodgepodge of USL and fingerspelling: "Where did you get this?"

"From my mother," Starla signs, and Toshiyo shakes her head in wordless wonder. "I don't know any more than that."

"It's our thing," Toshiyo signs. She looks up for confirmation. "The little buddy."

Starla nods. "I think so."

It is, she feels it with the core of her being. And

if Toshiyo sees it, too, maybe Starla's not making it up.

"Where did your mother get it?"

She wishes she could remember, wishes she'd asked for more stories about it. Growing up, she had focused entirely on creating her own stories, on battling the fear that she'd never have any stories to tell, that she'd turn out to be ordinary. A nobody. It simply hadn't occurred to her to probe into her parents' stories, to say, Mom, tell me how you found that weird necklace you always wear.

The one thing Starla *does* know about it is that Lasadi found it the day Starla was conceived. Which is definitely not a story a teenaged girl wants to go digging into.

Where the hell *were* you that trip? she wonders.

But this isn't a cheesy vid, and her mother doesn't appear lily white and glowing in the center of the conference table to answer her questions.

"They probably found it out in Durga's Belt," Starla signs. "Maybe from wherever the original researcher found her samples? I mean, that's a leap. I have no clue." She waves her hands over the mess of files open on the conference table: Sam's paper, the DNA research and sketches, her notes from the virtual museum. "I'm just hoping that one of these things will start to make sense."

Toshiyo rakes her long black hair over one

shoulder and leans over the conference table, ankles crossed on the seat beneath her, slippers in a neat pair on the floor under her chair.

She taps a black-varnished nail against the DNA research.

"Since we're sharing weird theories, this is mine," she signs. Or, mostly spells. Starla gets it. "The two samples in this paper are identical, right? And ours came back as identical, too. Different from the other two, but identical. I think they're sets of clones, at different stages."

Starla shakes her head. "Why?"

Toshiyo is slow to answer, but Starla can see by the tight line of her lips that it's not because she doesn't have an idea. She's just not sure if it'll sound crazy.

"Tell me," Starla signs. "Nothing is too weird now."

Toshiyo takes a deep breath. "Okay. I've been thinking. What if they were trying to find a new home, same as humans were on the *Ark Matsya?* Only we built a massive generation ship to make sure our offspring would get here. What if they sent scouts in a small ship?"

"What makes you think that?"

Toshiyo swipes up a keyboard and searches through a file structure that blinks in and out of Starla's vision before making the tiniest amount of sense. An image appears on the conference table. At first Starla can't see what it's supposed to be, but then she recognizes the name in the upper left corner of the image: Ximena Nayar.

It seems like months ago that Ximena was sitting at this same table downloading all the information she'd gathered about the Alliance terraforming efforts near Redrock — but it was only last week.

"You broke into her comm?" Starla asks.

Toshiyo shrugs. "I had it," she signs, and Starla gives herself yet another reminder not to leave anything interestingly hackable around Toshiyo. "But these aren't the images she gave us originally. Somebody sent her a new set of files today."

They're mostly photos of the terraforming site, but closer images than the ones Ximena had originally shown them. In the foreground they focus on the lush landscape, the incredible plant life, but there's something metallic far in the background.

Toshiyo swipes to the next set of images and Starla's jaw drops.

"I know, right?" Toshiyo says.

The metallic object in the background is a spaceship, but the lines are distinctive and strange. Designed for something with different dimensions than human — it has more . . . space to stretch out. Spread your wings, maybe. It also doesn't look like a shuttle meant to take its crew back up into orbit, rather more like a dart looking for a place to hit.

Humanity had cast nearly a dozen arks off its dying home planet, each peopled with enough humans to land a viable population on whatever planet the ark finally reached. What if another species had instead sent thousands of smaller vessels armed with one self-replicating genetic strain — and the means to terraform a new homeworld while it waited for others to arrive? Like a thistle, throwing out thousands of seeds, knowing that the odds of a single one sticking are infinitesimal, also knowing its survival depends on throwing out those seeds.

"If the creatures we have here are clones, are they meant to receive the original's memories somehow?" Starla asks. "Or, how would that work?"

Toshiyo glances at the ceiling, as though she could see the creature in its makeshift tank floating floors and floors above them. The creature that might be a blank slate just waiting for the memories of the creature it's meant to replace.

For a moment, neither of them move.

"'How great the multitude of truths which the garment of words can never contain,'" Toshiyo murmurs.

Starla frowns at the words on her lens. "What?"

"It's something Tae used to say." Toshiyo starts

to sign it; her fingers stutter as she signs Tae's name. "She wasn't really religious," Toshiyo says aloud, "but she never ate meat and she did the new-year fast. And she had all these quotes from Baha'u'llah. Like, you'd bring up something strange, and she'd just shrug and say, 'How great the multitude of truths.'"

Starla's staring at her. In the fifteen years she's lived with Jaantzen, this is the first time she's heard someone talk so openly about Tae Boroma. The woman who should have been her godmother. She's gleaned enough to know her parents' agreement with Jaantzen had been made while Tae was still alive, and had gone both ways: if something had happened to Jaantzen and Tae, Raj and Lasadi Dusai would have taken in their two children.

Intellectually, Starla knows she was supposed to land in the care of a happy family, not a broken-hearted man set on revenge. With how reluctant everyone is to talk about the past, that fact has been easy enough to forget — still, an undercurrent of complicated, painful history has shaped every moment of her last fifteen years. And at the heart of it all, a missing piece shaped like a woman whose name no one says.

"You knew Tae?" Starla asks carefully.

Toshiyo makes a surprised face. "Of course!"

Her surprise at the question muddies into something more complex and painful.

"I'm sorry," Starla signs. "Just no one talks about — " Anything, is what she wants to say. "Her. The past."

"It's fine," Toshiyo signs, though from the uncomfortable way she shifts, it's obviously not. "She was amazing. She was one of the best friends I've ever had." Toshiyo cracks her ring fingers. "I actually lived with her and your godfather when I first came to Bulari. I think they thought I would stay a week or so, but I stayed for almost a year. They were so sweet about it, but looking back it's kind of embarrassing how long it took me to get my own apartment. But Tae — "

Toshiyo clasps her hands together, thinking, and Starla almost tells her it's fine, they don't have to talk about it. This outpouring of history feels like a stolen taste of liquor as a teenager: forbidden and intoxicating and searingly painful all at once.

She needs more.

"Tae what?" Starla prompts.

"Tae was about to have Sora. They needed a little more space." Toshiyo laughs ruefully. "Even as oblivious as I was back then, I figured that out without them having to tell me."

"How old were you?" Starla asks, not yet

willing to let this brief window into her family's past close.

Toshiyo frowns at the ceiling. "Nineteen? Twenty?"

So, twenty years ago. Starla feels a sudden stab of jealousy that Toshiyo got to see a world Starla has only ever dreamed of. A world where her godfather was happy.

"What do you remember most about her?" she asks.

"Tae never treated me like I was made out of glass," Toshiyo signs. She smiles at Starla. "And neither do you." Her smile fades as she turns her attention back to the images of the alien spaceship on the conference table. Toshiyo traces a finger over the lines.

"We should go," Toshiyo signs.

Starla stares at her, startled as much at the change of subject as she is shocked by the comment. Toshiyo wants to travel halfway around the world, into the heart of the Alliance concession on New Sarjun? Toshiyo doesn't even leave the building — Starla checked the entry and exit logs last month, and Toshiyo had left Cobalt Tower on her own only a handful of times in the previous year.

Hell, she barely leaves the fourth floor.

"You want to go to Redrock?" Starla asks.

Toshiyo's eyes widen, real fear spilling into

them as she shakes her head. "No, no. You guys do that. I stay home." She points at the clock. "I mean it's time to go."

Of course. This impossible scheme of Jaantzen's isn't going to execute itself. A smooth sense of readiness fills Starla, covering over the flutter of anticipation in her gut. It's time.

"Thank you," Starla signs. "For telling me about Tae."

Toshiyo's smile is lopsided. "I miss her," she signs back. "I miss talking about her."

"I want to hear more."

Toshiyo takes a deep breath, then pulls Starla down into a hug. She murmurs something into Starla's collarbone, vocal cords vibrating, then gives her one more squeeze before letting her go.

"Go kick some ass tonight," Toshiyo signs. "Then let's get a bottle of wine and I'll tell you everything you want to know."

19

MANU

"The ramen at Food To Go is better," Oriol says.

Manu nods, noncommittal. Food To Go is three blocks closer to the casino drag, and its real name is written in a scrawl that nobody can decipher; the words *Food To Go* are the only legible bit. The noodles there may be better, but Food To Go is a cart in the middle of the street, and after the past few days, the place between Manu's shoulder blades itches expecting a bullet. There's no way he's taking lunch there today.

Anyway, this lunch isn't about the food. It's about scouting tonight's business with Acheta.

Manu and Oriol are sitting in a booth at Lucky's Palladium Coast. Faded and broke-down cushions in the booths, fake-gilt candelabras, a garish beaded fringe over the bar that catches the light and scatters rainbows like shivering confetti. Nothing about this place says the food will be good, but the strange thing about low expectations is that they're as good a seasoning as salt. Food that would be competent yet forgettable in a classier place stands out as unexpectedly decent at Lucky's.

Nobody Manu knows comes to Lucky's for the food. They come because it's a known neutral spot where you leave your grudges at the door. Lucky's is where you go when you don't care who sees you meeting someone in public and you want the security of knowing there will be plenty of witnesses around if somebody tries to double-cross you. Here you're less likely to run into an Indiran tourist and more likely to see a couple of the local casino bosses meeting for a business lunch or for a friendly dinner with their spouses.

Or men like illicit financier Teo Lordeur meeting with local crew boss Levi Acheta.

Lucky's doesn't depend on tourist traffic, and even though Manu and Oriol are here squarely between the lunch and dinner rush, there's a steady flow of customers. It'll be packed as usual tonight, which should relax Acheta enough to show up to his meeting with Lordeur.

You'd be crazy to attempt a hit in the middle of a restaurant crowded with neighborhood regulars.

Much easier to plan for an ambush on the way here.

Oriol reaches to snag a piece of Manu's shredded chicken with his chopsticks. "You're not hungry?"

"It's too tough," Manu says. "Here." He scoots his bowl closer to transfer the rest of the chicken over to Oriol's bowl.

"Sure you don't want me to ask Lucky to blend it up for you?" Oriol gives him a lopsided smile.

"Nah, the noodles are fine." Chewing anything more feels like a spike through the bruise on his jaw. But more than that, Manu's stomach just isn't into it. Between Toshiyo's fanged alien hell-beast, the attacks on Starla and the Lorelei, tonight's plan, Oriol's restlessness — all of it — Manu doesn't feel like eating. He was starving before they met for lunch, but the three bites he's taken are knotting in a lump.

Oriol tucks into the extra chicken, his appetite as bulletproof as ever.

"I got the name of the Arquellian woman from my guy on Acheta's crew," Manu says. "Norah é Vega, she showed up just a few days ago. You heard of her?"

Oriol shakes his head, a lock of brassy hair falling into his eyes. "I'll see what I can find out, but if she's Alliance, that's not her real name."

"My guy hasn't gotten close enough to find out what she wants from Acheta, but he says they got tight fast."

"He know her from before?"

"Doesn't sound like it."

"Then she's got a good cover."

"*If* she's Alliance."

Oriol's lips quirk to the side. "Right. *If.* You don't believe me? Or you don't want to believe me."

"I don't want to." Manu sighs. "Everything goes well tonight, we can all sleep a bit easier."

Oriol chews thoughtfully a moment. "That's a strange way of looking at it," he says finally.

Yeah, it is. If you'd told Manu even last week he'd be working to get Blackheart back in power, it wouldn't've even been laughable. It would've made his blood boil. And, yet . . .

Here we are.

"Lesser of two evils," Manu says. He scissors his boiled egg in half with his chopsticks, watching the yolk seep into the broth like blood.

"She gets things back on an even keel, then I'll put a bullet in her for you," Oriol says quietly. "You just say the word."

"Not tonight."

"I'm just registering my dislike of the plan."

"Doesn't matter," Manu says. Across the room the front door opens; a quartet of dealers in Horus uniforms push through laughing. "You've got the man's back, right?"

Oriol's pause is too long. Manu looks back sharply. Oriol's expression is relaxed, but Manu catches the sound of fast drumming of fingers on Oriol's prosthetic thigh.

"Did he even ask you?" Oriol asks.

Manu lifts an eyebrow. "I'm sorry?"

The noodles in Oriol's chopsticks break free and fall back to the bowl as his hand clenches tight. He sets his chopsticks on the table with careful deliberation, his relaxed facade is gone. "Did he even ask you," Oriol says evenly. "Or did he just give you the word, this is how it's gonna be."

"We talked about it," Manu says, though that's hardly true. But the decision's been made, and he's not going to defend Jaantzen to Oriol, any more than he'll defend Oriol to Jaantzen.

"You talked about it." Oriol's voice is low. "And Jaantzen told you it didn't matter what that asshole did to you, you should just suck it up and — "

"What she did to me? She killed his — "

"I don't need a fucking history lesson, Manu," Oriol cuts in. "I was there when Tae died. I was there when they found you." He leans forward, gaze narrowed. "And I'll be there the day she gets a bullet in her head."

"Will you be?" Manu asks through clenched

teeth, regretting the words before they're even out of his mouth. Just not enough to stop. "That mean *you're* going to start asking me first? Before you sign up for another ten months away?"

"What the fuck are you talking about." Oriol's golden eyes burn clear and steady.

"You got another adventure planned already? Offers on the table? When do you ship out?"

A muscle twitches in Oriol's cheek. "Still sorting out the details."

"Any place fun?" Manu should let it drop, bring it up later when he can keep the bitterness out of his voice. "Or just away from here?"

The rebuke lands; Oriol sits back as though he's been slapped. Manu bites down hard on whatever he was going to let fly next and pain sears through his injured jaw. He welcomes it.

This isn't how they fight, with barbs and venom. Though, to be honest, Manu can't remember the last time they had more than a quick disagreement. With how much Oriol's been gone the past few years, maybe they've forgotten how to fight at all.

He clenches his jaw to feel the stab of pain again. "Oriol — "

"I gotta travel," Oriol cuts in. "See things. You knew this about me from the beginning."

"And I'm not trying to keep you," Manu snaps. In the kitchen, something's started to burn, Manu can hear the clattering of pans hitting the sink and the tirade of the head chef berating a line cook. He catches a whiff of acrid smoke in the air.

Oriol's expression softens. "Then come with me."

"They need me here."

"Sometimes, sure." A quirk of the lips, it's not amusement. "But maybe sometimes you just need to be needed."

Manu narrows his eyes at that. "What do you mean?"

"It doesn't matter, I'm sorry," Oriol's hands are up, palms up in surrender. "I don't want to fight, babe. I love you."

"And I don't want to talk about this right now." Manu swipes marks from his comm onto the table to cover the tab, pushes back his barely touched bowl. "I need to get back downtown. And you should get back to Phaera."

Oriol catches his wrist, his fingers warm, his grip steel. "Don't walk away from me mad," he murmurs. "Two outta the last three nights you almost caught a bullet from Acheta's crew. Now you're talking about walking straight into his mouth."

Manu sinks back into the booth. Oriol's steel grip softens, hand smoothing over Manu's.

"I'm not mad," Manu says, because it's true. He doesn't quite have a word for the grief-betrayal-regret-fury churning in his chest. Their fingers catch in a complicated knot. "And I love you, too."

His comm is buzzing; he realizes with a start that it's been trying to catch his attention for the last few minutes. He lays it on the table to check, partly for convenience, partly so Oriol can see. He's got three missed messages from Jaantzen.

"I gotta run," he says, as gently as he can. "We'll talk tonight. And after this, we'll go somewhere. I promise."

The words are out of his mouth with the familiar taste of never-kept promises before he can stop them.

Oriol smiles sadly. "I'm looking forward to it," he says.

Same as he always does.

By the time he gets back to Cobalt Tower, he has another message from Jaantzen and one from Oriol: BRING UP A SET OF ARMOR FOR HER and I'M SORRY BABE, respectively.

He's not sure how to address the latter, but he can take care of the former. And so Manu exits the lift at the weapons lockers on his way to Jaantzen's penthouse, hunts through for a short-sleeved biosilk undershirt and a combat vest with a fully charged medpack. They're both small enough to fit even Thala Coeur's wasted frame — but armor in this situation doesn't just mean the ability to stop bullets. Showing up to face her old crew in a visible combat vest is its own signal of weakness. She'll need a jacket to go over everything, something that says she's wearing the crown again.

He opens his locker, closes it. Anything he owns will be too broad in the shoulders — especially with all the weight she's lost. Starla's locker is empty since she keeps most of her stuff in her apartment in the tower, and it would probably be too big anyway.

Simca Anahoy might be the better fit, and she's always leaving her shit here.

Manu opens a message to her, rummages through her packed locker a minute, then deletes the message without sending it. Simca's style is pretty heavy on the neons and metallics, and he can imagine the look on Coeur's face when he brings her a moto jacket printed with oversized rainbow poppies.

Let alone how her crew will react when she shows up in it.

He threads the moto jacket onto its hanger, crowds it back onto the rack, then shuts Simca's neon chaos away. He does a quick scan through the rest of the lockers. Out of luck.

Unless . . .

He makes the call. "Lo, you still here?"

Her laugh sounds on the other end of the line.

"I am unless you need me to talk to Cedra," she says. "'Cause then I went home for the year. Oh my god I had no idea what you'd been dealing with, please take my promotion back."

"Not a chance." Manu smiles; no one like Lo to make him feel normal again. "Though you're safe from Cedra — I just need a favor. Can I borrow your jacket?"

She doesn't even pause. "I didn't know we were swapping closets now," Lo says. "Can I borrow that blue silk vest Oriol got you? I have a date next week."

"It's not for me. And just for tonight." Manu frowns at that, thinking. "Actually, I'll buy you a new one."

"You do know that 'borrow' means you're giving it back?" Lo asks.

By tomorrow morning, it might be full of bullet holes. And even if it's not, that jacket will have spent more quality time with Blackheart than any decent thing should. "You might not want it," he says.

Here's the pause. He half expects her to ask why, but:

"Can the new one be real leather?"

Manu smiles. "Whatever your heart desires." Some people might take that as a challenge to purchase the most expensive thing they can find, but Lo's not the sort of person whose heart can imagine desiring something beyond a budget Manu would approve.

"Ordering it right now. You're going to love this one. I've had my eye on it for months."

"Great. Can't wait to see it. I'll be by in a sec." He's about to cut the connection when he hears her voice again.

"Hey. Manu?"

"Yeah?"

"Is everything all right?"

He takes a deep breath. "Just some trouble brewing," he says. "But it'll all be fine, def."

"Anything I can do to help?"

Absolutely not, dear sweet Lo. "You're doing it," he says. "Just finish up and head home for the night. I'll be by for the jacket."

He skips grabbing a cart, figures he can handle the armload of body armor and medpacks on his own, though he's juggling things by the time the lift door opens.

The lift isn't empty.

Giaconda Áte's propped against the back wall, arms and ankles crossed like she's auditioning for the part of bored background lift rider. She arches an eyebrow in genuine surprise to see him standing there.

"Hey," she says, coming off her lean to hold open the door.

"Hey," Manu says. "Thought you'd gone home?"

"I wanted to do one last check on my patient, but she's not in her bed," she says. "I figured I'd sound an alarm, but Tosh told me I should check with you." Gia looks pointedly down at his unruly bundle. "Planning a fun night?"

"Depends on how you define fun," Manu says. "Gia. I'm sorry I haven't been out to visit you and your man for so long."

She makes a face, ready to dismiss the comment. But whatever she sees in his eyes makes her pause.

"We'll make it happen," she says, then juts her chin at his barely contained armload. "Does your fun night have to do with why my patient is missing from her room?"

"Could be."

Gia sighs and reaches to help Manu carry his load.

20

———————

JAANTZEN

Coeur has looked worse.

The woman sitting on the couch across from him in his penthouse suite is gaunt and breakable in her short-sleeved hospital gown — though the muscles of her upper arms haven't lost their definition. After multiple surgeries, her hands are now bound in black therapeutic gloves, half the fingers on her left hand still splinted. Those gloved hands dangle over her knees, elbows braced on thighs like she's resting between bouts of a particularly rough boxing match. Deep, ragged breaths lift and drop her shoulders. A knit cap covers the bandages on her scalp; without her braids her face is skeletal.

But she almost looks whole.

Almost.

She's already made her snarky comments on his decor and bitched about the couch cushions, so now they've lapsed into a companionable silence punctuated by the faint clink of vials against the conference table. Gia's student, Elian, is doing a last-minute check on the meds he's packed for Coeur to take with her — no point in going through all this trouble just to have her die of complications later this week.

Even if they were alone, Jaantzen's not sure what he'd have left to say.

A courtesy knock on the stairway door before the handle turns: Starla and El, both dressed for whatever the night might bring in black fatigues and light combat armor. If things go smoothly, neither of them should see any action.

Of course, nothing ever goes smoothly.

"I just heard from Manu's headhunter," Starla signs. "Her crew's in place at Lucky's. We have an hour before we need to be there, too." She glances at El. "And we've got a squad already in place in Acheta's territory. El's team is prepped to shadow Manu."

"Thank you," Jaantzen signs.

Coeur cranes her neck to see who just entered, gaze latching onto Starla, tracking her as she crosses behind Jaantzen to pour herself a glass of water from the kitchen sink. Jaantzen's heart rate kicks up a notch, but there's nothing of the old predator in Coeur's gaze. She merely looks curious.

Coeur lifts her chin as the other woman turns back from the sink. "You must be Starla," she says.

Starla takes a sip of the water, watching Coeur warily.

"It's nice to finally meet you," Coeur says. With another person, Jaantzen would interpret the tone as genuine. He's still not sure how to read this new Coeur.

Starla glances at him sidelong, then looks back at Coeur. "Nice to meet you, too," she finally signs.

A chime rings and the light flickers as the lift arrives, and the awkward moment between Blackheart and his goddaughter is broken; Starla moves to the conference table to confer with El. Manu's out of the lift with an armload of gear, and though Jaantzen's not expecting to see Gia exit behind him, he's hardly surprised. If she'd truly been happy leaving them all behind, she would have gone back home to Tevi the instant Coeur was in the clear. Jaantzen should probably give her the push to let her set herself free again.

Soon.

Gia drops her armload on the couch beside Coeur and gives Elian a disappointed look. "I disapprove of whatever it is you're planning with my patient," she tells Jaantzen.

He smiles at her and is rewarded with a faint quirk of her lips.

"Noted," he tells her. He turns to Coeur, who's pawing at the ties of her hospital blouse. "Do you need help?"

Coeur rasps a laugh. "I told you she'd find me," she says to Jaantzen. "And I'm fine, Gia kitted my hands out nice." She waggles a gloved hand at him, then tugs off the blouse with a hissed curse and fumbles her way into a biosilk undershirt. Yellow bruises muddy the red-brown skin stretched over collarbones and shoulders.

She manages the undershirt, but she can't undo the buckles of the tactical vest. Gia sighs and reaches to help her strap it on; Coeur's nostrils flare with pain as Gia tightens it under her arms, but she doesn't complain.

"The medpack's topped off," Gia tells her. "It'll track your pulse, your blood pressure, and stick you with the good stuff if it thinks you need it."

"I'm fine."

"You're not fine, you're too thick-skulled to realize how wrecked your body is." Gia plugs a diagnostic terminal into the vest's shoulder port and types for a minute. "It's press and hold here to get the painkillers," she tells Coeur, tapping a spot on the vest just below the left collarbone. "And it's just mild stuff, nothing that'll dull your thinking — so don't be afraid to use it preemptively."

Coeur hesitates only a second before pressing and holding the spot, flinching at the needle. She closes her eyes a moment.

"Did you disable the other automatic medpack shit?" she asks.

"No," Gia says, unplugging the diagnostic terminal. "It's still going to monitor your vitals and keep you alive if you get horribly injured. Just your tough luck."

Coeur's eyes narrow. "And what's it reporting to you?"

"Your vitals," Jaantzen says. "You're welcome to supply your own tactical vest or go in without armor if you don't trust me, Thala."

"It's fine." She fidgets with a shoulder strap and hisses with pain, but bares her teeth when Gia reaches to help. Gia raises her hands in surrender and steps back, leaning a hip against the edge of the couch. Manu's been staying away from the whole scene, checking through the gear he brought and ignoring Coeur entirely.

Jaantzen studies his lieutenant as Coeur messes with the fit of the vest, but though Manu's clearly not happy, nothing in his manner shows hesitation. Now he settles next to Jaantzen on the couch, ankle crossed over his knee, as loose and easy as if he were at a party.

Jaantzen lifts an eyebrow at him and gets a solemn nod in response.

Coeur finally manages the row of snaps that's been fighting her, then leans back stiffly, hands cradled in her lap, eyes clamped shut.

"Tell me," she says. Over her shoulder, Gia gives Jaantzen an expectant look.

"We estimate that probably a third of your crew will turn if they know you're alive," Jaantzen says. "And we've been feeding the rumor mill to get them primed."

"One-third isn't enough." Coeur's eyes are still closed.

"One-third is a start," says Manu. "And we can guess Acheta will send his most loyal after Phaera tonight, or have them at his side when he meets with Lordeur. So that gets a few more out of your way. Plus, we don't know how many will turn if you actually show up and can talk them back onto your side."

"There's the other issue," Jaantzen says. Starla and El have rejoined the conversation, but he's too preoccupied with Coeur to attempt to sign as he speaks. He raises an eyebrow to Starla, taps the corner of his eye. She nods; her lens is catching the conversation.

Jaantzen turns back to Coeur. "You taught your crew to respect strength, and only strength," he says. "That's why so many of them stayed when Acheta killed Hinoja, even if they didn't agree with him. Your crew respects their memory of the fighter you were. How many of them will keep that respect when they see you now?"

Coeur's eyes open to slits. "Then we don't let them see."

"Look at yourself, Thala," Jaantzen says. "You've exhausted yourself putting on a vest. Maybe you can hide your injuries well enough for the first impression, but you've established a precedent: leadership is gained by fighting."

"Then I fight."

Manu's shaking his head. "You fight, you're dead." His voice is grim. "You've survived assassination attempts. You survived weeks being tortured by the Dawn. You survived Zacharia's attempt to kill you at Julieta's. You survived that crash. You survived surgery. And right now you're completely wrecked."

"Fuck you, too."

"You're wrecked, but you're alive," Manu says. "That's not weakness. That's proof that you're a tough-as-nails bitch who nobody can kill."

The words glitter with venom, but lightly enough that anyone who knew Manu less well might not notice. Jaantzen catches Manu's eye in warning, and a muscle tightens in Manu's bruised jaw before it smooths into a mask of relaxation once more.

Coeur opens one eye. "What are you, my cheer-leader or my speechwriter?"

"Whichever you need to get your ass out there and win tonight," Manu says easily. By his tone of voice, Manu could be discussing the weather. But one thumbnail scrapes across the pad of his index finger before he catches the gesture and stills.

"It's starting to sound like you're sweet on me," Coeur drawls.

Manu's scarred left hand clenches against his thigh.

"Thala," Jaantzen says sharply, and the mockery in her gaze sobers. "Apart from me, every single person in this room would prefer to put a bullet in your head tonight. The only reason you're alive is because I've ordered them not to." His voice is almost a growl. "Do not test the patience of my people."

Coeur legitimately looks chagrined. "Sorry. Habit," she says. She glances at Manu. "Sorry, man." She takes a deep breath and levers herself back up to a seated position, elbows braced on thighs, hands cradled on knees. She jerks her chin at Manu. "What else am I up against?"

Manu's answer is clipped, precise. "There's an Arquellian woman who showed up a few days ago, says she was part of your crew back on Indira, here to avenge your death. Called Norah é Vega."

Coeur's expression goes dark.

"Is she yours?" Jaantzen asks.

Coeur scowls like she's thinking about it. Or maybe thinking about how to phrase it.

"Was," she says finally. "Norah's dead."

Manu lifts his hands to Jaantzen. "Oriol believes the woman might be Alliance-trained," he signs, and Coeur glares at him.

"You got something to say?" she asks; they all ignore her.

Manu throws an image from his comm onto the coffee table to float in front of Coeur: a copper-skinned woman with shaggy black hair, a petite nose and pointed chin. "Is this her?"

Coeur studies the image, a flicker of emotion passing over her face. "No, not quite. Good try, though." She waves a gloved hand to swipe the image away. "Norah was killed by the Dawn when I got taken."

"So only the Dawn would know she's dead?" Jaantzen asks.

Coeur shakes her head. "The Alliance would know. They were at me, too."

"Of course."

"I did steal their toys for the Dawn."

"Anyone else 'at you' we should know about?" Jaantzen asks her.

"New Manilan gangster called Pirao," Coeur says. "But he could barely reach past his own border. No way he has the resources to come for me here."

"You make so many friends."

"Well, folks who know me best call me a tough-as-nails bitch." She winks at Manu. "Tell me about her."

"All I know is she got tight with Acheta quick, and a lot of your crew are upset about that. And she fights like she's Alliance."

"She's probably not Dawn, and if she's Alliance there's no way she's working for Acheta," Coeur says. "Which means Acheta's a goddamned idiot, falling for Alliance bullshit. But if she's here to 'avenge my death,' she doesn't kill me without blowing her cover in front of a couple dozen trigger-happy assholes who hate the Alliance. So I got her on the ropes there." She tilts her head at Manu. "You got a mole in my crew?"

"No clue what you're talking about."

"I find him, I kill him," she says.

Manu just shakes his head, gaze raised to the ceiling.

"Sounds like you're back in full form," Jaantzen

says, which earns him a long glare. "It's time to go. Everything goes right on our end, you won't have to worry about Acheta coming back to challenge you. But don't take your time. I don't want Manu in your territory any longer than need be." He glances over at the conference table. "Elian, are you ready?"

"Ready," he says, crossing to Coeur but stopping a healthy distance back to toss the packed med kit onto the couch beside her.

She cracks a smile. "Thanks, pup."

"Everything's labeled, just follow the instructions and you should be fine. If you experience any nausea with — "

"I know how to find doctors."

" — any nausea with the antibiotics, there's some crystallized ginger. I would've thrown in a nanite pack but I figured you'd be too paranoid to take it."

Coeur gives him a second look, then grins. "I like you, kid. You ever need a new gig, you call me."

"No, thank you, ma'am. Get someone to help you change the bandages on your hands, don't try to do it yourself."

Jaantzen clears his throat. "It's time. Ms. Ravi?"

There's a faint pop in his ear; around the room, people react to the connection being made.

"Ready to go, boss," Toshiyo says in his ear.

"Thank you. Elian, we'll need you here for at

least the next few hours in case anything goes wrong." The young medic nods tightly. "El, get your team on the road. Starla, you're with me. Thala, try not to goad Manu into killing you before he gets you to your people."

Behind Coeur, Gia shifts. "And who's got Manu's back?" she asks.

"El's team."

Coeur's gaze narrows, but if she has a problem with El bringing crew into her territory, she keeps it to herself.

Gia takes a deep breath. "I want to go, too." Manu starts to protest, but she's shaking her head. "No way I'm letting you all put your asses on the line without proper backup. Besides, you're probably going to need someone who can pull out a bullet in the field as well as put them in."

A grin tugs at the corner of Manu's mouth; Jaantzen realizes it's the first time he's seen his lieutenant smile in days.

"Thank you," Jaantzen says. "You'll report to El. Let's go."

He catches Manu's wrist before his lieutenant can rise, leaning close as the others begin to disperse. "No unnecessary risks," he murmurs. "The most important thing tonight is you coming back in one piece."

Manu's dark expression softens, and he reaches

his other hand to clasp Jaantzen's jaw and neck, drawing him closer until their foreheads touch. He's silent a moment, breath even and calm. "I'll see you tonight," he says, then releases him, a smile pulling at his lips. "Take care of the old man for me," he signs to Starla with a grin as he stands.

"You are all so adorable." Coeur grabs a black cane with a steel handle, uses it to push herself to her feet. Pulls a red faux leather jacket over her vest, her jaw clenched as she zips it up, fighting for each inch but not asking for help.

Both Gia and Elian are ready to catch her when she falls, but she takes steady steps, leaning heavily on the cane.

"Have fun, everybody," she says. "It's showtime."

21

ORIOL

The sun's going down, and instead of her usual evening wear, Phaera D's in a man's work trousers and a loose work shirt rolled up to the elbows, her hair pinned back in an unraveling, dusty knot. She's managed to scrape open a knuckle and has dirt smudged across one cheekbone, and for someone who runs her businesses with such elegance, Oriol's surprised to find out just how well she knows her way around a nail gun.

She lifts her end of a dead holopanel with a grunt and tilts her pointed chin to the far side of the lobby. "Over there." He leads, stepping backwards over rubble, the panel's edge biting into his fingers through his gloves.

They've been at it all day, overseeing the

cleanup of the Lorelei. There's shattered glass to be swept, doors to be reinstalled or at least temporarily sealed, wiring to be fixed. Security to be upgraded and bullet holes to be patched.

Bloodstains to be scrubbed.

Phaera hired a local contractor, but that didn't stop her from joining in, which means Oriol got to ditch the suit jacket and roll up his own sleeves, too. It's a nice change of pace from all the standing around bored or shooting at people, though he's not fooling himself that it'll last much longer this evening. Acheta gave Phaera three days to come up with the cash he's demanding, and that deadline comes to a close tonight. Maybe what Jaantzen's got planned will fix things in the end, but Oriol's betting more bullets will fly before the day's done.

Which is why Oriol's spent part of the day with the security chiefs of the Lorelei and the Devil's Table, Jae Bakshi and Hiro Matapang, going through the weapons shipment Manu's guy Beto dropped off this morning. Oriol had his reservations at first, but both security chiefs turned out to have military backgrounds themselves, and more interest in training and safety than in handing out weapons like candy.

Satisfied that Bakshi and Matapang had a handle on security, Oriol went back to keeping an eye on Phaera — which in this case meant joining the construction crew. Priority number one has been cleaning up the mess. They're working from the inside out, leaving the shattered, glitching facade and fading police markings for last.

It made a nice backdrop for the press, Phaera said.

And it has, for the few who braved the casino district to follow up on the damage. They've been cornering those of Phaera's people who are working outside — meaning, those she's prepped for interviews — to hear about how even though the casino is closed for the time being, Phaera is still paying everyone's salaries half-time, and time-and-a-half if they come in to help with the cleanup. Dealers sweeping up glass and bouncers carting away debris alike are ready to say how lean times have been since the police have failed to do anything about Dry Creek and Acheta's crew.

Phaera's even given a quote or two herself, carefully crafted barbs about how the businesses of the casino district need to support each other and drive out the criminal elements.

Her face has been in the news plenty before this, though she's normally played up her more extravagant and exotic side. Today, in minimal makeup and work clothes, she's just a local gal made good — she could be you, your sister, your aunt.

With anyone else, Oriol might start to wonder which persona was real: the ruthless backroom negotiator, the media darling, the elegant hostess, the bootstrapping businesswoman. With Phaera D, they're all equally true, faces of the same dice.

They set the broken holopanel on a pile with the others and Phaera tugs her gloves off; her scraped knuckle glistens red.

Oriol grabs a napkin off the nearby bar. "You're bleeding."

She kisses blood off her knuckle, then accepts the napkin and dabs it to the scrape. She wrinkles her nose, then starts on the buttons of her work shirt. "God, I stink." She shucks the sweat-dampened shirt, revealing the gray tank top beneath, and rolls her shoulders. "All day, and not a damned one of them has come," she says.

Any of the other business owners on the drag, she means. Despite the constant meetings over the past few days, not a single one of Phaera's peers has come to pay condolences or see how she's doing. Her barbs directed at the local business community have gotten more pointed with each interview she's done today.

"Acheta's attack wasn't just a message for you," Oriol says. "You can't blame them for being scared."

"*They're* scared?" She laughs derisively. "I'm fucking terrified, Sina. But I've never let that hold me back before." Her gaze shifts over his shoulder and her brows pull together. "Jae, what's wrong."

Jae Bakshi, a steel-haired, steel-muscled older woman, is picking her way through the debris-strewn lobby towards them. The expression on her face is grim.

"I'm sorry, ma'am," she says. "But I have bad news. Diana didn't make it."

Phaera's face falls, and Oriol steps back to watch the room as Jae wraps her arms around Phaera. He never met the woman they're mourning, one of the Lorelei's security guards, who took a bullet through the lung last night in the attack. That brings the total now to four dead, thirteen wounded. Mostly civilians, despite how quickly Phaera's security team had responded.

Oriol's comm buzzes and he takes another searching look around the lobby; clear.

It's a message from Manu.

GOING IN.

He's expecting the message, but it still hits him like a punch just below the sternum. Oriol takes a deep breath, lets it out; the feeling of dread pooling in the pit of his stomach doesn't follow. His duty is here, and that doesn't stop him wanting to break into a sprint and get to wherever Manu's about to throw himself to the lions.

COME HOME TO ME, he responds, then slips the

comm back into his pocket, schooling his face into a calm mask.

Bakshi has left; Phaera is slumped onto a bench near the entryway, her head in her hands.

Oriol knows he's been working with Jaantzen too long when his first thought is, Not in front of the employees. But he's been watching her all day. The loyalty she's built has nothing to to do with her stoic strength and everything to do with her willingness to wear her heart on her sleeve. One young woman — a bartender — lays her hand on Phaera's shoulder as she walks by, and Phaera squeezes it in her own, looks up with a sad smile.

Oriol scans the room once more, then sinks onto the bench beside her, realizing how tired he is, too. His ankle clicks and whirs as he straightens his legs.

"You should get yourself some food," Oriol says. He thinks she broke for lunch — he was unpacking fun crates of guns with the security team — but he knows she didn't stop for dinner.

"I'm not done yet."

"Everyone else is ready to call it a day," Oriol says, voice low. "And Acheta's crew will be here any moment."

Phaera's shoulders stiffen, but only for a moment. She lifts her voice. "Let's call it, folks. I'll see you all tomorrow."

Her employees slowly begin to clear out of the

lobby, little murmurs of thanks and squeezes of her hand as they pass. Even as the lobby clears, Phaera doesn't move.

Neither does her security team, Oriol notes with satisfaction. He catches Bakshi's eye across the lobby, and the older woman gives him a solemn nod. None of them are going anywhere until Phaera's home safe.

And as much as Oriol would like to be patient, would like to spend the evening sitting here beside her until Phaera's ready to head home, every fiber of his body is screaming that he has somewhere else to be. If he can just get her safely ensconced in her own home, then he can get hold of Jaantzen, find out exactly where Manu is, how he can help.

He realizes too late Phaera's watching him.

She tilts her head. "What's wrong?"

"It's been a long day for us all," he says. "And it's not over yet."

"You look worried. About Acheta?"

"No, ma'am."

"About Juric?" Her expression softens. "What's your boss planning?"

"You're right here, ma'am."

"Jaantzen, Sina. You take his money, you're taking his orders. What has he ordered you to do tonight?"

"Keep you safe."

"Because I'm bait while he takes out Acheta," she says, frustration coloring her voice. "I got that part. He wouldn't fill me in on the rest of the plan."

"He's like that."

Phaera tilts her head, studying him. "But I'm guessing you know. Since your husband — " And at Oriol's expression, Phaera lifts an eyebrow. "You're not married? Sorry I assumed, but seriously, Sina. Why wouldn't you tie a knot in your net once you've got a catch like that?" She waves a hand before he can answer. "No one's paying you to talk about *your* love life, either. Or about your boss's plans."

Jaantzen's told her — or she's guessed — that Acheta won't live through the night. But if Jaantzen hasn't told her about Coeur, he's got his reasons. Reasons that Oriol can't even begin to defend to Phaera.

"Tonight should go smoothly," Oriol says. "We're just giving him the money and letting Jaantzen take care of things on his end. Speaking of, we should probably go grab the . . ."

Phaera's gaze narrows defiantly, and a stab of unease pierces Oriol's gut.

"Ma'am," he says slowly. "You have the money?"

"For that pig?" she says bitterly. "He's not getting a cent."

"Phaera," Oriol breathes, but he cuts off at the voice in his ear. "Hold on, ma'am. Come again, Hiro?"

Across the lobby, Jae Bakshi is shouting orders to her team.

"Two spinners approaching," Hiro Matapang says again over the radio. He's been designated their lookout tonight, given he's got the sniper experience from his service and Bakshi's got the better knowledge of the Lorelei.

"It's Acheta's people," Matapang says.

"What is it?" Phaera asks. They're on a separate security channel tonight from the one the Lorelei normally uses.

"Acheta," Oriol answers. "Let's get you inside. If you're not planning on — "

"So they can, what? Firebomb the place this time?" Phaera pushes herself to her feet, then heads towards the door.

"Ma'am!"

"They want to talk with me, and that's what they'll get," Phaera calls over her shoulder, and as the two spinners glide to a stop, she's walking out to the curb to meet them, approaching like a queen despite her rough work clothes. Along the drag, the other casinos are standing strangely eerie in the absence of patrons, their facades lit like bonfires in the light of the setting sun.

"Get these people inside," Oriol says to the one of the remaining employees still working on the facade. The woman nods, fear in her eyes, and begins to herd the others indoors.

"We've got them covered from above," says Matapang.

Bakshi falls into step beside Oriol as they head after Phaera, her gun in her hand. "She's not going to give them the money," Oriol hisses to Bakshi, who sighs, but doesn't seem surprised.

"You get used to her. Be ready for trouble, Hiro," she says over the channel.

"Always am," Matapang answers.

Other security team members are taking up positions at the entrance, near barricades, and it's at least a demonstration that Phaera D comes with some muscle at her back — though that won't mean a damned thing if Acheta's crew decide to shoot her right here and now.

If Acheta wanted that, he would've done it already, Oriol tells himself. Acheta wants the money. And so long as they can convince him he's going to get it, they might just make it through tonight.

The spinner doors spread open like wings, and Acheta's nowhere to be seen. His lieutenant, Sjel, steps out with a lazy grin.

"Your boss couldn't make it?" Phaera asks. She

makes a show of looking around. "Well, why don't you come back tomorrow when he can join us."

Oriol sighs. Goddammit, Phaera.

"He's too busy for errands," Sjel says. "I'm just here for the money, Phaera. Then we'll get out of your hair." His gaze slides past her to the rubble. "Looks like you have a lot to do."

Phaera's nostrils flare, her shoulders back, her chin high.

"Unless you think you can cheat us?" Sjel asks lazily. He sweeps his hand up and down the empty drag. "Because if you think anyone else is coming to help you out, you're wrong. I've seen your little interview clips, all about having each other's backs? But then where's the rest of your little coalition? Where's your boyfriend? He doesn't even come himself, doesn't even send his good soldiers, just sends his gimp."

Sjel doesn't spare a glance for Oriol at the comment, just cracks his knuckles and squares with Phaera.

"You're all alone," he says, crew gathering behind him like rats. "Hand over the money, or you're coming back with me to see what Acheta has to say about people who try to cheat him."

22

MANU

Manu's driving an unmarked, unrecognizable spinner, but they've been marked anyway: somebody's been following since they reached the crux of the second and third Fingers, closing in on Coeur's — well, Acheta's, territory.

They've just passed the Sulila hospital, the one Gia trained at well before he ever met her, and now they're driving past the dingy bar where Manu met Arquellian special administrator Marquez ó Lauris and the cute barfly with the braids who hadn't waited for him. Manu changes lanes and the spinner behind him does, too.

As they head into the second Finger, Altamira, the main streets give way to residential areas, and it almost reminds him of where he grew up, Carama

Town, though the houses here are more crowded together and the streets are actually paved.

"This is getting to be a habit," Coeur says from the passenger seat beside him. She looks infinitely better than the last time he was driving her to a confrontation, on their way out to Julieta Yang's estate.

"Twice in one week doesn't make this a habit," Manu says. "It just makes it a really bad week."

Coeur slides him a smile; there doesn't seem to be any malice in it.

The residential street gives way to a brief commercial area, markets and restaurants and cafés and convenience stores all lighting up the night. He takes the opportunity for a few fast turns, slipping his spinner through the chaos of bicycle carts and moto taxis before ending up on a new arterial.

With no tail.

Good.

"Hey, Manu."

He glares at her, irritated. "What."

She's watching him, bands of light sliding over her face, glinting in her eyes. "I just wanted to say thank you."

What new hellish game is this? "For what?" he asks warily.

"For being the better person." Coeur's still watching him, her head rolling back and forth against the headrest at the bumps in the road. "Ain't many who would do what you're doing."

Manu turns his attention back to the road. "I'm doing it for him, not you."

"Oh, I know." A smile touches her lips; it looks genuine. "Still. I wanted to say thank you. And that it's been an honor getting to know you better."

He looks over, hunting for the joke behind her words. But she just nods solemnly to him and turns her face away, pointing a gloved finger out the window at a bar with faded paint and half-broken lighting. "Dezi's is still around? I used to love that place. I can't believe it's still running."

Manu forces his hands to unclench on the controls, forces his shoulders to relax, his breathing to come naturally. Grinds his jaw to feel the pain there, giving him the focus he needs to ignore the woman beside him.

Was that an apology?

Fuck her if it was.

The farther they go in, the higher the ravine juts up around them, blocking out the light of Bulari's downtown, blocking out swaths of stars, and casting the neighborhood in inky black with only sparse, sputtering streetlamps to light their way.

"The black heart of Bulari," Coeur says happily. Manu doesn't answer.

Coeur set up shop years ago in an old church

about a third of the way into the Altamira ravine. It had been abandoned for decades before that, all colonial chic in broad steel plates riveted together, pitted and rusting. The bell tower — or minaret, he's not sure what kind of church it used to be — has been converted into a guard tower. Manu catches a glint: somebody's goggles or the muzzle of their gun.

"I've got you, Manu," Toshiyo says in his ear. "Teams One and Two, I see you're in place. Check in." Manu relaxes slightly as they do. Team One is a trio of Jaantzen's soldiers who've been in place since early this afternoon. Team Two is El, Gia, and El's soldiers. Manu may be a sitting duck, but at least he's got plenty of firepower backing him up.

The church is on the eastern edge of a small city plaza, all cement and scraggly desert shrub in clumps that are meant to be decorative. There's a play structure, a half-sized soccer field, and a ball court for the neighborhood kids. Unlike those in the Dry Creek neighborhood where Coeur had been held prisoner, these actually look like they get used. There's a handful of kids here now, kicking a ball against the side of a graffitied utility building. They stop as Manu pulls the spinner up. Four of them remain, kicking the ball idly back and forth. The fifth takes off at a jog towards the church.

"Sentries," Manu says.

"Kids their age should be in bed this time of night," Coeur answers.

"Like you and me were, def."

Coeur smiles at his joke and he catches himself before he almost reflexively returns the smile.

"We're in place," says El in his ear. "Go when ready."

It's not going to be a matter of when they're ready, though. Coeur's old crew is ready for them. The side door of the church opens and a greeting party pours out, bristling with weapons. At the head is a man Manu has been reassured would be here tonight. A man he's been reassured is prone to asking questions before shooting bullets: Aden Damyati.

That's going according to plan, at least — even so, Damyati's brought plenty of firepower. He's flanked by six other crewmembers, all armed. The kid from the ballgame trails behind, curious.

Manu glances at Coeur. "Let me talk to them first," he says. He opens his door and steps out, leaning one hip against the hood of the spinner. A bit of excited chatter goes up from the kids in the park. They know who he is.

"Five more flanking on the left," Toshiyo says. Manu marks them coming around the side of the park.

Damyati has a pistol strapped to his thigh, but

he's not drawing it. Not yet. He tilts his head, considering, and this is the fulcrum the entire plan is balancing on: curiosity. He doesn't look worried about Manu, he's not wondering how Manu knew to come while Acheta was away. He's only wondering what's in it for him.

That's what Manu needs.

Manu holds up his hands. "I'm just here to talk," he says, and Damyati stops five paces away, his soldiers fanning out behind him, weapons ready but not aimed at Manu. Yet.

"Acheta's not here," Damyati says. "But I'm guessing you know that. Your boss thinks this crew is his for the taking, he's gonna need to think again."

"The man's got no interest in a fight with you, or with Acheta."

"I'm not talking with Jaantzen." Damyati's gaze flickers to the passenger door. He can tell someone else is in there, but he can't see who.

"You're not," Manu says. Damyati lifts his chin as Manu puts his hand on the controls to open the passenger door.

A prickly wall of weapons rise to point at the door as it swings open. Manu notes which barrels dip or fall as Acheta's crewmembers recognize the person inside.

About half. Good. They can work with that.

Manu also notes the ones who take a tighter

grip on their weapon, pointing it even more surely. Those are the ones he's going to have to watch out for.

A murmur goes up around them, and Damyati silences that with a sharp look over his shoulder.

"Hello, Aden," Coeur says with a smile. Because he's looking for it, Manu can see what effort it's taking Coeur to move with power, to make her slow, deliberate slide out the door look regal rather than convalescent.

He supposes she has a lot of experience hiding boxing injuries from a hungry crew. It's in their faces now, which ones are hunting for her weaknesses, which ones are taking solace in her strength.

She holds the cane like a weapon, bracing herself as little as possible. The tactical vest keeps her spine erect, helping her stand tall.

"You've been a good soldier, Damyati. Thank you."

It's not what he was expecting to hear, and he hasn't yet recovered from his surprise at seeing her, either. Damyati gets glances from others in the crew, and a few more lower their weapons.

"It was a long road here, but I've made it back to you," Coeur says. She's pitching her voice strong now, to the back reaches of the gathering crowd as she scans, exchanging slight nods, knowing smiles. "Devo," she says; she takes a few painful steps to reach out and palm an older man's cheek, ignoring the muzzle of his pistol pressing into her sternum. "I'm glad you're well."

Manu's watching the faces. He doesn't recognize all of them, but he recognizes a few, from fights, from being around. He recognizes a few more from long days being held and tortured back during the civil war. That big man in the back — Manu can't remember his name, but he was Coeur's chief enforcer at the time — is watching him with such cold satisfaction it makes Manu's skin crawl.

Manu forces his attention back to Damyati and Coeur. Back to making it out of here alive.

Damyati steps forward. "Last I heard you were dead."

Coeur's eyes go wide in surprise. "Acheta didn't tell you?"

Damyati glances over his shoulder, gets a confused shrug from the woman beside him.

Coeur's eyes glitter. "Dry Creek had me. Just a few kilometers away." She lifts her splinted left hand. "They broke my hands, a bone at a time, and the whole time I wondered why the help Acheta had promised me wasn't coming. Why none of my people were looking for me." A few more people shift uncomfortably as she spears individuals with her gaze, a few more weapons lower.

Manu resists giving Coeur an impressed look. It

wouldn't have occurred to him to claim Acheta knew she was alive, but the lie's landing perfectly.

"Vira, you would have come," Coeur says, and the woman beside Damyati flinches in shame. "Fang?"

"I'm sorry, Thala," says the man she addressed, banked anger in his voice. "I didn't know. No one knew."

"I don't blame any of you." She laughs bitterly. "That bastard Acheta let me rot."

Coeur lifts her chin again, raises her voice. "It wasn't an easy road home, as you can see. But I always told you I'd come back, didn't I? And you know I reward those who are loyal."

The little act is having its effect, but the reactions in the crew are still split. Manu can see Damyati calculating his move. Shooting Coeur here and now might win him Acheta's approval, but only if the people in the crowd who are still loyal to Blackheart don't get their revenge on him first.

And while chaos in this crew isn't the worst outcome, Manu's not sure he survives that shoot-out. He shifts, closer to the driver's door.

"This isn't your crew anymore," Damyati says, his tone still carefully neutral. "You planning on fighting Acheta?"

Coeur laughs at the suggestion, taps her cane against the ground. "Are we a pack of dogs, surviving purely on our ability to tear out the throats of our prey?" she asks him. "That attitude will put you — and everyone here — in the ground. This is a game of wits, Aden. The strongest may come out on top in the boxing ring, but you're not playing the smart game when it comes to keeping control of this city."

"What are you talking about, the smart game?" Damyati says. "We took out the Dawn, and now we control the production and the distribution of shard. We own this city."

Coeur laughs. "If you can beat Dry Creek without paying your crew." She raises her voice. "Any of you oldtimers ever go hungry under *my* rule? No. You think you own the city? You're getting owned. Look at Acheta. Inviting *Arquellian traitors* into this crew?"

Frowns and murmurs all around at that. "É Vega said she was part of your crew on Indira," Damyati says. But Manu can see that struck a universal chord. Nobody in this crowd is happy with their new Arquellian crewmember.

"Norah é Vega was part of my crew," Coeur says. "But I saw the Alliance kill Norah. If Acheta had taken even two minutes to ask any of my old crew back on Indira about her, he would've known the woman calling herself Norah is a fake. Whoever that woman is, she's playing with you, and how many of you are going to sit there and let yourself be played?" She lifts her chin. "That bitch around?"

But before anyone can answer, a shadow shifts just behind Damyati. Manu tenses.

The big man from the back — Coeur's old enforcer — pushes himself past the others, seeking eye contact as he goes. Some meet his gaze approvingly. Others are avoiding it. His shoulder hits Damyati as he passes — it's broad, with thick white scars in the warm brown, bulging, muscles. Sinewy forearms. His face is angular and fierce, and scored into Manu's memory: grinning down at him as blows come again and again.

Manu remembers that scar running down the man's right forearm, too. Manu gave him that, fighting for his life before Coeur's crew finally managed to take him in the first place. The man gives him a deadly look before turning his attention to Coeur.

"I'm done listening to you talk," he says. "You think because Acheta's gone, none of us are strong enough to challenge you?" The big man rolls his neck, slams one fist into the other palm. "You think again."

Coeur tilts her head back to study him, a faint smile on her lips.

"Hello, Bull," she says.

23

———

JAANTZEN

Sending Calanthe to talk with the others. Asking Lordeur to meet with Acheta. Hiring out the contract to a headhunter Manu trusts — Willem Jaantzen's signature may be all over this hit, but his fingerprints are wiped clean.

Not that it matters.

Acheta's not here.

And if he's not here by now, he's not coming.

It's taking all of Jaantzen's willpower to keep himself seated, and Starla gives him a sidelong look. She offers him her thermos of milky coffee. He waves it away and tries to relax against the seat of the spinner, staring at the dusty street stretching out from their vantage point in a parking lot three blocks down from Lucky's Palladium Coast.

When Acheta arrived at Leone's dinner party last week, he'd brought a gift, showed the proper respect to the others there. He'd indicated that he was ready to step into their circle seamlessly, as Naali Hinoja had done when Coeur was exiled.

But ignoring the bounty on his head. Trying to intimidate another member, then shooting up her place of business?

No — Acheta wasn't playing by the rules.

That's why he needs to be gone, more than anything.

"Headhunter just checked in," says Toshiyo in his ear. "Still no sign. Orders?"

"Tell her to wait," Jaantzen says.

The last time Jaantzen hired someone else to take care of trouble was during the civil war. He'd been there that time, too, sitting across the street in a darkened spinner right before a dust storm while one of Coeur's lieutenants, a woman named Danela, was drinking with a group of friends.

It hadn't been hard to make the decision. Along with her long list of crimes that didn't endear her to Leone and the others, she had also been the one tasked with bringing in Manu.

Of course, Starla hadn't been the one to sit beside him that day. She'd been a teenager, safe back home. He hadn't needed to be there, either — he had a reliable headhunter he'd worked with before, and a reliable driver who knew how to get a job done and get gone. But he'd wanted to be sitting across the street when the driver pulled up, when his man strolled into the bar, strolled back out followed by screams, and slipped into his ride and away into the night.

He'd wanted to hear for himself when people shouted, "Somebody shot Danela. Danela is dead."

He isn't getting nearly as much pleasure out of being the one to call this order as he did the day Danela died. Whereas that felt like a victory, retribution, this feels only like a job that needs to be done to bring things back into line.

But it's getting later. And Acheta still isn't here.

Starla's watching him, frustration etched on her face.

"If he's not here, where is he?" she signs.

Jaantzen opens up a channel to El first. Acheta probably didn't know about the plan ahead of time, but Manu is deep into his territory by now, and Acheta could have found out he was there and started to head back.

It's also possible that Acheta went to see Phaera himself, having agreed to this meeting as a ruse to make sure Jaantzen wasn't at her side. But Oriol and Phaera's security team should have a handle on that, and so long as Phaera's sticking to her role, Acheta shouldn't have any excuse to harm her.

Manu and Coeur, on the other hand, are completely exposed. There's not much El and Gia and the rest of the crew will be able to do for them if Acheta shows up with his loyal people.

Of course there's also not much anyone can do for them if it turns out that Coeur can't flip her old narrative about the best fighter getting the crown.

"El, no sign of our guest," Jaantzen says. "What do you see?"

The response is slow to come, but eventually it does. "Just checked with sentries. No sign of him here, either," El says.

"Check again."

"Copy," El says; this is the third time they've had this conversation, and each time he sounds as professional as the last.

Jaantzen leans heavily back against the seat, then messages Oriol: WE HAVEN'T SEEN ACHETA. WHAT'S YOUR STATUS.

"What about the Arquellian woman?" Jaantzen asks El again.

"Negative."

"Toshiyo?"

"I haven't put eyes on either of them, boss," Toshiyo says. "I've been tracking since Team One got into place. Either he got going real early in the morning, or he's slipped through."

But any further consideration they might have on the matter is cut short.

"We have a problem," El says quietly. "Coeur has a challenger."

Starla's gaze snaps up to meet Jaantzen's.

"Get Manu out," Jaantzen orders.

"On it."

He checks his comm, but still has no answer from Oriol.

Unease twists his gut.

"He could've gone for Phaera," Starla signs.

He sends another message to Oriol: *STATUS*.

No reply.

Jaantzen takes a deep breath.

Acheta isn't coming.

"Toshiyo, tell the headhunter to stay put and tell Team Three to get Lordeur home safely," he says. "Let's go," he signs to Starla.

24

MANU

Bull's got nearly a foot and two hundred pounds on Coeur, all of it muscle, all of it tensed for a fight. One blow and she's obliterated, and Manu's going down with her.

"Get back in the spinner," El says in his ear. "We've got you covered."

But when Manu's hand moves towards the door, half a dozen weapons move with him.

"You don't want to fight me, Bull," Coeur says quietly. Her tone is light, but there's steel beneath. "Think this through."

Bull's nostrils flare. He turns away from her.

"You all just going to let her come back in and take over?" he asks, sweeping his gaze over the crowd; there are guarded murmurs of agreement.

"She said herself she's not strong enough to lead. Look at her. She's walking with a cane."

"It's been a rough month," Coeur says. "But the Alliance couldn't break me, and neither could Dry Creek. Strength's more than a thick skull and a fist."

Bull turns back to her, closes the gap between them. He's close enough that she has to tilt her head back to make eye contact. The strain is getting to her; this close to her, Manu can see the sheen of sweat on her brow, hear her trying to control her breathing.

But Coeur doesn't move an inch. She's holding an easy boxer's stance, but there's no way she's fast or strong enough after everything that happened to her. With hands just out of surgery, she's not taking this guy down.

"Manu, get out of there," El says again.

"Used to be we had a way of choosing leadership," Bull says, voice still pitched to the crowd. Then he snarls in her face. "Used to be you cared about the strength of your crew. And then you go running off, let people like Naali run us into the ground. Acheta knows what it is, but as soon as he steps away for a minute, you think you can just hop the ropes and talk us into giving you the crown instead?"

He hauls back a fist, testing her, but Coeur doesn't flinch.

"Manu, get back in the spinner," Gia hisses.

The tension is thick, and one unexpected move — like him going for the door again — could turn this whole thing into a bloodbath. Manu slowly rests his palm on his pistol, senses more than sees the forest of weapons around him shifting in response.

This is going terribly, terribly wrong.

"You think we're gonna fight for you if you can't fight for yourself?" Bull snarls in Coeur's face. He kicks away her cane. It clatters to the ground, spinning across the cement towards the knot of ball-playing kids. Coeur stumbles but doesn't fall.

"Aren't you gonna fight me?" Bull asks. He bares his teeth, face inches from hers.

"A body needs muscle," she says quietly. "But a body dies without brains." Coeur's lip curls into a smile. "Somebody get this asshole out of my face," she calls.

A shot rings out. Bull crumples at Coeur's feet, blood blooming from the back of his skull.

Coeur takes a halting step back to steady herself on the side of the spinner. One of the ball-playing kids darts forward and picks up her cane, holds it out to her like a scepter. Coeur winks at the girl as she takes it.

Damyati lowers his smoking pistol. "Who's with Bull?" he calls.

No one answers.

Damyati steps forward to shake Coeur's hand. "Welcome back, Blackheart," he says. His gaze slides to Manu, who still has his hand on his pistol. Bull may be down, but not everyone else here is happy with the change of guard. Doesn't mean any more of them will challenge Damyati's decision, but he's not going to be caught unaware if they do.

Damyati lifts his chin to Manu. "Why is he here?"

"Because it's not fifteen years ago and alliances fucking evolve, Aden," Coeur says. "But that's a good question." She turns to Manu, a spark in her eyes like she's sharing a joke. Only thing is, Manu's not sure if he's in on it. His grip tightens on his gun, and she smiles.

"Juric is here because I want him here," she says coolly. "And you touch him" — she raises her voice to the crowd — "anybody touches him, or any member of Jaantzen's crew, and they'll answer to me. Times change. Grudges are buried. And the only reason I'm here today is because Willem Jaantzen and his people saved my life."

"So we're doing business with — "

Coeur turns a fierce grin on the speaker, a woman with short spikes of graying hair. "We have a truce, Mila. We're playing the smart game," she says. "Now. Where's this woman who thinks she can style herself after my old lieutenant? I tell you the real Norah é Vega fought like a demon. She was fierce as a wildcat, and she died saving my life. I won't see her memory made into a joke."

"She left an hour ago," Damyati says.

"With Acheta?" Coeur growls. "Find that Alliance bitch who's wearing my girl's name and bring her to me."

Damyati lifts his chin to Manu. "And him?"

"I should go," Manu says.

Coeur's eyes glitter. "You should go."

She's watching him, though, with an expression he can't quite place. And he's not sure what's going to become of this, whether giving the demon queen back her throne was the best idea. But it's suddenly starting to not feel like the worst.

"You afraid to turn your back on me, Manu?" Coeur asks quietly.

"Maybe."

She gives him a slow smile. "I know you don't give two shits for my word, but you and yours are safe from me."

He's sure it's meant to be reassuring, but it feels more like how even though if you actually survive the L_{43} virus you develop an immunity to it, you're still paralyzed from the waist down.

Manu opens the door, but El's voice stops him

before he gets inside. Coeur's watching his face; she lifts an eyebrow.

"You may have trouble heading this way," Manu tells her. "Acheta never showed."

"Appreciate the heads-up. Now get out of here," Coeur says gently, then turns back to her crew.

Manu gets in the spinner and drives.

His shoulders don't unknot, not until he can't see the glinting of rifle barrels trained on him from the guard tower. Not until he's out of the narrow warren of roads of the Black Heart of Bulari and into more familiar territory.

"Gia?"

"Yeah."

"Please tell me you left some sort of remote-detonate poison pill in her when you did surgery."

"I'm not suicidal."

"Well, we can always hope for the best."

"Not until we find Acheta," cuts in Toshiyo. "Oriol's not responding. Manu, get to the Lorelei. Everybody else get out of there and back to base."

Fear spikes through Manu's chest. He drives.

25

ORIOL

The sun's gone down, but the casino drag's as bright as day, flickering colors and streetlamps and the distant sound of music echoing strangely in the empty pedestrian street. There's none of the usual bustle of people and pedicabs and barkers and street performers, at least not on this end. Farther down a few pedicabs have circled up like the violence about to happen down here won't wash to that end.

"Where's the money, Phaera?" Sjel asks.

"You're not getting it," she says. "Tell Acheta to come see me in person and we'll talk. But I'm not having a conversation with a bunch of guns stuck in my face."

"I'll take you to him, then." Sjel's grin bares his

incisors. "And you can explain why you made us come all the way out here for nothing."

If she's at all afraid, it doesn't show. She might as well be ordering another round of drinks for how relaxed she looks.

Oriol is not relaxed. His grip tightens on his pistol and he catches Bakshi's eye. He's at Phaera's right, Bakshi's at her left. Matapang's stationed on the roof with a high-powered sniper rifle, and the best shots from this afternoon's target practice are at his back. But Oriol's goal is to get out of this without shots fired.

Handing a pile of silver ingots over to Sjel was supposed to accomplish that.

"I'm not going anywhere with you," Phaera says. "I suppose you'll have to shoot me. But then where will your boss get his money?"

"I'm not here to make a scene," Sjel says, and Phaera laughs. The sound is bright and bitter in the strange false twilight of setting sun and blooming holograms.

"You can't make a scene on an empty street, now, can you?" Phaera says. "Speaking of which, where do you think business owners are supposed to get the money to pay your boss if you've scared away our clientele?"

Sjel shakes his head. "That's on you," he says. "You were willing to let every other business in this neighborhood wither because of your own pride. I can't help you with that."

Phaera's eyes flash. "Damn right I have my pride. So tell Acheta to come see me in person and we'll talk. I'm not here to throw words around with you." Phaera turns to walk away, but Sjel is fast as a snake, grabbing her left bicep to pull her off-balance and back into his chest, his pistol to the base of her skull. Oriol and Bakshi have their weapons up in an instant, so do the rest of Sjel's crew. For a moment the street is oppressively silent but for the whir of warming pistols and tiny scuffs of shoes against pavement as stances shift. The rasp of Phaera's breath. The acrid bite of cooling asphalt and spiking adrenaline.

"No need for violence," Sjel says calmly, looking first to Bakshi, then to Oriol. "But the lady's coming with us."

"Get your hands off me," Phaera growls. "I'm not going anywhere."

"You want to see these people killed?" Sjel's voice is low and dangerous. "More blood on your doorstep?"

"I have clean shots, but not on the primary," comes Matapang's voice in Oriol's ear.

"Hold," Oriol murmurs. He has a clean shot on Sjel, and Bakshi probably does, too, but getting into a shoot-out here is just going to get more people killed — most likely Phaera included.

Sjel's grip on Phaera's arm is tight, her pale arm bloodless under his hand, his fingernails digging into muscle. His pistol is pressed with enough force that her neck bows forward, though her eyes are embers of fury. He takes a step backward towards the spinner and Phaera lets out an involuntary gasp of pain as he pulls her with him.

Oriol shifts, tracking him; out of the corner of his eye he marks Bakshi flanking to the left. Even if Oriol doesn't have the shot, she'll get it. Though that will likely leave both of them dead and Phaera still gone.

Sjel's watching him calculate the odds with a wicked smile.

"I'm not going anywhere," Phaera says, voice rough and low.

"You so sure?"

In a breath, Sjel shifts his weight forward and grip up so that his forearm is tight around Phaera's neck. He aims his pistol at Bakshi.

"Listen, lady," he says, into her ear but loud enough for the rest of them to hear. "What do you think the end game is here tonight? Do you think it matters if you order your people to kill me? Because you got a lot of nice folks working for you, dealing cards, serving cocktails, and if you don't get in, how many of them do you think will die?" Phaera's gaze is locked on Bakshi; the older woman hasn't flinched, her gun still trained on Sjel despite his aim on her.

"I have the shot," Matapang says.

Bakshi's gaze flickers to meet Oriol's; she knows the odds tonight.

"Hold," Oriol says under his breath.

"How many?" Sjel asks again, tightening his forearm against Phaera's throat. Her hands fly to his forearm, as much to ease the pressure as to hold herself upright.

"I don't know," Pharea rasps.

"As many of them as Acheta feels like killing," Sjel says. "Maybe we even bring some back with us so you can watch."

Phaera takes a harsh breath, but doesn't answer.

"Maybe we start with the old lady." Sjel shifts his weight as though to shoot Bakshi.

"No!" Phaera shouts, her voice coming strangled. "No. I'll go. Put your gun down, Jae. Sina. All of you, put your weapons down."

A grim smile spreads over Sjel's lips. "Good choice." He relaxes his grip and Phaera gasps for breath.

There are too many innocents here that could get hurt if Oriol tries to stop them. But get to a place where he only has to worry about Phaera and he'll feel better about his options.

"If she goes, I'm going with her," Oriol says quietly, and Sjel's attention shifts to him.

"An Arquellian putting his life on the line for New Sarjunian trash like us? Never thought I'd see the day." Sjel grins, and a few of his crew laugh along. "Fine, hero, you can come along." He jerks his chin at two of his crew, who step forward to disarm Oriol, digging the barrels of their weapons into his ribs.

"Let's go." Sjel releases Phaera but doesn't let his aim at Bakshi drift. Phaera stumbles a step away from him, then turns back, smooths her palms over her thighs. She meets Oriol's gaze, and for the first time since he's met her there's real fear in her eyes.

Sjel steps aside to hold the spinner's door for Phaera, then pauses, frowning down the drag.

A luxury pedicab is slowly approaching, determined fear on the rider's face. He knows exactly what sort of trouble he's pedaling himself into.

"Stop right there," Sjel shouts when the pedicab is just under a block away. "What do you want?"

The pedicab's doors spread like a gull's wings, and a broad woman gets out. Her glittering silver gown and diamond-studded hijab play off midnight skin as she turns back to the pedicab and holds out her hand to help her companion down.

Sjel's face tightens in recognition; the woman's face is unmistakable if you've been in Bulari for even half a day. Ayisha, famed singer and proprietor of Ayisha's Palace just down the road, is a legend.

Her companion is a slim man in a red top hat and a sharp suit that shimmers like pyrite, long silver braids framing his weathered brown cheeks. Oriol can't remember his name, but he recognizes his face as Ibn Rushd's partner, the co-owner of the Aterciopelado. The old man straightens his tie, leaning heavily on his polished red cane.

"What's going on down here?" Ayisha calls, voice belting down the block.

"None of your business, ma'am," Sjel calls back. "Why don't you head on home and we'll keep on with our arrangement." He lifts his chin to the old man with the red cane. "You too, Cavy."

"I see guns on my drag," says Cavy, quiet voice carrying in the stillness. He begins walking towards them, Ayisha at his side. "I don't want to see guns on my drag."

"Then we'll be gone." Sjel grabs Phaera's arm again, pulling her towards the spinner. "C'mon."

"Phaera, honey, these men bothering you?" Ayisha asks. She's come up beside Bakshi, who is standing motionless with Sjel's pistol pointed at her head. Ayisha is trying for calm, but Oriol can see her fear in the quickness of her breath, the pulse fluttering in her throat. "Tell your boss he's going to need to set an appointment to talk to us all if he wants to come to an arrangement."

Cavy steps into place beside Oriol; Oriol catches a whiff of leather and cologne. "Or tell him to fuck off," the old man says, his cane clicking on the pavement. "You do not come onto my drag and try to kidnap my associates."

Oriol can see the calculations running through Sjel's mind. He was willing to spill any blood but Phaera's to get his way before, but if a stray bullet so much as chips Ayisha's nail polish or punches a hole in Cavy's top hat, Acheta will be forced to serve Sjel's head up on a platter to appease the rest of the casino owners. Sjel breathes in sharply and lets Phaera go. She turns slowly, her fear washed clean by fury.

"Get the hell out of here," she says to Sjel.

And just then, the man who's had his gun trained on Oriol doubles over, puking. Cavy steps back, offended.

Sjel's face twists in disgust. "Get in the spinner," he barks, but if the man hears him, he's too miserable to do anything more than retch in the street. Sjel's nostrils flare. "You'll be hearing from us," he hisses to Phaera, then turns his poisonous gaze on Ayisha and Cavy. "You all will." He holsters his weapon, then slips into the spinner behind him. Both spinners peel away from the curb.

Oriol steps past Phaera, his weapon recovered from the retching man, training it on Sjel's spinner. Ayisha sweeps Phaera into a hug. "Honey, you're so cold," she murmurs.

"Please get inside, all of you," Oriol says.

But, "Look," Phaera breathes.

Twin lines of cabs are advancing down both ends of the drag, cutting off any exit for Sjel and his men. After a moment's hesitation, the driver of Sjel's spinner swerves sharply and tears across the pedestrian plaza towards a gap between the Lorelei and Herran's.

"I can get it," Matapang says in Oriol's ear.

"Do it," Oriol answers.

A sharp concussion, and the spinner's tire goes flat, the vehicle skidding with a crunch into a bollard. The other spinner had swerved in the opposite direction, but it skids to a halt of its own accord, the driver's side door opening and the driver vomiting out into the street.

Phaera laughs, though from the way she's shaking it's probably more nerves than pleasure. "Jaxon," she says to Ayisha. "He sent them a special delivery for me."

"Stay here, ma'am," Oriol tells her, then turns to

Bakshi. "I've got Sjel. Secure the other spinner. You three," he shouts back at the door. "With me."

Oriol doesn't hesitate to fire when the first of Sjel's soldiers takes aim at him; the man crumples back into the spinner with a bullet between his eyes. Another goes down with a bullet to the thigh from one of Phaera's security team. A third is retching miserably on the ground — but Sjel takes off at a dead run. "Secure them," Oriol shouts back to the guards following him. He sprints after Sjel.

Sjel darts through the nearby doors of Herran's to the sound of shrieks. Oriol follows, just in time to see Sjel jump a low barrier and plow his way through the crowd of gamblers watching a hologram of the cage match happening live several floors below. A massive man in the poison-green suit of a Herran's security guard steps in front of Oriol, a meaty hand on his chest.

Oriol shoves his pistol back into its holster. "Oriol Sina, I work for Phaera D. That man robbed the Lorelei," he shouts, pointing after Sjel. The big security guard straightens and barks a code into the cuff of his suit. He steps out of Oriol's way.

Sjel has pushed his way through the crowd gathered around the holostage. He's almost free when he skids to a halt as another, equally big security guard in a green suit steps up to block his path.

Sjel breaks left onto the holostage just as Oriol

vaults the railing. Oriol leaps for the stage, using the advantage of his prosthetic for extra distance, ignoring the sharp crack of the glass as he lands in front of Sjel. The larger-than-life hologram fighters whirl and kick around him, a crescent kick sizzling through Oriol's head. Followed by a real-life punch from Sjel.

Oriol blocks it, and the next, ducking as Sjel throws a wide right hook with enough force that it sends him off-balance.

Oriol uses Sjel's momentum to catch him by the shoulder, shoving him down hard as he brings his prosthetic knee into Sjel's gut.

Sjel doubles over with a groan, but recovers quickly. He shoves Oriol back hard, just as one of the larger-than-life hologram fighters sends the other crashing to the ground where Sjel stands. Blinding light sparks against Sjel as he whirls on Oriol, blending the true opponent with the false.

Sjel's next punch lands, and the crowd's cheering — at the holograms or at Sjel finally landing a blow, Oriol can't tell.

Oriol tunes them out, ducking Sjel's next punch and coming up beneath his outstretched arm, locking it over his shoulder and landing a punch to Sjel's throat. He pivots on his prosthetic to sweep his good leg behind Sjel. The man goes sprawling to the ground.

Sjel's gasping for air and the crowd's now booing and muttering unhappily — sure, a throat punch is dirty, but Oriol's not fighting for anyone's entertainment. He straddles Sjel, who throws a pair of wild punches Oriol easily blocks. Oriol snatches his karambit from its sheath at his lower back and punches Sjel once in the face with his hand wrapped around the handle. Sjel's head cracks back against the holostage, his right cheek bleeding where the karambit's metal ring around Oriol's index finger split the skin.

Before Sjel can move, Oriol pivots his wrist so the point of the curved blade is a centimeter from Sjel's left eye.

Sjel freezes.

"We done here?" Oriol asks him, and gets a fraction of a nod in return.

He resheaths the karambit, throws Sjel onto his belly, and wrenches his hands behind him. One of Herran's poison-green-suited guards tosses Oriol a pair of cuffs when he holds out his hand.

Sjel coughs up blood; it spatters across the holostage, smearing the images projected above.

The hologram boxing match mercifully finishes and the holograms flicker out to a chorus of cheers from those who won their bets, groans from those who lost.

"What the devil is going on here?" someone growls.

Herran Tarri is looming over the stage, face a mask of fury. Oriol can't tell if the man recognizes him as Phaera's bodyguard from two days ago, but his two bodyguards do. They're appropriately impressed.

"Catching a thief, sir," says the security guard who handed Oriol the cuffs. "This man stole from the Lorelei."

Tarri's face goes red. "And that requires a fistfight? In my bloody casino?"

Oriol drags Sjel to his feet and off the stage, exchanging nods with the bodyguards. "Just cleaning up the neighborhood, sir," he says to Tarri. "Sorry if it was any trouble." He thanks the security guard for his help and frog-marches Sjel through the crowd.

He can hear Tarri sputtering behind him, but no one stops him.

By the time he's returned with Sjel, Bakshi and the rest of Phaera's security team have rounded up Acheta's men and lined them up in temporary cuffs on the curb. Bakshi does a double take at the state Sjel's in and lifts an eyebrow at Oriol. "I can't wait to see that vid hit the feeds tomorrow," she says.

"What vid?" Oriol drops Sjel at the end of the line.

"Of whatever epic fight you two just had in Herran's." She grins at his confusion, then claps him on the shoulder. "It's the drag, Sina. Somebody's always got a camera out." She glances back at the Lorelei. "Get back to her. I'm good here."

When Oriol reaches Phaera, she's at the center of a small knot of other business owners on the drag who have come out to see what's going on — and who are getting an earful from Ayisha for not bothering to come sooner.

Phaera excuses herself from the crowd when she sees him approaching. "The police are on their way," she says softly, crossing her arms instinctively over her ribcage as they walk. The fingers of her right hand cover the bruises already blooming where Sjel had gripped her upper arm. She's shaken, and Bakshi's words about cameras echo in his mind.

He squeezes her shoulder. "People are watching," he murmurs, and she straightens, lifting her chin and sliding her hands down her forearms. She looks a bit less the victim, but not much.

Phaera takes a deep breath. "Thank you," she says. "For everything. But especially for offering to come with me. Jaantzen's surely not paying you for that."

"No, ma'am," Oriol says, and there's a strange feeling behind the thought. He's worked gig jobs his entire life since he was discharged from Alliance special ops. He's taken the money, gone home, and not spared a thought for an employer.

No, Jaantzen's not paying him to follow Phaera into the lion's den like that, and Manu's going to kill him when he finds out he offered. But the thing is, Manu would've made the same decision if it was his own boss's life on the line.

And Oriol would have had Phaera's back tonight even if there wasn't a paycheck in it for him.

Phaera's giving him a look he can't decipher. "I wanted to ask you something, Sina," she says. "When this is all done . . ."

Her voice trails off and he turns to follow her gaze. Another black spinner is heading towards them, and it's not the police.

Oriol recognizes it. "It's fine, it's just the man." He opens a channel to Bakshi, who's raising her weapon defensively across the plaza. "They're friendly," he says, and she lowers her weapon but doesn't put it away.

Jaantzen's come too late to do any good, but why is he here in the first place? Does that mean the business with Acheta is done? Oriol finds a few messages on his comm from Jaantzen asking for a status check and no word from Manu. He's fine, he's fine, he tells himself, but his heart is pounding in his chest.

"We'll talk later," Phaera says, and turns to stride across the plaza to meet Jaantzen.

He's not here for her, though.

Jaantzen's out of the spinner and has Sjel by the throat almost before Starla's stopped the vehicle. Bakshi raises an eyebrow to Oriol like she's wondering if she should intervene. Oriol shakes his head.

"Where's Acheta?" Jaantzen says, deadly quiet. He looks past Sjel's twitching form to Oriol, then Phaera. "Acheta's not here?"

Oriol shakes his head.

"What's going on?" Phaera asks. "Jaantzen, he can't answer you like that. Put him down."

Jaantzen almost does, but Oriol sees the moment his notice lands on the bruises on her arm. Fury kindles in his eyes; his grip tightens.

If Manu were here, he'd step in and stop Jaantzen from doing something to Sjel that'll come back to bite him. Oriol'd rather let him crush Sjel's windpipe and save them all the trouble later, but that's probably not the right move.

"He'll get taken care of, man," he says quietly. "Police are on their way."

Jaantzen's gaze meets his a moment, then he drops Sjel to his knees on the cement with a crack.

"What are you doing here?" Phaera asks him.

"Acheta never showed up to his meeting with

Lordeur. I thought maybe he'd agreed to the meeting to keep me from being here." Jaantzen glares down at Sjel, who's wearing a faint smile even as he gasps for breath. "I see I was partly correct. Phaera, I'm so sorry I wasn't here. Are you all right?"

"If he's not here, then did he . . ." Fear spikes in Oriol's chest. "Is Manu . . . ?"

"Manu's fine," Starla signs to him. "It's done."

Phaera narrows her eyes at him, then at Jaantzen. "And what have you all been scheming tonight?"

"I'll tell you when I know where Acheta is," Jaantzen says. From his fetal position on the ground, Sjel laughs. Jaantzen reaches for him again. "What do you know," he growls.

But Sjel only doubles over as though he's heard the funniest joke imaginable. Jaantzen draws back his arm, but Starla brushes fingers over his shoulder before he can strike.

Her eyes are wide with fear.

She makes Toshiyo's namesign. "He's at the tower," she signs, and Jaantzen lets Sjel slump back to the pavement. "Toshiyo just called for help," she signs to Oriol.

"He's attacking Cobalt Tower," Oriol tells Phaera.

"Go," Phaera says.

26

TOSHIYO

Toshiyo Ravi can see everywhere, go anywhere. She's soaring through the night sky on the wings of the drone she's slaved to Manu's spinner, slipping through layers of grainy government surveillance footage for signs of trouble, snapshots accumulating in her mind as she references them again and again for changes, for anything out of the ordinary.

But there's been nothing out of the ordinary tonight. Not until she gets the alert.

Toshiyo knows how to hack into a security system. She's obscured and erased incriminating footage, she's glitched out cameras so her people could move where they needed to without being detected. She knows systems' weaknesses, and she can skirt them easily.

So, damned right she's got backups built into hers. She's beaten systems with every trick in the book, and used each one of those tricks to shore up the security at Cobalt Tower.

Someone's trying to clone her video feed.

She leaves the feed on Manu running in a corner of her desk and watches the intruder's progress curiously. They're not going for historical data, they're trying to ghost into a real-time feed, trying to use the internal cameras as eyes.

Let them.

Whoever it is will encounter enough resistance to seem real, then get access to the dummy cameras showing a standard feed. It should take some time for them to realize they're not seeing the real thing. And by then, she should have a better idea what they're up to.

If she was trying to cover up a break-in attempt, she'd use access to the feed to begin looping it in disguise. When the intruder doesn't do that, she starts to wonder. They're just watching — well, watching her dummy system. Just getting their eyes on the place.

Maybe they're not trying to sneak in.

Then what are they trying to do?

She scans the rest of the system for anything

suspicious. Have they gotten into the communications with her team? Can they hear what she's saying to them?

No, that still seems solid.

But best to be safe.

"It's dinnertime, folks," she says, and in the comms screen, names blink out of the main channel and reappear in the backup channel. The knot in her chest loosens a touch at each switch. They're all homeward bound, but that can be when the worst happens. Toshiyo never breathes easily until everyone is back at base.

One name is stubbornly stuck in the wrong channel.

"El?" Toshiyo asks on the main channel. "Come in."

She can see Manu's tag, heading out of the danger zone of Coeur's territory and towards the Lorelei. See Jaantzen and Starla and Oriol on the satellite feed in front of the Lorelei. But El's tag hasn't moved for the last few minutes.

"El?"

The name blinks into the new channel.

Can't talk pinned down but fine, comes a message.

"Do you need backup?" Toshiyo asks.

No am fine, just waiting it out.

"I've got my eye on him," Gia says on the new

channel. "A couple of Blackheart's are camped on top of his location. Not hunting, just smoking. We'll be out soon."

"Copy that," Toshiyo says.

She checks the feeds again to see how her intruder is doing. They're still there snooping around in the dummy video channel.

It doesn't matter whether or not they're getting anything good. What matters is why they're poking around in the first place.

She's about to open a direct channel to Jaantzen to explain what's going on when chatter on Cobalt Tower's security channel catches her attention. On a normal day she'd only have it running in the background, with an AI instructed to alert her if anything that needs her attention comes up. Cobalt Tower's security staff have got it covered.

But during operations she keeps the channel open to make sure she doesn't miss anything important happening back home.

"Requesting backup in the lobby," says one of the night security team, her voice high and tense. "There's a spinner approaching, fast."

Toshiyo swipes to the lobby feed just in time to see a spinner crashing through the front entrance in a glittering hail of glass. It skids to a stop on the tile of the lobby, and the doors open with a hail of gunfire.

A spray of bullets — the security guard behind the receptionist's desk manages to take out one of the assailants before crumpling to the floor herself — and the backup she called for is holding the rest of the fighters in the spinner for the moment. One of the backup team goes down; the other two are getting pushed back.

"The tower's under attack," Toshiyo says over the new ops channel. "Spinner breached the front door, there's fighting in the lobby. At least two of ours down." She pushes the lobby's video feed through the channel. Over the tower's security channel, she can hear the chatter of the security team mobilizing throughout the building.

LOCK DOWN THE BUILDING, Starla messages. ON OUR WAY.

Toshiyo types in the codes to shut down the lift, lock out the doors to anyone without security clearance. But two figures in full battle armor have fought their way out of the spinner, one crouches over the first security guard's body and wrenches up her arm to open the biolock door behind her even as Toshiyo frantically works to block her from the system.

The door slips open a fraction of a second before Toshiyo deletes the clearance.

"Breach in the south stairwell, two climbing," Toshiyo says through the ops channel, adding in the tower's security channel for the moment. She doesn't normally do much with them — when she does break in to let them know things like this, they probably assume she's some sort of AI, except for the few who've been to the fourth floor and met her in person.

They've breached the stairwell, and it's probably Acheta or his team, they're probably here for the case. There's not a way they'd know how to find it, though. The only people who know about it are Jaantzen's core crew.

But the thought nags her. There's no way she'd send in her people to snatch something if it meant searching an entire sixty-plus-story tower for it. That would be suicide.

Which means these guys are stupid, they're a distraction, or they know exactly what they're looking for and where.

If it's the latter, Toshiyo can worry about how they found out later.

She expects them to continue up — all the way to the penthouse, maybe, or at least to the twelfth floor to the medbays.

She's reinforcing the security measures on those floors when she looks up to see that they've stopped in front of a door.

They're fast, she thinks, or they've stopped before the twelfth floor. They swipe the security guard's stolen pass over the door and it doesn't work; Toshiyo's shut her out of the system. But they've come with a plan B: a quick line of adhesive explosive on the edges of the door.

The explosion flares on Toshiyo's screen, and she feels the concussion of it in her chest, screaming in her ears.

Oh, *shit.*

Smoke pours through the open door of her office, and through the ringing in her ears she can hear the ping of cooling metal, the thud of boots on the stairwell, the wrenching shriek of the door being pulled out of the way.

"They're on the fourth floor," she says to both channels, as calmly as she can. "Going dark."

She slides her hand under her desk and taps the code into the kill switch. Her desk turns off, and light vanishes from the room.

Darkness falls with the weight of a cave-in.

Toshiyo clamps both hands over her mouth and breathes as deep as she can through her nostrils, fighting the crushing waves of panic she knows are coming.

Pitch darkness is strange.

It's claustrophobic, shrinking down the entire world to the amount that fits into your awareness, a palm-sized space where your breath leaves your body, your organs thrum in your chest cavity, you feel the tiny, disconnected sensations where parts of your body press against unknown objects. But it's also expansive, your potential environment no longer confined by the physical walls that once hemmed you in. Pitch darkness is what your imagination makes it.

In pitch darkness, you can imagine yourself in a coffin or in a cavern the size of a planet, and until someone turns the lights back on, whatever you imagine is the truth.

And for Toshiyo, every time, she can only imagine herself in a single place: the mines of her youth, freezing and terrified and hunted and hurting.

Toshiyo never lets her world go black.

But she remembers how it works, and fights to calm her breathing. Remembers that she can pick the coffin or the cavern, no matter who's stalking her through the black.

Toshiyo knows her warren of half-finished projects and machinery and tools like the back of her hand, and so that's the world she chooses to imagine.

Home.

It crystallizes in her mind.

She's finally breathing normally again; she slips from her chair and into a crouch, staying close to the floor. She hears the telltale click of someone trying to turn the lights back on, but the switch at the door won't work.

Only Toshiyo can turn this room back on.

She has that control, at least.

Her mind is racing. She just needs to get herself safe, get the creature safe, and wait for Manu and the others to get back — they're close.

But the ones who are hunting her are closer.

She creeps towards the wall farthest from the entrance. There's a secret door there, hidden behind an antique conveyor arm. It will allow her to climb the cleaning-bot shafts up to the twelfth floor. She's never done it before, but she's thought about it. Peered up and down the shaft and wondered if it would ever come in handy — cataloguing hiding spaces yet another habit left over from her early days in the mines.

These two either have some inside intel about where the cases would be stored, or they know Jaantzen's organization well enough to assume Toshiyo would have them in her office. She's guessing the latter — otherwise, they would have headed straight to the twelfth floor. She can get to the creature and secure it while these two are ransacking her office, and they'll never know where to find her.

She slips beneath a swag of conveyor chain she's been meaning to move, careful not to let her back brush the chains and set them to making noise.

Not that it matters much if she makes noise. The armored figures aren't talking, but they're crashing their way through her office without regard to finding a clear path, jagged shafts of light piercing painfully through the dark. Something crashes to the floor with the sound of shattering glass — probably just one of those nav panels — and Toshiyo fights down panic once more. It will be fine. She'll get out of here, and things will be fine.

Things go silent a minute, and she turns carefully to find out why. The flashlights have stopped on her desk, they're playing slowly over its surface for clues.

She's not breathing as an armored figure pushes a pathway through to stand in the heart of her space. They turn slowly, and then light falls on the silver case lying on the workbench nearby.

She never bothered closing it, so the lid's sitting on askew. The figure gingerly lifts it off, curses when it's empty.

Toshiyo breathes sharply in frustration. She thought she'd have another few minutes before they found it, another few minutes of them trapped in here while she figured out what to do. While Manu and the rest got closer and closer.

She has to get to the creature.

She slips back, towards that far wall and the cleaning-bot shaft, keeping her low crouch to stay out of the light playing over her office. Her hands brush against a stack of two-meter-long stabilizing film rolls and she catches one just before it falls, cursing herself for leaving them so precarious. Past a circuitry printer and she's home free.

But as she turns away from the film rolls she hears the whole mess of them begin to tip, unearthly thuds and clatter as they bounce against tables, hit the ground, and roll.

Toshiyo doesn't bother staying quiet anymore. She scrambles away, toppling over a stack of crates behind her, and through the pounding in her ears she hears the scrabbling of soles on the drifts of small electronics, the heavy crash as an armored figure catches itself against a table.

Toshiyo darts left where she knows there's a zigzagging path between a pair of old industrial rehydrators and she should be able to lose her assailant.

She ducks, grazing her own shoulder heavily against one of the rehydrators and biting back a cry of pain. She pulls a spare beetle drone from her pocket and sends it spinning noisily along the path she had been following, then pulls herself up on the rehydrator, slicing her hand as she climbs. She eases back on her perch, palm slick with blood, and tries to make herself as small as possible. Tries to breathe as little as possible.

"Hiding again? You know I always find you."

Her panic spikes, but that voice is long dead — she hopes — or at least long forgotten. That voice is lost in the mines, like she would be now if Jaantzen hadn't paid off her indenture and brought her to work for him. She forces her panic back down — no one has actually spoken, least of all *him* — and forces her breathing to steady.

"Toshiyo, come in," Jaantzen says in her ear, and it sounds like he's shouting. She thinks she hears the armored figure pause, as though it heard it, too, but that can't be true. Still, Toshiyo turns the volume down. Jaantzen calls for her again, but it's just a whisper. And she can't respond without giving away her location with the sound of her voice or the flash of her comm.

The figure walks past, guided by the sounds of the beetle drone Toshiyo had set off to cover the sounds of her climbing. One step, two, and they stop.

A grip like a vise comes down on Toshiyo's ankle, and Toshiyo scrambles for purchase with her blood-slick palm as the figure pulls her down off the rehydrator. The figure catches her before she hits the ground, then wrenches her hands behind her to send her screaming to her knees.

Pain shoots through her arms and wrists, unending fire, and for a moment past and present merge and she's back in the ice-cold and pitch-black mines, sleeping among the equipment because none of them want to expend the energy to head back up to the surface in the limited amount of time they have to rest, the lights out because even though staying the night is common practice the bosses won't pay for electricity after hours. Not that nights are restful, with all their dangers, the human ones that the bosses never take seriously — she remembers pain in her arms and wrists, being held in the dark, that voice in her ear, *"Just be quiet or I'll tell the foreman it was you that broke the conveyor."*

When she doesn't think she can take it anymore, the pain stops, but the feeling of iron grips on her wrists in the dark, her back crashing against a table, the arm around her waist, and she bites down like she wishes she could have back then, but her teeth make no difference. It's armor.

And someone grabs her throat — she's staring into the helmeted face of a woman, not *him*. Toshiyo fights away the panic.

The woman marches her back to her own desk, where the other armored figure is still searching, throwing things to the ground. They're about to drop the silver case, but Toshiyo screams for them to stop.

"It's explosive," she says. "The case. Oh my god, you almost killed us all."

The figure growls at her, but then sets the case carefully back on her desk.

"Where is the serum?" he asks, turning to her with a growl.

Acheta.

"I don't know what you're talking about," Toshiyo says, and the blow from his fist knocks her head back against the woman's armored chest.

"Tell me where it is."

He cocks back his arm for another blow — *"You like that, don't you?"* Did he say that or was that yet another ghost? But the armored woman holds up a hand. The woman turns Toshiyo so she can see her face, touches a button, and the helmet folds back into the collar of her suit.

"You'll tell us," she says in an Arquellian accent — Found her, Toshiyo thinks. "Because your people are on their way, and if you don't tell us where the serum is, we'll kill them all."

Toshiyo can't fight them, but she can tell Manu and the others where she is. She switches her transmit back on.

"I'll take you to the serum," she says. "Just let go of me."

For a moment she doesn't hear any response,

and she's afraid her emergency switch didn't work. Then:

"We're coming for you, kid," Manu whispers in her ear. "Do whatever they ask."

Toshiyo forces herself to breathe. Because things are still bad, but Acheta and the Arquellian woman need her.

At least for now.

And the others are on their way.

27

TOSHIYO

They've made Toshiyo carry the silver case — it's so light without the glass sphere of liquid and new life inside. They've got weapons trained on her, and she knows that running won't do anything. She saw photos of the crater that was left when Jaantzen shot the other case and destroyed Zacharia. This one has the same deadly combination of chemicals running through its shell.

If they shoot it — if Toshiyo drops it — she's a goner.

And not just her.

Her heart drops as she hears footsteps charging down the stairwell above them, and she takes a breath to shout. The Arquellian woman's hand clamps over her mouth, cutting off her warning.

"We have a hostage," Acheta roars, and the footsteps still. "Come around the corner with your hands up or she dies." Toshiyo's earpiece is only giving her the ops channel, not the Cobalt Tower security channel, so she can't hear any chatter of the guards there. But that must be who is approaching them.

Her suspicions are confirmed when a pair of guards in Cobalt Tower uniforms walk cautiously around the corner, hands raised.

The taller one raises his voice. "Whoever you are — "

A sharp report echoes through the stairwell and he stumbles back against the wall, blood dripping down between his eyes. The Arquellian woman shoots the second as quickly as she did the first; Toshiyo can only watch in horror as they both crumple to the ground.

The Arquellian woman releases Toshiyo and takes the silver case out of her hand. "Get one of their radios," she says, but Toshiyo can't make herself walk towards the guards' open-eyed stares. The woman grabs her arm and drags her up the stairwell. "The radio," she says again.

Toshiyo kneels beside the taller guard's body — she didn't recognize his face, but she knew his voice instantly, the other guards on the channel called him CJ, he was always cracking jokes. She reaches trembling fingers to close his eyes, then slips his earpiece off. It's sticky with his blood.

"Tell Jaantzen that if they set foot inside this building, we'll shoot the case and blow this whole thing up." The gleam in the Arquellian woman's eye says she's serious.

Acheta's brows draw together. "Once we're far away and have the serum," he says. The woman doesn't answer.

"It's going to be okay, Tosh," Manu murmurs in her ear. "We heard her, but make the call."

So she doesn't suspect. Toshiyo taps CJ's gauntlet to open a channel to the whole building — Manu and the rest who are on the ops channel tonight would have heard her, but there are other guards throughout the building who might come charging around the corner and lose their lives like the two who are lying next to Toshiyo this very moment.

She closes her eyes to shut them out, then holds CJ's earpiece up to her left ear. She doesn't want to risk feedback revealing she has a piece hidden in her right ear already.

"This is Toshiyo Ravi." She tries to keep her voice steady. "Everybody stay out of the stairwells, vacate the twelfth floor. No one comes into the building, they've accessed the primary feeds." Please god, Starla, remember what that means. Know that it means they can only see the dummy cameras. Know that you can come in. Toshiyo clears her throat. "They have a bomb and they'll set it off and kill us all if anyone approaches."

The Arquellian woman snatches the earpiece away and hands the silver case back to Toshiyo. She's blinking at something on her lens. "The twelfth floor is medical suites?" she asks. How did she get such detailed knowledge of Cobalt Tower?

But Toshiyo nods, because there's no reason to deny it. She only knows that she has to keep herself alive.

The Arquellian woman drops the earpiece back on CJ's lifeless chest, then prods Toshiyo up the stairs.

"What were you doing with the serum?" Acheta asks. "Trying to duplicate it?"

"You already tried that, it didn't work," says Toshiyo.

"We're almost there," Manu murmurs in her ear. "Starla says you have a dummy camera feed, that's probably what they're watching?"

She could cry with relief. "Yes," she says. She looks back at Acheta. "We were trying to duplicate it."

Acheta curls his lip at her. "You think you're so smart, maybe you can come back with us and help."

Toshiyo catches her breath, but keeps climbing. Manu is almost here.

She keys them into the twelfth floor, and feels a rush of relief that the guards who had been in front of Coeur's door are gone. Acheta and the Arquellian woman glance in Medbay 1 as they walk past, but don't comment. It's still in a state of disarray, having been recently evacuated by Coeur. But it's empty.

Or so she thought.

"Tosh? Hey, when — "

The Arquellian woman whirls and shoots, and to Toshiyo's horror, Elian slides down the wall, clutching at his belly, his gaze blank. Toshiyo screams, but the Arquellian woman yanks her arm so hard that she nearly loses her grip on the case. She stumbles after her; there's nothing she can do for Elian now.

Medbay 2 is dark — Toshiyo has been turning off the lights at night under the assumption that if the creature sleeps, it probably doesn't want to do so in the light. Just the faint glow of monitors, and the ever-present eerie fluorescent pink trails the creature's wings leave through the liquid it's suspended in.

"It's in here," Toshiyo says, then suddenly realizes what this will look like — a trap, a practical joke, a setup. "Wait, you need to know something — "

Acheta hits the light.

The creature whirls — it's been adrift, asleep or resting or dreaming murderous dreams — then rushes the front of the aquarium with teeth bared. Acheta screams.

Toshiyo sets the silver case carefully on a nearby table, but neither Acheta nor the Arquellian woman seem to notice. They're mesmerized by what's in the tank. It's just long enough for her to grab a pair of marble-shaped scanners off a tray. They slip up her sleeve, hovering, waiting, warming to her skin.

The woman turns on her first.

"What is this," she asks.

"Some kind of joke," Acheta snarls. He thrusts his pistol into Toshiyo's chin, digging into her throat; the table behind her cuts into her injured palm. "What kind of sick joke do you think you're playing on me?"

"It's not a joke," Toshiyo says, choking. "I swear, I swear. This is what was in the case."

But his eyes say he can't be reasoned with. She saw him scared — she made him scared — and he'll kill that weakness before he'll let her laugh at him. She's seen that look before, too many times.

"Acheta," the Arquellian woman snaps, and Acheta manages to pull himself free of his rage just before he pulls the trigger. It's anger at being interrupted that does it, but Toshiyo will take what she can get.

"Acheta," the woman says again. "She's telling the truth."

She doesn't seem to believe herself, but the Arquellian woman is staring at the second globe, the one that fits so perfectly in the silver case. And the fist-sized bean inside, which is now growing unmistakably into an egg.

Acheta stares at the egg a moment, then turns back to Toshiyo. She can see deep in his eyes that her original affront to him won't be forgiven.

"We found it," he says. "Goodbye." And the pistol digs in even deeper as he reaches for the trigger.

A shot rings out, and in the flash of white blindness of fear and adrenaline and clarity it takes Toshiyo a moment to realize that she's still standing.

That Acheta is on the floor at her feet.

Distantly, someone who sounds like Manu is shouting for her to talk to him, but her ears are ringing and she can't comprehend why she's still here.

Beside the creature, the Arquellian woman turns and shoves her pistol back into its holster, and Toshiyo's terror-soaked brain finally realizes what just happened.

"You shot him," she murmurs.

The distant shouting in her ear silences with a curse.

"Shot who, Tosh," Manu asks.

"Acheta," Toshiyo says, before remembering she can't just answer him. "You shot Acheta."

"I was done with him," says the woman. "But I am not done with you." She waves a hand at the creature, who's flapping through the aquarium with ferocious, angry sweeps of its wings. "Tell me what this is."

"How many are left, Tosh," Manu says.

Right. Pull yourself together.

"I thought the two of you were working together?" she says. "And then you shot him."

"We're almost there, kid."

Toshiyo has to fight not to answer him, and for a terrifying moment she wonders if the woman can tell he's in her ear. The way the woman is watching her, she could know anything.

"You work for the Alliance," Toshiyo says. "Don't you."

"Explain to me what's going on here," the woman says again, and Toshiyo takes a step backwards, realizing she's tracking Acheta's blood on her shoe.

Not just on her shoe — she's been caught in the spray, Acheta's blood is spattered in a fine mist down her arm and torso, speckling the back of her right hand, vivid on pale skin. It must be on her face, she realizes with a start, and her unblemished left hand flies to her right cheek, sweeping down her neck and coming away smeared with blood.

She gapes at it, not sure how to get it clean.

"Hey," says the woman, then again, more loudly. "You never seen a dead man before?"

Toshiyo blinks at her.

"Acheta may be dead, but you're not in the clear, sister," the woman says. "He didn't have the imagination to cause the kind of pain you'll feel if you don't cooperate with me. You and everyone you love. Now what. Is. This."

For the first time since she blew through the door to Toshiyo's office, the woman seems not to know what's going on. Toshiyo's been wondering this whole time if she and Acheta had backup beyond the crew in the spinner who helped them break in. But if it was Acheta's crew, the Arquellian woman is probably cut off now. And if someone besides her were actually checking the feeds, they'd have realized by now they were only seeing dummy cameras.

It gives her a glimmer of hope. This woman hacked into Toshiyo's system to get in and get around, and to have advanced warning if anyone else came in. But now she's far too preoccupied to realize her mistake.

The creature is charging the glass, gnashing its teeth at the Arquellian woman, but when Toshiyo approaches its tank, it swims to her side and gives her a sidelong look, like *Why did you let this horrible woman in here?*

"It'll be all right," Toshiyo signs to it. It whirls in a tight circle on her end of the tank, snapping its teeth daintily at the Arquellian woman.

"Where did this come from?" she asks.

Toshiyo frowns. "What do you mean where did this come from? You work for the Alliance, right?"

"Who I work for is none of your business," the woman snaps. But her Arquellian drawl is clear, and she definitely doesn't work for Acheta. "Answer the question."

"Tell her what she wants to know," Manu says. "We don't have any secrets worth more than you." He sounds like he's running, breath coming fast and ragged.

At least she hopes he's running, because she's heard his breath that tattered before, when he was injured. She desperately wants to ask, to check the feed from his tactical vest. Without her ops desk overseeing them all she feels like a sense has been cut off, a numbness like reaching out to touch a wall and feeling nothing, putting a spoonful of food in her mouth and tasting nothing, smelling nothing.

"It came from Blackheart," she says. "She stole it from the Alliance on Indira."

"And what is it?"

Toshiyo sighs. "We're still trying to figure that out," she says. "You see that bean? Well, an egg, but we thought it was a bean when it was littler. That's what we found in the globe of liquid that everyone seems to think is a special serum. It's not, though, it's just some sort of fertilizer."

The woman turns to her, frowning. "And this?" She points at the creature.

Toshiyo shrugs, smooths fingers down the case in a way that's meant to be soothing to the poor little guy. "He was in the other globe, fully formed. Smaller, though, when we first found him. Obviously. We're guessing that when the egg hatches, we're gonna get another one of these guys."

She watches confusion run over the woman's face. "The Alliance didn't tell you what you were going after?"

Instead, the woman just points Toshiyo at the tank. "Get that thing packed up," she says. "We need to get going."

The woman picks up the glass sphere with the

incubating egg and nestles it carefully in the silver case, then closes the lid. Toshiyo worries to see the little thing surrounded by darkness and potential explosives once more.

But Toshiyo can see the woman calculating. Her mission is to bring the creature back, but she can't carry out this entire apparatus.

"We're almost in," Toshiyo hears Manu say, and if she can just hold on, just make herself useful a few minutes longer, then the woman won't kill her before he gets to her.

"Can you sedate it?" the woman asks.

Yes, the tank is set up so she can corral the creature back into the connector tube, in case they need to take any more genetic samples or sedate it, but Toshiyo doesn't want to tell her captor that. Only, as she tries to think of a way to explain it, the woman can apparently see in her face that she's about to lie.

"I don't know how we can . . ."

The look the woman gives her chills her to the bone. "If you lie to me again, I will kill you and everyone you love," she says quietly.

The woman looks past Toshiyo and sees the mesh for corralling the creature, pulls the lever. As the mesh sweeps towards it — faster than the woman perhaps intended — the creature gnashes its teeth in fury. It's not moving out of the way in time.

The mesh snags against the tip of its wing, and Toshiyo jumps forward to pull the lever back.

"You're hurting it," she says.

The creature tugs at its wing to free it; faint milky-blue threads seep from the small tear in the membrane.

"I'm sorry," Toshiyo signs.

The Arquellian woman reaches for the lever again, and Toshiyo flings the two marbles out of her sleeve — the tiny drone scanners unfurl their wings midflight and begin their whirlwind holding pattern, right around the Arquellian woman.

The woman curses and bats at the drones. They won't do a thing to hurt her, but it might take her a minute to realize that. And Toshiyo dashes for freedom again.

She hears the whine of a warming pistol, ducks, hears the sound of shattering glass, the rush of water, and an unearthly shriek that chills her to her core.

The creature surges from the tank with a rush of liquid and shattered glass, leathery wings slapping wetly, screeching once more in fury or fear. It turns its gaze on Toshiyo, fangs bared and glinting, then launches itself at her, crashing into her chest and knocking her back. She catches herself on her forearms in the slurry of broken glass and liquid. It's perched on her chest, lighter than she expected, but its talons are deadly sharp, digging into her collarbones like needles.

She can hear distant shouting, familiar voices, but all she sees is the creature's malevolent eyes. It bares its fangs. It lunges.

28

JAANTZEN

On the feeds he can see that Cobalt Tower's facade is shattered, a spinner in the middle of the lobby, the bodies of his security guards crumpled on the floor. One woman is slumped against the reception desk, shotgun slipped from her limp hands.

Later. He'll think about all this later.

He can hear Toshiyo in his ear. Her voice has been a familiar companion for almost two decades, giving direction and reassurance, answering questions, initiating backup plans, warning him what's around corners.

She's still telling him what's happening. But she's doing it indirectly, and at gunpoint, and cool fury blooms in his chest. Acheta will die for bringing Toshiyo Ravi into this.

Toshiyo has disabled the lifts, but they can still take the stairways, the back ways that aren't accessible from the lobby but instead from the underground garage, where Starla pulled in just after Manu.

Starla charges up the stairs at the far end and Manu motions for Oriol to stay behind with Jaantzen as he races after her.

Jaantzen's fit, but not twelve-flights-sprinting fit. And his right knee is letting him know he should be thinking about surgery sooner rather than later.

Oriol leads the way up the near-end stairs, gun in his hand, and Jaantzen ignores the grating pain in his knee as he climbs, letting Toshiyo's voice lead him. "Wait, you need to know something — " she says, and in the background Jaantzen hears Acheta and the Alliance operative both reacting to seeing the creature for the first time.

"It's not a joke, I swear," Toshiyo is saying, her voice coming strangled, and Jaantzen starts taking the steps two at at time.

"We'll take the far side, boss," Manu says.

And then Jaantzen hears something that makes his heart stop, Acheta's voice as close as if he were standing beside him:

"Goodbye."

And the gunshot.

Jaantzen flinches, a hand to his ear, and Oriol looks up, towards the physical location of the noise.

"Tosh," Manu is saying. "Tosh, talk to me."

Jaantzen stops with his hand on the door to the twelfth floor, white noise buzzing in his ears. They're too late. He's failed Toshiyo.

And like a ghost she murmurs, "You shot him."

Jaantzen remembers to breathe again as Manu quietly questions her. Toshiyo is still alive.

Oriol is watching him. "Acheta's down," Jaantzen signs. "Just the Alliance woman left."

Oriol nods.

"We have visual," Manu says. "Approaching. There's a body down your end." His voice is dispassionate, and Jaantzen slips back into it, too. They have one chance tonight, they need to play it well.

The hallway is white and antiseptic as always, but for the body slumped against the wall near Medbay 1, a slick of blood spreading across the floor. Elian.

The boy's eyelids flutter at their approach and Oriol kneels beside him, hands pressing tight to the gut wound. Oriol glances up at Jaantzen, and he can see it: Elian isn't long for this world if they can't get him medical care. Jaantzen nods and Oriol disappears into the open medbay door, Jaantzen can hear him rummaging quietly through the cabinets for something to field-dress the wound.

There's nothing Jaantzen can do to help either of them, so he steps past Elian's prone form, inching towards Medbay 2. Now he can hear Toshiyo talking to the Alliance operative, and he cuts out her open channel. He'll still be able to hear Manu and get messages from Starla, but the disorienting feeling of hearing Toshiyo speaking so close in his ear while also down the hall vanishes.

Manu and Starla are approaching from the far end of the hallway, and Jaantzen can hear Toshiyo arguing with the other woman, a sudden whir and flurry of curses, then another gunshot, the shattering of glass as he reaches the doorway. Only part of Jaantzen's mind registers that the tank is in shards, water sloshing out over Toshiyo in a flood of broken glass and madly flailing wings; his main attention is on the woman in the middle of the room.

But she's not shooting anymore — her attention is on the creature.

"Move and you're dead," Jaantzen says, his pistol at her temple. The woman stiffens, turns her head just slightly so she can meet his gaze. Manu edges past her to help Toshiyo, but the creature swipes its claws like a desert cat defending its kill, slashing down his shoulder. Manu bites out a curse and levels his gun at it.

"No, Manu," Toshiyo whispers. She's fallen to the floor, propped up on her elbows, the liquid around her arms slowly turning pink as her blood seeps into it, glass catching the light like shattered rose salt. She doesn't take her gaze off the creature.

Which bares its fangs at Manu, wings spread and chest bared, and suddenly it doesn't seem so much like a predator defending a kill, but a parent defending its nest, shielding Toshiyo with its wings.

Manu lowers his gun and it clambers down Toshiyo's belly, gently, flesh-tearing talons held back until it's on the floor. It does a hopping shuffle as it turns to face the Alliance operative, flicking glass with what little remains of its tail.

The Alliance agent turns slowly towards Jaantzen, handgun still at the ready. She can't make it out and she can't take them down, and Jaantzen sees the moment that she decides that if she goes, they all go. She whirls to shoot the silver case.

She's fast, but he's muscle.

He blocks her shot, the bullet tearing into a wall as her gun hand meets solid forearms, her handgun flying into the slurry of water.

Starla charges her, but she's poorly matched, the woman is Alliance-trained and faster even than Oriol. Jaantzen's yelling for Starla to stay back when a leathery wind sweeps past his face in a rush of rasping, astringent air.

The creature lands with a screech on the woman's shoulders, tearing into her with its claws, throwing her to the ground and slashing at her face with talon-tipped wings.

"Stop!" yells Toshiyo, pulling it off as it dives for the woman's neck with open jaws and razored teeth.

It whirls on her with a hiss, then seems to realize who she is; it stops itself just before burying its claws in her belly, flinches back, a confusion passing over its face.

Jaantzen trains his gun on the creature in case it goes for Toshiyo again, and he feels as much as hears the stun pulse. Starla's taken advantage of the Alliance operative's distraction to hit her in the neck with an electric barb, and the woman goes limp on the floor, her face a ruined mess of blood. With a casual move, Starla flips the woman onto her stomach and binds her hands behind her.

"Don't kill her," Toshiyo says and signs, and Jaantzen's about to answer that of course they won't, he's not in the market for a one-way ticket to Redrock, but he realizes that Toshiyo's addressing the creature. It's swaying as it watches her, like a cobra about to strike.

"Toshiyo. Get back," Jaantzen says.

"I think it's all right."

"C'mon, Tosh," Manu says. "Get away from it."

At his voice, the creature spins and bares its fangs, hissing once more.

"That's Manu," Toshiyo says quickly, signing as she speaks. "He's a friend. Everyone here is a friend. Well, I mean, not her." She points at the Alliance agent. "But you can't kill her."

The creature swivels its head. Toshiyo makes Manu's namesign. "He's a friend," she signs and says. She makes the sign for *friend* again, pointing at herself first, then Manu, then Jaantzen, then Starla. "Friend," she says each time she signs it. She points at the Alliance woman's prone and bloody form, then makes a face. "Enemy," she says and signs to the creature.

"Can it understand you?" Jaantzen asks.

Toshiyo shakes her head slowly. "I, ah . . . I have no idea. But it's not killing us currently."

"It likes you," Manu says, and the creature hisses at him.

Toshiyo grimaces. "Maybe don't talk until it doesn't hate you."

Manu just lifts an eyebrow at her: *Whatever you say, kid.* He looks at Jaantzen. "Where's Oriol?" he signs.

"With Elian," Jaantzen signs back.

Toshiyo's face pales. "Is he . . ."

"He was alive last time I saw him."

Her breath catches.

"Secure the tower," Jaantzen signs to Starla, who's already typing into her gauntlet, presumably securing the tower.

She nods at him and sends the message. "I'll be downstairs," she signs, taking off at a jog.

The Alliance woman is bleeding, but doesn't seem to be in physical danger, which means their most urgent problem is the winged alien creature. Which is downright terrifying, but doesn't seem to be a problem so long as you don't try to injure Toshiyo. Jaantzen can appreciate that mission.

The creature takes a little hopping step towards Toshiyo and tilts its head, darting out a tentative black tongue to taste the blood on her wrist. Toshiyo flinches away with a little gasp of surprise. She opens her hand to it; it licks blood off her palm.

"Tosh," Manu murmurs. He reaches out to touch her arm, slow, nonthreatening. Toshiyo takes a step towards him. The creature cocks its head to glare at Manu.

Jaantzen's finger tightens on the trigger.

"We'll find you something to eat," Toshiyo says and signs. The creature sways, watching her. She mimes eating with bloody hands, pats her belly, and licks her lips.

If the creature understands her, Jaantzen can't tell.

"Let's go," says Jaantzen.

He drags the Alliance woman out the door, then covers Manu and Toshiyo as they slowly back out of the medbay and into the antechamber, where Acheta's body is already splayed on the ground. The creature takes a few hopping steps towards them, but it looks no angrier than usual when he shuts the door between them and throws the bolt.

"Holy shit," breathes Manu, shoving his pistol back home. Toshiyo spins and wraps her arms around him, burying her face in his shoulder. She's shaking uncontrollably as Manu strokes her hair, pressing his cheek to the top of her head. Rivulets of blood run out of the cuff of his sleeve and down the back of his right hand. He looks up, meeting Jaantzen's gaze with an expression that says things have only gotten worse.

Because the creature is loose now, and hungry. And they've taken an Alliance operative captive, which is certain to rain retribution down on their heads.

But at least Acheta is dead, and Toshiyo is alive.

Tonight he'll take small mercies.

"Oh my god," Gia says from the doorway. "I leave you alone for a fucking minute and you're all covered in blood." She slings her rifle over her shoulder and glances over Toshiyo and Manu, dispassionately professional, then starts to kneel beside the Alliance operative.

"Elian first," Jaantzen says. "Oriol's with him in the other medbay. Once Elian is stable, we can worry about the woman who shot him."

Gia bites out a curse and runs back out the door.

Jaantzen digs through the cabinets for wound sealant, then slowly kneels beside the unconscious Alliance woman, ignoring the protests from his bad knee. Even if Elian is the priority, it won't do to let her die. A row of slashes from the creature's talons have laid open the left half of her face, but her pulse is strong, and though her face is a slick of blood, most of the wounds seem to be shallow — except the gouge through her left eye.

He shudders, then sprays sealant over the lacerations and hoists himself back to his feet. That's going to be a mess to stitch up. He's glad it's not his job.

He catches Manu's eye; Manu nods and kisses the top of Toshiyo's head. "Let's get you cleaned up, kid," Manu says, gently loosening her grip on him and helping her over to the sink.

"Your arm is worse," Toshiyo says.

Manu shrugs. "Could be."

She lets him run water over her forearms — blood streams from a web of cuts of varying depths, tiny shards of glass still glinting in her skin.

El is checking in on the ops channel, down in

the lobby with Starla assessing the situation and triaging the wounded. Sounds like an ambulance is already on its way, but Starla and the tower's security team know what to do in that case, too. Jaantzen messages Starla to contact him directly if she needs him, then shuts off the ops channel.

"Manu, what do you need?" Jaantzen asks.

Manu rotates Toshiyo's wrist, plucking out a shining splinter with a pair of tweezers and dropping it in a tray beside the sink.

"Oh, I'm good," he says. "I'll wait for Gia." He plucks out another sliver.

Toshiyo yelps. "Ow. We should get some food sent up for our little buddy," she says. Her eyes are red-rimmed and face pale. "I told it we would."

"You don't know if it understood you."

"Sure. But if it did, we probably shouldn't start by breaking promises."

"Agreed. Any idea what it eats?"

Toshiyo laughs nervously, glancing down at her wrists. "Raw meat?"

Jaantzen sighs. "I'll have a variety of things sent up," he says. "Toshiyo."

She looks up at him, and her worried expression smooths into something that could be compassion, though he's not sure why.

"I'm so sorry," Jaantzen says. "If anything had happened to you — "

"I know." Toshiyo gives him a warm smile. "Can you ask the kitchen to send me up a sandwich? I'm starving."

"Of course."

"Make that two," Manu says. A faint clink as he drops another shard of glass into the tray.

He'll make it a dozen; they're probably all starving after this.

But first.

He hoists the Alliance woman to her feet and drags her out into the hallway. A pair of Starla's soldiers are at the far end of the hall, they come jogging over to help him. "Take her to a cell," he says.

Jaantzen makes the call to the kitchen, then goes to Medbay 1 to see how Elian is doing. Gia has the bullet out and is stitching him back up, with Oriol assisting.

"How is he?" Jaantzen asks.

"He'll live, thanks to Oriol," Gia says.

"I come in handy sometimes," Oriol says. "Did we win?"

Acheta is dead, but Coeur is standing in his place. Everyone he sent out tonight is safe, but those he left home are battered and bleeding, and at least five are dead. Toshiyo survived, but so did the Alliance agent — and whatever happens next with her will require a deft hand or they'll all end up dead or at the heart of an international scandal.

And the creature which was once content to glare at them from its tank is now roaming free in his medbay. And apparently it's starving.

Did they win?

"Maybe." Jaantzen slips off his suit jacket and rolls up his sleeves, then heads to the sink to wash his hands. "I can help Gia," he says to Oriol. "Go see your man, he could use some fussing over."

"Press here," Gia says as soon as he's in place, and Jaantzen holds a wad of gauze down where she points.

"I'm sorry I put your boy in danger," he says.

Gia's nostrils flare, but she continues stitching up her medic's abdomen. His skin is bloodless, pale and bruised. "I put him in danger recommending him to you."

"I didn't tell you why I needed him."

"It doesn't matter. Tevi was right, being involved with you at all is a risk." She looks up a moment, her gaze softening. "I'm not pissed at you," she says, her voice kinder. "You didn't go looking for any of this."

"Didn't I?" Jaantzen says. "You can tell yourself I'm doing the right thing in a world of people who aren't, but don't lie to yourself and pretend I got where I am clean, Giaconda. Tevi's the one saving the world. Not me."

Gia meets his gaze for a long moment, then goes back to her work in silence.

"Scissors," she says after a moment, and Jaantzen hands them over, takes them back when she's finished cutting the suture thread.

"Food is being sent to the meeting room down the hall," he tells Gia when they're done and she's scrubbing off Elian's blood in the sink. "Can you let the others know?"

She tilts her head, watching him. "You joining us?"

"I have work to do."

29

JAANTZEN

In the morning, the news feeds are still carrying Phaera D's emotional interviews, alongside reports of another tragic drive-by attack on a local business, this one in the heart of downtown.

Sweeping footage of the shattered facade of the Lorelei is interspersed with shots of the destruction in Cobalt Tower's lobby, where a local crew apparently drove a spinner through the front doors, shot up the place, then escaped on foot. That's all the detectives will say — and Lo é Njeri, Manu's secretary, who is apparently now being called Cobalt Tower's Chief Operations Director, has been carefully thanking the Bulari Police Department for their swift response while urging them to do more to make this city safe again for business and tourism.

A less reported story is that three of Dry Creek's highest-ranking members have been found dismembered in a Jet Park warehouse. Coeur's been busy.

Jaantzen switches off the feeds and the warehouse's graffitied facade fades from his desk.

An incoming call from Manu ripples through to take its place.

"Boss?" Manu sounds like he might have gotten some sleep in the last few hours. At least someone has. "You need to come take a look at something."

Jaantzen's had enough uneasy moments in the last few weeks that the note of worry in Manu's voice just triggers a feeling of resignation.

"I thought you were headed home," Jaantzen says.

"Was. We got a, ah. A weird delivery. I'm in my office."

With a sigh, Jaantzen levers himself out of his desk chair, plucks his suit jacket off the back of the couch, and hits the button for the lift.

Manu's got his feet up on his desk and the arm that's not in a sling behind his head. He's watching the feeds when Jaantzen walks in. There's an insulated food courier box on the corner of his desk.

"It's safe," Manu says, dropping his feet to the

ground with a wince. "Came by special courier after the cops left, and the front desk staff thought it seemed suspicious, so they called Lo. It's addressed to you, no return address. I checked it out, but no one else has seen it."

Jaantzen rests his fingers on the lid. "You opened it?"

Manu sighs. "Sorry to say I did. And like I said, it's safe. Just . . . wrong."

With a sense of dread, Jaantzen lifts the lid off. Sets it carefully on Manu's impeccable desk.

Nestled in the box is a man's severed head.

He's familiar, and it doesn't take Jaantzen long to place him: the second of the two men who tried to kill Starla. There's a note tucked carefully into his hair. Jaantzen tugs it out.

"Did you read this, too?" he asks.

Manu shakes his head. "I bet I can guess."

Jaantzen unfolds the note, smooths it out on the desk.

Kind regards, Thala.

Manu cranes his neck to read it. "How sweet of her," he says. "Bitch is unhinged."

"I agree," Jaantzen answers slowly. He slips the note into his pocket, then puts the lid back on the courier box.

"I'll take care of that," Manu says.

"Thank you. Then you should head home."

Manu nods; he looks exhausted. "Planning on it, def."

In the background, the feed is still looping, interviews with Lo é Njeri interspersed with pictures of the rubble, showing the world how Willem Jaantzen let his guard down, how he let someone strike at his home and murder his people.

He turns it off.

"Ms. é Njeri is doing well in her new role," he says.

Manu smiles wanly. "I know. I'm going to have to fill her in on some things soon. Not everything, but — she's curious and sharp, and if she's going to hear rumors, I'd rather her hear them from me."

"Understood. Let me know how things go."

Manu's smile fades, but he nods. Manu knows the position he's putting Lo in by relying on her, of course, by bringing her closer to the heart of what Manu actually does for Jaantzen. And he knows the consequences of making someone a liability if they're not able to handle it.

"How's Toshiyo?" Jaantzen asks.

"Sleeping, I think. Gia got her to take a sedative."

Jaantzen takes a sharp breath. "But how *is* she."

Manu smiles wryly. "Tougher than you think, man." He takes a deep breath. "Speaking of sleeping, the Alliance woman's still out, too. We need to figure out what to do about her."

It's one of the only things Jaantzen has been thinking about today. "I'll be seeing Julieta tonight for dinner. I'll ask her advice, but I'm afraid we'll need more time than we'll get. Someone is bound to come for her."

"I can buy us some time."

Jaantzen lifts an eyebrow, doesn't ask how. Manu's connections reach into the strangest corners of Bulari society; if he says he can buy time from the Alliance, he can.

"Thank you. Go home, I'll check on Toshiyo in a few hours." Jaantzen's gaze comes to rest on the courier box once more. "Is the polite thing to send her a thank-you card?"

"That might just encourage her." Manu stands and tucks the box under his bad arm, supporting the box's weight with his sling. "All right, I'm out. I'll see you this afternoon."

"Make it tomorrow, I'll be gone this afternoon."

"Have fun, then." Manu clasps his arm and leaves him at the lift, heading down the stairs with Coeur's gift tucked under his arm.

By the time Jaantzen reaches the penthouse once more another call is coming in, and he wearily decides to ignore it, until he sees the name.

His heart sinks.

"Yes?"

"Good morning! I'm just calling to talk," Phaera says, her voice floating softly from his desk. He frowns, glad she didn't make a video connection. He's not in the mood for small talk. "Just to catch up," she says, and his frown deepens as he tries to figure out her game.

"What did you want to talk about," he says finally, and on the other side of the city she laughs.

"I'm teasing you," Phaera says. "I can see your face right now. Don't worry, Jaantzen, I promise I will never call you just to hear your voice. Oriol gave me the short version of what happened last night, and of course I've seen the news. I wanted to make sure everything was all right."

Is everything all right? How does one even go about answering that question after this past week?

"It's complicated," Jaantzen says. "We lost some of my security team. But we'll recover."

"I also wanted to say I'm sorry."

"For?"

"I provoked him. And he knew — "

"Stop. Acheta's attack on me had absolutely nothing to do with you. I can promise you that."

"How can you be sure?"

"I'm sure."

"Because he knew about Blackheart?"

"Because of a number of reasons." And he'll tell

her some of them, some day. When he's ready to make her a liability, too.

She's quiet for a moment, long enough that Jaantzen checks the connection to make sure she hasn't terminated the call.

"Are you still looking for the other gunman?" she asks. "We'll be opening our doors again to-morrow and I can have my staff keep an eye out."

"That's fine, there's no need."

Another pause.

"Because you already found him?"

"You don't need to. But thank you for the offer."

Phaera takes a breath. "Did you kill him, too?" She says it with a bit of a laugh, like it's a joke, but it's not. He can tell she needs to know.

"Phaera — "

"Listen, Jaantzen. I don't need to think you're a saint. But don't keep me in the dark because you think it's for my own good. I already know who you are, and I want to get to know you better. If I ask you something, it's because I want to know it. If you have a good reason not to tell me, I respect that. But if you're trying to keep me safe from myself we can stop this right now."

Jaantzen takes a deep breath.

"Coeur sent me his head."

There's silence on the other end of the line.

"That's a figure of speech, right?" Phaera says after a moment.

Jaantzen wishes it were. "His literal head," he says. "It arrived by courier this morning." He's still not certain if it was meant to be a gesture of respect, a veiled threat, or merely unsettling. But Coeur succeeded in all three.

"What the fuck is wrong with her?" Phaera says, and the way she says it untwists something deep inside him that has been bound up for ages.

He begins to laugh.

"I have no idea," he says when he can breathe again.

He hears Phaera's quiet laughter on the other end of the line.

"Willem," she says after a moment.

A chill touches the back of his neck.

"Yes?"

"You've got to lighten up on the machismo shit," she says. "Putting guards on me, keeping me in the dark about your plans, trying to herd me like you're a big bad guard dog and I'm part of your flock." He sits straighter, frowning. "I get it, you've lost people. You're terrified of losing more. But that fear isn't doing you any favors, and it's not doing your crew any favors. You have to understand that we are not yours to lose."

She takes a breath; before he finds an answer,

she speaks again. "You tried to build a wall around yourself so you wouldn't get hurt again, but that didn't work. Now you're trying to build a wall around the people around you, but it's not just about their safety. It's still so you don't get hurt."

The silence lasts a moment, he can hear the faintness of her breath, the rustling of fabric. He doesn't have a response for her. He has arguments he could make, he's made them to himself, he's made them to Starla and Manu. But he realizes as he forms them that she's not the one that needs convinced. She's said her piece, and he can take all the time in the world to repeat his arguments to himself once they've said goodbye.

And instinctively he realizes she hasn't asked him to respond to her words. There's something lying under what she just said, some deeper question she's waiting to hear the answer to: Is there going to be a next time between them?

"Thank you," he says, and he hears her let her breath go. "I appreciate you saying that. I'll try to do better by you, in the future."

She takes a deep breath. "That said, I should have trusted you. I put people in danger because of my pride."

"You didn't know what I was doing."

"Don't defend me, Jaantzen," she snaps. "I need to say this. Your man Sina was willing to die for me.

Jae. The others. I could have gotten them all killed because I don't know when to step back and let someone else help me."

"Trust goes both ways, Phaera," he says quietly. "And this is how it's built. If you need anything from me in the future, please — "

"I want you to come over for dinner."

The quick change of conversation leaves him even more speechless. "I — "

"Tonight? I'll make my grandmother's famous korris chicken recipe."

"You cook?" It's a stupid thing to say, but it's out of his mouth before he can think of a better response.

"I'm a woman of many talents."

He hears her shift on the other end of the line and realizes she's waiting for an answer. "I can't. Not tonight," he adds quickly, realizing how that sounded. "I've already agreed to have dinner with Calanthe Yang and her family." And, god, what is he about to do?

He takes a deep breath. "Would you join us?"

"Thank you, I will," she says, and he senses something in her voice. Relief, he realizes; maybe her light air and teasing is her own way of hiding her nerves.

"I'll pick you up." He digs his fingers into the bridge of his nose.

"Good," Phaera says. She clears her throat. "I did have one item of actual business to discuss with you while I have you here."

"Yes?"

"I'd like to make a hire, but I need your blessing."

"My blessing?"

"It's Sina," she says. "I've appreciated having him around, and it sounds like he's looking for something permanent."

"Oh?" Jaantzen smiles. Manu will be thrilled, provided Oriol can calm his urge to wander long enough to say yes. "Of course, you're welcome to ask him. You don't need my blessing."

Phaera just laughs. He wonders how a sound he hadn't paid attention to before a few days ago could suddenly seem so necessary.

"I'll have to make it quick," she says. "Now that his fight at Herran's is all over the feeds, he's going to get plenty of job offers."

That he might, but Jaantzen's never seen Oriol so protective of anyone besides Manu and Toshiyo. "I think he'll take yours," he says. He hesitates at the next question, but he needs to ask her, especially since she apparently intends to continue spending time with him. "I have a business question for you, as well. What's your bad blood with the Demosgas?"

Phaera laughs again, and he relaxes at her reaction. "You mean did Lhasa stiff me on a contract, or Aiax knock up my sister? There are no scandalous secrets, I just can't stand them. Lhasa is a prickly old money snob and Aiax is a bombastic hothead who can't get over himself. They both make me crazy. Why?"

"I have a business opportunity. Nothing to do with the casinos."

"If you can handle talking to them, knock yourself out," she says without pause. "Go get some rest, Jaantzen. I'll see you tonight."

AUTHOR'S NOTE

When I wrote *Double Edged*, the first book of the Bulari Saga, I meant for Phaera D to walk onstage and back off as an interesting background character who might swing by again later.

But then Julieta Yang had to draw Jaantzen's attention to the romantic tension between he and Phaera, and as soon as he started noticing it I couldn't stop thinking about it, either.

Julieta was right: Phaera *is* good for Jaantzen. He needs the kind of woman who's not going to fall passively in line like crew, who's going to challenge him, who's going to require him to rethink his assumptions about himself and others.

Like Jaantzen, I didn't plan for Phaera. But I'm enjoying watching the waves she's created rippling out through the insular world of Jaantzen's crew. And I'm very excited to watch that shape up in the coming books.

Writing the Bulari Saga has been like feeling my way through the dark toward a destination that seems inevitable, but is also constantly surprising me. Because each book of this series is so tightly connected, my characters are constantly dealing with repercussions of past decisions even as more chaos gets thrown their way — and the third book, *Pressure Point* is no different.

If you're the sort who enjoys bonus excerpts, read on to find a sneak peek at *Pressure Point*.

If you're just dying to know WTF hellbeast, buy *Pressure Point* here:

WWW.JESSIEKWAK.COM/BOOK/PRESSURE-POINT

Thank you for reading!

If you enjoyed *Crossfire*, I'd love to hear your feedback. Leave a review on your favorite retailer to let me know what you thought.

See you in the next book,

Peace comes at a price, and this Pax Bulari could cost Jaantzen everyone he loves.

Turn the page to read the first chapter.

Buy at:
WWW.JESSIEKWAK.COM/BOOK/PRESSURE-POINT

"I'm not here to make trouble. I just have a few questions."

The figure freezes, silhouetted against the dim light of the hall. The office is dark, though if you've been sitting and waiting in that same dark, eyes adjusting as the evening light faded, it's easy to see the fear etched into the face of the old man standing in the doorway.

The old man's breath quickens, shallow at the top of his lungs. He's thinking about whether to call security. Whether the voice is lying. Why the voice sounds so familiar.

It's a few seconds before his breath deepens, control found again. He clears his throat. "May I turn the lights on, Mr. Juric?" he asks.

"Please," Manu says. "Make yourself at home."

A mildly amused laugh. "I think I shall."

The door closes, the lights bloom, and Alliance Deputy Chief of Mission Marquez ó Lauris is illuminated in the doorway to his own office in the Alliance embassy, a combination of annoyance and intrigue on his features. He crosses to his desk and hitches a hip onto the corner rather than settling in the imposing leather chair behind it. Steam twists gently from the mug of tea in his hands.

Manu has taken up residence on one of the stately armchairs by the bookshelf — one ankle over the opposite knee, his suit jacket unbuttoned, although his shoulder holster is covered. He doesn't miss ó Lauris's glance at where the weapon would be, though. He's been imagining that this chair is where ó Lauris settles with a cigar for a late night of reading, or to puzzle out thorny issues of interplanetary policy. As the deputy chief of mission to the Alliance ambassador on New Sarjun, ó Lauris must have plenty to puzzle.

Hopefully some of the chair's problem-solving charm will rub off on Manu Juric, deputy chief of Jaantzen.

"I didn't realize we knew each other well enough for casual drop-ins, Mr. Juric."

"I didn't think you'd want me on the visitors' log."

Ó Lauris takes a sip of his tea, steam kissing his glasses opaque a moment as he watches Manu over the rim of the mug. "Quite," he says finally.

The last time they met, it was in the back room of a seedy bar, Manu relying on ó Lauris's curiosity to draw him out to a meeting with Willem Jaantzen's right-hand man. Tonight, Manu doesn't have time for games.

Ó Lauris isn't the kind of man to waste time complaining that there were other options for meeting, or asking how Manu got in. Since he hasn't yet called security, ó Lauris has probably decided Manu won't kill him, and Manu's banking on not being thrown out until the man's curiosity has been satisfied. In fact, the way he's watching Manu, seems like he's more amused by a hiccough in his evening's schedule than angry at the intrusion.

Which means he probably has no idea that his government just declared war on Willem Jaantzen.

"I wanted to pick your brain," says Manu. "Run by you a hypothetical problem we might have."

Ó Lauris inclines his head. "A problem your employer has? Or?"

Manu touches a finger to his chest, tilts it to include ó Lauris. And, with a *What the hell!* smile, circles it to include the whole damn city. "We."

At this, the mild interest in ó Lauris's expression slips to serious. Good. Because what Manu's

dealing with is about to get disconcertingly international.

"Indulge me a minute," Manu says. "What's the
protocol when an undercover Alliance action
against a private citizen in a non-Alliance country
goes wrong?"

Ó Lauris considers him carefully, then sets his
tea aside. "I saw the news about your employer's
place of business. Another 'unfortunate incident of
violence by a local crew.'" He's parroting the phrasing; it's clear he doesn't believe that version of the
story. "Is everything all right?"

"Nah, man," says Manu. "I'm burying friends
tomorrow." He sets both feet firmly on the floor,
hiding his wince, watching ó Lauris. The old man
has no idea what Manu's about to say; the way his
torso leans forward, he's almost off-balance in his
desire for inside information. If ó Lauris knew the
Alliance was behind the events of last night, he
would be on guard. There'd be no way his fight-or-
flight response would let him stand so vulnerably.

"An unfortunate and unprovoked attack by a
local crew," Manu says. "But what if they'd had
help? What if that 'attack' was actually a covert Alliance mission, and the agent got caught?" His smile
is sharp. "Hypothetically."

Ó Lauris's expression becomes professionally

glass, but it takes him a few beats to properly react; this was not what he was expecting to hear. "And you have proof?" He straightens, hand clawed on his knee for support. "You have a prisoner?"

Manu lifts an eyebrow.

"Are they being treated well?"

"Course, man." Manu holds out his hands — *We're still friends*. "For the purposes of our hypothetical, let's assume we're not dealing with monsters. Just businesspeople trying to make a living without getting shot up by foreign spies."

Ó Lauris is still. "Mr. Juric, I can assure you that the Alliance doesn't perform operations on foreign soil. That would be in breach of the Eyes of Durga Treaty."

"Oh, I know that. Which is why we're having a friendly conversation." Manu shakes his head in mock disapproval. "Imagine the international scandal this would be if something like that had actually happened. I'm sure your side would be coming up with a plan to react in that case."

Ó Lauris clears his throat. "If they had proof of life."

"And how do they get that."

No answer from the old man; he doesn't know or he's not saying. Manu and Starla went over the Alliance operative's armor and Gia went over her body last night — if she has a transmitter, it's been shut down. Not to mention the room she's being held in is signal-blocked. That should keep her handlers in limbo, enough not to come in guns blazing. With all the effort they went through to embed her with Acheta's crew, they're not going to tip their hands on a rescue mission for an agent they don't know is alive or dead.

Manu knows enough from Oriol about the Alliance's attitude towards its operatives. Unless it becomes a scandal, they probably won't risk much on her.

Only thing is, she was supposed to come back to roost with the case in tow. The Alliance may not come for her, but they'll definitely come for it. The question is how soon, and what Manu can do to stall them.

"Well," says Manu, "in this hypothetical, let's assume the operative is still alive and being treated very fairly given the body count they left behind. And that their captors have pretty damning evidence."

He reaches into his suit pocket and ó Lauris flinches. But Manu's not reaching for a weapon. He produces a small holoprojector, small enough to nestle in his palm. He tosses it to ó Lauris, who presses the button with a dark expression.

He's probably expecting a threat: an Alliance

operative blindfolded and bound with a gun to her head. The clip he views instead isn't long, just long enough to show vid from the stairwell where the Alliance woman's face is clearly visible as she shoots two guards point-blank — they have their hands up, weapons on the ground. The footage cuts to the hallway of floor twelve. The woman's dragging Toshiyo with her when she spins and shoots Elian in the stomach.

"The kid she shot in that last clip was an unarmed medical student," says Manu. "Not a great look for the Alliance. Especially considering the man she's with."

Ó Lauris sighs deeply. "That was Levi Acheta?"

"Only one of the most notorious criminals in Bulari's underground."

"Who has seen this?"

"No one, yet." Manu leans elbows on knees. "I don't know what the standard Alliance special ops response would be in this case, but maybe it would be better to think about a diplomatic option. Particularly since the civilian target is pretty well-connected with people in New Sarjun's government. Oh — and since our governments are on the brink of negotiating a new trade deal." Manu shakes his head. "Terrible timing, yeah? Something like this could get out of hand so fast."

Ó Lauris nods slowly. He's gotten the message:

Tell whoever's in charge of black ops on this planet that there will be dire consequences to pulling additional shit. Now it's time to figure out what Manu and ó Lauris can actually do about it.

"I hope you appreciate the respect I did you by coming to you directly," Manu says. He'd already suspected that ó Lauris isn't much involved in whatever illegal tactical operations the Alliance has underway on New Sarjun — but he is in charge of administering the embassy under a parade of rotating ambassadors, and has been for two decades. The ambassadors and the black ops handlers may come and go, but ó Lauris is invested in this country. He's a man whose sole purpose is fixing things. Just like Manu.

"I do appreciate the gesture, Mr. Juric. And I will maintain absolute discretion. What's your next step?" Ó Lauris smiles. "Hypothetically."

"You'll know." Manu stands, straightens his cuffs, doesn't button his suit jacket. "Right now I just need a message sent. And to know there's someone in your government willing to work with us instead of just sending in the dogs."

"Consider it done," ó Lauris says. "In the interest of interplanetary peace."

"Thank you." Manu holds out his right hand to shake, ignoring the screaming pain in his bicep where Toshiyo's hell-beast tore into him last night. The arm should be in a sling, but that's not the way you make a proper impression on a fellow.

Ó Lauris stands to meet him, his grip firm. Polite. His hand is warm and dry.

"Do you have just a moment more, Mr. Juric?" he asks as he releases the handshake. He's feeling more in control of the situation now, Manu can tell, the edge smoothed from his amused Arquellian drawl. "I have a question for you."

"Ask away." Manu doesn't like ó Lauris feeling more in control. He keeps his shoulders relaxed, his gun hand loose.

"I've been hearing rumors over the last few days." The hint of a smile. "That a certain former mayor is alive? And — and this is what has me lingering at work when I should be heading home — that she may have rejoined her old crew?"

He knows about Thala Coeur, he's just waiting to hear Manu confirm it. And, what the hell. It'll be common knowledge soon enough.

"I've heard that, too," Manu says.

"When last we spoke, you came to ask me what we did to contain Thala Coeur when she sought asylum at the embassy. Did you know she was alive at that time?"

Voices pass in the hall, the click of heels rising

and fading, a woman's laughter. Ó Lauris doesn't break Manu's gaze.

Manu lets a smile tug at his lips. "I'll answer that question honestly if you do."

An intrigued arch of ó Lauris's eyebrow. "Agreed."

"Yes, I did." Manu lifts his chin. "Your turn."

A breath, ó Lauris considering his answer. "No," he finally says. And the follow-up question he wants to ask is plain in his face, but he'll never say the words: Should I have?

Manu watches him wonder if the Alliance was involved in Coeur's "death" and then revival. If the problem of Thala Coeur and the attack on Willem Jaantzen are, in fact, linked.

Watches seeds of doubt grow as ó Lauris wonders just how his own government is undermining his peace efforts, right under his nose.

Good.

"Life is cyclical, isn't it?" Ó Lauris picks up his tea once more, sipping contemplatively. "You think you've dealt with a problem, only to find it back on your doorstep."

"Do you think she has a grudge against you?"

Ó Lauris smiles faintly. "One can assume."

"Take a few days and ask some questions," Manu says. "Find out why your government might attack a private New Sarjunian citizen, and who else knew that Thala Coeur was alive. And let the appropriate people know what kind of shitshow they'll have on their hands if they go after the man again. I'll be in touch to set up a meeting, and we can sort this out like adults. Have a good night, Deputy Chief."

"Good night, Mr. Juric. Please convey my sincere condolences to your employer on the tragic loss of life, and let him know I have the best interests of international relations at heart."

Manu nods solemnly at that and lets himself out the door. Ó Lauris may honestly regret what happened last night, but Manu doubts that sentiment applies to the rest of his colleagues. He's still walking through a den of snakes.

This late, the hallways of the Alliance embassy are nearly empty. Manu leaves through the front doors — no one bothers to challenge you once you've gotten in, and the few people still milling about aren't likely to recognize him. Somebody'll check the security vids eventually, though. They'll wonder how he got in, marvel at how casually he strolled back out.

Manu's found that nothing helps a negotiation along quite so well as your enemy knowing just how close you can get to them.

Outside, the baking desert evening is finally starting to cool off as a slight breeze picks up, the air velvety against Manu's skin. It's the sort of night he usually loves, a night meant for sitting lazy in cafes, like the one across the street, where lanterns are strung above cafe tables, waiters pour wine, the kitchen fills the air with the scents of fresh-baked bread and garlic and bitter orange. The government district comes alive in the evenings, a safe place for tourists and the sort of Arquellians who style themselves expats rather than immigrants to sample the evening cafes without worrying they'll get mugged or have to rub elbows with a dirty local.

In the still night, Manu catches snatches of different accents and languages, mostly from Indiran countries, though there are plenty of tourists from throughout New Sarjun come to visit the big city of Bulari, too.

He pauses a moment on the embassy's steps; the first of New Sarjun's moons is rising full just down the street, perfectly framed in the gap between buildings, a deep burnished gold in the faint dust haze of the horizon.

Others have stopped to stare at it, too, others who are leaving the embassy at the end of the day, or stopping on the wide marble steps to enjoy their takeout meals or tie their children's shoes or rest their bones with a cigarette. It's such a captivating sight that, for a moment, it feels like the entirety of Bulari must be appreciating the beauty of the rising moon. It's stunning, both the vision and the sudden vertiginous feeling that everyone else in this city is enraptured by the same glorious celestial object.

Manu isn't looking back at the embassy, but even if he had been, he wouldn't've had warning.

The bomb had been ticking away for the better part of the day. Timed for the hour, not the transcendent distraction of the rising moon, the blast rips through the embassy's facade, thundering through glass and cracking marble, sending bodies tumbling down the steps like windblown leaves. Across the road, the cafe's windows shatter, patrons scrambling for cover.

In the wake of the explosion, an eerie stillness descends. Full minutes tick agonizingly by before bystanders begin to trust that they are safe, shocked onlookers slowly emerge, a few unbelieving moments more before emergency calls are made, before anyone who thinks they might be able to help approaches to see which — if any — of the unmoving bodies on the stairs can possibly be saved.

Through gently raining ash and shifting dust, the shattered facade of the Alliance embassy gapes like a maw.

Get PRESSURE POINT here:
WWW.JESSIEKWAK.COM/BOOK/PRESSURE-POINT

ABOUT JESSIE KWAK

Jessie Kwak has always lived in imaginary lands, from Arrakis and Ankh-Morpork to Earthsea, Tatooine, and now Portland, Oregon. As a writer, she sends readers on their own journeys to immersive worlds filled with fascinating characters, gunfights, explosions, and dinner parties.

When she's not raving about her latest favorite sci-fi series to her friends, she can be found sewing,

mountain biking, or exploring new worlds both at home and abroad.
Author photo by Robert Kittilson.

Connect with me:
www.jessiekwak.com
jessie@jessiekwak.com

DID YOU LIKE THE BOOK?

As a reader, I rely on book recommendations to help me pick what to read next.

As a writer, book recommendations are the most powerful way for me to get the word out to new readers.

If you liked this book, please leave a review on the platform of your choice — or tell a friend! It's the easiest way to help authors you enjoy keep producing great work.

Cheers!

Jessie

Nonfiction

*From Chaos to Creativity: Building a Productivity System
for Artists and Writers*